Frances Gordon is the daughter of an Irish actor and after a convent education worked in newspapers and the legal profession. She now lives and writes in Staffordshire.

She is the author of four acclaimed fantasy novels, written under the name of Bridget Wood, and three horror novels, *Blood Ritual*, *The Devil's Piper* and *The Burning Altar*. Her most recent novels in this series, *Thorn*, based on the legend of 'Sleeping Beauty', and *Changeling*, based on 'Rumpelstiltskin', are also available from Headline Feature:

'A superior example of the vampire genre . . . a pleasure from start to finish'

Time Out

'A chilling, blood-curdling novel'
Peterborough Evening Telegraph

'A quality novel of supernatural power through the ages . . . Blending well-fleshed characters and a strong story'

Bradford Telegraph & Argus

Wildwood

An Immortal Tale

Frances Gordon

First published in Great Britain in 1999
by HEADLINE BOOK PUBLISHING

First published in paperback in 1999
by HEADLINE BOOK PUBLISHING

10 9 8 7 6 5 4 3 2 1

ISBN 0 7472 5986 0

Typeset by CBS, Martlesham Heath, Ipswich, Suffolk

Printed and bound in Great Britain by
Mackays of Chatham plc, Chatham, Kent

HEADLINE BOOK PUBLISHING
A division of Hodder Headline PLC
338 Euston Road
London NW1 3BH

Author's Note

An ancient Derbyshire legend uncovered during a visit to Millers Dale provided the genesis for this book. But deeper investigation then revealed the unsuspected but intriguing existence of the Foljambe family, thus supplying the historical background.

The Foljambes are documented in old Derbyshire records, and although the records are somewhat fragmentary, their provenance appears to be authentic. Little first-hand evidence of their origins is available, but fascinating glimpses emerge.

In the time of William the Conqueror (1066–87) the Foljambes were enfeoffed as hereditary foresters – a royal appointment which certainly included the slaying of wolves in the dense forests that covered a great part of the land. The family was evidently successful in this part of its curious calling, since an entry in the Pipe Rolls of Henry II (1154–89) refers to a sum of 25/- being paid to them as an extra fee for pursuing their profession in Normandy – possibly at the request of the king.

In 1214, a Thomas Foljambe was knighted, and nearly a hundred years later, in 1301, Foljambe sons were summoned to the muster at Berwick-upon-Tweed, to fight the Scots in the armies of the glittering Edward Plantagenet – the infamous battle in which the Stone of Destiny was seized from Scone Abbey by the English.

My enquiries and research indicate that the family has almost certainly died out: if, however, there are descendants living today, I tender them my apologies for making so free with their history.

But it does not stretch the imagination too far to believe in their centuries-old battle against one of man's greatest and oldest adversaries.

Chapter One

It was raining on the day that Felicity finally knew she would have to leave Connor: a grey, despairing rain that poured ceaselessly down from a leaden sky, flattening the gardens and beating against the windows, so that you were not quite sure where the greyness of the weather ended and the greyness of your own unhappiness started.

The letter from the unknown finance company was part of the greyness. It said, in apologetic but official language, that the arrears on the loan Mr Connor Stafford had taken out three years ago were now such that unless they were settled within fourteen days, the company would very regretfully repossess the North London house which had been given as security. Their representatives would attend at the property on the twenty-fifth of the month. At 12.00 noon, added the writer. High noon.

Felicity made a pot of tea and sat down with the telephone. This was clearly a monumental blunder on somebody's part. The house was not mortgaged to anyone: it never had been. It had been left to her by her father, five years before she even met Connor, and she owned it outright. Con could not possibly have used it as security for a loan – the deeds were in her name. This would turn out to be the most immense criminal mistake ever. There would be a fulsome letter of apology and probably a computer would be blamed, and all would be well. They might even be able to laugh about it later on.

But it was not a mistake and there was not going to be any apology. There was certainly not going to be any laughter. Connor had indeed used the house as security: Felicity, beating down a mixture of panic and rage, understood in the first three minutes of the conversation that he had forged her name on any number of documents, that he had lied about the ownership of the house, and that he had not paid the finance company a

1

penny piece. The debt was a mind-blowing one hundred and thirty thousand pounds.

'Capital and interest,' said the voice at the other end. It sounded quite sympathetic by this time. 'The original loan was for seventy-five thousand – the house was valued for loan purposes at a hundred and seventy-five thousand, although in your part of London that's probably dipped a bit since. And then compound interest at 22.5%, although of course the APR—'

Felicity did not wait to hear about the APR, whatever the APR was. She did not wait to hear about house prices dipping and slumps and recessions. She slammed the receiver down in fury.

One hundred and thirty thousand pounds. *One hundred and thirty.* It was a monstrous sum. It was obscene.

It was the last straw in a long series of increasingly humiliating straws. It was no use railing at Connor, because it never was any use, and in any case he was not here. Felicity had no idea where he was. He would probably turn up around midday, having spent the night God-alone knew where, and he would probably smell of stale drink. That was an increasingly frequent occurrence. He might also be smelling of another woman's scent, which was also an increasingly frequent occurrence.

She thought she was entitled to feel furious. She thought she was entitled to feel murderous. She was not yet sure what she was going to do, although what she was not going to do was cry, because she had not cried yet, not even on the afternoon when she had come home unexpectedly and found Connor in bed with her best friend, the bitch. She had thrown the bitch's clothes out through the bedroom window, and then she had thrown the sheets after her as well. It had been an immensely satisfying gesture.

Felicity had no idea what took place when a house was repossessed. Would there be a silently gathering posse of men in the street, all checking their watches at intervals, waiting grimly for high noon to strike? And if she was in the house what would they do? Would they force their way in, and pick her up and carry her out bodily? What happened to the furniture? Did they take it away to sell to recoup some of the debt, or did they throw that into the street as well? She had wild visions of her very saucepans and Bryony's little Victorian chair that had been a godmother's present, standing piteously in the rain. Along with it was the heartbreaking vision of Bryony herself standing in the rain with the chair, determined not to cry, resolutely wearing the bright red cloak with the hood, which had been a seventh birthday present from Connor, and from which she would not be parted.

None of this could be allowed to take place. Felicity drank the rest of the tea, which was tepid, and sat down to think. The kitchen was bright and cheerful, and it was filled up with misery and furious anger. Misery smelt of lemon washing-up liquid and the scarlet geranium in its pot on the windowsill.

When Connor finally returned, it was a safe bet that one of two things would happen. If he had sobered up, he would almost certainly have switched to his charmingly rueful mood. He would explain how he had been on the track of a deal – 'A really good deal, Fliss, we're going to be rich' – and how clinching the deal had made it imperative to go along with a group of people to a club or a bar. He had done it for her and Bryony, he would say, and he would be unshaven and his dark hair would be untidy and he would look like a raffish Victorian rake. In that mood it would take a great deal of resolve not to listen to his excuses. It would take even more resolve not to let him persuade her into bed for a grand reconciliation.

But if he had been on a real binge, he might not return until tonight, or even the small hours of tomorrow, and he might still be drunk. And in that case, he would almost certainly force her to make love, and Felicity had already discovered that being made love to by somebody who was drunk was not making love at all. It was not far from being raped by a stranger. And if misery smelt of lemon washing-up liquid and geraniums, rape smelt of second-hand wine and garlic, and of Giorgio Armani for Men, gone a bit stale – and what was Connor doing using Giorgio Armani, for God's sake, when a hundred and thirty thousand pounds was owed to a finance company!

It did not matter which of these scenarios Connor thought he was going to be playing, because he was not actually going to be playing either of them. Felicity was simply not going to be here when he got back. She had no idea where she would go, but she would go somewhere where Con's dazzling erratic charm could not reach her. She would engage a solicitor and there would be a divorce, and whatever money could be salvaged would be salvaged.

She stuffed the hateful, humiliating letter into her pocket, and went upstairs to drag the suitcases out of the boxroom.

She had got as far as folding Bryony's scarlet cloak when the phone rang.

It was a completely strange voice – doctor somebody, Felicity never found out his name – but he was ringing to tell her that a man he was afraid might be her husband had been brought in to the Emergency Department of his hospital. The man was rather badly injured, and they were trying to trace his family.

'His driving licence and cheque book say Connor Stafford. And your phone number was in a pocket book.'

'Yes?'

'The car was a dark blue Renault,' said the doctor, and read out the registration number.

Felicity said, 'Yes, it's – I think it must be my husband. Oh God. I'd better come, hadn't I? Where exactly—?'

It was somewhere in Marylebone. Felicity had never been there in her life and as far as she knew, Connor had never been there either. There had been no reason she knew of for Con to be driving through that part of London at 3 a.m., and to crash the car into a wall. Except that Con did not need a reason: he would have been with the group of people who were going to set up the new deal ('We're going to be rich, Fliss') or he would have been driving away from the bedroom of some new female.

When she finally reached the hospital after an awkward and exhausting journey, she was met with the news that they were dreadfully sorry, Mrs Stafford, everything possible had been done, but Connor Stafford had died of his injuries half an hour ago.

The hospital pathologist bent over the naked body on the marble slab, and frowned slightly as he performed his slightly sad, slightly macabre tasks.

This had started out by appearing to be a routine drunk-driver post-mortem; even with safety-belt regulations and campaigns against drink-driving, you still got far too many of them. According to witnesses, the guy had driven at about eighty miles an hour, smack into a brick wall. According to the

4

reports from the lab, he had been four times over the permitted alcohol limit. The pathologist mentally halved the witnesses' reports of the car's speed, but the lab report would have to be accepted. You could not argue with a properly documented lab test.

You could not argue with the anatomical evidence of your own eyes, either. The pathologist reminded himself several times that you did get odd quirks in nature; you had only to work inside a large hospital for six months to know that. Peculiar blood groupings, and occasional weird placings of organs. Right-hand hearts were not as rare as all that, and it was not unknown to find the appendix – McBurney's point – out of its normal spot. Tragic, bizarrely deformed babies were sometimes born to apparently normal parents.

But he had never come across anything quite as strange as the young man whose label identified him as Connor Stafford, aged thirty-four, white Caucasian male, and who had been listed by the office as number 32709/M.

Whatever Connor Stafford had been in life, in death he was still startlingly good-looking; dark-haired and with the kind of soaring cheekbones that the poets called winged. When his eyes were open and looking out on the world, they would have had a slant to them. I bet you flurried a few hearts and a few bedrooms in your time, thought the pathologist.

He sewed up the torso, and checked to make sure he had labelled all the specimens. This was the kind of case that might rebound on the hospital; it would not do to miss anything, or skimp. Stomach contents, of course. It looked as if 32709/M had eaten a lavish supper as well as all the booze. Good for you, 32709/M; I'll be here until at least midnight by the look of things. Sections of liver, lungs and kidneys had been taken as usual, and also a small section of brain tissue. He had not missed anything. He had sent blood for analysis at the start of the autopsy.

Blood . . .

The lab had phoned an hour ago to demand irritably whether the path. department thought it was the first of April and had sent along a slide of something from the zoo, just to catch them out.

'Certainly not.'

'Oh. Well, in that case you've got something very peculiar

5

down there, and in your shoes I'd thank my stars it's dead. Whoever he is, I've never come across such an obscure red cell structure, in fact for recording purposes we've had to create a completely new reference. It doesn't fit any of the known classifications.'

The small scraping of skin that had been sent to dermatology for analysis did not appear to fit any known classification either. The word 'aberrant' had been used. The pathologist added this to his notes, and thought crossly that the entire histology department was beginning to echo with the sound of heads being stuck into sand and bucks being passed.

He had only the routine examination of the inside of the mouth to do now, and then he would have finished. By this time no freakish malformation would have surprised him. He adjusted the strong overhead spotlight and propped the jaw open.

It was then that he wished he had not lit on the word 'freak'. He also wished that he had not elected to work late tonight. It was close on midnight and he could hear rain lashing against the windows. His assistants had all long since gone, and he was alone with this—

With this dark-haired, slant-eyed creature whose blood fitted no known classification, whose skin formation was aberrant, and who had teeth so absolutely perfect that no dental work of any kind had ever been done on them.

He twitched the sheet up over the body, and returned Connor Stafford's body to its metal drawer to await removal to the hospital's small chapel of rest.

As he locked up, it occurred to him to wonder if 32709/M really was a one-off, a freak, or if there were any more like him anywhere in the world.

Night had long since fallen, but in the sketchily converted room that had once been a barn, it was warm and bright. The barn led directly out of the old-fashioned crofthouse kitchen, and despite the storm that had been raging for almost three days, it was a rather friendly place. There were half a dozen battered but comfortable chairs, and there was a large scrubbed-top table that somebody had not thought worth removing. This was littered with various people's notes. Oil lamps cast friendly golden pools of light, and heat was pumping out

6

from judiciously placed oil stoves.

Cruithin Island was getting the worst of the storm that was apparently afflicting most of Scotland's west coast: rain and hail lashed against the windows and there was the moaning rise and fall of a keening wind, so that at times the oil lamps flickered ominously. After a while, Nina got up to draw the curtains, because even the most objective mind could not help seeing eerie outlines in the darkness.

Piers Adair surveyed his team, and although he had a sheaf of notes in front of him, he did not appear to refer to them.

'I've come to the conclusion,' he said, 'that our original assumption about the inhabitants of Cruithin are wrong.' He paused, and then said, very levelly, 'You'll all remember that when we first came here, most of you thought this was an isolated settlement—'

'A forgotten tribe, beyond the frontiers of civilization,' murmured a male voice from the far end of the table, and Piers smiled.

'Are you writing copy already, Toby?'

'Of course. Go on, professor.'

Piers said, 'I think that at certain times a few of these people might very well leave Cruithin Island and go into the world.'

'What a sinister suggestion,' observed Toby, still scribbling his notes. 'I don't know about the rest of you, but the thought of any one of these creatures loose somewhere on the mainland gives me screaming nightmares.'

'You never had a nightmare in your life, Toby,' said Piers, grinning. 'And we're studying these people. Why wouldn't they study us?'

'Um – Dr Adair—'

'Yes, Nina?' Piers was aware that both the girls had not quite managed to shake off the lecture room yet and use his first name, but he thought they would do so eventually. He had been pleased to find that neither of them seemed to mind the rather spartan living conditions on Cruithin. He had worked under far more primitive conditions than these, and he knew they were lucky to have the use of the abandoned farmhouse with its workable cooking range, and even an antiquated plumbing system, but it was not a view that would necessarily be shared by everyone, and certainly not post-graduate female students.

7

Nina said, 'But even if any of them could get to the mainland, surely they couldn't survive for long? I mean – not among ordinary people?'

'Why not?' said Piers.

'But that's crediting them with a great deal of intelligence,' said Nina.

'You don't think they're intelligent?' said Piers, looking at Nina very intently, and Nina fought down a sudden blush, because like this, slightly unkempt and wearing scruffy corduroys and sweater, Dr Adair was a million times more attractive than he had ever been in the lecture room.

'I wouldn't have called them intelligent,' said the other girl. 'I'd have called them cunning.'

'Would you?' said Piers. 'Then you don't think it's possible for any of them to live among the humans?'

'Undetected?'

'Yes.'

'For a long period of time?'

'Yes.'

'No, of course not.'

'Why not?' said Piers again.

'Well, because people would know!'

'Would they?' said Piers, in a soft voice. 'Are you sure about that?'

There was an abrupt silence. Nina glanced uneasily at the curtained windows.

Toby said, 'Piers, are you saying these creatures might already have had some contact with the outside world?'

'Oh yes.'

'Why?'

'Because,' said Piers, 'from somewhere, at some time, some of them have learned human speech.'

This time the silence lasted considerably longer.

'You're right, of course,' said Toby, at last. 'I'd forgotten those early tapes you got.'

'Pure luck,' said Piers, shortly. 'I taped from the south side of the compound, where the ravine is narrowest. The recordings weren't all that good actually – the distance blurred the sound.'

'I couldn't understand what they were saying for most of the time,' said Nina.

'Oh, couldn't you? Dr Adair understood it very well,' said Priscilla.

'He's been studying these people for much longer than the rest of us!' Nina was not going to let that snooty Priscilla put her down.

'Well, intelligent or cunning, I wouldn't trust any of those sinister creatures from here to that door,' said Toby.

'You were the one who started off by insisting they'd turn out to be ordinary humans!' remarked Priscilla.

'I said they were human, I didn't say anything about them being ordinary,' objected Toby. 'Dietfreid agrees with me, don't you, Dietfreid?'

Dietfreid, who had been poring over his own notes, muttering to himself in a bumble-bee baritone, waved a large hand. 'I have not yet made an opinion. I study my notes in order to do so. Please not to interrupt.'

'Well, Piers can talk till hell freezes about human beings crossing genetic lines and inherited lycanthropy,' said Toby. 'They're a bunch of dangerous savages for my book.'

'The men are very good-looking,' murmured Nina.

'For myself I think they are spindles,' said Dietfreid, looking up disapprovingly. 'A man should have breadth and girth,' added Dietfreid, who was not thin.

'I didn't know you'd got that close to them, Dietfreid?'

'Oh yes, I have been to the edge of the ravine and looked across. It is like a moat girdling a remote civilization,' added Dietfreid, displaying an unsuspected streak of romanticism.

'Oh, how very—'

'But of course, it is due only to the geological fault that has given the conditions out here,' added Dietfreid firmly, and Nina sighed with exasperation.

Piers moved to the window and drew back the curtain in order to look out. His profile was outlined against the darkness and Toby glanced at him and thought: fine chance I've got of getting either of those two girls into bed while he's around, looking like the answer to a maiden's prayer! It's only the dark hair that needs cutting, and the translucent complexion so that he looks like Keats in the later stages of consumption, of course. No, be fair, it's more than that. He remembered all the accounts of *femmes fatales* who littered history and wondered if there might be a masculine counterpart and, if so, whether he was seeing one now.

The team's designated record-keeper, who was a final-year student on loan from Harvard University and who had been bowled over by Dr Adair's glossy British courtesy the instant he encountered it, hesitantly offered his own contribution. 'See, what I don't understand is how they would cope with the practicalities beyond Cruithin. It's pretty remote out here,' he added. 'In fact it's a whole lot lonelier than we were expecting.'

'Yes, it doesn't look as if anyone's lived here for years,' said Nina.

'You mean apart from the wolf-men?'

'Will you *stop* that, Toby!'

'I don't think anyone has lived here for years,' said Piers.

'This house *certainly* hasn't been touched for a couple of centuries,' said Priscilla, disdainfully.

'Well, anyhow,' went on the record-keeper doggedly, 'these guys have lived here all their lives, right? So even if they're second Einsteins, they probably can't read or write. And that'd be a very great obstacle to them going among – um – ordinary people.'

'That's a very interesting observation,' said Piers, coming back to the table and sitting down again, and the record-keeper turned fiery red and thought when the British were polite, they were *seriously* polite.

'I don't see reading or writing as a major difficulty,' objected Toby. 'The statistics show that a surprisingly large proportion of the population can't read or write. They get by with a mixture of bluff and cunning.'

'Oh God, trust a BBC man to quote statistics!'

'Also,' went on Toby, undeterred, 'there's no shame in admitting to word-blindness nowadays.'

'But to do that, they'd have to *know* about it first,' objected Nina.

'You're still pre-supposing that these creatures don't have any contact with the outside world,' said Piers. 'They might quite often take a trip into Scotland or even England. So might the rest of them for all we know. They could have boats – Cruithin isn't so very inaccessible. We managed to land here . . .'

'Eventually,' muttered Dietfreid, who was not the happiest

of travellers, and had suffered certain physical indignities during the attempts to land on the island.

The rare but infinitely sweet smile lit Piers's thin face, causing Priscilla and Nina to sigh longingly. Nina had confided to a girlfriend that she was thrilled at the idea of the Cruithin project, and the girlfriend had said, 'Oh, join the club, dear; most people fall a bit in love with Piers Adair – girls *and* men. But whatever he does for sex, he doesn't do it with his students, so don't hold out any hopes.'

'Dietfreid, have you made your opinion yet?' said Piers.

'I cannot make it until I have physiological specimens to study,' stated Dietfreid firmly. 'But there is one thing I find here; wait, I will show you. Where do the sketches discover themselves, please? Ah, I see, thank you, yes.' He perched his spectacles on his nose.

'There are many subtle variations within the genus *Canidae*,' he informed his audience severely. 'Also within the species *Homo Sapiens* as well, of course. Perhaps there are even more variations there,' he added, with unexpected, if ponderous wit. 'But it is in the species *Canis lupus* that is found the curious and very unmistakable eyes – narrow and slanting. I demonstrate, so,' said Dietfreid, contorting his face into an alarming grimace.

'Ah. Yes, of course.'

'I have seen that these people have such eyes,' explained Dietfreid, earnestly, and scuffled his notes again.

'Wolf-eyes,' murmured Nina.

'Yes,' said Dietfreid, pleased at meeting with such comprehension.

Priscilla said, 'That doesn't sound very wolfish to me. Don't all dogs have slanting narrow eyes?'

'No, no, I explain. A dog, a domesticated dog, has eyes with round pupils, like those of man. A fox or a jackal has pupils that are vertical – a straight narrow line up and down, so.' He jabbed the air energetically. 'But a wolf,' said Dietfreid, lowering his voice and unexpectedly infusing it with an extraordinarily sinister air, 'has thin pupils set on a slant. I do not have the word—'

'Oblique? Diagonal?'

'Yes, thank you, oblique. Very unmistakable. Here we find examples to compare.' He spread out several pages of illustrations and pointed with a chubby finger.

'Thank you, Dietfreid,' said Piers politely after everyone had studied the illustrations in respectful silence. 'These are beautifully clear.'

'So.'

'Exactly what kind of physiological specimens do you want, Dietfreid?'

'Blood. Hair. Bone. A section of brain would be nice,' remarked Dietfreid wistfully, and Nina rather hastily reached for the coffee pot to refill her cup.

'Taken from a living body?' asked Piers.

'Living would be better. But dead is not too bad.'

'I hoped you'd say that,' said Piers, with a grin that made him look much younger.

'Oh God, he's going to play Burke and Hare!' Toby reached for the coffee pot as well. 'Well, you're on your own there, professor, because if you think I'm going to start digging up the bodies of these bizarre things—' He put down the coffee pot and looked round the table.

Nobody spoke.

'I was joking,' said Toby.

'I wasn't,' said Piers.

'I *told* you he wanted to play Burke and Hare—'

'Exactly.' Piers grinned across the table. 'I'm going to go out to the burial ground and bring up the most recent corpse for Dietfreid to analyse.'

'But – they'll see you!' protested Nina.

'They've probably seen all of us a dozen times already,' said Toby. 'But she's right, Piers, you can't openly walk into the wolf's den.'

'I shan't do it openly. I shall do it at dead of night,' said Piers.

Chapter Two

Felicity thought it was somehow like Connor to die dramatically in an awkward place, so that a morass of bewildering formalities had to be grappled with.

It was like him, as well, to have a funeral on a day when London had suddenly taken an upward spiral into an Indian summer, with the sun blazing and humidity peaking, so that people in the church were stickily uncomfortable in dark suits and formal outfits. Funerals ought only ever to be held on bleak wintry mornings, so that the skies reflected your feelings, and so that although you were cold and miserable inside and out, you derived a little glow of comfort from going inside and getting warm, eating and drinking with the other mourners.

There were quite a lot of mourners, and among them were a number of females Felicity did not know and had certainly not invited. Some of them were extremely expensively dressed. They kept their distance, and whoever they were they could be frostily ignored, because Felicity was damned if she was going to be polite to Con's wretched women across his coffin. She was very glad indeed that she was wearing the black silk designer suit that made her legs look long and shapely, and that brought out the coppery tints in her hair. It was appalling to mind about looking good at your husband's funeral, but not when you were faced with a pewful of his girlfriends. At least feeling angry would help her to get through the service.

The arrival of a latecomer just after the vicar had started to intone the dismally bright message about rebirth and the celebration of a Christian life, was an annoying disturbance. Felicity heard someone enter the church and she heard a few heads turn to see who it was. She stared determinedly ahead of her, and it was only when the appalling moment for the procession behind the coffin came that her eyes were drawn to the lone figure at the back. The church was small and rather

13

dim, and for a moment he was in complete shadow. But even in the dimness there was the unmistakable impression of something very unusual indeed, and there was not the smallest doubt in her mind that this was the person who had caused that ruffle of interest.

As the coffin trundled towards the east door and the small cemetery in the church grounds, a pallid ray of autumn sunshine slanted through a window, and Felicity stared at the dark-haired young man, and felt as if a cold hand had suddenly closed around her heart. Just for a moment it might almost have been—

She smacked the thought down at once because ghosts did not enter churches, and ghosts certainly did not attend their own funerals and stand watching their widows with that blend of arrogance and speculation. But as she walked steadfastly out, her heart was beating so fast that it was difficult to breathe normally, and her mind was tumbling with wild visions of spectral bridegrooms who walked among the living, but whose real place was among the dead . . .

But Con really was dead, he had died in a drunken car smash, and he had left behind him mountainous debts and an appalling collection of ambiguous memories. Felicity forced herself to concentrate, drew in a deep breath and went forward to the graveside for the burial service. The expensively dressed females kept their distance, but Felicity was aware of them hovering on the edge of the group of mourners. She hoped they were all feeling miffed to discover that their numbers were legion.

She had managed to clamp the lid down on the seething disquiet churned up by the young man with the disturbingly familiar eyes, and after the service ended, she studiedly ignored him. There were a number of people who had to be thanked for attending; Felicity managed to endure the stifling embraces and the meaningful hand-pressings, but all through it she was strongly aware that the newcomer was watching her from the shadow of a cedar.

It was not until she began to walk back to the waiting car that he approached her. From the corner of her vision, Felicity saw him move forward and the resemblance scythed into her mind all over again, more startling out here with the sunlight dappling through the leaves, turning dark hair to sable, highlighting eyes so strange that the actual pupils looked slanting—

And then he stepped out of the rippling brightness into the deep well of shadow cast by the church, and whatever ghost might have walked for a moment walked no longer. It was not Connor, of course, but it was someone so strongly like Connor that Felicity thought she might be forgiven for those wild fantasies earlier on.

He came straight up to her and took her hand, murmuring something conventional about sympathy. His voice was faintly sibilant but it was attractive, and Felicity thought there was the faintest hint of a foreign inflexion.

She said, 'Thank you. Thank you for coming to the service as well,' and waited.

The unknown young man said, 'You don't know me, but I'm Connor's cousin.' He smiled at her. 'My name is Brother Karabas,' he said.

And then Felicity saw for the first time that he was wearing a black clerical suit with a small pectoral cross.

'It was debatable whether Connor was the black sheep of the family or whether I was,' said Karabas Stafford, seated in the room that had been Connor's study. The funeral guests had stayed for a correct hour, consuming sandwiches and sherry that Felicity could not really afford to give them. They had left some time ago, but Felicity had asked Karabas to stay a little longer.

When he said this about Connor being the black sheep she said, carefully, that she could well imagine Connor being the black sheep of any family, but that it was difficult to imagine a monk in that role.

Connor's cousin said lightly, 'Oh, we're the sinners and thieves of the world these days, didn't you know that, Felicity?' and Felicity looked at him and thought: yes, I can well imagine you being one of the sinners. What I can't imagine is what on earth you're doing inside a monastery.

Karabas was sitting in the slightly battered, deep old chair that had been Con's. He was drinking coffee with perfect equilibrium and Felicity found it eerie to see him there. He was several years younger than Con – perhaps he was twenty-eight or nine – but the resemblance was still startling. Felicity said, 'I didn't even know Connor had a cousin. Actually I didn't know he had any family living.'

'Our generation drifted apart some years ago. A stupid family feud.'

'I suppose you saw the obituary notice in the newspaper,' said Felicity, reaching for the coffee pot.

'News travels,' said Karabas. 'And my family likes to keep a close watch on its own people.'

This struck Felicity as a rather peculiar thing to say. She glanced up and found that he was watching her intently. Their eyes locked and held, and it was suddenly rather shamefully easy to understand why the appalling females at the funeral had been so ruffled. If he looked at them in the way he's looking at me now, thought Felicity . . . She heard her voice say calmly, 'More coffee?'

'Thank you.' He handed her his cup, and when he took it back his fingers brushed her hand. Felicity felt as if she had received a mild electric shock. She managed not to snatch her hand back.

Karabas said, 'When I heard about Connor's death, I wondered if there might be any practical help I could offer.'

He paused, as if considering whether he had used the right words, and Felicity said, 'That's extremely kind of you. Particularly since I'm a complete stranger.'

The smile that was so uncannily not his own touched Karabas's lips. 'There's a strong tradition in my family of helping our own,' he said. 'And even in the monastery in Cumbria—'

'Yes?'

'I've only been with them for a very short time, but they've got the same pack instinct,' he said.

Felicity remembered that the Catholic Church looked after its own, probably more zealously than any other institution in the world.

'Of course, it's more than likely that you're perfectly well provided for,' said Karabas, speaking carefully, as if he was reciting a prepared speech. 'If that's so, forgive me for intruding.'

You could not say to a monk – not even to this monk – that his cousin had gambled and drunk and womanized on money he did not have, and that he had committed fraud and forgery to get that money. You could not say that he had cashed insurance policies without you knowing – Felicity had found that out two days ago – and that because of all these things you were so broke you would consider anything, short of prostitution or murder. Not that monks were given to suggesting either of these activities as solutions to anything.

But Karabas had used the expression 'black sheep', which suggested he knew Connor's faults, and so Felicity said, 'When you say help—?' And paused, because a monk's idea of help might be anything from saying masses for the repose of Con's soul, to a donation from monastic funds.

Karabas said, 'I'm speaking without authority, you understand, but it has occurred to me that I could talk to Father Abbot about the possibility of some work for you.'

'What kind of work?'

He picked up the suspicion instantly. 'It would be a case of two needs – yours and the monastery's – being brought together, Felicity.'

'Yes?'

'There's a small school attached to the monastery,' said Karabas. 'There are only about three hundred pupils or so – but next spring it will be two hundred years since the school started.'

'Bicentenary celebrations,' said Felicity, more or less automatically.

'Yes. *Yes*, bicentenary celebrations.' It was disconcerting to find that as well as Con's eyes, Karabas had the same trick of snatching eagerly at a subject or an expression, and then focusing on it intently for a few minutes as if somehow absorbing it. He said, 'You were in advertising before you married Connor, weren't you? Public relations and promotions?' He used the terms as if they were unfamiliar to him. To a monk, they probably were.

'Yes, I was.' Felicity wondered whether she should ask how he knew this.

'I only saw Connor a few times, but we occasionally had news of him,' said Karabas, as if Felicity had voiced the thought.

This was slightly disconcerting, and so she said, 'Tell me about the monastery.'

'It's mainly a teaching order,' said Karabas. 'But I think they also have one or two retreat houses in various parts of the country. Places where people can stay for a few days to recover

17

from the stresses of modern living. Not necessarily the monks themselves, but people from various walks of life.' Again Felicity received a glancing impression that he was feeling his way through unknown paths.

She said, 'Tell me about the bicentenary.'

'I think the brothers are looking around for someone to organize it,' said Karabas. 'It's quite an important event for them – I was listening to some of the discussions.'

Felicity said, slowly, 'It sounds as if it would be rather interesting. And it's true that I'll have to find some kind of work.'

'I could ask if they would consider talking to you about it,' said Karabas. He was regarding her with his head on one side, almost as if he was listening for her response. Felicity felt an unexpected prickle of alarm. I suppose this *is* what it seems? I suppose he *is* what he says? And then – oh God, is he expecting to be asked to stay the night?

She said, carefully, 'If they really do want someone I'd certainly be interested in discussing it.' It would presumably mean a trip up to Cumbria, but Bryony would be back at school next week, and she could stay with schoolfriends. The schoolfriends' mother had been particularly kind since Con's death, and Felicity thought this would be all right.

Karabas said, 'I'm catching a late train tonight, but when I get back I'll ask Father Abbot if he'd see you.'

So he was not pushing it to stay the night. Felicity's relief was so disproportionate that she said, 'That would be very kind of you indeed. And you'll stay to supper before you go, won't you? And meet Bryony.'

He was suddenly still, and Felicity wondered if she had said something wrong. Ought she not to have invited him to supper?

But then he smiled and said very softly, 'Ah yes, Bryony. Yes, I should like to meet Bryony.'

Bryony Stafford knew about cousins and uncles, even though she did not have any of her own. People at school had them, and talked about them importantly, and Bryony had always wanted to be able to do the same. It was considered to be pretty boring to have a lot of relations: it meant you had to be polite and sometimes there were uncles who had too much to drink and aunts who got cross. Everyone said it was not so great really, Bryony was lucky not to have to bother. Mother said relations were not important, and anyway, a long time ago Bryony would have had lots of them. She told Bryony hugely exciting stories about the people who had lived in her family hundreds of years ago. Their name had not been Stafford, which was Father's name; it had been Foljambe, which was a pretty funny name, but people in those days did have funny names.

They had lived at the centre of an old forest, these Foljambe people. The king had given them the special task of hunting out the wolves – wolves were extremely bad things and so you did not want them prowling and roaming through your forests all the time. Anyone knew that. You did not get wolves any longer – mother had explained this very firmly – but in those days there had been a whole lot of them. It was pretty scary to have to hunt wolves, but you could not say no to the king.

The Foljambe people had been called the king's foresters and they had not minded about hunting wolves because they had thought it was an honour. They had exciting adventures in the forest and also fighting wars for the king, and their children had had lots of exciting adventures, and *their* children as well. There were lots of good stories about them, but the one that Bryony liked best was how the first Foljambe of all had been called to the king's court. His name had been Richard and the king's name had been William the Conqueror, and Richard had had to ride to the king's palace at Westminster, and he had to kneel down in front of everybody for the king to make him the royal wolfhunter. And then everybody had cheered and there had been music and dancing and a big party, and Richard had come home and built a house in the forest and started the adventures.

One day mother and Bryony were going to find the forest where Richard had lived. It would not be as big now, but mother thought there was still a bit of it left. It was in a place called Derbyshire. This would be a pretty good thing to do because Bryony could pretend to be Richard's lady, riding on a white horse with scarlet and gold reins. She would wear her red cloak with the hood, and they would probably kill a lot of wolves and then go home to have a specially lavish tea. When Bryony thought about belonging to the Foljambe family she did not really mind about not having aunts or uncles or cousins.

The cousin called Karabas was part of father's family. Father was dead since last week. Bryony did not absolutely understand about being dead, only that it was sad and it meant you did not see the person again. Mother had said it meant father was with God and all the angels in heaven, but Bryony did not think father was in heaven at all. Heaven was only for good people – they had learned this at school – and although father made people laugh a lot and everybody liked him and said things like, 'Oh, Fliss, *isn't* your Connor a rascal, but *what* a charmer,' Bryony knew that father was not good. He was really two people – Bryony did not understand how this could be, but when the bad person was there father's eyes altered and even if he smiled it was somehow an extremely frightening smile, as if he would like to do bad things. As if he would *enjoy* doing bad things.

She was not sure yet if Karabas was two people like father. He had smiled at her and said that she looked a lot like Connor – mother had said, 'Yes, I think that's one of the things that's going to hurt later' – and he had asked Bryony about her school and her friends, and what things she liked doing best. Bryony had explained about liking to draw and to write stories and Karabas said stories were important: people hundreds of years ago had told stories to one another, and the stories had been handed down and down, and that was what history really was. He said in his own family there was a very old tradition that you learned from stories handed down by your parents and grandparents. People in different parts of the country lived in different ways, he said, and knowing so many of his family's stories had helped him when he went to live in Cumbria. It was very nice in Cumbria; perhaps Bryony would come to see him there, or even to stay for a while?

Bryony looked to mother for guidance, and mother said, slowly, 'Would that be possible? For Bryony to attend the school, I mean?'

'I can't think why not. It's girls and boys.'

It was then that Bryony had known that Karabas was two people after all, because he had looked back at Bryony, who was curled up in her own chair in the corner by the fire, and he smiled father's scariest smile, and said, in a queer whispery voice, 'Because if you do come to Cumbria, Felicity, Bryony must certainly come with you.'

Chapter Three

The young Harvard record-keeper on Piers Adair's team was knocked out with pride to be the one accompanying Dr Adair to the burial ground. He was just knocked out, there was no other word for it.

His name, to his everlasting embarrassment, was Tybalt T Fogg, and everybody in the team called him Tybalt without appearing to think too much about it, but Priscilla called him Tibbles as if he were a cat, for Chrissake, and he just wanted to die every time she said it.

He had listened to the discussion about sneaking into the compound by night without saying very much; it was kind of interesting to see the way people responded to one another, and it was certainly fascinating to listen to Dr Adair.

Nobody had actually disagreed with Dr Adair's idea; the problem had been who should go along with Dr Adair to actually do it.

Toby Friedman declared flatly that nobody had better be expecting him to make one of the party. He was here to research a potential programme about the ways and the history of a remote group of people, possibly descended from an ancient North American Wolf Clan, possibly even some kind of peculiar genetic link between wolves and humans, discovered by Piers to be living on an even remoter island. He added firmly that his brief did not cover grave-robbing in any form at all, and said he would not go into the burial ground if all the television companies in the world went down on their knees and offered him prime time slots every week for a year.

Priscilla thought exhuming bodies at any time of the day was a crazy idea and exhuming them by dead of night was downright insane. This was one expedition where they could count her out, she said.

She could be pretty two-faced at times, that Priscilla. Tybalt knew perfectly well that if it had been a question of just Priscilla and Dr Adair going off together she would have leapt at it, because she would have seen it as a chance to get him in the sack. Tybalt did not much care who Priscilla got in the sack but he hated it when she was mean about Dr Adair's work.

Dietfreid was not going to join the party, either. He said, in jowly fashion, that he would happily analyse any remains they were able to find – he wrote down an extremely grisly list of what they should try to bring out for him – but he would leave the actual disinterring to other people.

'Also, I am not of a shape for bunnelling,' he explained, happily.

'You mean tunnelling, Dietfried. Or maybe burrowing.'

'Tunnelling, yes, thank you.'

Nina said, rather defiantly, that if Dr Adair wanted her to go with him she would; the only thing wrong with this offer was that Nina had so obviously had to dredge up all her courage to make it. Dr Adair looked at her thoughtfully, and said he did not actually need anyone to go with him, in fact too many people pussyfooting around the compound might attract attention.

It was then that Tybalt heard, to his horror, his own voice say, 'I'll come with you, Dr Adair. If you want me to.'

And at roughly the same moment, Toby said, 'Oh hell, I suppose I'd better come really. OK, count me in, Piers, as long as it's understood that this is for the sake of the viewing public only, and if there's any unpleasantness I beat it back to the farmhouse.'

Dr Adair looked at them both, and said, in his cool understated way, 'Thank you very much, both of you. I think that would be an ideal arrangement.'

'When do we go?' demanded Toby. 'Because if 'twere done at all, 'tis well 'twere done quickly.'

'Before you lose your nerve?' demanded Priscilla.

'Exactly.'

'We'll have to wait until the storm's blown itself out,' said Piers.

'I meant what time of day?'

'Midnight,' said Piers, deadpan. 'What else?'

But it was another three days before the storm abated

22

sufficiently for them to walk across the island to the compound.

The rain had stopped, but the wind was still sending the night clouds scudding across the sky. There was a cold, sharp scent in the wind, but a bright clear moon showed them the way.

'Full moon,' observed Dr Adair, glancing up.

'Of course there's a full moon,' said Toby. 'When else would you go grave-robbing?'

Tybalt thought that anyhow they were well equipped for the grave-robbing. He had found a small haversack, and they had packed into it two large flashlights, a hammer, a couple of chisels, and Toby's hip flask. Tybalt carried the team's video camera, in case they might want to record this crazy expedition.

As they went cautiously towards the compound, Tybalt began to entertain visions of capturing for posterity some amazing footage of them actually entering the burial chambers and making world-shattering discoveries there. Dr Adair would offer him a permanent job when he had finished at Harvard and wildlife societies would want him to lecture and be their president. His name would go down in anthropological and zoological circles: 'Tybalt T Fogg?' people would say. 'Wasn't he the guy who got that mind-blowing film of that wolf-tribe?' He was just visualizing himself on national TV when Toby handed him a large spade and told him to sling it on his shoulder, rifle fashion.

'We'll be like three of the seven dwarves going off to the mines,' he added.

Dr Adair said, blandly, 'If we find Snow White, we'll draw lots for her.'

The compound was near the centre of the island, inside the curious ravine that formed a practically unbroken circle around it, and that Dietfreid had likened to a moat. The team had studied this ravine as well as they could without getting too close, and had reached the conclusion that in Cruithin Island's remote past there must have been some kind of freak geological disturbance that had left these huge clefts in the earth. Nina was compiling some botanical notebooks with detailed sketches of the sparse but tough patches of vegetation. The storm was still grumbling to itself somewhere over the North Atlantic, and Tybalt shivered, and wound his woollen scarf more closely around his neck.

'Do we know where the burial ground actually is, sir?' he said, as they neared the ravine. He glanced at Dr Adair and in the dim light saw the narrow smile lift his lips slightly.

Piers said, 'Yes, I know where it is. I charted the island soon after we got here. There are what look like barrows on the north side of the compound. The shapes are too regular for them to be anything other than man-made.'

'I don't remember seeing them,' observed Toby. 'I certainly don't remember hearing you refer to them.'

'No, I haven't. There are times when it's useful to keep the edge on people,' said Piers, tranquilly. 'By the way, Tybalt, you don't have to call me sir every five minutes.'

'Oh, well, right,' mumbled Tybalt through a mouthful of woollen scarf.

'Piers, I suppose you have considered the most obvious explanation of all this?' said Toby, as they made their cautious way forward.

'That we're the victims of a gigantic hoax?' said Piers. 'Of course. But if this is a hoax, it's a damn good one.'

'Better men than you have been fooled, dear boy,' said Toby. 'Remember poor old Conan Doyle tricked by a couple of mischievous schoolgirl flappers into believing that fairies existed? And what about Piltdown Man?'

Tybalt, entranced, asked what Piltdown Man might be.

'One of the all-time greats in forgery,' said Toby. 'It was presented to the scientific community somewhere around 1910, and it was supposed to be a fossil of great antiquity – practically a missing link. But about forty years later somebody realized that the skull was simply an ape jaw fused onto a human cranium.'

'Wow,' said Tybalt, awed, and Piers grinned.

'I'll give you Piltdown Man, Toby, but this set-up isn't a hoax. These creatures have a sound provenance – listen, I did my doctoral thesis on the North American Wolf Clan, for God's sake! And James Frazer records them in *The Golden Bough*.'

Toby, mindful of his image as cynical TV man, said, 'Oh yeah? And just how reliable is *The Golden Bough* anyway?'

'Oh, people will argue that Frazer was sold at least a hundred elaborate fictions,' said Piers, dismissively. 'But there was a castaway in the seventeen hundreds, called John Jewitt, who published a journal of his captivity at the hands of the Tlokoalan Wolf Clan, and it describes some of the rituals he saw. I managed to track down a copy of it while I was doing my doctorate. It makes fearsome reading.'

'And you really think the creatures on Cruithin are connected to this Wolf Clan?'

'That's what we're here to find out,' said Piers. 'Jewitt's wolf-men were brutish, barely-intelligent beings, but from the little we've managed to see of this lot, they're a much more polished version.'

'You know, you're building up a fantastical ancestry for these creatures,' said Toby thoughtfully. 'I thought we'd agreed that what we've been seeing is some form of inherited lycanthropy – OK, maybe heightened by generations of in-breeding – but nothing more sinister than that.'

'Lycanthropy is pretty sinister on its own account,' Tybalt said.

'You're still putting it down to lycanthropy, are you, Toby?' said Piers, looking at Toby intently. 'That's very interesting.'

'Classic case, I should think,' said Toby. He paused, and then said, 'We're here.'

There ahead of them was the compound.

This was Piers's fifth or sixth sight of the settlement that he and his team generally referred to simply as 'the compound', but as they approached it tonight, he felt his heart quicken.

It lay on the other side of the ravine, and it was perhaps a hundred and fifty feet across at its widest point. The ravine enclosed it on three sides, and on the fourth was a sheer rockface, fifteen or twenty feet in height, with six or eight wide-mouthed caves at the foot. As far as they had been able to make out, the caves were used as sleeping quarters.

Piers and Toby had positioned two cameras in the trees, hoping to get footage of the subjects searching for food. Whatever had caused the curious gulch out here seemed also to have given Cruithin Island a degree of fertility that Piers thought unusual for this part of the world, and the creatures they were studying seemed able to grow roots and vegetables which they apparently stored. They also snared rabbits and hares with traps which they set up beyond the confines of the compound, and once a couple of the younger ones had been filmed slaughtering some sheep. The sheep had been roasted over a fire at the compound's centre, although none of Piers's team knew where the sheep had come from. The tribe might keep their own livestock somewhere inaccessible, or they might make periodic raids on neighbouring islands or even on the mainland. The nearest stretch of mainland was wild and bleak, but shaggy sturdy sheep were farmed there. Once the storm had abated, Piers was going to take the launch on a fact-finding tour and see if he could pick up any rumours about sheep-stealing.

He stared across at the dark compound. There had been a fire there tonight, and from time to time the embers were stirred into life by the wind, almost as if a giant invisible hand was shaking them.

'The wind's on our side tonight, isn't it?' said Toby, after a moment. 'It'll hide any sound we might make.'

'On the other hand, it might stir up the invasive scents,' said Piers.

'What invasive scents?'

'Humans,' said Piers.

As they stole around the edge of the compound, Piers's heart was racing. This is the maddest thing I've done so far, he thought. We're actually going inside the compound. What do I do if those creatures sense our presence?

Because they have night-sight, and they have the extra senses that make it all the easier to smell the presence of humans, my dears . . .

He had the feeling that slanting eyes were watching him from the shadowy corners. But nothing moved, except the softly settling embers of the dying fire, and for a crowded instant he remembered his own childhood: his father padding around the garden of the remote Derbyshire house, the two of them gathering dry grass cuttings and kindling and leaves, and then his father showing Piers how to stack everything so that the fire would blaze high up into the night sky. 'You have to have a good blaze,' his father had said. 'It's one of the rules of bonfires.'

Whatever kind of blaze this bonfire had made earlier on, now it had dwindled to a sullen glow at the compound's heart.

'Don't make a sound, either of you,' said Piers, softly, as they crept around the edges of the sinister compound. The dying fire cast mysterious shadows everywhere, giving the illusion of movement where no movement existed. Once Tybalt stopped dead, his heart in his mouth because he thought he had caught a darting movement from within the shadows. He turned round at once, expecting to find that something had slunk out of the shadows and was prowling along behind them, but there was nothing to be seen and the only sound was the scurrying wind.

'This is the stuff that nightmares are made on,' said Toby.

'Yes, but those creatures are all asleep inside the caves.'

'How do you know that?' demanded Toby.

'Instinct.'

'As well as a peculiar upbringing you've got some bloody peculiar instincts, then. I wouldn't know if they were asleep or turning cartwheels.'

'That's not the upbringing, that's years spent studying peculiar creatures, with special focus on television documentary-makers. Let's keep walking forward. Are you OK, Tybalt?'

'Um – yes.' Tybalt was not all right at all, but he would have been torn into pieces by wild horses galloping in four different directions before he would have admitted to it. He asked whether they were not nearly at the far side of the compound by now.

'Yes. The burial mounds should be directly ahead of us,' said Piers, and as he said this, Tybalt saw them.

They were extraordinarily sinister. There were about half a dozen of them, and they seemed to huddle together near the foot of the cliff-face. This is the back yard, he thought, and then: but there aren't many burrows. If these people have been here since Adam, there surely ought to be more?

Piers said, softly, 'But maybe they're deeper than they look,' and Tybalt jumped, because it was sometimes uncanny the way that Dr Adair picked up people's thoughts. To regain his composure, he volunteered the information that the barrows might actually be burial pits.

'Or even bone pits, like – uh – well, like Zoroaster's towers of silence where the bodies were picked clean by birds before burial.'

'You don't miss the chance to add a bit of atmosphere,' remarked Toby, and Tybalt grinned sheepishly.

Walking up to the burial mounds was easily the spookiest thing Tybalt had ever had to do. He kept thinking he was about to be leapt on by the creatures who lived in the compound, and who were even now sleeping inside the black-mouthed caves on the other side of the rock. It was only when Dr Adair said, 'Good God, look at that!' that Tybalt was able to jerk his mind back to the immediate present.

He said, 'What? What are we looking at?' and heard that his voice had risen a couple of octaves. He cleared his throat and said, firmly, 'I don't see anything—'

'There, on the nearest barrow.'

'What?'

'It's a slab of rock,' said Toby, peering through the darkness.

'Yes.' Piers walked towards the mound, which was roughly twelve or fourteen feet in length and about half as wide, bending over to examine it. When he straightened up Tybalt heard the suppressed excitement in his voice.

'The rock has been shaped to fit on top of the barrow,' said Piers, his eyes shining. 'It's been smoothed and honed to the exact right size as if somebody wanted to create a covering, or a lid—' He leaned over again, absorbed and intent, and after a moment said, 'Tybalt, you were right – this isn't a barrow, at all, not in the real meaning of the term. It's a tumulus – what some parts of the country call a how. I've seen similar ones in Derbyshire, where there was once a massive forest, teeming with wolves.'

Tybalt thought he had never seen anything quite so gloweringly sinister as this crouching hump with its lid of reddish rock. He produced the flashlight and waited for Dr Adair's decision, his heart thumping.

'It's a burial chamber,' said Piers at last. 'I'm almost certain of it. And I think this piece of rock is the roof.' He looked across at Tybalt and Toby. His eyes were blazing with excitement, and his dark hair was whipped into disarray by the wind.

Tybalt said, 'Does that mean we can't excavate it after all?' and knew, with a queer blend of sinking heart and spiralling anticipation, that it did not mean any such thing.

Piers said, 'Does it hell mean we can't excavate it! We're going in!'

'*Now?*'

'Now,' said Piers, and picking up the spade, he inserted it between the rock lid and the ground.

Chapter Four

The lid came loose far more easily than any of them had expected, but it did so with a nerve-jangling scrape of rock against stone that sent the fear scudding across Tybalt's skin all over again, and made him turn involuntarily to look into the shadows afresh.

'Nothing watching us?' said Piers, matter-of-factly. He sounded so unconcerned that Tybalt would have bet his pulse-rate was absolutely normal.

He glanced over his shoulder again. 'I don't see anything, sir – I mean, Dr Adair.'

It would be absurd to say that it was not a question of seeing, it was a matter of feeling. Tybalt felt as if the night was coming alive with little rustlings and scufflings, and as if inward-slanting red eyes were watching.

Between them they set about dragging the lid around, so that it would lie at right-angles to the tumulus. As it moved a sour, tomb-like stench gusted out, and Toby and Tybalt both stepped back at once.

'Nasty,' said Piers. 'All right, Tybalt?'

'Never better,' said Tybalt, faintly, and Piers grinned.

'Have a pull from Toby's whisky. While you're at it, give me one, as well.'

Tybalt said, 'If this project lasts much longer we'll all end up as raving alcoholics.'

And then Dr Adair pointed silently, and Tybalt saw that beneath the red slab was a rock-lined vault, going down and down into the earth. Piers flicked on the torch, shading most of the beam of light with his hand, and they saw the shallow stone steps, worn away at the centre. There was no need for any of them to say anything; they all knew they were going into the vault, and they knew they were going into it now.

Piers paused. 'One of us will have to stay up here,' he said.

'To keep watch and warn the other two if anything approaches.'

'That's for me,' said Toby at once.

'OK. Tybalt, how about it? Are you on for coming down there with me?'

'Uh – yes, sure.'

'Good for you. Toby, for the love of all the pagan gods that ever walked, sing out if anything nasty looks like appearing from the compound. But find yourself a bit of cover.'

'I'll lurk in the undergrowth,' promised Toby. 'Not that there is much undergrowth, but there's enough.'

'All right. Tybalt, here we go. Remember to tread delicately like Agag.'

'He means you've got to walk on eggshells,' said Toby.

'I *know* what he means—'

'Well, down you go, then.'

Piers went first, directing the torch carefully, and Tybalt followed, feeling the ancient darkness of the rock vault close around him. There was a brief feeling of suffocation and of a brooding silence that ought not to be disturbed, so that for a moment he thought he would not be able to go on.

And then common sense reasserted itself, because this was only a crumbly old burial vault, dug out of the ground by an extremely primitive set of people, and in the interests of scientific research – and Toby's TV programme – they were just going to take a look. No, be honest, it's not only that, thought Tybalt. We're curious as hell. He glanced at his companion. He's certainly curious as hell, thought Tybalt.

The steps went down and down. Tybalt had gone down quite a long way before it occurred to him that maybe he should be counting them, but they reached the foot without mishap and Dr Adair shone the flashlight around.

'Do we just go straight forward?' Tybalt had instinctively lowered his voice but the rock passage picked it up anyway and magnified it into dozens upon dozens of eerie whispery echoes.

'I don't think there's anywhere else to go,' said Piers. 'This is quite a narrow tunnel and unless I've lost my bearings it winds under the compound. We'd better be ready to scoot back out, Tybalt.'

'OK.'

'Be careful – the ground slopes downwards quite sharply.'

As they walked along, they both had the feeling that they were going deeper into a strange world where all the natural laws might have been suspended, and where far more ancient, far grislier ones might hold sway.

Piers suddenly said, 'The tunnel's widening— Dear God, look at that!'

They both stopped dead. The narrow rock tunnel had widened into a vast, high-ceilinged cavern, lined with the same reddish rock that sealed the entrance, but containing what looked to their astonished eyes like dozens upon dozens of rock shelves, cut into the sides.

And on the shelves . . .

'It's a small catacomb,' said Piers, softly. 'There must be ten or fifteen generations down here at least.'

'All laid out on rock shelves,' breathed Tybalt. He stared in fascinated horror at the skeletons, some of them half-mummified from the dark airless cave, so that shreds of leathery skin clung to the bones giving them a spurious air of life. 'And they're *seated,*' he said, forgetting to keep his voice low, so that the echoes picked his words up and sent them scurrying all around the cavern. *They're seated, they're seated* . . . 'They've been buried in a sitting position,' said Tybalt, his voice high and strained. 'Why were they put like that?'

Piers was moving cautiously around the cavern, shining the torch as he went. 'It isn't entirely unknown for human corpses to be buried in a sitting position,' he said. 'These look as if they were originally crouching.' He continued his exploration, moving a little away from Tybalt, his expression absorbed.

Tybalt, left alone, glanced uneasily over his shoulder. They had a flashlight each, and clearly it was up to Tybalt to share in examining the cavern. But the shadows lay like black sinister pools everywhere and anything might be crouching in them . . . He hesitated, and then was so cross with himself for being such a dork that he delved into his pocket and switched the flashlight on.

The cold electric light slithered in and out of empty eye sockets, creating a grisly impression of pale, watching eyes, but Tybalt determinedly swept the beam over the walls. There was nothing to see apart from the poor bones on their rock shelves, layer upon layer of them, and whether the shelves were man-made or not, they stretched all the way round—

They did not stretch all the way round at all. Directly behind Tybalt, low down near the ground, was a roughly hewn opening, so shrouded in thick choking cobwebs that for a moment it looked as if a musty grey curtain had been drawn across it. It looked as if it might be a small alcove scooped out of the rock face, and the entrance was barely three feet square. Tybalt knelt down and poked cautiously at the cobwebs with the butt of the flashlight, pushing them aside like a mothy curtain. There was a sad dry sighing, and the cobwebs stirred slightly as if a soft cold breath had blown onto them. Tybalt shone the flashlight cautiously, the light slicing through the blue and violet darkness.

The alcove widened beyond the narrow opening, and for a moment he thought there was nothing here, and that this was just an empty hollow in the rock. He moved the light again, and something cold and hurting seemed to close about his guts. They're more bones, but they're smaller. And although most of them look as if they've been shovelled in and that they've just lain where they fell, there are others—

He tore aside more of the shrouding cobwebs to see better, and said, 'Uh – Dr Adair – I think you should see this.'

'What? What have you found?' Piers crossed the floor and knelt down next to Tybalt, peering into the terrible cavern. There was a moment of horrified silence, and then he said, 'Oh, dear God.'

The two of them stayed where they were, kneeling side by side in silence, and then Piers said, very softly, 'They're children. Dozens of children's skeletons. How unbelievably pitiful.'

'But they aren't laid out like the others, are they?' Tybalt's voice came out a bit too loudly, and he took a gulp of air. 'Those on the ground – can you see?' he said, re-directing the flashlight.

'I see them.'

'They look as if they've tried to crawl towards the entrance – the skulls are twisted around as if they were trying to catch the last thread of light before they were left down here in the dark for good—' Tybalt broke off abruptly, and felt Dr Adair thrust Toby's flask into his hand.

'Drink it,' said Dr Adair insistently, and Tybalt obediently gulped down the neat whisky, shuddered, wiped his mouth with the back of his hand, and said, 'Sorry. But this is dreadful.

Oh God, it's the most dreadful thing I've ever seen—'

'It's the most dreadful thing I've ever seen as well,' said Piers, still staring at the heaped-up bones. 'It's like something from Belsen or a third world famine.'

'They weren't all dead when they were put here, were they? Those ones on the ground—'

Piers said, 'Bones can do strange things after death. There can be contraction or expansion, depending on the temperature. And there may have been landslides above that shifted the earth and disturbed things down here.'

Bullshit, thought Tybalt, but he was grateful all the same. He managed to say, in a fairly level voice, 'How long would you think they've been here?'

'Quite a while,' said Piers, his eyes still on the appalling skeletons. 'Maybe centuries. No, I'm not trying to make you feel better, Tybalt: if there'd been any mass murders lately the media would have nosed it out, even in such a remote place as this. Murder is news these days, and serial murder is big news.'

'That's true. Uh – some of the bones look as if they've been – gnawed by an animal—'

'Whatever happened to them, it probably happened years ago,' said Piers, still studying the heart-breaking bones. 'I'd guess that they're the victims of ritual killings, Tybalt – generations of ritual killings.'

'We shouldn't move them, should we?'

'Not really. There'll have to be a full forensic investigation – carbon-dating of the bones and the dust. It's like a cross between a Lady Chapel and an alchemist's crucible in here,' said Piers, still looking at the pitiful little bodies. He stood up, brushing the dust from the knees of his cords, and in a conversational tone said, 'We'd better get on with the body-snatching. One of those from the lower shelves, I think, don't you?'

'We're going to be offending about a hundred shibboleths,' said Tybalt, uneasily.

'Oh yes. But let's do it anyway,' said Piers.

Tybalt looked at him. 'You feel strongly about this, don't you? I mean – you feel that it's something you have to do.'

For a moment he thought he had stepped beyond an invisible boundary, but then Piers said, very quietly, 'Yes.'

'Well,' said Tybalt, after a moment, 'how do we do this body-snatching bit?'

'Empty out the large haversack,' said Piers, producing plastic sample bags. 'You weren't thinking I meant us to carry one of these things back with our bare hands, were you?'

'No, but I am truly glad to hear you say that, Dr Adair.'

Piers said, 'And I'm glad to hear that you haven't lost your sense of humour, Tybalt.'

'That would be the last thing to go,' said Tybalt valiantly.

It was as they were preparing to leave that Piers went back to the pitiful rock alcove, and shone the torch into it once more. He did not say it to Tybalt – he would not have been able to say it to anyone – but he wanted to make a silent farewell to the dead children and to explain to them that he would come back. It was the height of illogicality, of course; he knew the children had been down here in the silent dark for God alone knew how long, and he knew they had been dead a long time – from the look of them, most of them had been dead for decades.

But it was not the reasoning, logical part of Piers's mind that was driving him: it was a much deeper, much more secret part. It was the part that had compelled him to set out on this mad quest in the face of all odds; it was the part that had driven him to half-cajole, half-bully the necessary backing from the university and to set up the deal with Toby's TV company.

Standing in the dark cavern he felt the past rushing forward to engulf him – his own past and the past of the sad little victims left to die down here in the dark – and he felt the long-ago despair and helpless fear of the dead children pour down the centuries.

I know what happened down here, thought Piers, standing very still. I know that those children were herded into this dark grim place, and I know they prayed for rescue. They were terrified, but it was only later – when they knew that no rescue was possible – that they prayed for death because what was ahead was too appalling for them to bear . . .

And they're still here, those prayers, he thought, tilting his head to listen. They're very faint, but I hear the resonances.

Help us . . . Don't leave us in the dark with the wolf . . .

Tybalt was still in the outer tunnel, putting the bagged skeleton into the larger of the two haversacks, and Piers shone the torch into the alcove one last time. And then he saw what he had not seen before.

Stone jars. Six or eight of them, standing on a low shelf of rock just inside the cavern: large urns, similar to the funerary jars the Egyptians used for storing organs removed during the embalming process. For a moment he wondered whether these people followed the same practices, but then he saw that the jars were unstoppered. A chill of revulsion brushed his skin, and his mind churned with all the grisly rites and customs that were inextricably woven into mankind's history: the Ancient Egyptians feasting on the cooked limbs of the gods in the belief that they would imbibe the gods' divinity . . . The devouring of parts of the human body by primitive tribes – the liver for valour, the heart for courage, the testicles for strength, the eyes for the soul . . .

You fool! he said to himself. You know quite well what they are.

He glanced back at Tybalt, and then slowly and stealthily reached into the alcove and grasped the nearest jar. He drew it out, careful not to disturb any of the skeletons, and tucked it into his own haversack.

'Here we have an ordinary skeleton,' announced Dietfreid, firmly, frowning at the unpleasant fragments of humanity he had spread over the table. 'The skull is perhaps a little narrower than I have seen, but there is to find nothing extraordinary. It is the skeleton of a human.'

It was not until Dietfreid said this that Piers realized the extreme state of tension he had been suffering. He was aware of his taut muscles relaxing for the first time for forty-eight hours.

Toby said, 'Can you be sure about that, Dietfreid?'

Dietfreid regarded Toby over the top of his spectacles and said certainly he could be sure. He tapped the skull bone with a chubby finger. 'This is a young man perhaps of twenty, perhaps of thirty years,' he said. 'I have not the instruments here to be any better precise, I would need to use a laboratory on the mainland.'

'I don't think we'd want to put you to the trouble—'

'It would be no trouble,' said Dietfreid earnestly. 'Nina could assist me,' he added hopefully. Nina realized with a sinking of her heart that she had been right about a potentially awkward situation developing.

She said, 'I hate to say this, Dr Adair, but it's practically disappointing, isn't it? I mean – finding that they're ordinary human beings after all.'

'You're using that word "ordinary" about them again, Nina.' Toby frowned, and said, 'But I'll admit it's a bit of a let-down.'

Nina asked if anything else had been found in the catacomb. 'Anything to give us any other leads, I mean?'

Piers hesitated for a fraction of a second. Do I show them? he thought. And then – yes, don't be absurd, of course I do. He said, 'As it happens there is something.' He reached into his own haversack which was lying at the side of his chair. 'Dietfreid, would you take a look at this?'

'What is it?' demanded Dietfreid, suspiciously.

'It's just a stone jar,' said Priscilla, in a what-a-fuss-about-nothing voice. It was remarkable how patronizing Priscilla could sound. To counteract this, Nina leaned forward to see what Dr Adair had placed so carefully on the table. And felt at once as if malevolence was pouring into the room.

'It's more than just a stone jar,' she said. The large vessel with its bulbous body and narrowed neck was like a giant earthenware salt or sugar jar. It was a larger version of the storage jars you might have seen in your grandmother's scullery when you were small. Only there's no stopper, thought Nina, staring at it.

Piers said, 'Yes, Nina, I think it is much more than just a jar,' and he lifted it and turned it in his hands. Despite her wholly incomprehensible aversion Nina found herself thinking: I wish he'd turn me around in his hands like that. She glanced at Priscilla, and thought: oh bother, she's having exactly the same thought.

'I take a look,' announced Dietfreid.

'Let's all take a look,' said Priscilla.

As they took the jar in turn, Piers watched them closely. Neither Priscilla nor Toby displayed anything other than ordinary curiosity, although Tybalt seemed to hesitate slightly.

When it was Nina's turn she took the jar firmly and sat up straight, because she was feeling a bit dizzy and she was determined not to let Dr Adair see. But the instant she had touched the stone vessel, waves of sick revulsion had scudded through her whole body and she had to struggle not to throw it down. It's evil, she thought. And it's *old* evil. No, I'm being ridiculous. She forced herself to examine the jar minutely, even borrowing Dietfreid's strong torch and magnifying lens to look inside. There were dark smeary marks on the pitted interior, and as Nina bent over she half-thought that a soft tainted breath gusted into her face. It's blood, she thought. Old dried blood. But once it was fresh warm blood, and it flowed into this jar straight from someone's body . . . She shut off the thought before it could develop any more, and passed the jar rather abruptly to Dietfreid.

Dietfreid was ponderously thorough. He got up to bring one of the oil lamps nearer, repositioned his rimless spectacles, and politely requested the return of his magnifying glass which he clipped onto his right-hand spectacle lens.

'The pot it is perhaps coarse baked clay,' he pronounced, after a moment, and looked across the table, one eye hideously distended by the lens.

Piers said, lightly, 'I thought it might be. It was in the children's cavern in the catacombs.' He was aware of Tybalt glancing at him in surprise.

Dietfreid set the jar down on the table. 'The age is considerable,' he said, frowning at it. 'Again, we have not the facilities. But there is a trace of something that once has sealed up the top – animal fat, perhaps, such things were once used that way. The substance that lingers itself within the inner crevices, I do not know it.'

'It's human blood,' said Piers.

'Tsk, first there must be the analysis.'

Piers said, 'I know. But you'll find that it is human blood.'

'Are you sure?' said Toby.

'Oh yes. I think this is one of the sacred Blood Jars of the Tlokoalan Wolf Clan.'

'*What?*'

'It was one of their earliest rituals,' said Piers. 'Frazer refers to it, and so does John Jewitt in his journal. When the Wolf Clan killed for sacrifice, they always chose victims with descendants – children, or even grandchildren, who were approaching puberty. They drained the victims' blood into stone or earthenware jars, and the children were forced to drink the blood of their ancestors. If they survived it, they were admitted to the tribe as adults. If not—'

'Thrown into the catacomb?' said Tybalt, after a moment.

'I expect so.'

'Why?' asked Toby at length. 'I mean – what was the logic behind it?'

'At a guess it was an archaic form of genetic breeding and selection,' said Piers.

'They wanted to strengthen their lineage?'

'Yes. Whatever that lineage was.' He looked round the table. 'You're all looking shocked. But the drinking of an ancestor's blood was once quite a well-known custom. It crops out in folklore all over the place.'

'Yes, but hearing you say it, and seeing that jar—' said Priscilla, and stopped, and for the first time since arriving on Cruithin, Nina had a twinge of fellow-feeling for Priscilla.

'There is an old German tale,' said Dietfreid, looking solemn. 'Or perhaps it is French. Not good to give to children to read. But it tells of the capture of the child by the wolf, and then he forces her to drink blood.'

'I know that one as well,' said Nina, momentarily diverted from the jar. 'I came across it when I was doing my final-year dissertation—'

'English folklore?' drawled Priscilla, with the faint patronizing note of someone saying: oh yes, about the level I would have expected of you, dear.

Nina knew she would never have a fellow-feeling with Priscilla again, but she said, in a bright, friendly tone, 'Well, it was English and North European folklore as a matter of fact. But it comes in a nineteenth-century Brittany legend and I rather think it's one of the nastier endings to *Little Red Riding Hood*. The wolf puts the grandmother's blood in bottles and after he's eaten her, he induces the little girl to drink the blood.'

'Darling, would you *mind* not being quite so graphic,' said Priscilla, and Toby observed that he had thought somebody would bring Red Riding Hood up sooner or later.

Priscilla said, 'I suppose we aren't on the wrong end of some kind of massive fake, are we? I mean about the Wolf Clan and that eighteenth-century guy's journal?'

'If it's a fake, it's a very elaborate one,' put in Nina. 'And what would be the point of it?'

'Those catacombs surely weren't a fake,' said Tybalt, firmly.

'I saw them. You should remember that, Priscilla.'

'Tibbles, beloved, would I forget it?'

'But look here,' said Toby, 'if we're talking about fakes on this scale, we're getting into the territory of Piltdown Man again. To say nothing of William Ireland, Richard of Cirencester—'

'The moral of it all,' said Priscilla, 'is that you never go public with any discovery unless you're sure your ground is rock-bottom solid.'

'But I have a rock-solid bottom,' cried Dietfreid excitedly. 'I have said this is an ordinary human skeleton, and this is a clay pot, perhaps with blood once in its insides. I do not mistake about these things and if there is a fake I do not see it.'

'Then if any of those big bad wolves really do escape from their lair, it looks as if it's Red Riding Hood after all,' said Priscilla. 'More coffee, anyone?'

Chapter Five

When mother said they might leave London for a while and go to live somewhere else, Bryony at first thought this might mean the huge big forest where Richard and the Foljambes had lived. But mother said, no, unfortunately they were not going there, although they would one day. That was a definite promise.

Bryony knew definite promises could not be broken, and in the meantime, there was the place called Bracken, which was where mother was going tomorrow. Bryony would stay with the O'Callaghan twins while she was away which was always fun.

While mother was away there was a painting afternoon at school. You could paint anything you wanted, so Bryony painted the house in the forest which Richard Foljambe had built when the king made him the royal wolfhunter. The house was in a lot of mother's stories and Bryony knew how it looked. It was built of grey stone and it was a big, *big* house, not in a row with other houses like London, but all by itself. There were five doors to get inside. Two were at the very front and one was for visitors – that one was a wide oak door with a twisty iron ring for a handle, like churches had. Another of the doors was at one side of the house so that people could go from the sitting room straight into the garden, and one door went into the kitchen. Bryony thought Richard and his family would not have called it sitting room or kitchen.

Last of all there was a tiny door made of blackened wood tucked away in the darkest corner. It was almost hidden behind ivy and bits of stone and if you went close to it, it smelt very nasty indeed. This was the door to the cellars and the cellars were the scary part of the house, because that was where the Foljambes kept all the things they needed for trapping the wolves. If Bryony ever found the house she would make extra sure not to go through that door. Mother had not told Bryony about the cellars or the wolf-catching things, but Bryony knew about them anyhow. She did not know how she knew: it was just one of those things that you did know without anyone telling you. There were iron traps which were like giants' teeth – horrid grinning ogres' teeth that would chomp down on your legs and gobble you up if you were not careful.

The Foljambes hid the giants' teeth in the forest and covered them with bracken and grass so that the wolves could not see them. When the wolves came prowling through the forest they stepped on the teeth which came snapping down on the wolves' legs and broke them. This was not a nice thing to do, but if you were a wolfhunter you had to be practical. Sometimes the wolves were trapped in the giants' teeth all night and they howled in pain for hours and hours, so that people going through the forest whispered to each other to hurry along in case the wolf got free and came and ate them up.

The house made a good picture, and at the end of the afternoon it was chosen to be put in the art room for a display. They all went to the art room to see it fixed to the wall and it looked very splendid. There were grey walls and several chimneys, and there were stables at the back because Richard and his family had to have horses to ride out into the forest. You could not kill wolves without riding a horse; anyone knew that.

And Bryony had put in blobs of green for the ivy that grew over one of the walls, and brown and gold trees behind the house that were the forest in autumn, and everyone in her class stared at it and said things like, Ooh, what a *spooky* house, or, I can see *ghosts* through the windows.

Several people instantly began playing at ghosts, and the O'Callaghan twins found the dust-sheet that Miss Wilson used to cover the windows when there was a film show, and they danced around making wailing noises, until Miss Wilson came back and told them to behave, because she was not having her class acting like a lot of savages, and if Caroline O'Callaghan had torn that dust-sheet she would have to stay in at playtime tomorrow and mend it.

Richard's house was not really haunted. The cellars were not very nice, but the other parts were all right. People had lived there and been happy.

Bryony was a bit sad to be leaving London and her friends, but it was only for a little time, and the twins said she could come to stay with them in the holidays and Miss Wilson was going to have a letter-writing lesson so that they could all write letters. She told Bryony that it was very exciting to be going to live in a new place: Cumbria was very beautiful and Bryony must write a description of it, or paint a picture. They would all look forward to that.

This was all pretty good. The only bad part about going to this new place was that Karabas would be there as well. Bryony wondered whether mother knew about Karabas having the same bad person behind his eyes as father. She wondered whether she ought to tell mother, and then she remembered that mother was still trying not to cry about father being dead. It would be better not to say anything.

Bracken village was twenty miles or so from Caldbeck. Felicity had to take three wearying train journeys, and then an expensive taxi to reach it. She normally enjoyed train journeys, but she had a twinge of shameful anger against Connor who had crashed the car beyond all redemption when he died. It would have been so much easier to drive up here.

The interview with the finance company had been a nightmare but they had agreed to delay the repossession, and although they were trying to sell the house as quickly as possible to pay the debts, the truly colossal interest on the loan was soaring by the day. Felicity did not think there would be much money for her at the end of it. There might be fifteen or twenty thousand pounds. It sounded quite a lot regarded as a lump sum, but from the point of view of being homeless it shrank alarmingly. It would not buy so much as a cupboard in London and Felicity did not think it would buy much more than a cupboard anywhere else. She spent the first half of the journey trying not to hate Connor who had put her in this humiliating situation, and the second half trying to work out where she and Bryony would live after this thing with the monks was finished. Always supposing that this thing with the monks came off in the first place.

The first sight of the school was insensibly cheering. Felicity, who was still thinking in terms of sordid coinage, thought that the view by itself had to be worth about a thousand pounds.

The school was called Bracken Hall and it was a grey stone manor house with huge grounds and sprawling outbuildings that Felicity thought would once have been stables or coachhouses. The house looked as if it had been built in the early seventeen hundreds, perhaps for some nouveau riche landowner who had wanted to found a dynasty but had not managed it. Behind the house were smudgy blue and purple hills, threaded here and there with shining glimpses of lakes.

'Tarns,' said Brother Dominic, smiling kindly at Felicity and handing her a cup of tea across his desk. 'They call them tarns up here. It's a nice word, isn't it? We try to teach the children a bit about the local geography and geology, although of course, we have to stick to the curriculum pretty fiercely.'

He was plump and genial and he did not look as if the word fierce could even be in his vocabulary. His study was lined with dozens of books – mostly on Catholic doctrine and lives of various saints, although Felicity made out a few works of fiction – and his desk had the kind of pleasant clutter that made her think of an old-fashioned university don. The rooms all smelt of polish and sun-soaked fruitwood and there was a feeling of immense contentment everywhere.

'I expect Karabas explained what it's all about, didn't he?' said Brother Dominic, who took his tea well sugared and had made sure that a plateful of scones was on the tea tray. 'Remarkable, isn't it, the way God provides? You're meeting our need and we're meeting yours.'

'I hope so,' said Felicity, accepting a cup of tea.

'The thing is, it's by way of being our bicentenary year,' explained Brother Dominic. 'And Father Abbot thought it might be rather nice to mark it accordingly. We haven't too much money – well, I daresay you'll understand that – but we could pay a tiny salary although it'd probably be a pittance to somebody like you, Mrs Stafford—' He paused to butter a scone and added a spoonful of honey. 'I should explain that I'm the Bursar, so I can talk about our finances with reasonable authority.'

'Yes, of course.' I'm going back in time, thought Felicity. I'm stepping into a world that I didn't think existed any longer: a gentle, scholarly world where people still use nice old-fashioned words like 'bursar' instead of 'finance director' or 'company secretary', and where afternoon tea with home-made

44

scones and honey is served at four o'clock.

And although it seemed improbable that this nice pink-faced monk would ever have had even a nodding acquaintance with the kind of financial situation that was staring Felicity in the face, she met honesty with honesty, and said, 'Even a pittance would be welcome.'

'Ah. That's a worry for you,' said Brother Dominic, with cosy sympathy. He named a figure and Felicity did some frantic mental arithmetic. It wasn't quite a pittance, although it wasn't riches either. But it was enough.

'I should say there's a staff flat vacant just now which you'd be welcome to have,' said Brother Dominic, happily. 'That would help a bit, maybe?'

'Oh yes. Yes, it would.'

'Our predecessors turned part of the old stables into flats, and they're a mite small, but really quite nice. You've a daughter, I think Brother Karabas said?'

'Yes, she's just seven.'

'Well, there's the Primary Two class,' said Brother Dominic, at once becoming businesslike, and then, as Felicity was relapsing into some more mental arithmetic to see if the brothers' idea of a pittance would stretch to cover the fees here for a couple of months, he said, 'And of course, since you'd be on the strength for a time, your little girl would be our guest as a pupil. Miss Mackenzie takes that age-group, and she's really a very good teacher indeed. She has a wonderful way of firing the children's imaginations.'

Felicity liked the sound of this, although Bryony's imagination did not take much firing at the best of times. 'Don't you – do the brothers not teach?'

'Oh yes, but only some subjects. There's a great dearth of young men entering the church these days, Mrs Stafford, and so we're a mixed bag. Lay teachers in the main. But we take the religious instruction classes ourselves, of course, and also languages. We have two French brothers here and also a young Italian who's halfway through his novitiate, although he has his teacher's diploma, thanks be to God. And we try to give the children a smattering of Latin although they pick up a good deal of that from the music sessions.'

'Plainchant?'

'Yes, and some of the great Masses – Mozart and Verdi and

Bach. We're quite keen on music here – there's a school choir and a school orchestra.'

'How lovely.' Bryony would adore all this; she would love the rich pageantry of the religious ceremonies even if she did not understand it all. Felicity set down her teacup, and said, 'It's all sounding too good to be true. Perhaps we should talk about what you're wanting for your bicentenary and find out if I'm what you want. Have you any particular ideas? Apart from the school activities, that is?'

'Oh, I haven't a single idea,' said Brother Dominic, cheerfully. 'And neither has Father Abbot. He's not so young as he was, you see, and we try to save him as much as possible.' He leaned forward, and Felicity quenched an impulse to look over her shoulder to check that nobody was listening. 'He tends to have memory lapses,' said Brother Dominic. 'And he gets fixated on things. He'll probably talk to you about St Columbanus. Don't worry if he does.'

'Well—'

'He has a fixation on Columbanus just now,' said Brother Dominic. 'It's all perfectly harmless. He's eighty-eight, and please God he'll reach ninety-eight without getting any worse.'

'That's a great age.' Felicity wondered whether abbots were allowed to retire, or whether they just went on forever like the Pope.

'Oh it is. And really, he's done a great deal of good work for the Order,' said Brother Dominic. 'He set up two of our retreat houses practically single-handed – although that was nearly twenty years ago, I'd have to say. Of course, he could travel about more then.'

Felicity remembered Karabas mentioning the retreat houses. She asked if the Order had many.

'Four,' said Brother Dominic. 'It was nearly five – Father Abbot wanted to create a retreat centre on some remote Scottish island somewhere; I don't know how he got to hear of the place, but Brother Andrew went out to take a look and he said it was so primitive it was like stepping back two hundred years. We had to abandon the idea.'

'But wouldn't people want somewhere tranquil if they were retreating from the world for a while?' said Felicity.

'Yes, but they'd want electricity and drains,' said Dominic. 'And means of getting to and fro. Brother Andrew said they had to wait on the mainland for two days before they dared take the motorboat anywhere near the place.' He poured himself a second cup of tea, and said, 'But let's talk about the bicentenary. We don't know much about creating publicity in the Catholic Church. We attract it from time to time, of course, but it isn't always the sort we want.' He grinned, rather engagingly. 'So we'd much prefer to hand this thing over to somebody who knows what to do. If you can come up with the ideas, we can choose the ones we think will suit best, and then leave it to you to follow them through.'

It was several years since Felicity had given a presentation for a new account, and she had certainly never given one in such surroundings, but she said, 'I've thought about it a bit and I think there are several ideas you could consider.'

'That sounds splendid.' He opened a notebook and flattened it out, looking up at her with an alert expression.

Trying not to make it sound too much like a prepared speech, Felicity said, 'Most of this is largely off the top of my head – but I tried to see it from the aspect of children and education. So starting at the top, if you wanted to venture on something on a national level you could sponsor a national schools event – a drama festival or a music festival. Where it's held would depend on the facilities you've got, of course – you might need to involve the nearest large town—'

'Caldbeck,' said Brother Dominic, promptly. 'Maybe even Keswick,' he added, looking slightly awed at the enormity of this. He made a note, and said, 'I think we'd like the music festival idea very much.'

'I like that one as well. But if it turns out to be impractical or just too large-scale, you could have an essay-writing project for children – I don't just mean a couple of pages of scribble, but properly presented projects for a whole class or a study group. Bound folders or booklets, maybe illustrated by the children themselves, perhaps printed on the computers they all have in classrooms these days. That would involve several areas of work for them. Photography, art, research. Desk-top publishing even.'

Brother Dominic wrote this last phrase down carefully and studied it from several angles.

Felicity grinned, and said, 'The subject ought to mirror the bicentenary: perhaps it could be something like the progress

47

of education during the last two hundred years. Ragged schools to writing slates to computers.' She glanced at him and saw that he was listening with intense interest.

'Next is that you've got terrific grounds here,' said Felicity. 'I saw them from the taxi window. Your school choir and orchestra might give a really up-market open-air concert with food and wine, like Glyndebourne. Mostly for parents and friends but also any local dignitaries. I don't know about funding for the expense, but—'

Brother Dominic said funding could probably be squeezed from somewhere.

'You could sell tickets,' said Felicity. 'That would help. And it wouldn't need to be too highbrow, some of it could be pop. I don't mean the way-out stuff. The winners of the music festival could perform – that could be part of their prize.' She hesitated and then said, 'You've probably already thought about a celebratory Mass at some point, but it would be lovely if that could be an open-air ceremony as well – I'm sorry, I'm not terribly familiar with that side, but if it could be the highest Mass you've got, sizzling with some really marvellous music—'

Brother Dominic grinned, and jotted this down as well. 'This is all wonderful. Anything else? Not that we need it, but—'

'It might be nice to mount an exhibition of the school's two hundred years – if you've got sufficient space, which it looks as if you have. If not, perhaps there's a local town hall or good library nearby, which might come in on that – in fact they might do so anyway. The present pupils could get involved there. Then there's ex-pupils. Are there any distinguished ones, and if so, would they give talks or contribute to some kind of charity auction for the school's benefit – maybe to build a new swimming pool or equip the gym or something like that.' She paused for breath and grinned at him. 'How am I doing?'

Brother Dominic laid down his pen, shut his notebook, leaned forward, beaming, and said, 'When can you come?'

Felicity drew in a huge breath of relief, and smiled back. 'Would tomorrow be too soon?'

Tomorrow was too soon, of course; Felicity knew neither of them had taken that seriously.

After the meeting, there had been supper with the other

monks and several of the lay teachers, and the fifty or so boarders.

'We haven't the space for more boarders,' explained Brother Dominic. 'But we take some.'

Supper was taken in the refectory, with the pupils sitting at five or six scrubbed-top tables, and the monks and teachers at their own table at one end.

'We don't make it a rule that everyone attends supper,' said Father Abbot, who was old, with the pale, polished look of gentle old age, but who greeted Felicity warmly. 'It isn't always possible. But if we can, we like to have this little hour together at the end of each day. It's a time when we can exchange our bits of news: sometimes there's been a problem, and it might help to take a look at it between us. Or something amusing or interesting might have happened and it's good to share that, as well. This is a community, you see. And we're all friends in God. St Columbanus taught us that.'

'Yes, of course. It's rather a comforting arrangement.'

Felicity had been expecting that Karabas would be in the refectory, but it still came as a shock when she saw him. He was standing a little apart from the others, but he smiled at her with the smile that had been Connor's, and came over to her at once.

'I'm glad to see you here,' he said, giving her the brief platonic kiss that seemed to be a mark of greeting in religious life. There was a moment when it felt very far from platonic and when his hands closed on her shoulders with sudden hard strength. His body brushed Felicity's and she was aware of a strong warmth emanating from it.

She experienced a sharp jolt of emotion at the pit of her stomach and to cover it, said, 'I'm beginning to think I'm glad to be here.'

'Yes, it's a beautiful place.' He stepped back and the impression of sensuality vanished. 'Is Bryony looking forward to coming?'

'I haven't told her much about it in case it didn't happen. But,' said Felicity, looking round the narrow, rather austerely furnished room, 'I think she'd like to live here.'

'I'd like it as well.'

There was absolutely no reason why this should sound faintly sinister. Felicity started to make a vague, polite response, when they were interrupted by one of the younger brothers pronouncing grace.

The food was brought in and set on the tables by four of the pupils and it was plain but good. Vegetable soup, obviously home-made, was followed by shepherd's pie. There was stewed fruit and custard to finish, and tea or milk afterwards. The pupils fetched this for themselves from two large urns at one end of the refectory. Felicity noticed that they were lively and apparently perfectly normal and happy. There were a number of gigglers among them, but they were all quite well-behaved.

I could live here, she thought. I could live here and I could enjoy working here, and Bryony would love it. Please let it happen. I even think I could forget Connor here. And then she looked up, and saw Karabas watching her out of Con's eyes, and a horrid little voice inside her said: oh, could you now?

When Brother Dominic brought a cup of tea to her, she asked how long Karabas had been with them.

'See now, it would be . . . about a month.'

Felicity stared at him. '*One month?* I mean – is that *all*?'

'Yes, he came from one of our other houses – somewhere in Scotland, I think. Unusual character,' added Dominic, glancing across the room.

'In what way?'

'Well, he's a curious mixture of naivete and worldliness,' said Brother Dominic, lowering his voice slightly. 'Things you'd expect him to know, he doesn't, and *vice versa*. But of course,' he added, 'that does sometimes happen with very young men who come to us from remote regions where they haven't kept too much pace with the times. I believe Karabas is compiling some botanical treatise or other, and we have quite a good library here, so that's probably why he came. We're treating him as a rather raw new recruit, because between you and me, he hasn't a huge amount of theological knowledge. But then,' said Brother Dominic, with the happy simplicity of the true religious, 'if he's a crofter's son or something of that nature you wouldn't expect it, and as Father Abbot says, a great many of the Early Saints weren't what you would term theological scholars. It's the faith and the commitment that counts.'

'Yes, of course.'

'You didn't know Karabas until now?'

'No. My husband lost touch with his family and I hadn't

met any of them. Karabas came to the funeral. He was a complete surprise.'

'As a matter of fact,' said Brother Dominic, 'he was a bit of a surprise to us as well. We'd never heard of him, until he turned up one afternoon, thinking we were expecting him and that we knew all about him.'

'But – you did know about him? About his background?' I'm being absurd, thought Felicity.

'Karabas said when he was very small he saw Father Abbot once, and it influenced him,' said Brother Dominic. 'Father Abbot doesn't know if he remembers him or not, although of course, he doesn't know what he does remember half the time. And there was supposed to have been a letter of introduction, not that anyone actually saw it. In the end we decided that Father Abbot had probably lost it.' He sent a glance to Father Abbot in which affection and exasperation were about evenly mingled. 'I did tell you he was forgetful, didn't I?'

'Yes, you did.'

Felicity looked across the room and met Karabas's eyes again. She said, slowly, 'So neither of us had heard of Karabas until he turned up out of the blue.'

Chapter Six

Bracken Hall was just about the best place Bryony had ever seen. It was pretty funny to live in part of a stable so that all you had to do to go to school was walk across a courtyard, but mother had explained that it was all part of the arrangement with the monks. And although the house was smaller than the one in London, there was plenty of room for them both, and Bryony could have the twins to stay at half-term if she wanted – there were only two bedrooms in the stable house but Brother Dominic had said they could usually find space for the odd guest in the school.

School here was not the least bit like school at home. It was a big old house with rooms with names Bryony had never heard before, and there was a chapel where they had Mass on Sundays. Mother had said Bryony did not absolutely have to go to Mass, but it would be polite to the monks who had been so kind. Bryony quite liked Mass, especially if it was the evening one, when the sunset came pouring into the chapel through the coloured pictures on the windows. There was the most beautiful music, and something called incense was burned in a round golden ball.

The stable house was pretty good. Mother had brought some of the things from London – Bryony was pleased about that; she had her same bed and the dressing table with the crinkly mirror. There was a sitting room with windows that had lots of tiny panes with swirly glass in them. Bryony's bedroom was the tiniest room you ever saw, and it had a sloping roof over her bed, so that when she woke up in the morning she had to remember not to sit up because of banging her head on the slopy bit.

Mother had a tiny office in the school where she worked all morning, but she was always back at half past three when Bryony came home. Mother often brought work back for the evening – she said it was very interesting work and she was liking it very much – but sometimes she went back into the school to have supper in the refectory. Bryony was not allowed to go in to supper, but on the nights mother went, one of the boarders came to sit with her for an hour. They watched TV or played games or made a jigsaw. It was pretty good when this happened.

Karabas was here. He sometimes waited for Bryony after her last lesson; he seemed to know the time her lessons finished and that she always went back to the stable house through a courtyard with wooden benches which was where the monks sometimes sat, reading small books with shiny leather covers. He walked back to the stable house with her sometimes. Bryony was not sure yet about this, because of Karabas having the same evil, frightening person as father had had behind his eyes, but after a time it began to seem as if this person had gone away. Still, it would be as well to be careful.

And Karabas was actually pretty interesting if you could forget about the secret evil part. He knew a lot of things about the countryside, and about trees and plants, and he had good stories about forests and the people who had lived in them. He said that there was a forest near Bracken – he called it a wildwood, which he said was a very old word for a particular kind of forest.

This was interesting. Bryony explained about the Foljambe people and how they had lived in a forest hundreds of years ago, and fought wolves for the king. That might have all happened in a wildwood, what did Karabas think?

Karabas thought it was sure to have done. Anyone wanting to hunt wolves would have to live in a wildwood, because those were the forests that wolves liked best. You got a certain kind of darkness in a wildwood which wolves found useful, and because wildwoods were so extremely ancient you sometimes got the lingering fragments of things that had lived in the world thousands of years ago. Because once upon a time there had been magic on earth, and if you were very lucky or if you could look at the ancient forests in the way that the wolves looked at them, you might catch glimpses of that magic.

When Karabas spoke about darkness in forests Bryony had a horrid feeling that the evil person was starting to peer out through his eyes, and she got ready to say she had to go in for her tea. But then he said, Once upon a time there was magic on earth, and she forgot about the evil person and listened, entranced. Nobody really believed – not absolutely truly believed – in magic, but Bryony and the O'Callaghan twins and one or two others privately agreed that you could not be sure. In all the good stories people were always falling into other worlds. They did it by getting into magic wardrobes, or by finding enchanted boxes or magic stones, or exploring ruined caves or castles, but they did it.

But best of all Karabas knew about the Foljambe people, which was pretty lavish because Bryony had thought only she and mother knew about them.

But Karabas knew; he said they were what had been called hereditary foresters. What was even better than best was that he knew about Richard, who was Bryony's absolute favourite Foljambe. He said Richard had been a very good hunter of wolves, and the house he had built in the wildwood had become very famous. People had liked to be invited to Richard Foljambe's house on account of the wonderful time they always had there. There would be wolfhunts in the forest all day, and then at night there were immense banquets with more food and wine than Bryony could imagine. Richard brought in troupes of jugglers and acrobats to entertain his guests during the banquets, and sometimes there would be a dancing bear and gypsy musicians. And Richard's wife would be there as well – her name had been Madeleine – and she had been so beautiful that people had travelled miles just to see her. Bryony was glad to know all these good things about Richard and to know he had a very beautiful wife with a name like Madeleine which was not a name she had ever heard before.

And then Karabas said they could go to the wildwood near Bracken one day.

'You have a half-day holiday next week,' he said. 'We could do it then. We could go together and take a picnic.'

The funny thing was that Bryony had been thinking she would quite like to go to the wildwood with Karabas, and hear some more about Richard. But when Karabas said about having a half-day holiday and about them going off together the evil came back at once, and this time it was not just his eyes that changed: his voice changed as well. It went whispery and treacly, and it would be just about the worst thing in the world to go with him into a wildwood where there was magic and stuff like that. Bryony remembered that you had to be very careful about magic. Everyone said so.

So she said, in her best voice, that she would have to ask mother, and wondered if it would count as what Father Stephen called a mortal sin if she told Karabas that mother had said no.

The house in London had been sold quite quickly, although Felicity suspected the purchase price was a good bit less than the real value. She heard, with a feeling of wry irony, that her estimate had been almost exactly right: when everything was paid off and all the people who were apparently entitled to a percentage had taken it, there would be just on seventeen thousand pounds left to her.

Seventeen thousand pounds. On its own this might buy a pantry somewhere. Put with a mortgage it would probably represent a reasonable deposit. The trouble with mortgages was that you had to be in fairly secure employment. This was something that Felicity would have to worry about when Bracken's bicentenary was over. For the moment, she stowed the money in a deposit account, sent off a reminder to the Pensions Department of the DSS that she was still waiting for them to start paying her Widow's Pension, which seemed to be taking them a very long time to do, reminded them of her new address, and burrowed back into work.

The bicentenary project was shaping well. Felicity was enjoying being at the centre of it: she thought the monks were pleased with what she had done so far, and she was quite pleased with it herself.

The monks had liked almost all of her original suggestions, and had decided on the music festival as the centrepiece of the celebrations. The school choir would start rehearsing a *missa solemnis* next term – Felicity gathered that this was an extremely High and fully choral Mass – and Brother Martin, who was the abbey's precentor, was anxiously consulting with Mr Lucas, the music teacher, as to whether they could venture on Beethoven's Mass in D Major, or whether they had better play safe with J S Bach. It was reported that Father Abbot had transferred his allegiance from St Columbanus to St Gregory, the father of sacred chants.

A large part of the bicentenary would be the choral competition for schools and youth groups and clubs. Felicity had managed to reach most of the county education departments, sending them details and asking them to circulate schools in their area. There had been a gratifying response so far. Qualifying heats would mostly be held in the schools' county towns, and local judges would be used: Felicity was compiling lists of suitable people.

They hoped to get a minor music celebrity for the semi-finals and the final itself, which would be here in Cumbria. Father Abbot had unexpectedly announced over supper one evening that he had a cousin who had married a relation of the Earl of Beck, whose country seat was about forty miles west of Calder. They would ask if the house might be used for the final, said Father Abbot, beaming.

Nobody had quite liked to question this, because nobody had known if it was another of Father Abbot's fantasies, but in the end Felicity and Brother Andrew the sub-prior had composed and sent a careful letter to the Earl's estate manager, and a very friendly, very positive response had come back. The Earl would be delighted to make Beck Old Hall available for the occasion; the old ballroom which was seldom used these days should provide sufficient space, and it would be rather nice to open it up again. They opened the Hall to the public on certain days during the season and so they could provide a modest supper with wine on the night.

'For a fee, I suppose,' said Brother Andrew.

'Yes, but quite a small one.'

Brother Andrew, a Scot to his toes, said you could trust the aristocracy of England never to miss an opportunity to add to their coffers.

The Earl also said that if they wanted, he would be very happy to present any prizes to the finalists, and Felicity, after consulting with the brothers again, rummaged in the etiquette books for the correct way to address a belted Earl and wrote back to accept, enclosing a programme of events and suggesting dates. Morag Mackenzie, Bryony's class teacher, said with a hopeful glint that the Earl had been a bit of a lad in his youth and was still known to have a roving eye.

'Isn't there a countess?' said Felicity, but Morag said even if there was it would not bother His Lordship, and did Felicity think that her brown velvet would be going over the top?

'Morag, nothing's over the top these days.' Privately Felicity thought she would tactfully try to get Morag into something really stunning for the Earl's supper. She was a bit homely looking and she had nondescript-coloured hair, but her skin was good and she had nice eyes. She suggested, carefully, that velvet might be a bit warm for March, had Morag considered that aspect?

Morag said glumly that it was all very well for Felicity. 'It's easy for you. You'd look good in a sack with your figure and your hair.'

The first time Felicity had met Connor he had said, 'You have hair the colour of an autumn sunset shining through copper beech trees. You're someone I'd be apt to fall in love with, and I suspect that I'm going to marry you.'

'Don't be absurd.' Felicity had not been expecting to meet a lunatic at this very ordinary drinks party in Fulham.

'I'm not being absurd. You aren't married already, are you?'

'No, but— How much have you drunk?' Felicity had said to this maddening, charming stranger.

'I'm not drunk. But don't you think there are chords in the human mind, Felicity, and that sometimes they can be made to sing? Don't you believe that our souls quietly spin their own webs, and that sometimes the webs brush against one another?' He'd grinned. 'I truly am not drunk,' he'd said.

'Then I must be.'

Neither of them had been drunk that night – Con's drinking had started much later – and when he took her home in a taxi they had both known where the evening was going to end. Felicity had been twenty-six, and she had been on her own for seven years. Her mother had died when Felicity was fourteen, her father when she was nineteen. She had lived and worked in London for four years, and she thought she was pretty level-headed. There had been several men in her life and two had been serious and one had been disastrous, and some had been brief adventures. But she had known perfectly well that even if the wildest madness in the world gripped you, you did not take home unpredictable strangers whom you had only met two hours earlier, and you certainly did not end up in bed with them.

Except that she had taken the unpredictable stranger home,

and they had ended up in bed, and it had been shameless and abandoned and rapturous. It had been midsummer madness, of course – well, all right, it had been mid-September madness. Four weeks later, the madness had culminated in marriage with the unpredictable stranger.

Bryony had been conceived on the afternoon that they had run out of petrol when they were driving to a friend's weekend cottage in Wales. Instead of setting off down the road in search of a garage or a phone they had free-wheeled the car off the road, and Con had pulled her down in the long grass and made wild love to her with the rooks wheeling in the blazing blue sky overhead, and the cool grass under her bare skin, and the scent of heat and love everywhere . . . And the thudding weekend traffic only a couple of dozen yards off, for God's sake!

But there had been the heart-shaped leaves of wild bryony plants twining around some shrub or other nearby, and when Bryony was born she had Felicity's heart-shaped face and burnished-copper hair and her name had been pre-ordained.

If Con had lived – if Con had stayed as the Con she had met – that afternoon was something they would occasionally have mentioned with a pleased chuckle or a sideways grin, and every time they had driven along that road one of them would have suggested stopping, and sometimes they might even have actually stopped—

Felicity felt bitter anger all over again, because she ought to have been able to grieve properly for Con; she ought to have found the memories painful and poignant, but they should have been memories she could store away. They would have been good memories, as well; made up of passionate dawns and sudden parties, and of wine and music in front of log fires in winter . . . And the crazy expedition to Northern Spain when the car broke down and they ran out of money . . . The night of Bryony's birth when Con had cried in her arms . . .

But it was no use wrapping any of the memories up and hoping they would emerge, dimmed and cobwebby with the years, but sweet and good. (*'Because there are chords in the human mind that can often be made to sing . . .'*) It was no use, because the good things were inextricably muddled and muddied with the bad. The violent drinking bouts – the frightening changes of mood when a stranger had looked out of Connor's eyes, like the line by somebody-or-other about the devil behind the looking-glass . . . And then the women, oh God yes, the women . . .

The whole thing was false; it was a sham. Con was a cheat and a liar and a screwer-around – all right, he was a *charming* cheat and liar and screwer-around, but he wasn't the person Felicity had believed he was when she married him.

But whoever Connor had been, or whatever Connor had become, it was still intolerable and unbearable to have the sadness tarnished, and to have the ache of loss all snarled up with bitterness. Go away! cried Felicity in silent anguish to Con's memory. Go away from me, and go quickly, because I can't bear it!

Chapter Seven

The monks were as carefully efficient about her post as they were about everything. Felicity's letters were always brought to the tiny study that had become her office, shortly after the service the monks called Terce.

'The third hour of the ancient world,' Brother Stephen had said. 'When the Holy Spirit came down on the Apostles at Pentecost.'

There was unexpected comfort in hearing these time-worn rituals, and in realizing that despite the modern world, the monks of Bracken still adhered to the framework that had gradually evolved over twenty centuries. I'm pushing you back, Con, thought Felicity, I truly am.

The letter was one of several that morning; there were more entrants for the choral festival, which was pleasing, and there were estimates from two different printing firms for the commemorative brochure that was going to be on sale locally. Some ex-pupils had sent in old photographs, and Brother Dominic and Brother Andrew had written a very good potted biography of the school and the Order. Felicity had spent two absorbing days in the local archivist's office, unearthing all manner of old press cuttings and bits of information about Bracken Hall's first owner; the archivist had discovered an account from the builder who had built the original house in the early seventeen hundreds, written in a faded sepia copperplate hand for £2,226.17s.6d. This put Felicity's seventeen thousand in a different light, although not when you remembered that approximately two hundred and eighty years separated the two amounts.

The last letter was a brown, anonymous-looking missive, stamped with the insignia of the Department of Social Security. It was from the Pensions Department, from someone with an indecipherable signature. This person explained, in tones of businesslike regret, that they had no record of Connor Stafford having paid any kind of National Insurance contribution during the years that Mrs Stafford had notified to them. A computer search had been run on Connor Stafford, and the only person of that name it had yielded was a gentleman from a small village on England's north-east coast. This Connor Stafford had died in 1975 at the age of eighty-two, and appeared to have been without any family whatsoever. If Mrs Stafford could write again, confirming that the details already provided were accurate – that was, full name, date and place of birth – and giving any other information she could, they would re-check their records. In the meantime, very regretfully, they had to inform her that she was not entitled to the State's Allowance for Widows. If she was suffering any kind of hardship, they recommended her to get in touch with her nearest Social Security office at once, quoting this reference number.

'Of course there's been a mistake,' said Karabas, gesturing Felicity to a chair in his small, but surprisingly comfortable bed-sitting room in the monks' dorter wing. 'I didn't know Connor terribly well, but he certainly existed, and he certainly wasn't an eighty-two-year-old man in 1975.'

Felicity had taken the chair facing him, with a small electric wall fire between them. It was already dark outside, and Karabas had switched on a small desk lamp and drawn the curtains. The fire gave out a little glow of warmth, shutting them in. There's intimacy about that, thought Felicity, involuntarily. I think I'd better be a bit wary here.

She said, 'Do you know, I was beginning to have wild ideas that Connor wasn't Connor at all, and that he had borrowed this other man's identity. I even began to wonder if I'd fallen into a John le Carré book.' She glanced up, and for a split-second saw a blankness in Karabas's eyes. He doesn't know what I mean, thought Felicity, and felt a tug of unease.

To cover it, she said, 'But I expect that it's nothing more sinister than a computer error somewhere – it's always happening these days. But it might help if I could get more details about Connor's family. I thought you might be able to put me in touch with someone – your father, perhaps, or if there are any other cousins— It's just to find out a bit more information and pass it on.'

There was a pause. Then Karabas said slowly, 'What kind of information do you want, Felicity?'

It was absurd to think that his voice altered when he said this. Felicity said, in as practical a tone as possible, 'Well, things like where Con was born or where his family lived. Even his mother's maiden name.'

This time the pause lasted a good deal longer. He doesn't like me asking this, thought Felicity. But Karabas said, slowly, 'My father died some years ago. I don't think there's anyone alive now who would remember Connor's side of the family. He was always a bit of a mystery creature,' said Connor's cousin and looked at Felicity with his head on one side. Felicity stared at him, and felt his words stir up all the things she had been forcing her mind to banish. Because Karabas was right; Con had been a mystery creature, he had appeared from nowhere, but somehow that had been part of his attraction.

'You don't want to know about family, Fliss,' he had said to her once. 'Nothing that happened before I met you matters. It scarcely even exists. Isn't it more fun to think I might be anybody? I might be illegitimate royalty, or a gypsy prince. Or I might be the heir to the Romanov throne, Fliss, or the descendant of King Arthur or William Shakespeare.'

Only once had he spoken seriously about his family. 'I left them a long time ago,' he had said, his eyes suddenly dark and inward-looking. 'And I learned about the world in my own way, and at the start I made a lot of mistakes, but as I went on and grew older, the mistakes grew fewer.'

Felicity had met Con's wilder flights of fantasy with pragmatism – even though it would have been blissfully easy to let him carry her into those fantasies with him – but for all that there had been an undeniable air of dark romance about him. It had been something that made you remember all the eerie tales of demon lovers, and of silver-tongued seducers with chill faery blood in their veins who lured their victims into the dark greenwood and then cast aside their human disguise . . . However pragmatic you forced yourself to be, it was still uncomfortably easy to cast Con for the role of any one of these. Because whatever he might have been, he had had the ability to set a spell working and he knew about the chords deep within the human mind.

None of this could be admitted, of course, but Felicity,

looking across at Connor's cousin, who also knew how to set a spell working, said, 'You're quite right about the mystery.'

'Oh yes. I daresay he traded on it a bit.'

'Yes. Yes, he did.' And so do you, thought Felicity, meeting the strange eyes.

But monks surely did not deliberately surround themselves with mystery or mystique, and they most emphatically did not send out lures to females. You read about the occasional vicar going off the rails with a woman – there had even been a couple of bishops recently – but monks were the gentle, scholarly side of Roman Catholicism. They were the contemplative side. Celibates. Felicity stared at Karabas and thought: if you're a celibate I'm the Archbishop of Westminster.

And then Karabas smiled and Felicity saw that he, like Connor, possessed the ability to summon a dark and faintly dangerous charm; and that he too had at his beck an eerily seductive will o' the wisp, a satanic shadow-self who might be roused by firelight and aroused by moonlight, and who would beckon to a victim with eyes that were set aslant. And the poor victim, if she was not careful, might find herself lured deep into the dark tanglewood land of legend . . .

Felicity said, in a slightly too-loud voice, 'How is your work going? Brother Dominic said you were making a study of botany, or – or wildlife, was it?'

'A little of both. This is an interesting part of the world,' said Karabas, and Felicity felt the clutching unease recede a little, because the glint was fading, and he was sounding almost ordinary again.

She said, 'You didn't know this part of England before?'

'No, my branch of the family are from farther north.' He smiled, and said, 'A fairly remote part of Scotland.'

This chimed so well with what Brother Dominic had said that Felicity began to relax. A remote part of Scotland probably explained several things, among them the accent which Felicity had not been able to quite pin down. She said, 'Do you use this room as a study?'

'Some of the time,' said Karabas. 'Although I've been out exploring the area – collecting samples and studying the different species which inhabit this part of England. That's particularly interesting.'

'Yes?'

'Oh yes,' he said, softly. 'There's a great fascination in how so many plants and creatures mirror their surroundings. In some cases, they alter over the centuries to blend with them, did you know that, Felicity?' He made her name sound almost like a caress.

'No,' said Felicity.

Karabas leaned forward, the false fireglow casting its crimson shadow over the upper part of his face, and Felicity remembered all over again about the not-quite-human seducers who lured unsuspecting females into the greenwood. She had the sudden irrational thought that his dark hair was worn rather long for a monk. And if I look, I almost believe I might see that his ears are slightly pointed. Only I don't think I'd better look.

Karabas said, 'Nature has a remarkable way of adapting. Where I come from, there are forms of life that have altered to blend with their backgrounds.'

For some reason, this was vaguely sinister. Felicity said, 'Forms of life? Plants and animals?'

'There are butterflies which can masquerade as flowers. There is even a species of spider that bears the imprint of a human skull on its back – a case of nature stamping a villain with a warning.'

He hasn't answered my question, thought Felicity. She said, 'Does that often happen? That creatures change their shape to deceive?' And thought: I don't believe I just said that.

'Nature often marks the more rapacious of her creations,' said Karabas, his eyes never leaving Felicity. 'If you look, Felicity – properly and deeply look – you will see nature's bloodied paw prints in the most unexpected places. They are meant as omens. They mean, This one is clawed and toothed. That one enjoys the blood and the flesh of humans. Do not venture too close to them.'

This was straight out of *Grand Guignol*. Felicity forced cool politeness into her voice, and said, 'How very interesting. Do you – um – collect any specimens of those creatures?' And thought: well, that was just about the most outstandingly stupid thing I could have said, because now he'll say, in that slurry voice, Oh yes, I have some here, my dear, and it'll turn out to be the twentieth-century equivalent of 'come up and see my etchings', and I think, I really do think, that I'd better get out of here fast! She stood up, and saw for the first time the large stone jars standing on a shelf by the window.

'What are the stone jars for?'

'Certain species. Special ones.'

There was another of the pauses. Felicity said, 'They're killing bottles, aren't they?'

'Yes. Of a kind.'

'They look rather large.'

Karabas said, softly, 'Yes, they are large. But if a large species of life is being killed or preserved, that is necessary, Felicity.' The caress was back in his voice.

Felicity stared at him, and thought, well, that settles it, I've absolutely got to beat it out of here before—

The rest of the thought was cut off as he put his hands on her shoulders. He's going to kiss me, thought Felicity, wildly. Only it isn't going to be platonic this time, it's going to be something much more than that . . .

But Karabas's lips just brushed her cheek, and his hands rested lightly on her upper arms. Felicity was just drawing a shaky breath of relief when his grip tightened and he pulled her against him.

Barely four seconds passed before he let her go, but in those seconds she felt the hard insistent press of masculine arousal against her thighs.

And then he stepped back and smiled at her, and there was absolutely no doubt about the intimacy of his smile. He's acknowledging it, thought Felicity, her emotions tumbling so frantically she had no idea of what she was really feeling.

'Goodnight, Felicity,' said Karabas, softly. He opened the door and stood back to let her leave.

Bryony was writing a composition for Brother Stephen. It was part of Primary Two's weekend homework and it was quite important. A composition was a story, and the story was to be about one of the saints. It did not matter which one: they could go to the school library and read about all the saints, and then choose whichever one they wanted.

The library was full of the nice smell of old leather and you had to be very quiet. Miss Mackenzie showed them the shelf with books that had titles like *A Children's Guide to the Holy Saints*, *The Life of the Little Flower*, and *The Picturebook of Saints*.

Most people chose saints who had their own names, or well-known saints like St Theresa, or St Francis, or Joan of Arc, but Bryony chose St Barnabas. There was not a huge amount of stuff about St Barnabas in *A Children's Guide to the Holy Saints* but there was some, and anyhow Bryony knew about St Barnabas already, in the same way she knew about the dark, evil-smelling cellar below the forest house.

St Barnabas's Day had been an extra-special day for the Foljambe people, because it was the only day when they were allowed to kill wolfcubs in the forest. Generally the Foljambes had hunting parties in March and September which was OK with the king who wanted all the wolves dead, but he had said that wolfcubs could only be hunted on St Barnabas's Day which was the eleventh of June. In those days you had to do what the king said or you might be taken off to his castle and shut away in the dungeons for ever.

Bryony was not going to put any of that in the composition; she was only going to tell about St Barnabas's Day in the forest and the Foljambes being able to hunt wolfcubs. She wrote this down in her jotter which was what you had to use for rough notes.

Everyone in the forest house prepared very carefully for the St Barnabas Day Hunt, which did not set off until the evening – the time when it was nearly but not quite dark. The right word was twilight, but when Madeleine came to the forest house to marry Richard she had called it the Purple Hour, and said that at the very heart of all true wildwoods you got a smudgy violet and dark blue twilight, which was very beautiful.

The night before St Barnabas's Day, Richard's page, whose name was Edmund, was always sent down into the cellars to bring up the iron wolf-traps. Bryony did not know quite as much about Edmund as she did about Richard and the other Foljambes: this might be because Edmund had not been part of the family. But she knew quite a lot and one of the things she knew was that Edmund hated the cellar. He was not a whole lot older than Bryony – Bryony thought he might be ten – and he had been sent to live in the forest house with the Foljambes and be brought up by them. He had to wear the Foljambe livery which was like having a school uniform, and it was green and gold and very splendid. Edmund liked it very much. He liked living with Richard and Madeleine Foljambe and learning about things called archery and falconry. In fact the only thing in the forest house he didn't like was the cellar. He always tried never to go through the evil-feeling door after dark, and he tried to absolutely never go through it by himself. But on the night before St Barnabas's Day, which the king called St Barnabas's Eve and the Foljambe people called Wolf Night, it could not be avoided. Richard Foljambe had told Edmund to go down to the cellar and bring up the giants'-teeth wolf-traps, and so it had to be done.

You could smell the evil as soon as you got near to the black door; a sour, wet smell like an old drain, but on Wolf Night Edmund pretended to himself that it was not there. He got the key and went around the outside of the house to the horrid black door. The ivy had grown over it since the last hunt and Edmund had to push it aside. The door creaked when he opened it and the creak was like somebody scratching a nail across a slate.

Inside the door were steps going down and down, and with every step the smell and the frightened feeling grew worse. Bryony expected Edmund had taken a candle so that he could see the way. It was a bit spooky how she could see it all so clearly: Edmund, shielding the candle flame with a cupped hand because of the snatchy whispery little wind down here that blew backwards and forwards like something invisible that chuckled to itself and leaned forward to huff its blood-smelling breath on you.

Edmund was careful about the candle flame because if the whispery gustiness blew it out he would be in the absolute dark and being in the dark in the cellar would be the worst thing ever.

When he was almost at the bottom of the stair, he stopped. From here the candle flame picked out the spears and hooks all stacked against one wall. It picked out the giants'-teeth traps as well, glinting redly on them so that it looked as if they were smeared with blood. There was a bad moment when Edmund thought they moved, grinning and working their jaws up and down, and saying to one another, *Oho and aha, here is a nice little human boy to gobble up.* And, *Come closer, little human boy, so that we can see you all the better.* It was only the candlelight flickering, of course: Edmund knew this and Bryony knew this as well, but it was a bit frightening; well, it was very frightening indeed.

And then the light fell across the little door at the foot of the stair, and Edmund shivered because this was what he had been trying not to look at.

Behind the door was a cupboard, an old, old place, and it was a *bad* place. It was the place where the first wolf of all – the creature the Foljambes had come to the forest to hunt – had had his lair, which was a black kind of cave in the ground. Richard had built the forest house over the lair, and he and Madeleine and all the other grown-ups thought the wolf-creature had been killed. But they did not know that the wolf-creature had had a son who still lived in the wildwood, and who sometimes caught children and carried them back to his lair to eat.

Edmund knew it was important to tiptoe past the terrible black door in the cellar, and never, on any account whatsoever, peep through a crack in the door. If you did that, you would see down and down into the lair, and you might see the wolf-creature crouching on the pile of raw bones that was all that was left of the children he had eaten. What he usually did, that bad old wolf, was to drain the children's blood out into big stone jars and then drink it down. Sometimes he saved it for his wolfcubs to drink, but mostly he drank it himself because he liked the taste. It ran down his face onto the ground and sometimes it came puddling out beneath the space under the door. It did that tonight as Edmund tiptoed past, trying not to let the candle be blown out. He was not looking at the door but he knew that the blood was trickling out, thick and oozy and bad-smelling, and he knew that if he listened carefully he would hear crunching sounds from inside the cupboard, which would be the wolf crunching on the children's bones. It was important to be very quiet, because if the wolf heard him it would call out: it would say, *Come over here, my dear*, which was what wolves always said.

But if Edmund did that, the wolf would come bounding out, and it would pour his blood into huge jars so that it could drink it, and then it would chomp him up.

But Edmund was very quiet tonight, just as Bryony would be quiet if she found that house and went into that cellar. He scurried across to the traps and the spears, grabbed the nearest, and then ran as fast as he could back up the stairs and out into the garden. And then he was all right.

None of this came in mother's stories, which were always exciting and happy, and Bryony was not going to put any of it in the composition. Brother Stephen might not like a composition about wolf-traps and people being chomped up by wolves.

But Bryony wrote about St Barnabas's Day in the forest and the Foljambes being able to hunt wolfcubs then, and how the twilight had been called the Purple Hour. It was a pretty good composition. *A Children's Guide to the Holy Saints* said that St Barnabas had lived in Cyprus and that his name meant comfort, so Bryony put this in as well.

When it was finished she showed it to mother who said it was a very good story indeed.

'What possessed the child to choose Barnabas I can't imagine,' said Brother Stephen, reading Primary Two's compositions in the monks' common room on Monday evening. 'Of all the saints, he's the one we know the very least about.'

Brother Dominic, who had been looking over some of the children's endeavours, said that Bryony had a remarkable imagination.

'Yes, she's a bright little thing.'

'Where on earth did she conjure up this business about hunting wolfcubs in the wildwood on St Barnabas's Day?'

'I can't imagine.' Stephen marked Bryony's composition with a red 'A' and made himself a mental note to ask Miss Mackenzie if Bryony's story mightn't translate into one of the little playlets that the younger children sometimes acted at end-of-term concerts. It was nice to give them such a creative project, and also it taught them about the lives of the saints and the simpler Bible stories. Primary Two had done The Last Supper the previous Easter, with the senior domestic science class providing food and raspberryade for the wine, and it had been very successful.

'Have you read your niece's literary efforts, Brother Karabas?' said Dominic, glancing up.

There was a fraction of a pause, and then Karabas said, 'Not yet.'

'Do read it.'

'Yes, I will.'

It was probably forgetfulness on Brother Karabas's part that

he went into supper half an hour later without having looked
at Bryony's story.

Chapter Eight

Piers had known that he would have to return to the catacombs and the pitiful bodies in the children's cavern; what he had not known was that he would feel so strongly compelled to do so almost immediately. It's as if they're calling to me, he thought, in mingled horror and panic.

On the night after the conference over the skeleton and the blood jars, the team had thrashed out the question of an investigation into the catacombs. In the end they had agreed they would have to return to the mainland.

'We'll have to abandon the project,' said Piers, his voice expressionless. 'We'll leave the island as soon as the sea swell subsides—' On the other side of the table Dietfreid nodded in firm agreement. 'And I'll report on what we've found and get a proper investigation set up,' said Piers. 'Toby, you still might have a documentary, but it'll be a different one than you expected.'

'I always expect the unexpected, professor.'

'There must be many forensic samples taken from the catacombs,' decreed Dietfreid. 'Also scrapings of rock and earth as well as bones. It is Piers's discovery and so he will certainly be asked to head the investigation—'

'I hope I will, Dietfreid.'

'But I should like to help,' added Dietfreid, hopefully.

'Yes, of course.'

'Before anybody can head anything, those people in the compound will have to be neutralized,' offered Tybalt.

'Any suggestions, Tibbles?'

'I'm working on it,' said Tybalt, glaring at Priscilla with set teeth, while Dietfreid rumbled happily on about sifting the soil and the necessity for good photographs of all stages of the excavations.

Nina thought they should contact the nearest police at once, but Piers said, 'Why? There was no evidence of violence. And the bones have been there for a very long time. Another week or two won't hurt them.'

'Police there must be,' agreed Dietfreid. 'But not before it is assured that the caverns are properly sealed by experts.' He accepted a second plateful of the very good goulash that Nina had cooked for supper, tucking his napkin into his collar in businesslike fashion.

Piers thought: Dietfreid's right, of course. We mustn't disturb a single speck of dust without having a properly trained team and controlled conditions for an investigation – and permits to excavate the cavern properly, of course. Oh God, bloody bureaucracy, it'll take weeks! He allowed none of his thoughts to show. He declined a second helping of goulash, refused coffee, and eventually escaped to his own bedroom at the front of the half-dilapidated farmhouse, where he lay awake, listening to the others coming to bed at various times over the next hour. There was a *sotto voce* interchange between Dietfreid and Nina: Dietfreid's tuba voice rumbled suggestively, and Nina said something soft and regretful. Piers heard Dietfreid stump disconsolately off to his own room, and he smiled wryly.

But as silence closed down on the old house, Piers stared up at the cracked ceiling, trying to push away the memories of the murdered children who had been lying so patiently in the dark for so long. I promised them I'd go back. I promised I wouldn't leave them in the dark with the wolf . . .

Save us from the wolf, they had cried to him that night, their terror echoing and spinning painfully around the caves, and Piers knew that it had not been the sleek, silky-flanked animal with its sable coat and pricked ears the children had been so afraid of, but the macabre creation of the darkest of all the dark fairy stories: Perrault's '*Old Gossop Wolfe who met the little Red Riding-Hood in the forest, and had a good mind to eat her up*'. It was the slavering wolf who could walk upright like men, and who had the wit to dress up in grandmamma's clothes, and to don grandmamma's frilled mob-cap and lie in grandmamma's bed with the sheets pulled well up, and wait for the trusting little girl to knock at the door, *toc-toc* as Perrault put it . . .

I understand, thought Piers, staring up at the cracked ceiling. I understand because once upon a time it happened to me . . . *Once upon a time, when I was perhaps no older than those children,*

and when I still thought nightmares were real and that they could
walk into your waking life ...

The Derbyshire house had been filled with nightmares. The days were safe, because there was light and sometimes sunshine, and because there were other people coming and going. And the days were filled up with school and homework, and with all the things that children had done in those days. Piers had not done quite as many of those things as his school friends, because his mother had died when he was very small and there had only been his father and the two aunts who lived nearby and had shared his upbringing.

His father had been part of the nightmare.

The aunts had been unmarried ladies; sisters of his mother, and both considerably older than her. They had not understood children very well and they had imposed on Piers the rules that had applied when they had been children in the nineteen thirties, but that were wholly inapplicable to the nineteen sixties. Had he really to go gallivanting off to all these clubs and sports and after-school things? they said. Could he not enjoy some quiet hobby? In their day stamp collecting and nature study had been things that children enjoyed. And reading – they had a shelf-full of their own childhood books which he could have. Piers had since wondered many times what the aunts would have made of today's youth.

But they had done their duty, Aunt Vera and Aunt Monica, because poor Helen's boy must be given a proper upbringing, and also – although they never said this aloud – also the man Helen had married in a fit of madness could not be trusted.

A gypsy, they said, pursing their lips and lowering their voices. A tinker who had come to the door one day, selling something or asking for work, they had never discovered exactly what, but who had wormed his way into Helen's affections and ruined her. Romantic, of course, and dazzlingly good-looking – neither of the aunts had ever denied that Helen's husband was either of those things, or that he possessed the silver tongue of so many of his kind. He had filled Helen's head with wild impossible ideas about his background and how he was not really a gypsy at all, and she had been swept along by it all. Gullible, said Aunt Vera, clamping her lips tightly together. Helen had married him in the face of her sisters' opposition, but now that she was no longer with them it was their bounden duty to share in the upbringing of the boy. Romantic ideas were all very well in their place, but they were of no help to a growing child. Anyway, there was no one else to take on the task.

While one or other of the aunts was in the house during the day the nightmares stayed away, but once they had left – once the door had closed behind them and night descended on the isolated house – the nightmares had come crowding in.

The nightmares lived in the sprawling woodlands behind the house. The young Piers knew this, just as he knew that every couple of weeks his father went out there at night, waiting until everywhere was dark and quiet, and then stealing out of the house, leaving Piers alone. He had not much minded being alone, because he had believed that the nightmares could not break out of the forest and come into the house.

There was an old legend that told how the forest had once been inhabited by creatures who were not human, but who sometimes walked upright like humans, and there was another legend that said that even today the tread of humans had never fallen in the real heart of the forest. Piers always tried not to remember these legends, but sometimes at night it was difficult.

The house at night felt quite different to the house by day, and on the nights his father went out it felt even more different. There were creakings and odd sounds you never heard in the daytime. When he was very small Piers had dealt with this by burrowing under the sheets so that he could not see or hear, but after a time he began to sleep lying on his right side so that he would be facing the door.

It had been just before his ninth birthday that the nightmares began to become real. He had lain awake, waiting for his father to return from the forest, and he had left the curtains open because he liked to see the pattern made by the old oak tree outside his window. When the moonlight shone through it, its outline lay across the bed.

There was a wind tonight and the oak tree's branches were moving gently. Once or twice a twig tapped at the windowpane; normally this was a gentle, rather friendly sound but tonight it was not friendly at all. It was getting mixed up with other sounds: creakings and whisperings. Sinister scratchings that made you think of clawed feet scraping on the bare floorboards of the old staircase . . . He heard the outer garden door open and close very quietly. His father had returned.

Piers sat bolt upright in bed, pulling the sheets around him. The bedroom door was partly open and moonlight slanted across the large landing outside. It showered a cold pale light everywhere, picking out the shape of the huge gloomy-leafed plant that Aunt Vera had placed on the half-landing. Piers could see the plant's shadow clearly: a distorted shadow that looked as if some grotesque creature was crouching on the stair. When the creak of the stair came again he shuddered violently.

Creeping up the moonlit stair, mingling horribly with the malevolent nodding plant-shape, came a human outline. It came very slowly and very stealthily, pausing to listen after each tread, but each time it moved, its shadow on the far wall came a little more sharply into focus. He's trying not to wake me, thought Piers, frantically attempting to control the hammering of his heart.

He did not believe in fairy stories any longer: fairy stories were for very small children and girls. But the aunts' collection of books had included several of the staggeringly unsuitable fairy tales whose origins were grim in two senses of the word, and lying in the moonlit bedroom, his eyes on the dark stair, Piers remembered every one of them. He remembered one in particular, and he remembered how he had sat in the downstairs room called the study and how he had turned the pages slowly and fearfully, not wanting to come to the terrible picture. The book had smelt musty and the paper had been slightly foxed. Aunt Vera had said the book had been her grandmother's – Piers's great-grandmother – and he must treat it carefully because it was extremely old. Piers had had to pretend to be grateful and interested and not let the aunts know how absolutely terrifying he found the illustration of the wolf who had followed the small pretty girl through the forest.

The wolf had been able to don human guise and talk with human speech and reason with human logic, and it was this that Piers had found so sinister. Because the human disguise had not been complete: in the illustration you could see how the dripping-fanged muzzle and the sly red eyes showed through.

The figure creeping up the stair was his father, of course; Piers knew this sensibly and rationally. He could see that the shadow was that of a man, dressed ordinarily in trousers and shirt. But it was not the body that worried him; it was the head. It was just very slightly blurred. If the figure turned its head to one side, it would show in profile and that would be the worst thing imaginable, because the profile would not be a man's, it would be a long thin muzzle with huge snapping teeth . . . Because sometimes the human mask slips and the wolf glares through.

The figure reached the top landing and crossed the small stretch of floor, moving softly and lightly. Piers held his breath, and then his father went quietly into his own bedroom and closed the door.

One day he was afraid that his father would come from the forest straight into this bedroom. Then he would know that the nightmare about the wolf hiding behind human skin and human bones and hair was real.

The nightmares had continued for several years: Piers thought he had been seventeen or so, preparing for university, before they had really faded. His father had been dead by then and the aunts had sold the dark old house on his behalf.

Unhappy memories, they had said firmly. He would do better to invest the proceeds carefully and buy another house when the time came. It was better to let the past go.

Only I can't let it go, thought Piers, staring up at the crazed plaster on the old farmhouse ceiling. I couldn't let it go then, and I'm not letting it go now.

He knew that the sad, lost little skeletons in the cave had stirred up his own long-ago nightmares, and he knew that the dark time of his childhood had spun forward to surround him, preventing him from thinking rationally. He even wondered whether the half-buried memories might be affecting his sanity, because it could not possibly matter to the dead children whether he went back or not.

But on a different level he knew it did matter; his work had too many times taken him into ancient burial places, where sometimes there had been serenity among the dead but sometimes there had not. He remembered how the burial rites of the appropriate religion could often disperse the unquiet turbulence, leaving a gentle peace in its place. The children's cavern was the most unquiet place he had ever encountered, and he knew that until he had done something about it, he would not sleep.

Christian burial? But it seemed unlikely that the dead children had been Christians anyway. Bring them out of the dark evil-drenched catacombs and put them somewhere clean and tranquil? But he could not do anything with the skeletons – he certainly could not disturb such a valuable find other than under properly controlled conditions. At worst I'm being unprofessional and at best I'm being emotional about this, thought Piers, angrily. But the thought of the blinding flashbulbs of photographers lighting up the piteous cavern, and of detached efficient hands moving the fragile bones to laboratories and marble slabs, was suddenly unbearable. And while it was a fool's action and a romantic's folly to return to the cavern, Piers would rather be a romantic fool than lie awake with the beseeching cries of the dead children echoing in his mind.

He considered and almost immediately rejected the idea of taking someone with him again. Too dangerous, said his mind with firm logic. Oh sure, said the sneaky little voice that was not logical. How about you don't want to admit to sentimentality? Well all right, I don't.

He pushed back the bedclothes, and moving quietly so as not to wake anyone, pulled on a thick sweater and corduroy trousers and then went softly out through the silent house.

A thin ground-fog was forming outside; Piers shivered, and turning up the collar of his waterproof jacket began to walk warily through the cold, dripping night. The mist clung to his hair and icy moisture ran down his neck. He hunched his shoulders against the seeping cold and paused to forage for gloves. Tonight Cruithin Island was the most desolate place on God's earth.

He paused on the outskirts of the compound. It was shrouded in silent darkness tonight, and there was no eerie flickering wildfire to cast mysterious shadows and create prowling shapes where no shapes existed. Piers went stealthily towards the crouching outlines of the burial mounds. The rock slab moved easily under his hands, and the opening yawned blackly.

It was cold below the ground, but not as cold as it was above. Piers went down the stone steps, switching on his torch as he did so, picking his way carefully. The beam was a bit watery in the Stygian darkness. Damn, I should have brought the larger torch after all, he thought. But he had been fearful that too-strong a light might have been seen.

He felt the echoes as soon as he reached the foot of the steps. They were stronger and more immediate this time, almost as if that earlier experience had laid down stepping stones and as if, once laid, the stones made a permanent bridge. For a wild, heart-stopping moment, Piers almost believed he could hear the ghosts tiptoeing across the bridge, and he fought the impulse to turn and run. They're only poor pitiful ghosts, and ghosts can't hurt anyone.

And I'm here to reassure them. That's what this is all about. I think I might have crossed a line between sanity and madness somewhere tonight, but if I can hear them, then maybe they can hear me. And if only I can make them hear me – if only I can tell them they're safe, then surely I won't hear the ghosts any longer.

Oh yes you will, said a treacherous little voice. Oh yes you will. Because the ghosts and the echoes go much farther back than this cavern – they go farther back, even, than the dark old house of your childhood . . .

It was at this precise point that the watery beam from the torch flickered, and then abruptly went out. Blackness, thick and impenetrable, closed in.

Chapter Nine

Piers spent a whole minute in pointless cursing. He cursed himself for not bringing a back-up torch, and he cursed the others in the team for not checking the equipment, and then he cursed the makers of torch batteries who ought to be banned from selling goods that left people stuck in the pitch dark with a collection of grisly skeletons and a clutch of ghosts.

The ghosts were here, of course. Piers, hopefully waiting for his vision to adjust and to find that after all there were a few threads of light down here, felt his mind reel with the ancient pain and terror.

Save us from the wolf . . .

I really am in the wolf's lair, thought Piers, beating down panic. Oh God, I really am. But somehow I've got to find my way out, even though it means walking through the pitch dark, even though I can feel the clustering shades of the murdered children as strongly as I ever felt anything in my life. I can smell the spilled blood and I can hear the squelching bones as the victims are eaten . . .

He thrust the horrific images away, and stuffed the useless torch into a pocket so that he could concentrate on finding his way out. The blackness was still absolute: it was the darkness of the stone-blind. It ought to be relatively easy to feel back along the wall and find the steps. Piers thought he had retained his sense of direction, and he thought the tunnel wall was on his right. So if I reach out with my right hand, I should touch it – yes, it's there! And now if I turn completely round, and keep that wall on my left I should be retracing my steps.

He began to move cautiously forward, keeping his left hand firmly against the rockface. Even though he was reasonably sure that his sense of direction had not betrayed him, it was still appallingly nerve-racking. But he thought he was going in the right direction. Surely this was the jutting spur of rock that

79

meant he was nearing the steps. And this had to be the sharp curve in the tunnel, in which case he should see light filtering down from the opening at any second. He went on, his left hand still feeling its way along the rock wall. The ground was a bit uneven now; it was rutted and there was a rather unpleasant crunchy feel to it. Piers's heart began to beat faster. There was absolutely no reason to feel afraid; it was a bit unpleasant down here – well all right, it was bloody nightmarish! – but he would find his way out, even if it took longer than he had originally thought. And even if he did not find his way out – but of course he would – at least the others would realize where he was. When he did not appear at breakfast they would come out here to look for him. He remembered that he had left the slab at an angle. Anyone seeing that would know that he was down here.

Anyone seeing it . . . Supposing the tribe themselves saw it? But this was so comprehensively dreadful an idea that Piers dismissed it instantly. In any case, none of them ever came out here. No? How can you possibly know that from studying them for a bare month?

It was then that a shelf of rock, three feet or so from the ground, seemed to suddenly rear up and smack him hard against the knees. He gasped and tumbled helplessly forward.

He fell onto a painful, ugly jumble of thin, stick-like objects, and his mind spiralled in a vortex of new horror. A dry mouldering breath seemed to gust into his face, conjuring up unspeakable images, and he grasped wildly at the vanishing remnants of sanity. I've fallen onto one of the skeleton shelves in the dark, that's all, he thought, and shivered.

He tried to back away, but the fall had sent him sprawling almost flat out amidst the bones and he had to scrabble with both hands to lever himself upright. This was terrible. His right hand closed over the unmistakable shape of a skull, his fingers sliding into the eye-socket, and he snatched his hand back at once as if it had been burnt.

Logically, it did not make the smallest difference, and rationally it simply meant his sense of direction was wildly off course. But Piers's nerves were scraped raw by the dark and by the swirling invisible currents down here, and panic threatened to overwhelm him. He scrambled to his feet, and gasping with nausea clutched at the rock wall, forcing himself to remain calm. He stood very still, waiting for his hammering heartbeats to slow down, wiping the sweat from his forehead with the back of his hand. In another minute he would begin the journey all over again, and this time he would get it right, he *would* . . .

It was then that he caught, from somewhere behind him, a whisper of sound. He froze at once, and turned his head in the direction of the sound, the hairs lifting on the back of his neck. Had it been simply the disturbed bones settling back into place? Or had it been a light, soft footfall? Was something creeping up on him through the darkness?

Even before he saw the first smeary lights, Piers knew that the strange people he had spent so many years seeking, and that he had tracked to Cruithin Island, were entering the catacombs.

Bizarrely, it was the very fact that he had stumbled onto one of the shelves that saved him. His sense of direction had not been too far off the mark after all, because the lights were coming from his left. The second Piers saw them, he darted back into the deep shadow, half-kneeling, half-crouching on the rock. His heart was hammering so furiously that he thought it might break through his ribs at any minute.

Between one breathspace and the next, it seemed, they were inside the cavern; moving with an almost ritualistic solemnity and slowness. They carried burning torches, and there were at least thirty of them – Piers thought there were about an equal number of men and women. They were tall and slender, and although they were perhaps a little leaner than most humans, perhaps a little sharper of feature, that was the only discernible difference. They wore garments made from what looked like roughish-spun wool – mostly brown or green. The men had loose trousers and jerkins and they almost all wore dark ragged beards that made their teeth look sharply white. The women had skirts and jerkins, and long dark hair, and a few of the younger ones had twisted their hair on the top of their head and threaded it with tiny coloured berries. It occurred to Piers that they might easily pass for gypsies or New Age travellers, and he experienced a hideous jab of self-doubt. Supposing I'm wrong? Supposing this is nothing more sinister than the last people of a primitive tribe – a lost race, stunted by generations of in-breeding? Progressively warped by a form of inherited lycanthropy – the clinically recognized, delusional illness, not the horror-film, shape-changer stuff?

But as they filed past the wolf-cavern, firelight fell across their faces and Piers caught his breath, because for the first time he had seen their eyes, and they were the eyes that Dietfreid had painstakingly described in the farmhouse kitchen.

Narrow eyes, with slit-like pupils, set on a slant. By ordinary light they would be green, but in the firelit caverns there was an unmistakable red glint. Wolf eyes. Piers felt a real jolt of primeval fear. The legend is real, he thought. They're *wolves*! They walk upright like humans, and some of them can talk and understand human speech, but in reality they're wolves who occasionally go prowling out into the outside world to rape unprotected females and sometimes kill . . .

He remembered again the slab at the entrance which he had left dislodged, and for a moment he tensed, fearful of discovery. But there was no indication that these people suspected an intruder. Piers wondered briefly if their unconcern could be a ruse to catch him off guard, but he dismissed the idea almost instantly. He had no idea yet how logically they could reason, but he did not think they had this kind of human subtlety. The unwelcome thought that they looked sufficiently intelligent to be able to learn human subtlety flickered disturbingly across his mind, but for now most of them probably assumed that one of the others had removed the slab in preparation for tonight's meeting.

And then he saw that framed in the cavern entrance, the mingled darkness and torchflares cascading over it from above like a twisting black and crimson mantle, was a creature so monstrous, so utterly and wholly impossible, that for several crowded seconds his reason spun wildly out of control.

It's the creature of the fairy stories, he thought: the half-human, half-wolf. It walks upright like a man, and its body is that of a man. But its head is a wolf's. It's the thing that once crept through an old Derbyshire house and cast its warped shadow on the wall of the stairway . . .

Reason reasserted itself almost at once, and he knew the wolf-head was false, because anything else was biologically impossible. It was the head of a slaughtered wolf, cleaned and emptied of all brain and muscle, and jammed over the head of the tall man. It was fantastical to the point of insanity to believe, even for a second, that somewhere in their curious ancestry these people might have crossed a genetic line, or that at some time during the tenuous process of evolution there had existed an unsuspected link, a macabre ford that bridged the chasm between men and wolves.

The tribe formed a circle, some seated cross-legged on the ground but a number flinging themselves on their fronts. The women shook back their hair, and some of the younger ones glanced over their shoulders, their heads tilted. The similarity to large dogs, checking that nothing was behind them, was impossible to miss.

Piers had been studying these people for a long time. He had read and re-read Jewitt's amazing account of his experiences as a castaway at the hands of the North American Tlokoalan Wolf Clan. Since coming to Cruithin Island he had studied the film footage that the team had managed to get of the compound, and also the diary that Dietfreid and Tybalt had created, which charted the creatures' movements and their whereabouts at different hours of the day and night.

But none of this had prepared him for what he was seeing now. None of it had prepared him for the strange emotions that these creatures were awakening in him. He thought they were wild and obviously dangerous. But he also found them mesmerizingly attractive.

The tall man with the wolf-head stepped into the centre of the circle, and reached up to remove the grisly head. Piers saw that he had the black hair and slanting eyes of the others, but that there was a more rounded, more human look to him. Unmistakable authority streamed from him. I believe he's the shaman, thought Piers. The soothsayer or the sorcerer. He's the one who safeguards the tribe's secrets and rituals – he'll have inherited the role from his father, who got it from his father, all the way back to God-knows when. He's the one whose word goes, even above an elected ruler.

The shaman held out his hands, and a low growl of anticipation, scarcely human, and very nearly sexual in quality, came from the watchers. Piers, leaning forward as far as he dared, caught the glint of light and, at first, thought that what the shaman carried was a lump of quartz. It was roughly the size of a damson, and although it did not precisely shine, it glowed, with a deep purple-and-blue radiance. Piers thought it might be amethyst and then was not sure.

And despite the snatches of speech the team had been able to record, it came as a shock when the shaman said, in entirely comprehensible English, 'Prepare for the ritual. Prepare, so that one of you may take into his body the fragment of the timeless magical *Lia Fail*, the *Saxum Fatale* brought into the ancient wildwood by Edmund, servant of Richard Foljambe, nearly ten centuries ago, and wrested from him as he lay vanquished and dying beneath the wildwood.'

Piers could not have moved if his life had depended on it. He felt as if he had been down here for an entire lifetime – several lifetimes – and his mind was racing at top speed. *Lia Fail*, he thought, wildly. Oh God, what wouldn't I give for a camera and a tape recorder, or even pencil and paper!

A stillness had fallen on the cavern. The shaman spoke into it with the precise timing of an actor. 'Tonight, one of you will receive the *Lia Fail*,' he said. 'And it may please the gods to let that one rise from the death trance, and follow those of our people who have already gone out into the world.'

'Karabas,' murmured a number of voices, and Piers felt a ripple of delight stir the people.

'Karabas,' said the shaman, and this time there was a kind of reverence about the way he said the name.

He began to move around the circle, looking into the faces of each one as if seeking the one who would be put to the ritual.

'Do you all vow, as you aspire to take on Fenrir's spirit, that if you are chosen and if you are honoured with rebirth, you will enter the world of men and there seek and destroy all descendants of the accursed royal wolfhunter, Richard Foljambe? As our brother Karabas did recently, and as others have done down the ages?'

'We vow it.'

The shaman lifted his hands above his head.

'Then let the ritual commence.'

'I waited until I was sure they were too intent on preparing for their ritual to notice me,' said Piers, sitting in the warmth of the farmhouse kitchen, his cold hands wrapped gratefully around the mug of steaming coffee, hastily brewed by Nina.

'And then I slunk back down the tunnel and got the hell out of there.'

'You didn't stay to watch the ritual?' asked Priscilla.

'I did not.'

'Why not?'

'Because,' said Toby, in the patient voice of one explaining a simple fact to a child, 'he was afraid of the big bad wolves.'

'Exactly,' said Piers, shortly, and thought: oh, Toby, if you only knew exactly *how* afraid . . .

'Well, I don't blame you,' said Nina with a shiver. 'I wouldn't have stayed down there if you'd paid me a million pounds.'

'No? How very unmercenary of you,' purred Priscilla.

'You'd have stayed, of course?' Nina was not going to be put down by Priscilla.

'To the bitter end, dear.'

'Myself I would not have contemplated such a thing,' rumbled Dietfreid, who was a remarkable sight in a mammoth silk dressing-gown of rainbow hue and dubious qualities of concealment.

'Oh, me neither. The Beeb doesn't like dead heroes on its payroll.'

'Admit it, Priscilla, would you honestly have stayed?' demanded Tybalt. 'Knowing you were only inches away from them, for goodness' sake? Because I *certainly* wouldn't have.'

'No one asked you to, Tibbles my love. But,' said Priscilla, 'if Piers *had* stayed, we would at least have known what the ritual was.'

Piers, thought Nina, staring at Priscilla with dislike. So it's *Piers* now, is it?

'I know what the ritual was,' said Piers, and Nina repressed a childish urge to stick out her tongue and say, So pooh to you, Priscilla Perfect.

'What?' demanded several voices together, with Dietfreid a syllable behind.

Piers said, 'They were going to kill one of the young men and then wait to see if he would be reborn.'

There was silence. Everyone stared at Piers, and then Toby started to say, 'But that's absurd—'

'No, it isn't,' said Nina, eagerly. 'It's one of the old resurrection rituals, isn't it, Dr Adair?'

'Yes. Jewitt's journal actually records seeing it: Jewitt says that at intervals the Wolf Clan used to place what they believed to be a magic stone in the mouth of one of their number, and then kill him and wait for his rebirth. If he was reborn, they counted him as their leader. They regarded him almost as a demi-god. That's why I didn't stay, of course. If they'd caught me, they'd have killed me as well, and I didn't rate my chances of resurrection as very good.'

'Is that what happened to the one they referred to?' asked Priscilla. 'Karabas?'

'That's the obvious conclusion,' said Piers. 'Karabas, whoever he is, whatever he is, went through the ritual and because he survived, he was sent out into the world.'

'He survived being killed?' demanded Priscilla.

'It sounded like it. In any case,' said Piers, 'the ritual must succeed enough times to make it believable, or nobody would ever submit to it.'

'More likely people cheat,' remarked Toby, cynically.

Dietfreid gave this his support. 'Because it is likely that their method of killing would be a knife, and I am thinking it would be an easy matter to substitute a blunt blade or wear beneath the clothes some form of armour. This is your point, perhaps, Toby?'

'It's my point precisely.'

'And from the sound of it,' said Tybalt, 'Karabas has gone in search of these Foljambe people.'

'Hotfoot after the ancient enemies of his family, on a timeless quest for vengeance?' jeered Priscilla. 'We are sure, are we, that we haven't fallen into something by Tolkien and not noticed?'

'Royal wolfhunter,' said Nina, thoughtfully. 'That's what they said, wasn't it? I've never heard of such an appointment – has anyone else?'

'It's a very old term,' said Piers. 'In fact it's at least medieval, and I'd guess it was an hereditary office. They'd be foresters, mostly, or bailiffs – I mean bailiffs in the old sense – who received various perquisites for taking on wolf-hunting as a sideline. The usual payment was a grant of land.'

Tybalt, entranced by this newest nugget of information, gazed at Dr Adair in delight.

'So,' said Dietfreid, who had been making ponderous notes, 'our next move should be?'

'We've got to set up an investigation into the bodies we found,' said Piers, thoughtfully.

'But that will take some time, won't it?'

'Well, it won't happen overnight.'

'So we could go after Karabas?' said Tybalt, hopefully.

'Or the Foljambes,' added Nina.

'Both,' said Piers, and grinned at them. 'Remember what I told you: always pursue more than one line of enquiry at a time.'

'First rule of research,' affirmed Toby. 'Piers, d'you really think this character, Karabas, could reach the mainland?'

'Oh yes.'

'But how would he get a place to live and all stuff like that?' asked Tybalt.

'Quite easily. For starters, there are Salvation Army hostels and Centrepoint, and God-knows how many other charity centres,' said Piers. 'If he could fathom the system, he could live pretty well for a time.' He paused, and then, speaking very deliberately as if he was testing each word before letting it go, said, 'But if I was Karabas, or one of his people, once I'd got clear of this island I'd latch on to the first suitable lone man I could find. There are thousands of them – drifters, drop-outs, solitaries. Most of them are more or less homeless or even stateless. Karabas could kill one of those and take his place. Once he'd done that, he could take over his victim's identity and move to another part of the country. He'd have National Insurance number, birth certificate, everything he needed to pass unnoticed in the world.'

'All I can say to that,' said Toby, after a moment, 'is that if you really can put yourself in Karabas's place and imagine what he'd do, you must have a pretty peculiar mind.'

'I have. It's the fault of a peculiar upbringing.'

Toby said caustically, 'More likely you've read too much Frederick Forsyth and John le Carré.'

Piers grinned. 'OK, maybe I'm stretching imagination a bit. What I do think will happen, though, is that the pack instinct will take over.'

'He'll head for some kind of community?'

'Yes. It would give him protection, and also it's what he's used to.'

'If he's spent all his life on this island he'd have to learn a 'whole lot of things very fast,' observed Toby, thoughtfully.

'I don't think that would be a problem. I think these people can learn fast,' said Piers, in a voice so completely devoid of expression that Toby looked up sharply.

'It's odd, isn't it,' murmured Nina, 'how real Karabas seems to us. I mean – we're talking about him as if we know him.'

'I think we're focusing on him as a symbol of the whole clan,' said Toby.

'Oh yes, I hadn't seen it as that.'

'Piers, remind us what that creature chanted in the catacombs.'

'He said, "Richard Foljambe who lived in the wildwood ten centuries ago".'

'"And who had a servant called Edmund".' Nina took up the refrain.

'"Who was killed by one of Karabas's ancestors beneath the wildwood",' finished Tybalt. 'Whatever a wildwood is.'

There was a pause, while everyone digested this. Then Toby said, with heavy sarcasm, 'Well, clearly, it's going to be childishly easy. All we've got to do is find records for a thousand years ago – assuming there are any still in existence – in a part of the British Isles, if not the entire world, that we haven't yet identified. And if anyone so much as *mentions* needles or haystacks—'

'I can think of a few ways of starting the search,' began Tybalt.

'Oh God, Old Glory to the rescue.'

Tybalt thought that one day he was just going to completely lose his temper with Priscilla, and when that happened, he was going to tell her exactly what he thought of her. He had reached this very gratifying decision, when, to his blissful confusion, Dr Adair said, in his cool English voice, 'Can you really, Tybalt? That would actually be very helpful. And I do think we can allow ourselves a little time to follow this one up; it might be several weeks before we get permits and all the rest of it for excavating those catacombs.'

Tybalt ascended instantly into a celestial dream, in which he and Dr Adair together discovered the truth about these people and shared the podium when accepting the Pulitzer Prize for the amazing book they would write about their work.

Nina said, 'Dr Adair, what's the *Lia Fail*?'

Dr Adair looked at her, and the rare sweet smile that always knocked both those girls out and that Tybalt would have sold his back teeth to possess, suddenly lit his face. 'I was wondering when someone was going to ask that,' he said.

'But what is it?'

'Literally translated it's Celtic for Stone of Destiny,' said Piers. 'In a way it's not so curious to find a reference to it on an island called after the Cruithin.'

'The Ancient Kindred,' murmured Nina, and Piers sent her an appreciative glance.

'Yes. The Cruithin are generally reckoned to have been the most ancient people of the British Isles who were given a definite name.'

'I read it up before we came here,' confessed Nina. 'The Greeks called them the Pretani and the Romans called them Picts. They mostly settled in Ireland, but there're traces of them along England's east coast – Lindisfarne is one – and also on Scotland's west coast. Hence the name of this island, I suppose.'

'Yes. Cruithin is Scottish, but it's actually closer to Ireland's coast than you realize unless you look at the map,' said Piers.

'And even then it is only a blot,' said Dietfreid, who had tried to do this.

'You mean blob, Dietfreid.'

'So.'

Tybalt asked to be told about the Stone of Destiny.

'It's possible that its origins lie in the Irish ceremonial Stone of Fal,' said Piers. 'Priscilla, you once wrote quite a good paper on that, didn't you?'

'Yes, the Stone of Fal was used as a kind of testing process for kings of Ireland. They used to have wild orgies on the Plain of Fal, and the culmination was for the would-be king to embrace the Stone. If it cried out, then he was hailed as the rightful sovereign.'

'And there were probably even more orgies to celebrate the fact,' murmured Toby.

'It's Arthurian sword-in-stone stuff, isn't it?' demanded Tybalt, in delight.

'Yes,' said Priscilla. 'It's half-myth, half-fact.'

'I've always seen the Stone of Fal as a link with what we know today as the Coronation Stone of Scone,' said Piers. 'We know for certain that came from Ireland. Tradition says it was the stone used as a pillow by Jacob in the Old Testament when he saw the ladder leading up to heaven – and for centuries it was the coronation seat of the Irish kings of Munster. It's immensely old. It was as late as eight hundred and something that it fetched up in Scone in Scotland. *Saxum Fatale* is its Latin name, although the *OT* calls it the Stone of the Covenant.'

'Whatever it's called, it sounds as if Karabas's people have got hold of a fragment of it,' observed Toby.

'From Richard's servant, Edmund,' said Nina, thoughtfully. 'Which means they thought it was worth having.'

'Yes, and from what I saw, they seem to regard it as possessing magical powers,' said Piers. 'But I'm not sure I heard everything properly.'

There was a thoughtful silence. Then Toby said, 'It's a bit of a wild-goose chase to go after Karabas. I suppose it *is* the right thing to do, is it? I mean, shouldn't we concentrate our efforts on what we've already got?'

'Stay on the island?' asked Nina, with a shudder.

'Frightened of the wolves?' demanded Priscilla, scornfully.

'Terrified,' said Nina, shortly.

Piers looked very directly at Toby, and said, 'I think it would be safer for us to leave the island.'

'Ah. You think they know we're here?'

'I think it's possible. And I think Karabas ought to be found,' said Piers.

'Why?'

'Call it a hunch.'

You're stone-walling again, thought Toby. But he said, peaceably, 'OK, you're the boss.' And then, 'Listen, I don't want to forever play the cynic, but this – this magic stuff—'

'Magic once lived,' stated Dietfreid sternly. 'That is to say people once believed that it lived.'

'Dietfreid's right,' said Piers. 'And soul-stones and resurrection stones spatter the history of man.' He grinned, and Nina thought he suddenly looked more like a mischievous schoolboy than an eminent professor of anthropology. 'If you'd been born into a different culture, Toby, not too long ago,' said Piers, 'you might have found that an empty coconut had been hung over your cradle so that your soul could shelter there until you were strong enough to fight off demons. Or if you were sick, your soul might have been temporarily stored in an

Eskimo medicine man's soul-box until you recovered. Or in the Gazelle Peninsula there's a secret society who bestow a soul-stone on entrants and then watch to see if the stone is split by the elements. And—'

'Thank you, professor,' said Toby.

Nina said, 'So that stone you saw, whatever it was, was regarded by the tribe as a resurrection stone?'

'I think so,' said Piers.

'Jeeze, I wonder how Edmund came to have it?' said Tybalt. 'I mean, Karabas's people talked about wresting it from him as he lay dying beneath the wildwood—'

'Yes, and d'you realize there's another untapped story there?' said Toby, pouncing. 'Because if that stone really was regarded as having magical powers, how did a lowly servant come to have it in his possession in the first place? If you ask me, there's more to that Edmund than meets the eye,' he added darkly. 'If this was a book, he'd turn out to be a pretender to the English throne or something.'

'And you scoffed at Tybalt for being romantic,' said Piers, sounding amused. 'You're falling into the realms of fantasy yourself now, Toby.'

'Oh, we all fell into those ages back, didn't you notice?'

'But,' said Nina, thoughtfully, 'Tybalt's right. I do wonder how Edmund came to have a fragment of the Stone of Destiny.'

Chapter Ten

One day Bryony was going to write a story about the magic stone that had belonged to Edmund. She would have to find out a bit more about it, of course, but it would make a good story.

Edmund's mother had given him the stone just before he went to live with Richard and Madeleine Foljambe in the forest house. It was not a stone like you found in the garden, but a most beautiful violet stone, worn as smooth as silk on account of all the people who had owned it. It had belonged to hundreds and hundreds of people; Edmund's mother had said it was a tiny tiny part of something called the Stone of Destiny which was immensely ancient and very magical. It had come from Ireland, and Edmund's mother's own great-great-several-times-great grandmother had brought it to England. This several-times-great-grandmother had been attacked by wolves in a forest, but before the wolves had eaten her up, she had managed to hide the fragment of the stone so that her daughter, who was a tiny baby, could have it and be always safe.

'The wolves have always wanted it,' Edmund's mother had said. 'They believe it would give them great powers. But we have to guard it and pass it down through the generations and never let the wolves steal it.'

Bryony had asked mother about the Stone of Destiny, and mother had looked it up and said that it was a big slab of stone that once upon a time had been used for the crowning of all the kings of Ireland, and had come to be called the Coronation Stone. In the year 843 it had been taken to Scotland, to a place called Scone.

'Where did you unearth that one?' mother had said, and Bryony had said vaguely that it was something somebody at school had said. It had sounded pretty interesting. 'I do hope,' said mother, sounding a bit worried, 'that you know the difference between daydreams and reality, Bryony.'

'Um – yes.'

One day Bryony would probably be able to explain to mother about being able to imagine things; like the forest house and the wolves and the Stone of Destiny. It was not exactly like telling yourself a story or watching a film: it was a bit like looking down into your mind and letting your mind speed you back to Richard's time.

Scone was a pretty funny name for a place, and eight hundred and forty three was an extremely long time ago; Bryony knew this. Just as Edmund's time was a long, long way before Bryony's, so the time of the Stone being taken to Scotland was a long way before Edmund's.

Edmund had been at the forest house for two years when there was a specially hot Wolf Night. Summers had been very hot then, but they had been nice hot, because there had not been cars and machines, and there had been a lot more trees to keep everyone cool.

The trees in the forest had kept the house very cool indeed. Madeleine Foljambe had asked the cook to bake pies for all the guests who were coming to be part of the wolfcub hunt, so there was a good smell of apples and quinces everywhere. There were meat pies, as well, and huge wheels of cheese and freshly baked bread from the ovens. Richard had told the servants to put flagons of cider in the dairy where it would be cool. After supper there would be mulled wine, which was heated wine with tingly sounding spices sprinkled onto it – ginger and cinnamon and nutmeg.

Edmund was going out with the hunt, of course. He would carry things for Richard, and he might be allowed to carry a falcon this time. He did not really mind about having to go down to the cellar to fetch the wolf-traps on the night before the hunt – well, he did mind, but he was getting a bit more used to it. But on this night it was much scarier than Edmund had been expecting. He might have left it a bit later than he had done last year, or perhaps there was a storm brewing up. Bryony thought it could have been a storm, because the sky was a horrid purply colour – like huge bruises – and it seemed to be much lower than usual, as if it was coming down onto the forest so that you believed that if you stood on your tippiest tippy-toes you might be able to reach up and touch it. The branches of the trees were all hanging down as if a huge weight was pressing on them.

When Edmund went around the side of the house to the little half-hidden door he noticed how extremely silent everywhere was, and he paused to look out into the forest. Usually there were hundreds of little rustlings and patterings of feet which would be squirrels or foxes, or even badgers. At the Purple Hour there were always lots of birds singing as well – Edmund knew about the different bird calls. Bryony did not know them as well as Edmund, but she was trying to learn them. Karabas was going to teach her about them, which would be good.

But on this Wolf Night the forest was very quiet indeed, and as Edmund went towards the terrible door, where the ivy grew more thickly every year, he had the sudden feeling that people – or maybe only one person – was watching him from between the trees. It was odd how you did sometimes know this. For a moment Edmund was quite sure he could just see a glimpse of something dodging back behind the old trees. Bryony knew how he would have felt, and she knew how the trees would have looked on that Wolf Eve as well: they would be old, old trees, with huge purple and grey and twisty trunks.

Edmund thought that something was certainly out there, slinking in and out of the trees, and it took quite a lot of courage to turn his back on the forest and go through the cellar door. Even then he felt as if whatever had been creeping around the forest had followed him. As he went down the rickety steps, he kept having to turn round to make sure that nothing was tiptoeing after him.

Bryony knew exactly how the cellar would have looked to Edmund because it was one of the mind-pictures she saw the most clearly. There would be evil black shadows creeping across the old wooden floor but there would be a trickle of forest-light from above, because Edmund had propped the door open so that he could carry the traps out more easily. The forest-light came into the cellar in a slanting blue-grey swathe and millions of tiny dust-motes danced in and out of it. This blue forest-light lay half across the wolf-traps so that parts of them glinted horridly. Edmund was going to grab as many as he could in one go and scoot back up the rickety steps as fast as possible. Bryony thought this was a good idea. She wanted

Edmund to get right out of that place.

He was level with the black *evil* door at the foot of the steps, and he was just thinking that it was going to be all right this time because there was nothing there tonight, and he was even thinking that there was not the bad, sick-making smell here tonight and that perhaps the thing had gone away. He went purposefully across the floor, towards the pile of wolf-traps, and it was then that he heard the faint creaking sound from behind him.

Edmund was halfway across the cellar but he stopped at once. It was *just* possible that it was only the upper door he had heard creaking, but it was not very likely, because he had propped it open. His heart started to beat very fast, and he began to feel sick and cold with fear. In another moment he would have to turn round and see what the creaking sound was, but he did not want to do that because he might find that the black door was starting to swing open all by itself. For what seemed to be a very long time indeed nothing happened, and Edmund was starting to hope that he might have imagined it when something else happened, and this time it was something that made the blood in his whole body turn to ice.

A wet thick-sounding voice from behind the black door said, very softly, '*Come over here, my dear . . .*'

And then, as Edmund turned round in panic, it said, '*Pull the bobbin and the latch will go up, and open the door, my dear . . .*'

Where Bryony always thought Edmund had gone wrong was in doing precisely what the voice told him. If Bryony had been down in that cellar, with that horrid treacly voice telling her to go over there, my dear, and open the door, my dear, she would not have done it, not for anything in the world. She would have run as fast as her legs could carry her, right back up the rickety steps, and out into the forest, and back to the house.

But Edmund had not run away. It might have been something to do with him being a boy because boys were supposed to behave bravely in those days, or it might have been that he had the magic stone with him and he thought it would protect him. Bryony would not have trusted the most magic stone in the world in that cellar and she especially would not have trusted a magic stone that the wolves wanted to steal.

But Edmund seemed to trust it. He had taken it from the

pocket of his jerkin, and to Bryony's horror he had clutched it firmly, and he had gone across to the door. And then he had done the one thing he should absolutely never have done: he had peered through the crack in the cupboard door, and there, crouching in the dreadful dark, had been the wolf-creature.

It had been a million times worse than he had ever imagined. It had been worse than his worst nightmares. The wolf had been waiting for him. Edmund heard it tell him so; he heard the dreadful voice say, '*Hello, Edmund . . . I have been waiting for you . . .*'

The wolf had been seated cross-legged in the dark bad-smelling cubbyhole, but as soon as he saw Edmund looking through the crack, he reared up on his hind legs so that he looked exactly like a tall man. But his head was not a man's head at all, it was a huge, dripping, grinning wolf's head, and the wolf had just finished eating his last victim, because his jowls were all smeary and wet with blood and his hands were dripping with blood as well.

And he had been sitting on what was left of all his victims just as Edmund had always known he did, so that for a moment it looked as if it was a heaped-up bonfire. But it was not a bonfire made of twigs and dead branches, it was made of bones and skulls, and some of them were stained with blood, and here and there were wet squelchy bits of the victims' insides – kidneys and liver and bulgy stomach bits.

And the terrible voice was saying, '*Pull the bobbin and the latch will go up,*' and Edmund saw his own hand move up to the latch and pull it up, and the wolf was slavering with greed because he liked eating children, and best of all he liked eating fair-skinned beautiful children, and Edmund was fair-skinned and beautiful . . .

He said, '*And now open the door, my dear . . .*' and Bryony understood that the wolf could not get at you unless you invited him in, or unless you opened your door to him, but that there was a thing called hypnotism and Edmund had been hypnotized by the wolf, and he could not help lifting the latch and opening the door to the wolf.

As soon as he had done it Edmund realized his huge mistake, and he started to back away, but to his horror the door started to swing slowly open. He scrabbled backwards but he had forgotten about the wolf-traps behind him and his foot went straight into one of them. There was a sudden clanging snap, and then sickening pain in his ankle as if teeth had crunched down on it, and he knew it was the ogre-teeth trap, and it hurt, *it hurt*, nothing had ever hurt so much in his entire life . . .

As he lay helplessly there, a huge black shadow fell across him; it blotted out the dusk-light of the forest that had been pouring in from above so that the cellar was suddenly and frighteningly very dark indeed. A voice said, '*What a very pretty human boy-child you are, my dear . . .*'

Edmund looked up and saw the wolf smiling down at him and this was the worst thing yet, because wolves did not smile, any more than dogs or cats smiled. But the wolf was smiling because he was pleased at having caught a pretty human boy-child to eat, and juices were running out of his mouth.

The wolf said in his slurry blurry voice, '*And now, Edmund, give me the* Lia Fail, *and when you have done that I will eat you up.*'

It was better really not to think too much about Edmund, who had been nice and brave, and who had enjoyed wearing the smart Foljambe livery, and who had had a mother who gave him the magic stone so that he would be safe. He had not been safe at all, in the end; the wolf had got him. Bryony did not know what had happened afterwards, and she did not know if the wolf had left anything of Edmund for Richard and Madeleine to find.

Brother Karabas knew about the magic stone. He said it was a tiny part of the *Lia Fail*. He told Bryony that the lady who had brought the fragment of the *Lia Fail* to England had been an Irish princess who had married a prince of England called Bertelin. Bryony thought this princess was sure to have been the lady that Edmund's mother had talked about.

Brother Karabas said that places in England had been called by different names then, and Bertelin's father had been the king of Mercia, which had been where Derby and Stafford and Nottingham were today. The middle parts of England, anyhow. Mercia meant march lands, said Karabas. It had been a kingdom all by itself and Bertelin had been bringing his princess back from Ireland to live with him there.

Bryony asked whether they would have had the Stone with them on the journey, and Brother Karabas thought they pretty certainly would. He thought this was why the wolves had attacked them on the journey. Journeys in those days had been difficult and had taken a long time, and Bertelin and the princess had rested in a forest on their way. That was when the baby had been born, and while Bertelin had gone to get help, the wolves had come out of the forest and eaten the princess.

And the little baby as well? Bryony asked, round-eyed.

Karabas said that this was the really interesting thing, because most people thought the baby had been eaten as well – it was quite a well-known legend in that part of the country. But what most people did not know was that there had not been one baby but two. Twins. And the princess had managed to hide one of the babies under the bracken before the wolves got it, and tuck the stone in its shawl so that it was hidden. And so the wolves did not find the baby and they did not find the stone, although they had gone on looking.

This was all new and it was lavishly good. Karabas said one day he could take Bryony to the place where it had happened: it was called Ilam and he had an ancestor who had lived there a long time ago. Bertelin's tomb was there in a church. Bertelin had become a hermit and then a saint on account of being so upset at his wife being eaten by wolves. Bryony thought this was entirely understandable.

They talked about this some more on the day before the half-holiday. Karabas had remembered about having promised to take Bryony to a wildwood; he had waited for her after the last class of the day, which was arithmetic and spoilt the whole day as far as Bryony was concerned.

Karabas listened about the sums as they walked across the courtyard to the stable house. He did not like sums either. He liked nature study best, and as it happened he was going to take some people from Primary Three on a nature study afternoon tomorrow. They were going to a wildwood which was quite nearby and there would be a picnic if it was not raining. Bryony could come with them if she wanted to.

It was pretty important to go on an outing with Primary Three when you were only Primary Two yourself, and Bryony would quite like to go. It would not matter about Karabas sometimes being a bit scary, because other people would be there. So she said she would like to go and thank you very much. Karabas said not to wear her school uniform, but something that she could scramble around in. Strong shoes or boots, and woolly socks and trousers. And it might be better not to mention the expedition to any of her own classmates – they might be jealous or they might think that Bryony was getting special treats on account of Karabas being her uncle. Bryony quite saw this.

She did tell mother about it, of course, and mother said, a bit sharply, 'With Karabas?' as if she did not like Karabas very much. But then Bryony explained about Primary Three and the wildwood, and mother said slowly, 'Oh, I see. Oh yes, in that case of course it's all right,' and asked what time they were going and when they would be back. Bryony said they were going at half-past one, and they would have a picnic tea when they got there, and be home before it was dark. Mother said she would have a word with Mrs Simmonds, who was Primary Three's class teacher, just to make sure that it was all right for Bryony to join in the ramble, but Bryony thought Mrs Simmonds left the school before mother could do it.

Mother said she would make sandwiches for the picnic, which Bryony could take in her lunch-box, and she would put in some chocolate biscuits, an apple, and a large slab of cherry cake. It might be the kind of picnic where everybody contributed food, and if so, Bryony could share the cake and the chocolate biscuits.

Bryony thought it was going to be a pretty good afternoon.

Chapter Eleven

Felicity was immersed in the proofs for the bicentenary's commemorative booklet. The monks had chosen several photographs, mostly of the house at its various stages and one showing it decorated for VE Day, and there were articles about its history and the school's opening in 1797. She was just marking a photo from the early 1900s for the printer to reduce to the appropriate size, and adding a firm note that it positively *must* be shown in the original sepia, when Morag Mackenzie looked in to say she was going to walk down to Beck village for a breath of air, and would Felicity like to go with her? They might treat themselves to a ploughman's lunch at the Beck Arms.

'I'd like that.' Felicity had meant to work through the day, and just have a sandwich at her desk, but she was pleased at the small invitation. Morag was companionable and intelligent and it was nice to have found a friend up here. 'I've just got to go across to the stable house and see Bryony off on the nature ramble, but it won't take more than five minutes—'

Morag said, 'What nature ramble?'

'Brother Karabas is taking Primary Three, and he asked Bryony to go with them. It—' Felicity stopped, because Morag was staring at her. 'What's the matter?'

'You did say Primary Three?'

'Yes.'

'A nature ramble?'

'Yes.'

Morag had been halfway out of the small office but she came back in. 'Felicity, the whole junior school is playing Trivial Pursuit in the gym. It's an inter-school contest. They did it last year at the half-holiday – the junior version of the game, of course – and it was such a success that Sue Simmonds and Brother Stephen decided to repeat it.'

Felicity heard her own voice saying, 'I must have got it wrong. Maybe it's your lot that went on the nature ramble. Or one of the other classes.'

Morag looked at Felicity across the littered desk. 'Felicity, none of the children are going on a nature ramble.'

'But she was definite. She said they were setting off at one-thirty—' Felicity looked at the time. 'I'm meeting her at the house at ten past one – straight after school lunch, when the bell's gone to mark the half-holiday—'

Morag said, 'That's the bell now. I'll come with you to the stable house, shall I? I expect there's been some mix-up somewhere.'

Felicity heard her own voice saying, 'I expect that's all it is.'

There was no sign of Bryony in the stable house, and there was no sign of her anywhere in the school.

The two novices who helped Brother Joseph in the refectory were unsure whether or not they had seen her. One thought he had, but the other one said no, it had not been Bryony Stafford but another little girl. The rest of Primary Two thought she had not come in to dinner at all: she had gone off somewhere after the last lesson, which had been reading. Somebody had seen her putting on her outdoor shoes, but somebody else disagreed with this. Felicity could not decide how far to trust the evidence of a group of seven-year-olds.

Brother Dominic, cosily sure that there had simply been a crossed line somewhere, sent the novices off to search for Brother Karabas, and Felicity and Morag walked back to the stable house. Felicity went into Bryony's minuscule bedroom.

'What are you doing?'

'Checking if her outdoor things have gone.'

Morag came into the room. 'Have they?'

Felicity sat down on the bed. 'Yes. Her red cloak and boots aren't there,' she said.

It was very important not to panic. It was absolutely vital not to jump to any wild, erroneous conclusions. Felicity thought she must try to remain very calm. She must try not to be emotional, or embarrass people by becoming hysterical.

Even so, it felt as if the strength had suddenly drained from her legs so that she had to stay where she was, sitting on

Bryony's bed. After a moment, she said, 'Oh God. Oh God, Morag, where's Karabas taken her?'

There was a moment of silence. Felicity saw that Morag had not exactly been catapulted into panic but that alarm bells were ringing inside her head. The thought: she doesn't trust Karabas any more than I do, formed briefly.

Morag said, slowly, 'Let's just look at this sensibly for a moment. First of all, are you sure Karabas actually was going to take her out this afternoon?'

'Yes. *Yes.* They were going to have a picnic,' said Felicity, forcing her voice to sound calm. 'I made her favourite sandwiches and—' She stopped, because this sounded perilously like babbling. She made an enormous effort, and said, 'Of course there'll be a perfectly ordinary explanation.' But she thought: such as?

And of course the most obvious and ordinary explanation was that Bryony had misunderstood Karabas. The next most obvious was that Felicity had misunderstood Bryony. But when she suggested this, Morag at once said, 'I don't think you would get it wrong, and I don't think Bryony would get it wrong, either. She's unusually bright,' so that Felicity very nearly wished that Bryony was not bright; that she was dull, because that might have meant the child had got it wrong about the nature ramble with Karabas, and that she was consequently perfectly safe somewhere.

'Tell me exactly what Bryony said.' Morag perched on the narrow windowsill, and folded her arms with a businesslike air.

'Well, that Karabas was taking her and Primary Three into a wood somewhere near here and that they were going to have a nature study afternoon, collecting wild flowers and trying to identify different bird songs. It seemed a perfectly ordinary thing for them to be doing – I mean, it wouldn't be quite as normal in London where there aren't woods and fields and things, but out here—' But this was teetering towards babbling again, so Felicity brought the sentence to an untimely end and said, 'I was going to speak to Mrs Simmonds, just to make sure it was all in order, only she went off earlier than I was expecting. But Bryony seemed to have all the details – she said she didn't have to wear her school uniform, but that she had to wear outdoor shoes and she thought it would be best to put on her wellingtons—'The thought of Bryony's little feet in the brave scarlet wellingtons was very nearly too much to bear. Felicity took several deep breaths.

Morag said at once, 'Listen, there's no cause for alarm, I'm sure there isn't. All that seems to have happened is that Brother Karabas has taken his niece out for a couple of hours.' Morag's voice was calm and brisk, both at the same time, and Felicity was grateful to her.

She said, 'Put like that, it sounds entirely normal.' And thought: yes, and so it would be if it was anyone other than Karabas.

'It is entirely normal, Felicity. We certainly shouldn't get in a state about it, and I don't think we should call the police or anything like that.' She did not say 'yet', but Felicity thought they both heard the word.

She said, 'Oh no, of course we don't need the police.' And hoped Morag did not realize that she wanted, above everything else, to telephone the police there and then and go rushing off in search of Bryony. Because I don't trust Karabas an inch, he's Connor over again, and towards the end – maybe even from the beginning – there was something very sinister about Connor.

Morag said, 'You stay here in case she turns up, and I'll go along to check if anyone knows about the expedition. It's possible that Karabas really has taken a small group of children out – unofficially, I mean. He hasn't been here very long, and he might not have realized he should have cleared it with Brother Stephen or Brother Dominic. And I'll ask Brother Dominic if those two novices have found anything.'

These were all obviously sensible things to do. Felicity waited in an agony of impatience, trying not to look at the telephone which would summon the forces of radio cars and large reassuring policemen who would pat her shoulder and say things like, 'Now there's no need to worry, Mrs Stafford, we'll find her in a trice.'

Felicity suddenly desperately wanted someone to pat her shoulder and tell her in a warm comforting voice that Bryony would be found in a trice. She wanted to believe it was what would happen.

She discovered that she wanted Connor very much. He had loved Bryony; he had cried with emotion on the night she was

103

born, and he had told her stories by the hour when she was much too young to understand what he was saying, only it had not seemed to matter, because she had adored listening to him . . . Was that where she had picked up her odd, occasionally disturbing snippets of folklore and the wild half-myth, half-fairy tales?

If Con had lived he and Bryony might have had a lot of fun during Bryony's teenage years: Con would have met her from parties and discos, and pretended to be horrified at her outrageous clothes and hairstyles and music, and listened indulgently to the dramas and crises that all teenagers endured, and mopped her tears when she broke her heart over some boyfriend . . .

Except that there might have been other kinds of problems when it came to boyfriends, because girls with dazzling fathers sometimes had difficulty in forming normal relationships, and Con, at his best, had been dazzling: he had been spectacularly attractive and outrageously charming, and he had been the last of the romantics – he had told Felicity so on the afternoon Bryony was conceived . . .

But how much of all *that* was a rose-tinted view, because Con was turning out to be the worst kind of villain ever – he was working some kind of unsavoury scam with the Social Security people, and there was that monumental debt with the loan sharks in London. And towards the end he was out of the house more than he was in it. All the half-buried memories relentlessly paraded through her head one after the other.

But whatever Connor had or had not been, on this misery-drenched afternoon it was agony to know that he had not lived to see his bright, pretty daughter grow up. Oh damn, why aren't you here to help me through this? cried Felicity angrily to Con's memory. It's *exactly* like you to die and leave me to cope with this nightmare on my own. But, she thought, even if Con had not died there was no guarantee that he would have been here with Felicity now. And with his track record, it was a racing certainty that by the time Bryony was twelve, he'd have gone off with some blonde bimbo.

When Morag returned with Brother Dominic, to report that the rest of the junior school was intact – the blasé Primary Fives who considered Trivial Pursuit beneath their dignity were listening to pop music in the junior common room but everybody else was well away on the quarter-finals of the contest – Felicity tried to cling to the remaining shreds of self-control. She said, 'I'm sure we're worrying unnecessarily. But—'

Brother Dominic said, 'Certainly we are. But to be on the safe side, we'll phone the local police.'

Morag glanced towards the window, and Felicity at once started up. 'Have you seen something outside?'

'No.' Morag looked at Felicity compassionately. 'It's only that it's starting to get dark,' she said.

The police thought there was almost certainly nothing to worry about, as well. Almost certainly it would turn out to be a misunderstanding, they said. But just to be on the safe side, they would set the normal missing-child machinery into operation. They were all very kind.

The inspector was large and fatherly. He said that first of all his men would take a look over the school; it would all be very low-key, and they would not alarm the other pupils. But it was not unknown for children to get locked in a lavatory or fall over and knock themselves out. They would first make sure that that had not happened. And then a woman police officer would question all the children so that they could put together a timetable of Bryony's movements during the last half of the morning. It was the routine they followed in these situations, said the inspector cosily, and Felicity was grateful to him for making it sound as if he dealt successfully with missing children every day of the week.

An hour crept by, and Felicity sat on in the little sitting room and tried not to keep looking out of the window to where the light was draining from the dull November afternoon. She tried not to think how Bryony had disliked this premature night; coming home from school in London she had always wanted to scurry past a group of houses that had laburnums and thick old yew hedges enclosing them. You never knew what might be hiding in the hedges, she had said solemnly.

Felicity switched all the lights on, but left the curtains undrawn, because if Bryony came along the drive – *when* she came along the drive – she would see the lights in the windows and it would be welcoming for her. She stood at the window, staring out into the darkening afternoon, her hands pleating and unpleating a fold of curtain. Please, *please* let her suddenly appear, prayed Felicity, and in uncanny echo, Brother Dominic, who had stayed in the stable house while the police set about their routines, said, 'We're all praying that Bryony's all right, Felicity. The younger brothers are helping to search the grounds – well, you know that – but the older ones are in the chapel.'

This was immensely touching. Felicity, a Christmas and Easter church-goer, with the usual sprinkling of weddings and christenings and funerals in between, did not trust herself to speak for fear of breaking down altogether.

'And of course,' went on Brother Dominic, 'we're praying for you as well, so that you're given the strength to get through the ordeal.'

Felicity managed to say, 'That's very kind of the brothers. There's one thing I don't understand though . . .'

'Yes?'

'Can't we – or the police – simply drive out to all of the places you'd go for a nature study walk? And search? If several of us went—'

Brother Dominic said, very gently, 'Felicity, this is National Park area. Beck's Forest is the nearest and also the smallest, but even that covers between five and six thousand acres. We could search for a year in Beck's alone and still never find hide nor hair nor whisker of Karabas – or of Bryony.'

'Oh,' said Felicity, bleakly. 'Oh yes, I see. I didn't realize . . .'

Dominic looked at her with compassion. 'Is there anyone we could telephone for you?' he asked. 'Anyone you'd like to have with you?'

The woman police officer had asked this, but Felicity had not been able to think of anyone. There were friends in London, but you could not ask people to travel three hundred miles just out of the blue. By the time they got here Bryony would be back anyway, and so she said, 'No, there's no one, thank you. Morag's being a great help.'

'Yes, she's a good soul, Morag. Would you rather I left you on your own?' asked Brother Dominic. 'People have different ways of coping with ordeals, and if you'd prefer it—'

Felicity managed to say, 'It's quite helpful that you're here. But if there are things you should be doing—?'

'Not a single one,' said Brother Dominic calmly, and retired inconspicuously to the corner chair, where he drew out a small breviary and quietly read the daily Office to himself.

Felicity found this extraordinarily soothing. She was just thinking how kind everyone was being, and she was trying not to notice how dark it was becoming, when the large inspector tapped at the door and she turned from her stance at the window, her heart leaping. Except that he would not tap if he had Bryony, he would only tap if there was something unbearable to report . . .

Her voice was perfectly steady when she called to him to come in. He looked – Felicity sought for the word, and realized he looked puzzled.

But it was Brother Dominic who spoke. 'There's some news?'

He sounded so calm that Felicity was able to say, 'Have you found something?'

'In a manner of speaking, we have,' said the inspector. He looked at them both, and then said, 'We've found Brother Karabas.'

'"Found"? Does that mean something's happened to him?' said Brother Dominic.

'Oh no. No, he's perfectly all right. He's been into Beck for the afternoon, to look something up in the local archivist's office. He's only just got back by the late bus.'

'What about Bryony?'

'Brother Karabas doesn't know anything about a nature ramble,' said the inspector, looking at Felicity with the same compassion that Morag Mackenzie and Dominic had displayed.

There was an abrupt silence. Felicity was aware that she was shrinking into the chair she had been sitting on, as if she were trying to fold herself into a dark silence so that she would not hear what the inspector was about to say. Because once he had said it, it would put Bryony into the terrible ranks of all those children one read about in newspapers and heard about on TV news bulletins: '*Missing from home since twelve o'clock on Tuesday* . . .' '*Last seen leaving school with a friend* . . .'

It was then that the inspector said what she had not wanted to hear. He said it very gently but the intent was unmistakable.

'Mrs Stafford, have you got a recent photograph of Bryony?'

It was almost completely dark by the time the police inspector left the stable house and rain was lashing against the uncurtained windows. It was warm and bright and safe in the little sitting room, except that if Bryony was dead Felicity would never be able to feel warm or safe again.

The inspector had taken the photograph that had been taken at Bryony's seventh birthday. It would be copied and distributed, he had said, to petrol stations, bus depots, railway stations. And of course they were already searching the immediate area.

'Couldn't I help with the search?' It was unbearable to just sit there and wait. But the inspector said, carefully, that this was not a good idea; for one thing Bryony might turn up at any minute and Felicity must be there for that, and also his men knew the area and they were trained in these things. He said the same things that Brother Dominic had said about the vastness of the National Park forests, patted her shoulder, and went purposefully away.

Morag and Brother Dominic went with him. Morag had to supervise the junior school's supper but would come back later. If Felicity wanted anything – anything at all – she had only to ring through to Brother Andrew's office.

Felicity had thought she would prefer being alone, but as soon as the door closed panic swept in all over again. Bryony was somewhere out there in the dark, frightened and cold. The electric lights reflected in the window pane, making a solid oblong so that Felicity could no longer see along the drive. She switched them out, leaving only the glow from the little two-bar electric fire. Yes, that was better. She dragged a quilt off her bed, and curled up on the window seat, wrapping it around her. If Bryony came plodding along the drive, Felicity would not miss her.

She leaned her aching head against the cold window pane. Little rivulets of rain ran down the outside. The night weeping because Bryony was lost. But I don't dare because once I start I might not be able to stop.

She did not exactly sleep but she drifted for a time in an uneasy half-consciousness where sly-faced creatures tried to lure Bryony into the tanglewood thickets of ancient forests so that they could do unspeakable things to her. Con was there as well, padding between the whispering trees, uncannily part of the macabre greenwood . . . Oh Con, *why* aren't you here now! She wrapped her arms around her body to stop the ache of loss for Con who would never come back.

It was raining in that nightmare forest, just as it was raining here: a thin hopeless drizzle that poured ceaselessly down from a leaden sky, and dripped off the branches of the old trees so that the only sound was the soft steady patter of it onto the ground. Felicity, exhausted by fear, her mind roaming the dark hinterlands of nightmare, heard it clearly. She heard it subtly change, like a car shifting gear, so that it was no longer the drip of water; it was icy fingers against a frozen window pane, or frozen tears dropping from the black skeletal trees outside . . .

Tap-tap, tap-tap . . . And now it was almost as if something shut outside somewhere was trying to find a way in. Connor, answering that earlier, lonely cry of pain . . . ? Coming to find her, because she had let Bryony be lost? – don't be absurd!

The sound came again. Tap-tap-tap. Or was it, *let-me-in, let me in*? Was it the soft insidious plea of a dead man, who had dragged himself through the storm-tossed night, to the door of his erstwhile love? In the moment between sleeping and waking, Felicity saw Con's face very clearly indeed, and it was not the dark sardonic face of the man she had married, it was the remote, sunken-eyed thing that had lain on the mortuary slab.

In that instant dread cut through the smothering visions, because supposing, just supposing that after all Con really had been the spectral bridegroom of Gothic legend, and supposing that tonight he had cast aside his wormy shroud, and risen up from his stone coffin-couch to make his way through the storm-ridden night . . . ?

Felicity gasped and opened her eyes. The room was dark, and although nightmares still stalked the shadowlands they were no longer the surreal nightmares of eerie menace-laden wildwoods. She was in the warm, ordinary sitting room at Bracken, and the tapping was nothing more sinister than someone knocking to come in. She turned her head so that she could see the door.

Someone was standing out there, waiting to be invited over the threshold . . .

There was no reason to feel a sudden thudding apprehension, and there was no reason, either, to feel the hairs prickling on the nape of her neck. But Felicity did feel it; she remembered with a fresh jag of fear that she had not drawn the bolt. Whoever was out there tapped again, very lightly.

Furtively. As if not wanting to be heard by anyone other than Felicity.

It was probably someone who thought Felicity might have managed to fall asleep, and did not want to disturb her. Felicity seized this thought with relief and drew breath to call out, and as she did so, whoever was standing outside began to lift the latch very slowly. Felicity shrank back against the cold window pane, one hand flying to her mouth. The door swung open, and as Felicity saw the dark figure standing there, for a confused, heart-stopping second she really did think Connor had returned. Even when he stepped into the room and the fake firelight cast its spurious shadow across his eyes, her emotions continued to perform the most extraordinary somersaults.

It was not Connor, of course; Connor was dead, he was mangled up in the crushed metal of his car, and he was buried – Felicity had stood over his grave and seen the coffin lowered into the ground. And outside of Lovecraftian fiction and the cobweb-draped romance of Lefanu, the dead did not walk.

And yet, and yet.

'May I come in?' said Karabas, softly, and waited for her assent before stepping into the room.

Chapter Twelve

The situation reverted to normality almost at once. Karabas said, in an ordinary, concerned voice, 'Did I startle you? I'm sorry. I did want to see you, but I won't stay if you'd rather be on your own.'

He sounded so genuinely compassionate, and he stood looking down at her with such solicitude that Felicity felt instantly guilty because she had been harbouring unspeakable suspicions against him.

She got up from the window seat and came across to the little sofa that Morag had drawn up to the fire. 'You didn't startle me – it's all right.' She sat down and Karabas sat next to her. He was wearing a dark sweater and dark trousers and this gave him a tougher, more urbane look than the normal brown robe of the Order.

He looked at her for a moment, and then said, softly, 'Weren't you afraid to invite me in, Felicity?'

This was so unexpected and so extraordinary, that Felicity thought she must have misheard. She said, 'I'm sorry you've been involved in this muddle. But Bryony seemed so sure about the outing—'

'I did tell her we'd make an excursion to one of the National Park forests one afternoon,' said Karabas. 'We didn't make any definite arrangement, but she seemed to think she'd like to do it. I'd like to do it as well.'

He made it sound as if it was still a possibility. 'You think she's alive?' said Felicity, and realized that it was the first time she had dared voice the question.

And Karabas said without the least hesitation, 'Oh, she's still alive, Felicity.'

Silence. Felicity had been staring at the glowing bars of the fire, but she turned her head to look at him, and at once the ice-thin veneer of normality cracked and a dark menace began to ooze through. Karabas was watching her; not openly as if he wanted to convey sympathy, and not covertly as if wary of upsetting her. He was watching her slyly and calculatingly from the corners of his eyes. Felicity stared at him, and felt the past swoop forward to engulf her again.

Because that's how Con used to look, she thought. It's how he used to look towards the end – all those nights when he played mind-games: when he used to frighten me to death, and become wildly aroused as a result . . . And those times when he came slinking home in the small hours of the morning, smelling of drink and other women's perfume, and when the sex took a bizarre turn – and sometimes a *violent* turn – and he jeered at me for flinching . . .

Hold on to all that, Felicity thought. Hold on to it and stop pretending that this would have been easier if Con had been here, because it wouldn't have been easier at all, it might even have been worse. Because the real Connor was cruel and selfish and irresponsible, and it's as well, really, that he's gone.

Only Connor had not gone: he was here in the room now – he was part of the shadows and he was part of the fear. He was looking out of Karabas's eyes, and when Karabas leaned forward and slid an arm around Felicity's waist, a tiny fragment of comfort slid through the icy misery. She leaned against him, because for a moment she could let herself believe that it was Connor – the Connor she had married: dazzling and charming and intriguing. I shouldn't be doing this, thought Felicity. It isn't fair to him. She remembered that night when he had held her against him and she had felt the unmistakable swell of arousal. She had long since dismissed it, because presumably even the most devout of monks had involuntary responses to females.

Still, I'll sit up in a minute, thought Felicity, determinedly. But leaning against him was so comforting; it was so reassuring to feel that warm masculine strength once more.

Karabas said, very softly, 'You do know that you really *shouldn't* be alone with me like this, don't you, Felicity?'

'Yes,' said Felicity's voice from the depths of the dream. 'We'll stop in a minute, won't we?'

'Oh yes,' said Karabas, and this time his arm tightened. His fingers brushed Felicity's breast and lingered there, and alarm bells began to ring. I'm misunderstanding again, she thought wildly. Or I'm misjudging. He's a *monk*! A celibate! This is surely nothing more than a clumsy attempt to comfort me.

But when he pulled her more firmly against him she knew she had not misread or misjudged, and she knew that she had to deal with this instantly and firmly, but, if possible, tactfully.

She sat up, disentangling Karabas's hands in the process, and said, in an off-hand voice, 'You're being so kind, Karabas – everyone's being so kind. Let's put the lights on, shall we? – it would be more cheerful. And I'll make us some coffee or tea.' Had that signalled 'hands off' sufficiently politely? Had it indicated, 'We'll pretend this didn't happen'? Oh God, I don't think it has. What strange eyes he has. I don't think I'd better look at them for too long. And what a thin-lipped smile he has. Con used to smile like that sometimes.

Karabas said, 'Are you afraid of me, Felicity?'

'I – no. No, of course I'm not.'

'Oh, but you should be,' he said. 'Oh Felicity, you should be very, very afraid of me,' he said, and although the words were soft, this time Felicity heard the wet snarl in his voice. Panic, nearer to the surface than she had let herself admit, welled up and she put out a hand to ward him off.

He slammed her back against the arm of the sofa, pinning her against the cushions, his body half on top of her, and Felicity said, in a furious voice, 'Let me go! Karabas, let me go *now* or I'll call for help!' I'm not really in danger, she thought frantically. I'm within call of several dozen people, and if this gets out of hand all I've got to do is yell for help.

She said, 'Stop this, please! You don't mean it, and I don't want it! If I made you think I did, I'm sorry—'

For answer he struck her across the mouth, and Felicity gasped and instinctively threw up her hands to shield her face. At once he grabbed her wrists, imprisoning them easily and painfully.

'Don't scream,' he said. 'Don't turn me over to the police, either. If you do that, Bryony will certainly die and she'll die tonight.' He looked down at her. '*Now* are you afraid?' he said, and Felicity, her face still stinging from the blow, stared up at him in mingled horror and disbelief.

'Oh God, you took her! She really did get it right about the nature walk— Oh, let me *go*!' She renewed her struggles, half sobbing with fury and frustration.

113

'She came with me so sweetly,' said Karabas. 'So willingly. You can have no idea how easy it was.' His voice was slow and slurry almost as if he was drunk, and his eyes were catching the red glint of the fire again, they were crimson glaring eyes. Felicity stopped struggling, her mind in turmoil. Bryony's still alive – he said she was, which means there's still time to find her. Oh God, let me keep my head and, oh God, let him tell me where she is!

She forced her voice to normality. 'Tell me why you took her.' Had that sounded sufficiently unthreatening? Yes, he had relaxed his iron grip a little. Enough for her to twist out of his hands and dart to the door or the phone? No. She said, 'I mean, why Bryony particularly?'

'Because I come of an old, old lineage, and there is a vow that my people take,' said Karabas.

'What kind of vow?'

'To seek out and destroy the descendants of Richard Foljambe,' said Karabas, as if explaining a very simple fact to a very stupid child.

The old family name – vaguely French, somehow medieval-sounding – was the last thing Felicity had been expecting to hear. Her mother had believed the name had died out.

But the legend, the stupid, glossily sentimentalized legend had not died. Felicity could remember her mother spinning the stories for her, just as, twenty or so years afterwards, she had spun them herself for Bryony. They were splendid, harmless tales: tales to fire an already-imaginative child's mind. Adventure and bravery and parfait gentil knights and glittering golden kings . . . Richard who had built the forest house, and Thomas who had been knighted just before Magna Carta was signed. The twins – their names lost and only their courage in battle remembered – who had followed Edward Plantagenet into one of the later Crusades, and then had gone with him into battle against the Scots in 1301 . . .

The royal wolfhunters purging England of wolves, all the way back to William the First . . .

Except that she had taken care to edit out all reference to the wolves when telling Bryony the stories.

Karabas was watching her, his head to one side. After a moment, he said, 'That was the vow that Connor took ten years ago.'

The clustering memories vanished. Felicity said, '*Connor* took a vow to destroy my family?'

'Oh yes. But he lost sight of his mission. He became—' A pause, and again the terrible thin-lipped smile. 'He became humanized,' said Connor's cousin. 'He married and he sired a child on the family he had sworn to destroy.'

'Bryony,' whispered Felicity.

'Yes. You see we hadn't allowed for her,' said Karabas. 'Genetically her birth ought not to have been possible, in fact. We considered whether you might have had an affair, of course—'

'You did *what*?'

'But we discarded the idea,' said Karabas. 'She's clearly Connor's daughter.' He looked at her very intently. 'And she has the race-memories,' said Karabas, softly. 'The race memories from both parents. Once we realized that, we knew that Connor really had committed the ultimate betrayal. He had fallen too deeply into your world, Felicity, and he had crossed over a very dangerous line. So he had to die. We watch our own, you see. When one of our people enters your world, we keep in very close touch. Connor returned to us several times over the years and we knew exactly what he was doing. We knew that he had taken the identity of someone who had no family and who had died twenty years ago – that was all according to plan, of course.' He smiled, briefly. 'We have long since worked out our own ways of entering your world,' said Karabas. 'We have found pockets where we can blend in without too much difficulty, and where we can be accepted without too many questions being asked. This place – Bracken Hall – is one we found some years ago, although this is the first time we have used it.' He studied her. 'We have to adjust a little at times, but we hardly ever get it wrong,' said Karabas.

Felicity felt that the whole of her married life had suddenly been unravelled in a wild confusion of threads, and as if the threads were lying all around her in tangled disarray. The unexplained absences from home. The curious blanks in Con's knowledge and in his understanding of ordinary, everyday things. The fact that the only Connor Stafford registered for National Insurance was some long-dead old man who had had no family. Con took his identity, thought Felicity. I was right about the Frederick Forsyth plot, at any rate. And as the tangle

115

began to weave itself into a new pattern, two thoughts fought for mastery: how much of this do I believe? And – far more disturbing – if this is true, how greatly have I misjudged Con?

She picked one fact out of the welter of confusion. 'Did you kill him?'

'Yes. If one of the pack offends, it must be cast out,' said Karabas, and Felicity heard the eerie parallel with the Christian religion. If thine eye offends thee, pluck it out.

'But – Con died in a car smash.'

'Con died because when he got into his car that night, I was there as well,' said Karabas. 'He had been with some female, of course – that was always Connor's weakness.'

'Yes,' said Felicity, in helpless misery.

'I was hiding in the car – it was thoughtful of him to drive an estate car, by the way; it made it easier for me to crouch down in the space behind the back seat. Once the car reached speed, I reared up. He saw me in the driving mirror and he swerved violently and lost control of the car.'

Felicity was starting to feel punch-drunk at this nightmare sequence of revelations, but this last one conjured up such a vivid image that for a moment it blotted out everything else. She saw, with dreadful facility, Con driving through the night – reaching the badly-lit stretch of road where the crash had happened – suddenly catching sight of a pair of alien eyes in the mirror.

'He died,' said Karabas, slyly. 'But it took a little time. I watched him die, Felicity.'

The thought: he didn't need to tell me that! thrust its way upwards, and with it came a spurt of anger, unexpectedly strengthening. I'll beat you yet, you evil thing! thought Felicity, grabbing this welcome surge of fury and hanging on to it for all she was worth. I'll find out where you've taken Bryony if I have to bargain with the devil to do it. And when this is all over, then I'll face this question of Con stepping over some kind of genetic line, and I'll even face that searing image of him dying alone and helpless while this monster watched . . .

She said, 'But mightn't you have been killed as well?' and heard with gratitude that her voice was wholly devoid of emotion.

'Yes, certainly,' said Karabas at once. 'As it happened, I was only slightly bruised. I walked away before the ambulance

116

arrived. But I was prepared to die, and if I had it would have been for my people. It would have been an honourable death.'

'And Bryony would have been safe.'

'No. Someone else would have come looking for her.'

'Why?'

'We need to study her. To test her.'

'What kind of test?'

Karabas said, very softly, 'Have you never heard of the ancient ritual of drinking the blood of the ancestors?'

Sick horror threatened to overwhelm Felicity, but she fought it, and said, 'Ancestors—?'

'The ancestors of her father's people,' said Karabas. 'And that's where I'm going to take her. I shall take her to my people and she will be kept among us until she is thirteen. Then she will be brought to the ancient ritual. It will be the final test. If she has truly inherited the traits of my people, she will drink the blood and join in the ritual without hesitation.'

The thought of Bryony, so pretty and fastidious, being kept captive for six years by some outlandish tribe, and then forced to take part in such a repulsive act was practically unbearable. Felicity, grasping at straws, said, 'But why did you take her now? Why didn't you wait until she's thirteen?'

'By then she would have fallen too much under the sway of your world. We want her as she is now – malleable. Teachable. Still believing in fairy tales and magic.'

'Suppose she fails your test?'

'Then she will die, as all the children who fail the ritual die. Also, by that time she would have seen too many of our ancient secrets to be allowed to live.'

Felicity knew that if she had not been sitting down she would have fallen. She managed to say, 'Where is she now?'

'In a place where she will not be found.'

Felicity felt another lurch of sick panic, but she said, 'Where do you really come from? What are you?'

'Every so often – perhaps only once in every ten thousand years, or even once in every hundred thousand years – evolution takes an unexpected turn,' said Karabas. 'Sometimes it makes a jump between one stage of development and the next. It misses a link here and there. But sometimes,' he said, softly, 'sometimes it misses more than a link: it misses its way altogether and stumbles into a dark, thorny dead end. And strange things can be born out of those darknesses.'

'Nature falling into a blind alley,' said Felicity, softly.

'Yes. For many generations there has been a clear dividing line – the humans on one side, the animals on another – and my people have been in the shadow world that lies between the two,' he said, and for the first time Felicity was aware of a brief sadness within him. But please let him keep talking like this, because at any minute somebody might come in and then I'll be safe and Bryony will be safe, and providing we can find her—

The glint of sanity and logic that had shown in Karabas's eyes while he talked was dissolving, and the menace was pouring back into the room. Karabas tightened his grasp on Felicity's wrists, leaning nearer. His breath was warm on her cheek. And his face is changing, she thought, incredulously. It's becoming thinner and more pointed . . . No, I'm imagining it.

She said, 'Why did you come back here? Why didn't you just take Bryony to your people?'

'Oh Felicity,' said Karabas, genuine amusement in his tone. 'I came back to cover my tracks. I came back to kill you.' He studied her, and then said, 'You know too much, you see, and once the real enquiries start about Bryony— And even if I hadn't told you about my people, the police would start looking into Connor's background. You might tell them things about him that would be dangerous for us.' He released her wrists and padded across the room to the outer door. There was the scrape of the bolt being drawn across.

Felicity sat up at once, her mind working at top speed, considering and discarding half a dozen courses of action. She could snatch up a makeshift weapon – the table lamp, a marble bookend – but she could not do so without him realizing her intention and pouncing on her. He'll overpower me easily, she thought. Whatever I do, he'll overpower me.

'And now,' said Karabas, leaning back against the door, 'and now, my dear, no one can get in.' He looked her up and down. 'But before the killing, the pleasure. I've been savouring you for a very long time, Felicity. Get undressed.'

'*No!*'

'Do it!' He crossed the room and stood over her. Felicity willed herself not to flinch. 'Do it,' he said very quietly.

'Remember Bryony out there in the cold and the dark? If you turn me over to the police you'll certainly never see her again. She'll die of cold and hunger before you can find her. Keep remembering that, Felicity.'

'But – someone might come to the door—'

'Send them away. Say you're trying to get some sleep.'

Felicity stood up and, forcing her mind to some kind of detachment, slid quickly out of her clothes. The false firelight cast its red glow on the room, and rain was dashed against the uncurtained windows. It was a dreadful travesty of the nights she had shared with Con: winter nights when they had banked up the fire and piled up the cushions, and made slow sensuous love half the night . . . Only I daren't think about Con. I'll keep thinking about Bryony – I'll keep remembering that this is going to keep her alive, at least for tonight – yes, that's the way to get through this. And I will get through it, thought Felicity determinedly. I'll get through it and I'll find her. I *will*.

He's going to rape me – yes, of course he is. He's going to do it now, on this sofa, and whether all that stuff about vows and the Foljambes is true or not, I daren't call his bluff. If I yell for help I really won't get Bryony back. Oh God, she's out there in the dark somewhere . . . I haven't got a choice about this, thought Felicity in silent anguish. And I'd screw the devil himself if it would save her!

Karabas was watching her, his eyes narrowed, and Felicity's muscles began to ache with the strain of waiting for him to make the next move. She was just wondering a bit dizzily if he would undress, when he pulled the sweater impatiently over his head, tousling his dark hair in the process. He unfastened his trousers and stepped out of them. Dark hair, glossy and soft, grew on his chest and between his legs, curling down the insides of his thighs. The hot hard masculine arousal jutted upwards.

He walked towards her, and incredibly he was smiling and unbelievably it was Con's smile – rueful and charming and tinged with that faint hint of danger, so that you remembered all of the old nursery tales: you remembered that there were slender beautiful young men who wore an air of dark romance like a cloak, but who sometimes suddenly changed so that evil hungering beings looked out of their eyes . . . That once upon a time there had been creatures who could don human guise but who had a taste for human flesh and human skin. *Because sometimes evolution takes an unexpected turn, and sometimes, mankind branches off down an unexpected bypath . . . And the human disguise makes it all the easier to screw you, my dear . . .*

Only now the human carapace was melting. Oh God, I'm hallucinating, thought Felicity. This can't possibly be happening . . .

He moved on to her at last, bounding forward, half-smothering her, thrusting his hand between her thighs in unspeakable intimacy. Felicity's stomach was lifting with nausea but she clung to the thought that it would be over quickly. Wasn't rape normally quick on account of the inordinate excitement of the rapist? Please let him be so violently aroused that he'll climax within seconds, she prayed silently.

He jerked her thighs wider with one hand and then forced into her and Felicity cried out, because at once there was a tearing bruising pain. The thought: I can't endure this! surfaced, and with it panic. But then he began to move, not jerkily or bruisingly as she had been expecting, but smoothly, as if his body was made of polished silk. There was the warm golden scent of something wild and feral and blazingly masculine and for a treacherous moment Felicity was aware of a tug of response.

And then the response was swept away as memory flooded back, because this was not the romantic mysterious lover; this was the aberrant, the mutant creature born in one of the eerie bypaths that evolution sometimes wandered into by mistake, and it was the monster who had stolen Bryony away and killed Con. Hatred, bitter and violent, curved upwards and Felicity grasped it unhesitatingly. Through the measureless time that followed – through Karabas's smooth unhurried movements, and through the ascending excitement radiating from him – Felicity held on to that bracing hatred. When he finally shuddered in climax, there was a moment of sick revulsion – he's a *wolf*! – and for several seconds Felicity was aware of her own sanity spinning crazily away from her. But I've got through it, she thought. It's over, he's done it, and I'm all right. And now I can concentrate on reaching Bryony.

Karabas stood up and looked down at her. The firelight was casting eerie shadows over his face, but it was casting them in the unmistakable outline of a wolf's mask, so that for a hideous moment it was as if a creature with a man's body but a wolf's head stood there.

He was facing her, his legs apart, and she saw that despite his assault – despite the never-to-be-forgotten ejaculation of that alien seed into her body – he was still violently and obscenely aroused. Felicity's skin crawled with repulsion, and the tenuous belief that at least now she was safe began to splinter. She understood that she had been wrong to believe that the dark inner creature born from that grisly tanglewood bypath had gone, and wrong to believe that the rape was over.

He moved again, and this time he knocked her to the ground in a whirling tumble of warm golden body-scent and snarling teeth, and Felicity felt his nails – hard curving wolfnails – raking her skin, drawing blood. For a brief blinding moment it was as if the present was disintegrating all around her, so that she could see through to the distant past – to the raw battles fought between her long-ago ancestors and wild, inhuman forest beings they had vowed to vanquish . . .

In the sullen light of the deceiving fireglow he moved behind her, forcing her to a kneeling position, and as he pushed her thighs apart again, she knew that the real rape was still to take place.

Chapter Thirteen

Bryony's afternoon had started out by being pretty good. Karabas had met her out of school at quarter-past twelve, and said there was a slight change of plan: they were going to the wildwood earlier, in fact they were going right away. The idea was to have lunch there instead of tea, because at this time of year it would be dark too early to have tea comfortably.

Bryony saw the point of this, and the sandwiches and cherry cake and chocolate biscuits would do just as well for lunch. Also, it was Wednesday which meant sausage and bacon toad-in-the-hole and Brother Joseph often got the mixture wrong so that although the sausages and bacon were OK, with them you got a plateful of what Primary Two called sog.

She wondered about explaining to mother about the picnic time being changed, but Karabas said it was all right: he had been along to her office and told her himself. So Bryony went back to the stable house to change out of her school uniform. She put on a woollen jersey and a grey skirt, and over that she put the red cloak. This would be a good thing to wear in a wildwood and there were scarlet wellingtons that matched. It was going to be pretty exciting.

After all Primary Three did not come. This was a pity, but Karabas said they had a lesson to go to. He and Bryony would have just as good a time on their own, he said, and there would be more to eat. Bryony would have preferred not to be on her own with Karabas, on account of the spooky *other* person who sometimes peered out of his eyes, but it would not be polite to say this.

She thought they would go to the wildwood on a bus which would be fun. Buses here were not like buses in London where everyone was impatient. Mother had taken Bryony into Caldbeck on two Saturdays since they had been here, and both times the buses had bumbled happily along between the stops.

Quite often the driver pulled up along the road if he saw someone waving him down, and people travelling all knew one another; the drivers knew them all as well.

Bryony was surprised when Karabas led her around to the garages where the school minibus was kept, along with a couple of cars belonging to lay teachers; Miss Mackenzie had a red Mini, and Mr Lucas who came in to teach music had a sports car. All the girls in the senior school were in love with Mr Lucas and all the boys were in love with the sports car.

But they would certainly not be going to the wildwood in any kind of car today because Karabas could not drive, Bryony knew this. But then Karabas wheeled out something that had been standing in the shadows by itself, and Bryony saw with astonishment that it was a motorbike.

It was gleaming black with silver streaks here and there, and it was sleek and very big. Bryony thought it was not the kind of thing that monks usually rode, but Karabas said it would get them there very quickly, and it would be fun to ride. Bryony could sit on the pillion, and she must wear a waterproof cape over her things, because that was what people always did on motorbikes. There was a spare waterproof all ready for her, and there was a spare crash helmet as well. The waterproof was dark green and it covered Bryony all the way down to her toes. The helmet was a bit big and it bumped her nose if she was not careful, but she could see out under the rim pretty well. They wheeled the bike all the way along the drive and out of the school gates, and then Karabas started the engine.

Until now Bryony had been managing not to think about being frightened; she was sorry that Primary Three were not coming, but she was quite looking forward to seeing the wildwood and to searching for wild flowers and horse chestnuts which might be used in Primary Two's conker tournaments, and to listening to bird song. Karabas knew about the different bird songs; he said that all animals had their own language, which was not in the least like human language. Once upon a time humans had been able to speak the animals' language and there had not been such a difference between humans and animals. It was a pity that this understanding had long since been lost, he said, although occasionally you came across people in very remote country districts where the secret still lingered.

This was interesting. Bryony said hopefully, 'Are there people in the wildwood who know it?' and Karabas said that was one of the things they were going to discover this afternoon. You never knew what you might find in a wildwood.

When Karabas talked like this – when he told about secret, lost languages, or how you tracked a fox or a badger to its lair – he was so interesting that Bryony found it easy to forget about the other person behind his eyes. But when he sat astride the motorbike's leather seat and revved its engine, she remembered and started to feel very frightened indeed, because something was happening – it had started to happen as soon as he got onto the motorbike – and it was something that was part of the bad person who lived behind Karabas's eyes.

Whatever it was that was happening was not something you could see with your eyes, but Bryony knew, absolutely positively, that he had changed. He had changed inside – as if the secret cruel *other* person had climbed quietly up out of a dark hiding-place, and as if it was that person who was sitting astride the motorbike watching her.

For a moment she hoped it was just because Karabas was not wearing the brown robe that the monks normally wore during the school day.

What really made Karabas look different was the crash helmet; Bryony would bet that if he took it off he would not look frightening at all. But it was a black helmet and someone had painted feathery shapes on it in dark red, so that if you looked at it for long enough, you started to imagine the scarlet shapes were evil, slanting eyes.

'Get astride the rear seat, Bryony,' said Karabas, and Bryony knew at once that this was the voice of the evil, greedy person who lived behind Karabas's eyes. She took a fearful step backwards.

'Bryony,' said the greedy voice, very softly, 'aren't you going to come into the wildwood with me?'

'Well, actually I'm not sure if I want to come after all,' said Bryony, hesitantly, and at once the motorbike engine growled louder.

'But you promised,' said the dreadful thing. 'You promised to come to the wildwood with me, Bryony, and it isn't very far. It won't take us very long to reach it.'

Bryony saw that there was no way of getting out of it, and

so she walked up to the growly machine and clambered onto
its back. She was pretty unhappy about doing that, and when
she had finally scrambled into place it was just as horrid as she
had known it would be. The seat was covered with some harsh
bristly stuff and the machine purred and hummed, so that it
was exactly like riding on the back of something that had a
coarse matted skin but hard knobbly bones underneath that
you could feel shifting and rippling. It was even nastier to have
to put her arms round the black-clad creature with the glinting
helmet-eyes, who was so spookily not Karabas any longer.

As the snarly machine roared off down the road the wind
whipped into her face, snatching her breath away, and the
houses and the trees all zoomed past so quickly that you could
hardly see them. Bryony thought they went through Bracken
Village, and she thought there was a signpost pointing to
Caldbeck, but it was difficult to be sure about this because
they were going so fast. You had to cling very tightly to the
driver on a motorbike, and when you went round a corner you
had to be sure to lean over with the bike so that you did not
wobble it over. It took a lot of concentration.

When they had gone what seemed to be quite a long way
the motorbike snarled to a halt, and Karabas got off and helped
her to climb down. And there in front of them was the
wildwood.

It was exactly how Bryony had thought it would be. There
were the trees – hundreds and hundreds of trees – and they
grew so closely together that you knew that the deeper you
went into them, the darker it would get. And there were little
windy paths in and out of the trees: not paths that people had
made, just narrow little tracks that had been made by the
animals who scurried to and fro when nobody was watching.

Best of all, it was the kind of place where you might very
well find magic things – Bryony remembered that Karabas
had said wildwoods were so extremely ancient that you could
sometimes find scraps of magic in them.

Anyone could see at once that this wildwood was a place
where you might tumble into a magic world, or step into an
enchanted land. You might even come upon a witch's house,
or meet someone who had been put under a spell by an evil
wizard. Bryony knew, really, that these were only things out of

fairy tales, and that those kinds of fairy tales were for very young children indeed and not really true, but a bit of her thought you could not be absolutely sure.

They wheeled the bike quite a long way into the trees so that it would be hidden from anyone who might come along and steal it, which Karabas said was a thing that might easily happen. He took off the crash helmet and the waterproof, and Bryony risked a cautious glance at him and saw that he did not look as frightening now. This was good.

She was pretty pleased to be able to take off her own crash helmet and the waterproof. Now she could stomp through the forest in her scarlet wellingtons and jump into piles of leaves without getting splashed. She began to feel better, and when they started to talk about the Foljambes she felt absolutely lavishly better. They walked along, going deeper and deeper into the wildwood, talking as they went. Nearer to the wildwood's heart the trees grew so closely together that some of the branches were all twined up together over their heads. It made it dark, but Karabas said wildwoods were almost always dark. Bryony knew this, of course.

It was a good wildwood; Bryony was pleased with it. The ground was covered with fallen leaves so that it was like walking on a spongy carpet, and there were good smells everywhere; warm golden smells that made you think about bonfires and crunchy golden leaves on the ground.

Karabas was telling Bryony about Thomas Foljambe, who had been made Sir Thomas Foljambe by the king. This had not been Richard's king; Thomas had lived a lot later than Richard.

'As much as a hundred years later?' It was important to get these things exact.

'Oh yes,' said Karabas, and Bryony wriggled her toes in the scarlet wellingtons in delighted anticipation of hearing about Thomas. Mother had not known much about Thomas either. She had said that the mainly interesting thing about Thomas was that he had become so rich he had been able to make the forest house much bigger, but Bryony knew that the best part about Thomas's life had come right at the end, when he was an extremely old man, and the twins had been born. Next to Richard, Bryony liked the twins best of all the Foljambes.

Karabas knew about the twins, but he did not know their

names, and so, as they walked through the trees, Bryony told him about them. Their names had been Robin and Alain, which were good names, and it was a pity that Thomas had been so extremely old when they were born because he would have liked to see them, and they would have liked to have a great-grandfather. Anybody would like that, on account of great-grandfathers knowing about things – interesting history things – that happened before you were born.

Robin and Alain had lived in the forest house, which was bigger by that time. A place called a buttery had been built, which was where cheese and butter were made in a wooden churn. And there was a still-room, where the ladies of the house dried sprigs of lavender and rosemary and pounded up spices. The still-room always smelt beautiful, although if you stood just outside the door and half-closed your eyes you could just smell the squelchy-blood, crunched-bone smell of the wolf-lair. The new rooms jutted out from the wall, and the low, ivy-covered cellar door was always in deep shadow so that people walked past it almost without knowing it was there.

But the twins had known it was there, and they had known about the wolf-lair being down there as well. They had not liked it, but they had not been as frightened of it as Edmund had been, because they were twins and almost always together. Thomas had known about the cellar as well, because there was a legend in the family about Edmund by then: it was handed down, from father to son, and everybody thought the cellar was haunted. Thomas said that it was Edmund who haunted it and that *his* great-grandfather had offered Masses for the repose of Edmund's soul. Bryony was not too sure what this meant.

The twins knew what had really happened to Edmund. They did not know how they knew it, any more than Bryony knew how she knew it, but they knew about the magic *Lia Fail* which Edmund had had from his mother, and which the bad old wolf had stolen when he had finished eating Edmund.

The twins were twelve when they made their solemn vow to get the *Lia Fail* back for their family. Alain said and Robin agreed that it would be a way of avenging Edmund's death. In those days, people had minded about things like that, and taking a vow was a very solemn and important thing and you were not allowed to break it. And if they could not get Edmund's

Lia Fail back, then they would try to get a tiny fragment from the real Stone of Destiny. Robin said and Alain agreed that that would give them as much power against the wolves as the wolves had against them.

They took the vow in the cellar on the night before their thirteenth birthday, creeping down while everyone was at supper. Tomorrow they would be expected to eat at the long table in the great hall, along with the rest of the family and some of the servants, because in those days, when you were thirteen, you were regarded as grown-up. So they were taking the vow on the eve of their grown-up life, so that they could get on with the job of avenging Edmund the instant they were thirteen.

They lit candles and set them all round the cellar in little curvy silver candle-holders. Bryony would not have done that, not for a hundred pounds, but Robin and Alain did it because they hated the horrid old wolf who had eaten up Edmund. There were no grinning giants'-teeth traps down here any longer, because the wolf-traps were now kept in the stables, and there were stable boys who looked after them and kept them polished and oiled. So the cellar was just a dusty old room, and once Robin and Alain had lit the candles you could see the dusty bare floor.

Except that it was not empty at all really, because the wolves still sometimes came prowling into the black tunnelly place below the cellar, and found their way into the cupboard and lay waiting for nice little children. It was a good thing that none of them had been crouching there on the night that the twins took their vow.

They both knelt down at the very centre of the cellar, facing the door that led down to the lair. They called it the wolf-door, and there was a moment when Robin thought that he heard a sound from behind it – a horrid scratchy sound that might be wolfnails scraping impatiently at the door to get out. And then there was another moment when Alain thought he saw the door start to inch open all by itself. They waited, their eyes on the door, both of them holding their breath with fear, but nothing else moved and no more sounds came, and so they got on with the vow. Bryony could see them very clearly, kneeling in the bad-smelling cellar. They both had red-gold hair; Alain's was a bit brighter red than Robin's, and Robin's eyes were a vivider blue than Alain's.

They said a prayer first, and then they repeated, very solemnly, that they swore before God that they would avenge Edmund who had died in this house a hundred and fifty years ago; they swore that they would seek out the descendants of the wolf-creature who had killed him and destroy them all. Finally, the candles now burning low so that shadows oozed across the floor, they swore that they would search the land for the ancient magical Stone of Destiny, the enchanted *Lia Fail* that Edmund's several-times-great-grandmother had brought from Ireland, and Edmund's mother had entrusted to Edmund to keep him safe from the wolf.

They did not yet know how they would do this, but they knew they would do it somehow.

It was only when Bryony and Karabas stopped talking about the twins and about the Stone of Destiny, that Bryony realized how dark it had got.

They had eaten their picnic lunch seated in a little clearing, and when they had finished Karabas leaned back against the trunk of one of the old trees, and started to talk about the ancient magic in wildwoods.

But it was not until he said, 'Don't you feel the magic stirring all about us, Bryony?' that Bryony remembered about being frightened. There was a creepy half-light everywhere now – the Purple Hour – and the wildwood was starting to feel pretty scary.

Karabas said, 'Come with me deeper into the forest, Bryony,' and when Bryony drew in a breath and started to say she thought they should go home, he moved suddenly, and his arms closed around her, and there was the sound of hot panting breath in her ear as he hugged her against his chest.

He lifted her up and began walking slowly into the deepest, darkest part of the wildwood, and Bryony, frightened to death, managed to glance up at his face, and suddenly saw that this other person who had climbed out was not a stranger after all: this was one of the wolf-creatures who had hidden in the cellar of the forest house, and who had eaten Edmund and all those other children.

She gulped and said, 'Where are we going?' and the wolf-creature smiled down at her.

'I'm taking you to the hut at the wildwood's heart,' it said. 'And I'm going to lock you up and leave you there.'

He smiled at her again. 'And then,' he said, softly, his lips close to her ear, 'and then, my dear, when it's the middle of the night and there's no one about I'm going to come back and take you to where the real wolves live.'

Chapter Fourteen

Felicity had only endured Karabas's renewed violation of her body by clinging to the fierce burning hatred that had so unexpectedly ignited somewhere in her mind, and by holding hard to the knowledge that the only way she would save Bryony was by surviving on her own account.

After the final obscene thrusting he withdrew and Felicity was aware that her body was her own again. She half fell forward onto the hearthrug before the fire, intensely aware of him still standing behind her. And although she had vowed not to display any weakness, for several minutes she could only crouch there, gasping and trembling, expecting the final assault at any second. But the minutes stretched out agonizingly and he did not move, and at last Felicity nerved herself to turn round to look up at him.

He was dressed standing with his back to the fire, watching her. The light surrounded him like a crimson nimbus, but she could see his face and his eyes; she could see that his head was tilted to one side as if to hear her thoughts, and that there was charming, deprecatory regret in his eyes. Felicity, her arms and neck scraped and bleeding from his nails, her mind as well as her body scoured and stinging, saw that it was exactly the way that Connor had sometimes looked. But Con couldn't help what he did! she thought, and beneath the fear she was aware of a thread of confused gratitude. For the first time she saw Con's convoluted deceptions in a different light, and for the first time she understood that Con had been struggling to pass unnoticed in a world that was alien to him.

Except that once Con had lived among the humans for a time, he fell too deeply into their world, and an invisible genetic line was crossed when Bryony was conceived . . .

Karabas suddenly turned his head, and looked towards the window. He's heard something, thought Felicity. He heard it before I did, but I hear it as well now. Voices. People running across the courtyard. She grabbed her discarded sweater and pulled it on, and as she did so, Karabas moved to the window and stood in the shallow recess, looking down.

'It's the police,' he said. 'They're coming back. They're crossing the courtyard and in a moment they'll be at your door.' He came back into the room and grabbed her wrist again, his eyes glowing. 'Listen, Felicity, I'll make a bargain with you. Let me get clear of the grounds and I promise you Bryony will be safe.'

'I don't believe you—'

'You don't have any choice. Call them off. If they try to follow me, I'll still reach her first, and I'll kill her there and then.' His face swam sickeningly close to hers. 'And I can kill very quickly indeed if I have to,' he said.

'No!' cried Felicity, fighting to remain in control. 'No! The police are here – they'll be in the room at any minute – they'll charge you with kidnapping and you'll be taken away—'

Karabas said, very gently, 'And locked up? Would you let them put me behind bars, Felicity? Would you really do that to me?'

Behind bars. Caged. The image, startling in its suddenness, shocking in its clarity, rose up unbidden. But it was not Karabas whom Felicity was seeing staring out through a cell window; it was Con. Con's dark eyes staring with hopeless pain . . . Forgive me, Con, because I didn't know – I didn't know that I had to make allowances for your behaviour—

Karabas said, 'And if you did that, how would you ever find Bryony?'

'Of course we'd find her—' But Felicity glanced at the dark night beyond the window, and remembered all those acres of dark forestry.

'Would you really find her? She's very well hidden, Felicity.' Their eyes met and held, and Felicity flinched again, expecting another attack. Supposing he took her as a hostage? Would he even know the concept of taking a hostage?

But he released her wrist and went back to the window. 'She'll be out there on her own,' he said. 'In the dark and the cold—'

'They'd find her!' cried Felicity. 'In the end they'd find her!'

'But supposing they didn't? Or supposing they found her too late?'

This time the image was of Bryony, frightened and alone, her little white face struggling not to cry but fright and bewilderment in her eyes. Felicity felt her strength drain again, so that she sat down abruptly on the sofa. Oh God, what do I do?

Karabas said, 'If you hand me over to the police you'll lose Bryony for sure. That's the bargain, Felicity,' and leaning forward, he unlatched the window and swung his legs over the sill. As he dropped effortlessly to the springy grass below, Felicity heard the footsteps outside. She called out to them to wait a moment, dragged on the rest of her clothes, and shivering so violently she felt as if she might break apart, finally managed to get to the door and unlock it.

Brother Dominic with Morag Mackenzie and the police inspector stood on the threshold.

There was a moment when Felicity's mind spun back to Karabas's words: *If you hand me over to the police you'll lose Bryony for sure . . .*

I don't know what to do, thought Felicity. I don't know whether he was speaking the truth. I don't know whether I can trust him. Oh God, I'll die if I lose Bryony! (*She'll be out in the dark and the cold, Felicity . . .*) Supposing I do let him get away, would we be able to find out where he takes her?

And then reason reasserted itself because of course she did not trust him, and because the ordinary human standards – honesty and promises and truth – simply did not apply to him.

She looked at the police inspector and said, without preamble, 'Karabas has got Bryony and I think he's going to take her to some remote place where his people live. There isn't time to explain about all that now. He's attacked me, and he escaped through the window when he heard you coming. He said if I called off the search she'd be safe, but if you tried to imprison him she'd die tonight because we'd never find her.' Morag Mackenzie started to say something, but Felicity shook her head in agony. 'And he said that if you tried to follow him now, he'd reach her first anyway, and he'd kill her before you could get there— Only I don't trust him, I really don't—' Her voice wavered treacherously and she took a deep breath, and

133

then said, 'Please – I don't know what to do.'

There was a brief silence. She was aware of the inspector weighing up the situation, considering and discarding various courses of action. She thought: he looks heavy and a bit dull, but I don't believe he's either of those things.

'If he leaves the school premises my men can follow him discreetly,' said the inspector, with the air of a man making a considered decision. 'No, it's all right, we're trained for this kind of thing, Mrs Stafford. If he's on foot, it'll be easy enough to go after him without him knowing.' He crossed to the still-open window and peered through it, and after a moment, said, 'I can't see him but he might be skulking somewhere in the shadows. Are you absolutely sure he's got Bryony, Mrs Stafford?'

'Yes.' Explanations could come later.

'And you think he's making for wherever he's taken her?'

'*Yes.*'

'Does he drive?'

'No, he doesn't,' began Brother Dominic, and at the same time, Morag said, 'Not officially.'

Felicity said, 'He's almost certainly going straight back to where he's hidden her. And I've got to go after him – you do see that, don't you—?'

Morag started to say, 'But you can't possibly— Felicity, you're hurt!'

'It's only surface scratches—'

'But you're bleeding—'

'I'm all right.' Felicity was already halfway across the room.

'Hold on, Mrs Stafford.' The inspector spoke urgently into the small intercom he carried, and Felicity heard him say, 'He's still somewhere in the grounds. Keep him in sight but don't let him know you're watching him. That's absolutely vital for the child's safety – understand? It couldn't be more important. He knows we've been called in, but he thinks he's frightened the mother into getting rid of us.' He paused, and the crackly voice at the other end said something that sounded like, 'Bloody naive of him, sir.'

The inspector looked across at Felicity, and started to say, 'Don't worry, they all know what to do in these situations—' when the phone crackled again and Felicity heard the same voice say in a low urgent tone, 'We've spotted him.'

'Good man! Don't lose him—'

There was a pause and then the voice came back. 'Bit of a problem sir; our man's taken a motorbike from the stable block and he's wheeling it down the drive to the main road. If we take a car after him he'll see us at once—'

'Of course you mustn't take a car after him!' said the inspector instantly. 'Did he know you were watching him?'

Again the pause. Felicity waited in an agony of impatience, and then the disembodied voice said, 'We're fairly sure he didn't. The garage is at the back and he seems to be using the footpath along by the playing fields – it's wide enough for a motorbike. He hasn't fired the engine yet – he's free-wheeling it across the playing fields.'

'Then he's making for the back exit,' said Brother Dominic. 'The one that joins the lower Caldbeck road.'

'How long will it take him to reach the road that way? Wheeling the bike?'

'Ten minutes at least.'

'Then,' said the inspector, frowning, 'that means—'

'It means I can go after him,' said Felicity. 'I'll take one of the school cars—'

'That's entirely against routine procedure—'

'Sod routine procedure,' said Felicity.

'You'd be better staying here and let us deal with it—'

'I'm not staying here!' said Felicity furiously. 'I'll steal a car if I have to,' she said.

At once Morag chimed in with, 'No need, Felicity: we'll take mine and I'll drive you.' She glanced at the inspector. 'It's a Mini and Karabas would never suspect a Mini bouncing along the road.'

The inspector looked harassedly from one to the other of them. 'There's something in that,' he said. 'It's absolutely against all the rules, of course, but we haven't got time to abide by rules in this situation and we absolutely mustn't risk putting Bryony into any further danger—' He stopped, thinking hard, and then said, 'Yes, all right, we'll do it. But I'll come after you – no, it's all right, Mrs Stafford, I'll take the CID car which is unmarked, and we'll keep at a safe distance, I promise. They've all got radios so we can alert other divisions as we go, and swap cars if he rumbles us.'

'What will you do when he reaches – wherever he's going?'

'We'll decide that when we know where that is,' said the inspector. 'But listen now, Mrs Stafford, Miss Mackenzie; I've got to have your strict promise that once we reach him you'll stay well back, and if there's any rough stuff, you'll drive straight back here. Will you promise me that?'

'I'll get my coat,' said Felicity, diving into the bedroom and not waiting to hear Morag's response.

Brother Dominic said, 'I'll go with them, inspector. I know the roads around here fairly well, and I'll make sure they keep out of trouble.'

The inspector ran a hand distractedly through his hair. Felicity could almost hear him thinking, 'Two females and a bloody monk, the Chief Constable'll dismember me if anything goes wrong,' and then he nodded and said, 'All right, but don't set off from here until you get my OK that our man's reached the road. I'll go down now, and I'll shine the torch twice when it's safe to leave – if you stand at the window I think you'll see it.' He went swiftly from the room, and Felicity experienced an overwhelming affection for him because he had grasped the situation so swiftly, and understood that the need to protect Bryony outweighed the rule book.

'You'll need something to staunch those wounds, Felicity,' said Morag, practically, and Felicity remembered that she was probably bleeding in half a dozen places from that last dreadful attack when she had felt the nails that were not human nails on her arms, and when she had felt the teeth that were not human teeth on her neck. And those were just the visible marks.

She flinched from this thought and darted into the tiny bathroom, grabbing a box of tissues and a damp face flannel and hand towel from the rail. Morag, following her, rummaged in the medicine cabinet for antiseptic.

As they came back into the sitting room, Brother Dominic, anxiously stationed at the window, suddenly said, 'There's the signal,' and they ran out of the stable house and across the quadrangle to the garages.

As they went, Felicity heard Morag mutter to Brother Dominic, 'Pray to God that the car starts straight off.'

God – or someone – was on their side so far tonight, because Morag's Mini started at the first turn of the ignition.

As they went down the long wide drive towards the main school gates, Felicity managed to mop the worst of the scratches, using the tiny passenger mirror to see what she was doing. It could not have mattered less what she looked like, but it might alarm Bryony if her mother appeared to rescue her bleeding and distraught. When they did reach Bryony Felicity would have to be very careful indeed not to overwhelm her; all her instincts would be to snatch the child up in her arms and hold her so tightly that nothing harmful could ever touch her again. But to do that might be harmful in itself, because it might signal to Bryony just how severe a danger she had been in. If Karabas had behaved normally so far, it was just possible that Bryony, with her wild, fey imagination, would be seeing this as a great adventure and would have missed the danger altogether. Felicity was trying to decide how likely this was, and how much emotion she dared show, when Morag leaned forward over the steering wheel, and said, 'I believe that's him up ahead.'

Felicity saw him at the same moment, and the atavistic fear came flooding back. The lower road rose steeply all the way to Caldbeck and beyond, but in several places it looped back on itself so that there was a stretch where the motorbike was above them, but practically facing them. It was completely dark by now, but they could see the motorbike clearly; they could see that it was low and sleek and powerful. As it streaked through the night the creature astride it was bending low over it, so that for a nightmarish moment it was impossible to tell where the streamlined snarling machine ended and the rider began. Oh God, I don't believe any of this is really happening, thought Felicity.

Morag said, 'Are the police with us, Brother Dominic?'

'They are,' said Brother Dominic after a moment, having turned with all the difficulty attendant on a back-seat Mini passenger to look through the rear window. 'But they're quite a long way behind us. If he sees their lights at all, he won't think twice about it.'

'Felicity,' said Morag, as they sped along, 'I don't want to pry, but I don't understand why Karabas took Bryony and then came back.'

Felicity hesitated, and then said, 'It's an extremely long story, Morag, and I don't think I understand it all myself.'

'The man is not sane, of course,' volunteered Brother Dominic.

Felicity said, 'No, of course not.'

'But doesn't he realize that he'll almost certainly be caught and charged with – with kidnapping?' said Morag, and Felicity knew she had substituted the word kidnapping for a stronger one.

She said, carefully, 'Well, as Brother Dominic says, he isn't sane. He probably isn't reasoning on those lines.'

And the truth is that Karabas doesn't care so very much about being caught or being found out, and he doesn't even care much about being put into prison if he is caught, because if that happens his people will simply send someone else to get Bryony . . . And our standards of law and of justice simply don't apply to him, because he isn't wholly human.

'He's turning off,' said Morag, breaking into her thoughts. 'Look there – he's swung off the road—'

'Yes, I see—'

'Oh hell and the devil, it looks as if he's going into the forest!' said Morag furiously.

Brother Dominic, with not so much as a trace of reproof in his voice, leaned forward and said, 'Put your foot down, Morag! Because once he's entered Beck's Forest we've lost him!'

It was very silent and very still in the wildwood. Bryony was not wholly sure what time it was, because it was quite hard to know the time once it started to be dark. It was not absolutely dark yet, but it was nearly so.

It was important not to be afraid, even though she was entirely on her own and even though Karabas had locked her into this horrid old hut and said he would come back as soon as it was properly dark.

He had gone away then, locking the hut, and padding softly through the thick undergrowth, and Bryony had listened hard and thought she just heard the snarly sound of the motorbike starting up.

It was pretty horrid in this hut and it was even horrider to think about Karabas coming back in the middle of the night to take her to where the real wolves lived. Bryony gulped and determinedly wiped her eyes with the back of her hand. There was no need to feel afraid. Mother would come to find her before Karabas came back: she would be wondering where Bryony was, and she would come out to the wildwood and find the hut and she would know where to get the key to unlock the door. Probably this would happen pretty soon.

The forest was all around the hut. When a little wind blew through the trees, the branches leaned over and tapped at the hut's windows – tap-tap, so that it was as if someone was creeping around outside trying to get in. It might actually be the trees themselves. In books, trees sometimes came to life, but in any of the books Bryony had ever read, the trees were always good. But the trees in this wildwood did not look as if they would be good: if they came to life they would be evil and frightening.

Bryony started to think about Alain and Robin, because she could imagine they were here with her now. They had spent a lot of time in their own wildwood, and they had got to know about the trees while they practised their archery. They had worked very hard at this, because there was a new king: a golden-haired, golden-bearded magnificent man called Edward the First, who everyone said was going to fight a lot of wars, and who said himself that he was going to have a crusade when there was time. Alain said, and Robin agreed, that a crusade might be a good place to start their search for the stolen *Lia Fail*, and that the way to join a crusade would be to be the best archers ever.

It was always a summer's afternoon when the twins walked through the wildwood: golden sunshine poured through the trees and there were usually birds singing, and the twins' hair shone like huge shaggy chrysanthemums.

Thinking about Alain and Robin and their own wildwood made Bryony forget for a while that Karabas was coming back to get her. She had explored the hut and she had tried to get the door open, but it was a thick, strong door and the lock was a thick, strong lock. The hut belonged to the people who looked after the forest, and there was a sign on it: Bryony had managed to read most of it, and it said, 'National Park Property – Forestry Maintenance Division. Strictly Private.' She had stumbled a bit over 'Maintenance Division', because these were quite big words, but she thought she had got it right in the end.

It looked as if it was a place where the forest people kept the tools they used to lop branches off dead trees, and sweep leaves away from the little winding paths which visitors to the forest would like to walk along in summer.

In one corner were some large stone jars; there was nothing in them, she had peeped inside to see, but they smelt horrid. Bryony actually felt pretty sick from the smell. They looked a bit odd standing there by themselves. Bryony did not like them one bit.

In the other corner were pots of paint and a pile of signposts with little arrows painted in red. Some of the signs had the names of places, like Patterdale and Troutbeck and Stickle Tarn. These were nice names; they were like names out of fairy stories, and Bryony could imagine exactly what the places would look like.

She thought about these places determinedly for as long as she could, because it stopped her from looking at the stone jars, and it stopped her from noticing how extremely spooky the wildwood was becoming. But at last she ran out of these thoughts. She could hear the trees whispering to one another outside, and she could hear the tapping against the window again. Tap-tap . . . tap-tap . . .

It was beginning to look as if mother was having trouble finding her. Bryony had not bargained for that, and she knew that mother would come in the end. But she was starting to think it might be better to get out of this hut and into the forest. The trees were a bit frightening, but when Karabas came back he would not be Karabas any longer, he would be the wolf again. Bryony would rather face the trees than the wolf.

The door of the hut was locked, but in stories people escaped through windows. The stories did not tell you how they managed it if the windows were as high as this one, but Bryony thought that if she dragged the largest of the paint pots underneath and stood on it, she could reach. This was what was called making a plan, and it made her feel a whole lot better.

The paint pot was very heavy and so she kicked it a bit at a time until it was under the window. It was a good thing she was wearing her wellingtons today. The paint pot scraped across the floor with the kind of sound that made your teeth hurt and so she was glad when it was in place, and she could clamber up onto it and reach up to the window catch.

It was a bit horrid to find that the window was locked as

well as the door; Bryony was not happy about that. She sat down on the paint pot to think about breaking the window. You could not just smash a pane of glass with your hand, but you might break it by throwing something at it, like the O'Callaghan twins had done in the summer when they had all been playing rounders in the garden and Susie O'Callaghan had batted a ball straight through the kitchen window. There had been a big row and no pocket money for a week.

There were no rounders balls in here but there were the signposts. Bryony took a huge breath, and lifting the Patterdale sign, she threw it as hard as she could at the window.

It hit the window pane smash in the middle, and the glass broke at once, showering little shiny bits all over the floor. The Patterdale sign went sailing out into the forest and landed with a thud on the ground. Bryony waited cautiously to make sure that no more bits of glass were going to fall down on her head, and then got back onto the paint pot. This was the hard part, but she managed to knock the rest of the glass out with the sign that said Troutbeck, and then she climbed out. There was a bit of a drop to the ground outside: she landed on her heels and there was the horrid jerking pain that went up from her heels to her head, but after a minute it went away and the important thing was that she was out of the hut with the evil-smelling stone jars.

It was then that she heard the growl of the motorbike coming through the trees towards her.

Chapter Fifteen

As soon as she had got her breath back from climbing out of the window, Bryony ran a long way into the forest, away from the growling motorbike, and away from Karabas who was really the wolf, coming to eat her up.

Her cloak swirled out behind her as she ran, and the brambles snatched and snagged it, so that it felt as if long snaggy fingers were trying to stop her from escaping. But she was not going to stop, not for anything. She ran very hard indeed, looking back over her shoulder to make sure that Karabas was not chasing her. After a while she got a stitch in her side, and she had to stop and bend down to touch her toes. Then she looked to see where she was. She thought she had been running towards the road, but this was a very big wildwood indeed, and it was a completely strange bit of the forest. This was extremely worrying.

It was pretty spooky everywhere; Bryony had not expected the trees to be quite so frightening. They were old, *old* trees, and if you looked carefully, you could see that they had horrid leery faces at the centre, and you could see that the faces were all different, just as people's faces were all different. It would not take much for those faces to suddenly open in dreadful tree-giants' grins, and for their roots to drag themselves up out of the ground so that they could come lurching towards her. Bryony thought that if she was to walk under those trees now, the branches would suddenly dip down to snatch her hair, and nasty, woodsy-sounding voices would say, '*Hello, little girl*,' which was what all bad things in wildwoods said when they were about to snatch you up.

And then the trees would drag her down into the ground, and she would be trapped in the earth for ever with all the grisly tree roots and the worms and slugs. It would be very bad indeed to be buried with worms and slugs, but it would be worse to be eaten up by Karabas.

She could not hear the growly motorbike any longer which was good but she could hear other sounds, which was not good at all. She stood very still for a moment, listening. You often got bad magic in old forests; it had a way of hiding itself for hundreds of years and then of creeping out to catch you. It would be as well to keep a sharp lookout for anything that seemed like magic.

The sky was black but there was a bright moon shining through the trees, and Bryony could see her way. Moonlight was pale and rather pretty; you could pretend that it was melted silver sprinkled over the trees' branches, with sparkly bits falling onto the ground. Probably the Foljambes had hunted the wolves by moonlight sometimes. Thinking about the Foljambes made her feel a bit braver. She would pretend that Alain and Robin were with her, like she had pretended in the hut, and then if anything bad happened she would try to think what the twins would do, and she would do that, because it would be bound to be the right thing.

After a little while the trees stopped being silvery green and started to be darker, as if something had washed them in thick red light and they had not quite dried. Bryony did not like this.

The redness was coming from a clearing a little way ahead, and it was a rather nasty-looking light. If it was the bad magic Bryony was going to run as fast as her legs would carry her away from it. But it might not be. It might be a house where she could knock on the door and ask the people to help her to get home. She was not supposed to approach strangers – mother was very firm indeed about this. But when you were lost in a wildwood you had to find your way out somehow.

But the red light was not a house; it was a small bonfire, a dull smeary fire with a black cauldron of something bubbling over it. It made you think of the insides of caves and dark secret animal lairs where grisly enchantments were brewed by wicked witches. Bryony remembered and then wished she had not, all the tales of witches who lived at the heart of ancient forests and caught children and put them in cages to fatten them up for the oven. The smell from whatever was in the cauldron was exactly the smell you would get from children being cooked. This was probably being very silly indeed, however. Bryony managed to creep a bit nearer to see what was going on.

Six men were seated around the fire and even though they were sitting down you could see that they were tall and broad. They wore greasy-looking clothes with large flapping jackets or leather jerkins. The jackets had deep pockets and they were all stained and matted. Two of them had knives slung on their belts and one had a hat with a turned-down brim. They wore big clompy wellingtons and the hatted man was smoking a pipe; the smoke drifted into the trees – it smelt of old man and feet that needed washing.

A tiny night-wind ruffled through the clearing, and Bryony stopped smelling unwashed-old-man and smelt the bad cooking smell again. The men did not look very nice. They had small eyes as if they squinted at things, and their faces were lumpy and lopsided. When one of them spoke he had a scrapy kind of voice as if his throat might be filled with gravel.

He jabbed a finger at the cauldron and said, 'They're making us a nice bit of supper, those two.'

'Juicy,' said another. 'We did well to catch two together.'

'You sure nobody saw you do it?' said the pipe-smoking man.

'Naagh. Quick as a flash, that's me.'

'I caught three last week,' said the pipe-smoking man.

'That's good, three.'

The one who had said about doing well to catch two together picked up a long-handled fork and, dipping it into the bubbling mess in the pot, lifted out something caught on the prong. It was pink and meaty-looking.

The lumpy-faced men nodded at one another as if pleased. 'Both done to a turn,' said one. 'We'll have a drop of swipes to wash them down, shall we?'

'That'd go down very nicely,' said the hatted man, and it was then that Bryony realized with horror what the men were.

They were not witches and they were not wolf-creatures like Karabas, but they were something just as bad. They were *trolls*. Bryony knew it absolutely at once. They were forest-trolls – sometimes you got trolls living under bridges but these were forest ones – and they waited for children to come along and they caught them to cook for their supper. These trolls had caught two earlier on – they had said so – and now they were cooking them and quite soon they would eat them and drink something called swipes to wash them down.

Bryony had just realized all this when one of the trolls turned its head and peered into the darkness.

'Someone there?' said the one with the hat.

'I heard something.'

'Imagination.'

'No it was not.' The troll got up – he was as tall as Bryony had known he would be – and lumbered away from the fire, peering into the shadows. In another minute he would see her, and then he would grab her with his huge paws and she would be thrown into the cauldron and cooked—

The troll said, 'Why, it's a little girl in a red cloak. Hello, my dear.'

Bryony gulped and stumbled blindly back into the safe swirling darkness of the trees.

Felicity had known, at approximately the minute that Karabas went through the window of the stable house, that she was going to go after him, but it was not until he turned the curiously macabre motorbike off the main road, and vanished into the dusky wastes of Beck's Forest, that the plan slid into her mind. It did not form gradually or untidily; one minute it was not there and then the next it was – instantly understandable, its edges neatly trimmed and its surfaces buffed smooth.

She leaned forward, peering through the darkness. 'Morag, pull off the road, will you, onto the grass verge? Just here – yes, that's great. Switch off the engine and the lights, and listen, because this is what we do next.'

Brother Dominic, worriedly mindful of the surety he had given to the police inspector, said, 'Wait a minute, we're not going to be doing anything next. There was a promise made that you'd both keep well away from any confrontation—'

'I didn't promise anything,' said Felicity, at once.

'Well, I did,' said Brother Dominic. 'And I think we'd better stay here and wait for the inspector's men.'

'We can't,' said Felicity. 'We daren't let them go crashing into the forest and alert Karabas – it'll kill the whole thing.'

'But – hasn't Karabas vanished into the forest anyway?' began Morag.

'Yes, but we can still follow him, because we can follow the bike tracks. Even if he's wheeled the motorbike into the trees and left it somewhere, it'll have left wheel marks.' Without giving either of them the chance to speak she opened the passenger door and swung her legs out.

'I'm going after him,' she said. 'As a decoy. I'll be just loud enough to make sure he knows I'm there, and you two will be following at a distance. *Discreetly.* Will you do that? I truly don't think there'd be any danger to either of you – it's me he wants.'

'Of course we won't do it,' said Dominic. 'The one thing we mustn't do is separate.'

'Sorry, Brother Dominic, but it's the very thing we must do.'

'Then let me be the decoy.'

'No, if he saw you he'd be instantly suspicious. But he wouldn't be suspicious of me – or not in that way.' Felicity sent an agonized glance towards the sprawling black and green mass of Beck's Forest. With every second she wasted talking Karabas was getting farther out of reach. But it was important to convince Morag and Dominic and to enlist their help, and so, speaking rapidly, she said, 'Karabas thinks he frightened me into calling off the search – it was monumentally unsophisticated of him, but then he hasn't – he is monumentally unsophisticated in a lot of ways. Now, as long as he didn't know the police were watching him leave Bracken – and we don't think he did – when he sees me he'll think I simply pelted out of the house straight after him. He'll probably assume I borrowed a car – he might even have recognized your Mini, Morag – and he'll pounce on me and carry me off to his lair.'

'It's the pouncing part that's worrying me,' began Brother Dominic.

'Lair?' said Morag at the same moment.

'Hideout,' said Felicity, privately cursing herself. 'And I *want* him to pounce on me. It's the only way we'll find out where the hideout is. For heaven's sake, the police often do this kind of thing!'

'Yes, but with trained policewomen,' said Morag. 'OK, I accept that it's a good idea, but why can't we let the police set it up?'

'It would take too long – he's got Bryony in there somewhere!' said Felicity, and heard the note of panic rise in

146

her voice. She beat it down because panic was not going to help Bryony, and taking a deep breath, said, 'A police decoy would involve too many people and cars coming and going, and maybe those radio phones crackling all over the place. But I can be into the forest in about thirty seconds, and if you two follow at a distance, as soon as you see where he's taken me, you can beat it back to the road and bring the inspector's men riding to the rescue.'

Morag said slowly, 'It *sounds* all right.'

'It is all right.' Felicity stood up before either Brother Dominic could start to extricate himself from the depths of the back seat or Morag could get out and come around to the passenger side. Closing the Mini's door sufficiently loudly for it to be heard on the forest's outskirts, she vanished like a shadow into the dark wastes of Beck's Forest.

Brother Dominic, a genuinely devout monk who had embraced celibacy with less of a struggle than many of his brethren, sent up a prayer for guidance as he got out of the car. He added a second, rather more impassioned, prayer that they would reach Bryony Stafford before Karabas did, and beneath it all was guiltily aware that one of the minor advantages of being inside a monastery was that you did not have to cope with the devious machinations of females.

But it was not to be thought of that he should let two females go into danger – it was strongly against his instincts to have let one go, but Felicity had dashed off before he had been able to stop her – and so he said, 'Now Morag, listen to this. You're to stay here in the car and I'll go after Felicity on my own.'

'But—'

'One person following Felicity will attract less attention than two,' said Brother Dominic firmly, 'and you'll be the liaison between us and the inspector.' He paused, and then said, 'Felicity's right about the danger being minimal; once we see where Karabas has taken Bryony we can call the police in and have them swarming all over the forest on the instant.'

Morag said reluctantly, 'Well, all right. The inspector's parked about two hundred yards back down the road, as a matter of fact. I don't know if you can see him – he's switched off his lights, but he's there, all right.'

Brother Dominic immediately felt much braver. He straightened up and said, 'Then you'll help us all better if you

147

drive back and tell them what's happening,' and as Morag nodded and switched on the ignition, he crossed the grass verge and went into the forest.

A thin mist was clinging to the trees, making the entire wood shimmer with black and silver. Brother Dominic could just see Felicity; she was a goodish way ahead of him, but he could just make out the green jacket she had put on earlier. So far so good. He remembered that it was important to keep well back, and he waited to let her get farther ahead before going warily on once more.

It was queer how a man's footsteps echoed in the forest at night, even when it was soft bracken he was walking on, and it was queer, as well, how night noises were different to the ones you heard by day. By day the forest was a good place; they often brought the children here and the forestry people were always pleased to help with wildlife projects. But the forest was not a good place now. There were rustlings, the scurrying of feet. Brother Dominic glanced nervously over his shoulder again, and wished he had been firmer with Felicity Stafford about this mad plan.

It was then that he realized two things. He had lost sight of Felicity. And something was padding through the forest after him.

He knew then that he had been hearing the stealthy footsteps, one layer below consciousness, for several minutes. He looked back over his shoulder. Of course it would only be a fox or a stoat. It would be more frightened of him than he was of it. Not that he was frightened really.

But there was an air of menace and a sense of purpose about the footsteps, as if whatever creature they belonged to had sensed the presence of a human, and was saying: *here* is a tasty morsel! Brother Dominic wished he had not lit on that word morsel.

There was a low snarling sound from behind him, and he swung round at once. The undergrowth parted and the snarl came again, and something launched itself across the forest towards him – something that might once have been a man but that was a man no longer: something that was lean and hungry and that had reaching claws and slavering teeth . . .

There was no time to cry out and there was certainly no time to think. Panic flooded his mind, and then the creature was upon him, and there was a whirling blackness and the feel of teeth and claws tearing into his throat. The forest swam in a sick dizziness, and the darkness became shot with crimson, because crimson was the colour of pain, and it hurt, it *hurt* . . . His neck bones were being crunched by the creature's teeth and his flesh was being torn away, and somebody must help him . . . He clutched helplessly at the words of a prayer, but something deep inside him was collapsing and he felt a warm wetness between his legs and knew that bowels and bladder had given way.

The pain was roaring out of him in a pulsating flood, screaming as it went, only it was a silent scream because the thing had torn out his throat. There was the sudden bruising feel of the hard forest ground beneath him as he was flung down and then his assailant was bending over him, and through the tearing agony he was aware of hot breath on his neck, and then of teeth biting deeply into his throat again . . .

The pain began to dissolve into a cold darkness and as sight and hearing both dimmed and the final darkness swept in, he did not know that he had finally been released.

He certainly did not see the undergrowth shiver as his dark assailant vanished into the forest once more.

Felicity had expected Beck's Forest to be sinister in the way that any forest would be sinister by night, and she had expected it to be filled with scutterings and rustlings. But she had thought she would be concentrating so fiercely on attracting Karabas's attention and reaching Bryony that none of it would bother her.

It did bother her. As soon as the trees closed around her, she was aware of a menacing darkness descending about her, so strongly that for a moment she could almost feel it, like a huge smothering weight. The deeper she went the more she became aware of this menace, and the more she looked at the trees the more they seemed to be subtly changing. To Felicity's fearful eyes their branches began to resemble long poking fingers, and the tree trunks were gnarled and wizened so that if you were extremely fanciful you might see leering sly faces in them. Oh God, had Bryony, with her wild, fey imagination, seen that?

She was starting to feel as if she had been walking for quite a long time and there had been no indication that Karabas was nearby. Felicity hesitated and then walked on, listening and watching, but apart from the scufflings of night-creatures nothing moved and nothing stirred. But she had the impression that as she walked, the past was waking all around her, and that the shades of her fabled ancestors were with her, leading her forward to where Bryony was held prisoner at the heart of the twilight greenwood. Bryony's beloved Richard was here, of course . . . And Thomas who had been present at the signing of Magna Carta . . . The attractive-sounding twins who had ridden with Edward I into battle . . . Felicity could not see them and she could not hear them but she was increasingly aware of them. The disembodied, walking at midnight by wizard oaks and hungering trees . . . ? Only it was not midnight by a long way yet, and by the time midnight was here Bryony would be safely back home and— *There's something watching me from under that tree!*

The knowledge smacked against her consciousness, and she froze instantly, her heart bounding up into her throat. Was this it? She thought she had come quite a long way from the road but it was difficult to be sure. The knowledge that Brother Dominic was nearby, invisible but surely within call, was comforting. She stared at the thick patch of undergrowth and saw it move slightly. Some small innocent creature scuttling to its burrow? Or something else? She stepped nearer, and the bracken parted, and Felicity saw something that looked like the glint of staring eyes watching her . . . *Huge, hungry eyes, because there are some eyes that can eat your soul, my dear . . .*

At first she thought she had imagined it, and she was just trying not to remember that other dangers might walk abroad here, when from within the thicket came a low throaty growl. Ice trickled around in the pit of her stomach, and the sound came again. Felicity stared at the undergrowth but it was impossible to make out more than a thick tangle of leaves and roots and the winter ghost-shapes of tree mallows. She reminded herself that Brother Dominic would be nearby and took a step closer.

The entire pattern of the undergrowth altered and she saw beyond it to the sable and black motorbike, crouching like a feral animal within the bramble. The growl came again, and this time she recognized it for the bike's engine. Then he's there, thought Felicity, torn between panic and welling anticipation. He's there – and has he been circling around me all the time, and has he somehow led me to this spot? He's revving the engine very gently and then letting it die so that it sounds like something snarling.

The bike's single headlight suddenly blinked into dazzling brilliance, like a solitary demonic eye staring out of the trees, and Felicity gasped. And then between one breathspace and the next Karabas was there, springing up out of the bracken, silhouetted in the scything white glare of the headlamp. He was wearing the dark clothes he had worn in the stable house earlier and his head was uncovered. A thin night-mist was forming and the beam of the bike's headlight poured through the darkness, violet and blue smoke swirling outside it, shrouding the ancient trees, so that it was as if he stood in a spotlight at the centre of a stage set.

Moisture clung to his dark hair, so that it resembled an animal's pelt, and as he advanced towards her Felicity saw that his mouth was smeared with something dark and sticky, and that when he raised his hands to reach for her, his fingers dripped with something red and thick . . .

A violent pain lanced her mind at the sight of the blood-drenched hands and the terrible jowls and for the first time she felt her resolve waver. But she stayed where she was, and she even managed to meet the mad eyes, bereft of all humanity, as Karabas reached for her.

He carried her deeper into the trees, striding forward as if he knew his way through the forest very well. At length he stopped in front of a small building, not quite pre-fabricated, but constructed from sections of timber. Felicity, trying to take in as much as possible, thought it would be something to do with the National Park people or perhaps a centre for ramblers or bird-watchers. She said, furiously, 'Is Bryony here? Is this where you brought her?'

'She's here,' said Karabas. He set her down, keeping tight hold of her with his left hand. 'If you run away now be sure I will catch you, Felicity,' he said. 'And remember that wherever you run to, I'll always find you.'

'For someone who comes from a remote branch of humanity you're very well versed in clichés,' retorted Felicity.

But her heart was hammering because in just a minute she would be with Bryony and she would know if Bryony was all right or if this monster had hurt her . . .

As if aware of her churning emotions, Karabas took his time. He produced a key from a pocket, and with his free hand, he unlocked the door, and pushed it open.

The first thing Felicity saw as the door swung inwards was the smashed window with the paint pot standing beneath it, and at the same moment she saw that the hut was empty. Relief rushed in, because Bryony had escaped – she had done what she always did when she wanted to reach something from a shelf. She dragged the paint pot across the floor and smashed the window and climbed out! thought Felicity, and the flood of relief was so overwhelming that for a moment the hut tilted and blurred and she had to put out a hand to the wall to steady herself.

It was several minutes before she became aware of Karabas again. He had bounded into the hut, searching it as if he thought his quarry might be hiding. But there isn't anywhere to hide, thought Felicity. She said, aloud, 'You've lost her, Karabas. She's got away.'

'Yes,' he said, turning back to look at her. 'But you haven't, have you, Felicity? And now I'm going to tie you up and leave you here.

'Then I'm going out into the forest to find Bryony.'

Chapter Sixteen

Bryony had thought she would be able to run away from the trolls, but even though she had run as fast as she could from their bad-smelling fire and the dreadful black pot with the cooked children she must have made a noise, because almost at once she heard them coming after her.

The ground shook with their huge heavy tread, and they called to one another as they came.

'After her!' they cried.

'Don't let her get away, chaps!'

The one with the gravelly voice shouted, 'Keep her in sight at all costs!' and Bryony gave a sob because these were all the things trolls did say. They were catching her up – this might be because they were wearing magic boots that let them run fast like ogres – and it was when they began calling out about not letting her get away that Bryony suddenly remembered one of the stories about the twins. Alain had liked keeping a diary, and once when the twins were fighting battles with the golden king called Edward, he had written: '*The king told us to go not from, but towards the enemy, whether the enemy was the wolves or only men, and that is a very good ploy. To go towards the enemy, the king said, is the action of a fighter.*'

Robin, who was not as serious as Alain, had added, '*Also, it is not what the enemy will be expecting you to do, and that is always a good idea.*'

The trolls would be expecting Bryony to keep running away; they would not expect her to stop and hide, and so she plunged into a small patch of undergrowth and dropped flat to the ground, her heart thudding. She could not see anything through the undergrowth, only the tiny dancing specks that Brother Stephen had told them were fireflies. The moon showed them up clearly; they were zigzagging back and forth everywhere, leaving thin sprinklings of radiance on the darkness.

Following Alain's plan made Bryony feel a bit safer and a lot braver. It even made her think that the trolls might go running and running through the forest, and that they might even run until it was dawn, which would be pretty good because trolls had to hide away from the daylight or they melted away. Everyone knew that.

But the trolls were quite near: they were swishing the undergrowth and calling to one another that the little girl must be found.

Bryony laid her cheek flat against the springy ground, her heart pounding. Please don't let them find me. Don't let me down, twins: I've done what you did.

Above her head, the darting friendly fireflies suddenly shot wildly in several diverging directions, and the ground rippled more strongly under her listening ear. The trolls were coming straight towards her.

There was absolutely nothing to be done but lie still and hope they did not see her. Bryony was managing not to cry, but she was very frightened indeed.

And then the bracken parted and a troll-voice said, 'She's here,' and troll-arms reached down to lift her up, and the entire forest began to spin all round her as if it was a merry-go-round, only it was a sick-making merry-go-round spinning her towards a huge black mouth that was starting to open. As it yawned wider and wider Bryony struggled, and the troll said, 'There now, dearie, no need to bite me,' which was the most alarming thing it had yet said.

The black mouth gulped her up, and from a long way away, Bryony heard the troll say, 'Bless my boots, she's fainted.'

The six men with the unhurried rural voices and large-pocketed jackets agreed that this was a situation where you needed to decide very quickly what was the most important thing. Priorities, that was the word. It did not need too many brains to know that the priority here was to get the little girl safely out of the forest and find out who she belonged to. They picked Bryony up rather gingerly, and then set off in solemn procession. Jack, who was reckoned their leader, in as much as they had a leader, said they should go along to the main road where there was a telephone box and phone the police.

But the curious thing was that although none of them was

what you might call fanciful, as they went along they were all aware of the unpleasant atmosphere in the forest tonight. As if something a bit nasty was watching them from a hiding place – it was. They'd be glad to get out, even though their supper had just been coming nicely to the boil. They were glad, as well, to think there were six of them against anything that might come bounding out of the darkness.

But it was not until they were approaching the little clearing that folks called Beck's Glade that the unpleasant feeling got worse, and it was not until they were actually in the clearing itself that they saw what lay half-on, half-off the path.

They stood for a minute staring at it, because even seen in the dim light, it was plain that something very nasty had happened here. Even Jack, the eldest, who had been in Burma and could tell a few ripe tales after the fifth pint, scratched his head and said he had never seen anything as downright *messy*.

'It's an animal,' he said, at last. 'A large animal that's been killed and partly eaten.'

'Not it. It's too big for an animal.'

'And the wrong shape.'

'Well, what else is it, then?'

'I don't know, but I'll take a look. Stay back, chaps.'

'What about the little girl?' She was still asleep or in a faint, and they were worried about getting her to a doctor.

'It'll only take a minute. And there might be something we could do—'

There was nothing anyone could do, they all knew that, really, but you could not just walk away. And close up, it was unmistakably human – they had known this as well. There was hair and there were eyes. And there were dreadful wounds – great gaping tears in the flesh, and skin and bone shredded to bloodied tatters. The mouth – what was left of it – was stretched impossibly wide in a despairing silent scream of agony, and the hands were flung out as if in final entreaty. Whatever had shredded the skin had finished its work by biting out the throat – actually biting it out! There were lumps of gristly flesh lying on the ground, crimson-stained and veined with white.

They saw all this, and then they recognized with sick horror the familiar brown habit of the Bracken monks.

For a moment none of them knew what to do. There was

the little girl to be got to safety, but now there was this. And truth to tell, they were all feeling a bit scared, with the silly kind of scaredness that made you keep looking over your shoulder in case anything might be hiding in the trees. Jack reminded them that several times during the evening they'd heard stealthy movements within the forest. Supposing it had been the killer? Best if three of them take the little girl to safety a bit sharpish, he said, and the rest could go along to the phone box. Best not to separate too much, but to split up into two parties of threes.

It was Jack who suggested that rather than carry the little girl all through the forest, especially since it was a pesky cold night, three of them could take her along to the Forestry Commission hut. It was not far away, and it would be all locked up, of course. But in this situation they would surely to God be justified in breaking it open. And once in there, the little girl could be wrapped up and kept nice and warm and safe, while they got help.

Somebody was calling to Bryony, and although it was somebody a long, long way off, it was a safe voice.

Bryony considered the voice, because it was one she knew very well, and if she could just climb up out of the black mouth it would be all right to answer it—

And then she opened her eyes and there was no black yawning mouth after all, and she was in her own little bed in the stable house and mother was sitting at the side of the bed and of course it had been mother calling to her.

Mother said at once, 'It's absolutely all right, Bryony, you're here with me and you're completely safe.' Her voice sounded trembly as if she might be trying not to cry. But then she said, 'Have a tiny sip of this,' and there was the chink of a glass and the taste of cool orange juice.

Bryony sipped the orange juice obediently, and discovered that her throat felt dry and crackly. With the idea of getting everything straight, she said, 'I was in the wildwood.'

'I know you were. But as soon as I knew where you were, I came to get you.'

'There was a hut with horrid stone jars only I broke the window—'

'I know all about the hut, darling.' Mother gave her a hug.

156

It felt pretty good to be hugged and to smell the nice scent mother always used.

Bryony said, a bit uncertainly, 'It was actually pretty frightening.'

'I know it was – I know most of what happened and I saw the hut, and you're quite right, it was a dreadful place. You can tell me the rest if you want to, in fact we can spend a whole day talking about it and you can tell me all the bits I don't know. But I have to say,' said mother, her voice going trembly again, 'that you were very brave in the forest. Really very brave. I was extremely proud of you, getting out through the window and running away from Karabas.' Mother's voice trembled a whole lot and her eyes went shiny with tears.

'I wasn't lost.' Bryony thought this should be made clear. 'Not ezzackerly lost.'

'No, of course you weren't. Miss Mackenzie and a nice police inspector came with me to bring you home. And some poachers helped us – did you know about that?'

'Poachers?'

'Yes, they were very worried about you. They found you in the forest, and they brought you back to the hut while they went to get help.' And thank God they did, thought Felicity to herself fervently, and knew she would never forget how the faces of the men had broken into beams of delight when they broke into the hut and found her.

She said, 'The poachers are in the sitting room now. It's awfully crowded but they didn't mind. Miss Mackenzie's making them all cups of tea. They're sitting on the floor, mostly.'

Bryony wondered whether to say about them really being trolls. It might not be very polite if mother thought they were nice and Miss Mackenzie was making tea for them. Poachers might be another word for trolls, of course. And then she remembered about trolls melting in daylight, and said, 'Is it morning yet?' which would be a good test, although it might not be very nice to have melted troll all over the carpet.

But mother said, 'It isn't nearly morning. It's only about midnight. You've never been awake at midnight before.'

'No, I meant – the sky will still be dark for ages, won't it?'

'It won't start getting light until about six o'clock. Why?'

'Just wondered. What's swipes?'

'What?'

157

'Swipes. It's something you drink, isn't it?'

'I think it's a word they use up here for beer,' said mother. 'We'll ask Brother D—' She stopped very suddenly indeed, and bit her lip. But then she said, 'Bryony, listen, you aren't seeing things in double or anything, are you?'

'No, why?'

'Well, you fainted when the poachers picked you up, and—'

'Did I faint? Did I really?' Bryony was so impressed that she forgot about the trolls for a minute.

'Yes, you really did. Dr Barnes came out to take a look at you.'

'Was I all right?'

'Completely fine.'

'What about—' Bryony gulped and said, 'What about Karabas?'

Mother said immediately, 'Oh, he's gone a long time ago.'

'He took me into the wildwood.'

'Yes, I know. I didn't think it was a very good thing to do, that's why I got Miss Mackenzie to drive to the forest to bring you back.'

Bryony's lower lip trembled. She said, 'Actually, it wasn't lavishly nice in that old hut.'

'I know it wasn't, darling, but I promise it will never happen again.'

'He's bad, isn't he, Karabas? I mean really bad.' She looked down at the bedsheet, and said, 'He's the wolf.'

There was a pause, as if mother was trying to decide what to say. Then she said, in what Bryony thought of as a *careful* voice, 'He's not very well. Some people – only a very few people – get sick in their heads and it makes them act a bit strangely. It makes them think they're all kinds of peculiar things.'

'No, he really was the wolf and he was going to—' Bryony paused at this point, because remembering about Karabas being the wolf was truly dreadful. It might be better not to think about it. She said, 'Anyhow, it was pretty frightening.'

'Yes, and that's why I'm so proud of you for being so brave and clever and managing to run away. In fact,' said mother, 'I know that dad would have been proud as well.'

And this time mother's voice wobbled right over into crying, so that it was as well, really, that Miss Mackenzie tapped at the door to ask if Bryony was all right, and to see if mother would like a cup of tea.

'Bryony's fine,' said mother, trying to find a hankie. 'Damn— Don't take any notice of me, darling, I'm only being a bit silly.' She blew her nose, and then said, 'We're both fine, Morag, and we've been talking a bit about what happened, and we're going to talk a bit more tomorrow if Bryony wants to. But we'd both love a cup of tea.'

Bryony said, hopefully, 'I wouldn't mind something to eat as well.' She added, reproachfully, 'On account of I didn't have any tea when I was in the wildwood.

Mother said, 'Oh darling, you can have a ten-course banquet if you want!'

Felicity surveyed the crowded sitting room and thought that happiness – real undiluted happiness, so strong that you could practically see it – was a roomful of the most ill-assorted people imaginable, and Bryony safely in her own bed, eating scrambled eggs and banana ice-cream with industrious pleasure.

Dr Barnes, arriving somewhere around eleven o'clock and making a careful physical examination, had talked sepulchrally about counselling and child psychologists, but Felicity had said firmly that they would think about that if it seemed necessary. To herself, she thought that the best thing for Bryony would be a return to absolute normality, with the entire episode left to quietly dissolve. They would talk about it as much – or as little – as Bryony wanted, and Felicity would try to give the child answers that were honest but easily-understood, and definitely not frightening.

(And Karabas? How will you explain Karabas to her? How will you warn her that he got away, and that he's still out there somewhere . . . ?)

She beat this down, and turned her attention to the extraordinary collection of people packed into the stable house's little sitting room. Morag Mackenzie, that good stalwart soul, was dispensing tea from a huge teapot with as much aplomb as if she was presiding over a school tea party, and Brother Stephen and Brother Andrew were closeted in the window seat in anxious consultation with the police inspector. Dr Barnes was with them, and he and the inspector appeared to be explaining the bewildering processes of coroners' courts and inquests. Oh God, Brother Dominic. My fault, of course, thought Felicity. If I hadn't formed that mad plan of acting as decoy— He tried to dissuade me, as well. I'm going to be pulverized with guilt about that, once the relief at having Bryony back wears off.

The poachers sat happily at the centre of the room. They had taken their wellingtons off at the door, shocked at the thought of trampling all their dirt into Mrs Stafford's nice carpet, and they had carefully hung up their incredible jackets. The eldest had courteously asked permission to light his pipe; Felicity had instantly said, Yes, of course, and had tried not to think uncharitable thoughts about the efficacy of incense burners and room perfumers because the whole house would certainly smell of strong pipe tobacco and sketchily washed men for days.

The poachers had told their story several times now: Felicity thought they would probably tell it several times more, especially in the local pubs; it was likely that none of them would have to buy a drink for the next month, in fact. They had been having a bit of supper, the poachers had said – never mind what, they added with a sideways glance to the inspector. There was no law against making a fire in a picnic area of Beck's Forest, and no law against cooking *your own rabbits* over that fire.

'No law in the world,' the inspector had said, cheerfully, and Felicity had liked him all over again.

So there they had been, the poachers said firmly, stirring their rabbit stew and looking forward to a drop of beer with it as well, and truth to tell they'd been a bit uneasy for a while, they said; there'd been what you might call furtive movements in the forest.

'Probably my men searching,' said the inspector. 'I'll send them all on a course on silent surveillance next month.'

Ah, said the poachers. Anyhow, they'd looked up and that was when they'd suddenly seen the little girl watching them from the bushes. Well, they had been gob-smacked as you might say, for you did not often see little ones wandering about at that time of a night, not by their little selves, you didn't.

Felicity said warmly, 'I'm so very grateful you did see her,' and the poachers looked pleased. They told how they had got up at once – quite forgetting the rabbit stew – and given chase.

They hoped they had not frightened the little girl, they said, what with having to crash along, shouting, but they had been feared of losing her in the forest.

'I'm sure you didn't frighten her,' said Felicity, tucking this away in her mind to discuss with Bryony tomorrow.

They'd run after her as fast as ever they could, they said, right through Beck's Forest, and it had been just as they'd reached her, that they'd come across the other thing.

'Brother Dominic's body,' said Felicity in a whisper.

As the poachers went off down the drive of Bracken Hall, they thought how funny it was to think that they'd helped the police tonight instead of trying to avoid them. If the inspector had guessed they'd been after rabbits and hares in Beck's Forest tonight, he had turned a blind eye.

They had not told Mrs Stafford or that Miss Mackenzie the details about the body, of course: you hadn't to upset ladies with descriptions of suchlike. The really dreadful part about all this was that the mad thing who had taken Bryony Stafford and savaged poor good Brother Dominic – yes, and shut Mrs Stafford up in the forestry hut – had escaped, and was still at large somewhere. The poachers shivered a bit at the thought, even though it was practically morning, with a cold grey light creeping across the eastern sky.

It was as they were passing the Black Boar that it struck them that really, they'd been heroes tonight. It was not many folk as could boast of rescuing not one, but two ladies all in the same night. They began to plan how they would drop in at the Black Boar that very night, and how they would tell the tale. A good tale had to be properly told.

Chapter Seventeen

Tybalt was in the seventh heaven of bliss. He had been invited to stay with Dr Adair at his apartment in London, and Dr Adair had already said that their search for the Foljambe descendants would almost definitely mean spending some time in the British Museum Reading Room and the Public Record Office in Richmond. Tybalt spent the first few hours of the journey from Cruithin in a happy daze, murmuring the words, *British Museum, Reading Room*, as if they were magical incantations.

Dr Adair had warned that they might search for a month and find nothing at all. Or, he said, they might turn up exactly what they wanted in the first day; there was no knowing, and Tybalt would have to be prepared for anything.

'But that's part of the thrill,' said Dr Adair, as they drove onto the ferry bound for the mainland, and Tybalt glanced covertly at him and saw the glow that lit his eyes. *That's* how he does it with the women, he thought. That's how he gets them! It's that unexpected glint of something under the surface that's wholly different from the façade, and whatever it is, it certainly isn't a studious anthropologist.

They had closed up the farmhouse on Cruithin Island, and they were driving to London more or less in convoy, with Tybalt and Toby sharing the driving with Dr Adair, and Nina and Priscilla following with Dietfreid in Priscilla's car. Dr Adair was just about the worst driver Tybalt had ever come across, and he was at first terrified and then resigned. At least when it was his turn to drive he could not be any worse.

As they travelled down what Dr Adair said was called England's spine, and which turned out to be a straggly little range of hills called the Pennines, they discussed how to set about finding the Foljambes. First off, said Dr Adair, they would try to track down references to forester appointments and enfeoffments. He used the term 'Pipe Rolls' several times, and Tybalt waited hopefully for clarification of this weird expression. He was grateful when Toby said, 'What on earth are Pipe Rolls, Piers?'

'The Great Rolls of the Exchequer of England,' said Dr Adair, as carelessly as if this did not conjure up an entire medieval tapestry of wonders. Tybalt, trying not to wince as they overtook a lorry in the teeth of oncoming traffic, willed him to go on and after a moment he said, 'The records go back to Henry I. He was the first king to order public records to be kept. That was around—'

'The twelfth century,' said Tybalt, awed. 'Oh wow.'

'The Rolls contain accounts of revenue collected by sheriffs,' said Dr Adair, spinning the car along at a forbidden eighty-five miles an hour. 'If we're really lucky we might find entries for the Foljambes. If we're even luckier, we might then manage to track down the present generation.'

'Oh God, yes, of course, we're assuming that Karabas has gone hotfoot after the descendants, aren't we?'

'That was the vow his people took in the catacombs,' said Piers.

'But listen, aren't we making a lot of assumptions?' demanded Toby. 'Supposing there aren't any descendants of Richard Foljambe? I mean any still living.'

'If Karabas's people are still taking the vow to hunt them down and kill them they think they're still alive,' volunteered Tybalt. 'It sounds almost as if it's a regular thing for them – keeping watch on the Foljambes over the centuries, and sending scouts out to find them.'

'I wonder if that's how they got the *Lia Fail* from that servant,' said Toby. 'I could still bear knowing how he came by it, you know. And I could bear knowing if the tribe planned the theft as well. I mean – how calculated do we think that was?'

'Oh, I should think it was very calculated,' said Piers, vaguely, and saw Tybalt turn to look at him. He said, 'If they believed it to be a resurrection stone they probably plotted to get it for generations.'

'Yes, because— Piers, if you're going to get onto the motorway, you do know you're in the wrong lane—'

A hair-raising interval ensued. Tybalt hoped devoutly that

British motorways were safer than British ordinary roads.

Toby said, 'I rather jib at this part about the tribe keeping a watch on the Foljambes. Karabas's people aren't telepathic, for God's sake.'

'What makes you think that?' said Dr Adair, very softly, and Tybalt saw him glance at Toby in the driving mirror.

Toby, who had been looking out of the window and had missed the odd expression in Dr Adair's eyes, said, 'Well, I don't imagine they sit up there on Cruithin Island with a crystal ball and tune in to what's happening in different parts of the British Isles! At least, I hope they don't because it's a nightmarish idea!' He broke off and Tybalt saw that Dr Adair was staring very intently at the road.

'You won't have to actually go back all the way to Henry I to find the family, will you?' demanded Toby. And then, 'Or will you?'

'If you read your notes instead of scattering them all over my car,' said Piers, 'you'll see that Richard Foljambe's servant—'

'Edmund.'

'Yes, Edmund, thank you, Tybalt – you'll see that Edmund apparently brought the *Lia Fail* to England "nearly ten centuries ago".'

'Which means that Richard lived in – well, say, eleven hundred and something,' said Tybalt.

'Yes. And Henry of Normandy who was Henry I of England, and Henry of Anjou who was Henry II, pretty well split the twelfth century between them when it came to ruling England,' said Piers. 'Which means that at least we've got a date to start from.'

'What kind of references will we be looking for?' asked Tybalt.

'Payments out. Extra fees for services to the Crown. And payments in – rents, maybe. Probably taxes – there were still some Norman statutes in place in the early eleven hundreds – in fact, I *think* that Danegeld was even still in force.'

'Oh wow,' breathed Tybalt, adding *Danegeld* to his growing list of magical words, while a sepulchral voice from the back was heard to say something about income tax and a rose by any other name. Tybalt grinned, and then said, anxiously, 'But would the Foljambes be – um – wealthy enough for all that? I was kind of visualizing them as woodcutters living in a hut in the forest.'

'What a romantic child you are,' said Toby.

'I think they'd have had to be people of some substance,' said Piers. 'Remember that Richard apparently had servants – Edmund was a servant.'

'Oh, right.'

'Forest's a bit of a misleading term in this context, of course,' said Piers, frowning as he negotiated some kind of cross-over between motorways. 'In the days of the Normans and the Angevins it meant a royal demesne set apart for the preservation of the royal beasts of the chase, and – did you say something Tybalt?'

'No,' breathed Tybalt, who was putting the words *Norman* and *Angevin* into his litany.

'It was really a ploy to give the court facilities for hunting,' said Piers, 'and it was only called forest because forest law applied to it. In the twelfth century it might only have meant a hunting area. Are you taking notes, Toby?'

'Is the Pope Catholic? But,' said Toby, 'I don't want to bring up the subject of needles and haystacks again, but in eleven hundred and whatever surely most of England was covered by forests and woods, wild or otherwise. Piers, do you usually drive so recklessly?'

'Only when I have difficult passengers in the back. And worse men than you have survived my driving.'

'Speaking of surviving, isn't it time we thought about stopping for something to eat?'

'There's a diner about five miles ahead,' said Tybalt, who was on map-reading duty.

'He means a service station,' said Toby, grinning. 'Extortionate petrol prices and over-priced drinks and plastic salads. They're all part of our quaint English way of life, Tybalt.'

Tybalt hoped that Toby would stay with the project. It was not always easy to know when he was joking and when he was serious – that was laid-back British humour – but he was good company, that Toby.

This is where the past is stored, thought Tybalt, as he and Dr Adair were conducted to a long room with leather-topped tables and an air of being soaked in scholarly serenity. A great deal of it's here – and what isn't here is in other places exactly like this – as if, when each century ends, it gets folded away into a labelled carton, and the carton gets catalogued and filed on a shelf.

This is what happens to England's history, thought Tybalt; it preserves itself, not because anyone folds it in camphor or lavender, or scatters magic charms in and out of the creases, but because of its actual substance; because so much of it is set down in crabbed writing on curling brown parchment. And when the attendant murmured discreetly about computer terminals in a separate room, Tybalt understood that the preservation process had even managed to adapt and to metamorphose to suit the age of technology.

As he took a seat at one of the tables, Tybalt thought that if you really could find a way to unseal the past – if you could find the magical password to bring it tumbling out – it would not be scented with lavender or crumbling rose petals or magic talismans; it would be scented with bloody wars and black revolutions, and with intrigues and plots and counter-plots. Because this is a country that's steeped in piracy and heroism and legend, thought Tybalt. It's sprinkled with regicide and riots, and it's threaded with poets and peasants and kings, and, oh God, I'm actually going to turn up a tiny fragment of it.

Dr Adair moved with authority among the bewilderingly complex catalogue sections, collecting what looked like several armfuls of record books and privately printed manuscripts and then filling out request dockets for a couple of dozen more. Within the hour these were delivered to the table by a soft-footed attendant. They were presented at the table with as much reverence as if they were Holy Writ. Hell, they practically were Holy Writ. Tybalt was suddenly glad that he had not brought along the laptop computer which had been his father's leaving present to him. It would have been crass and clumsy. He carefully opened a plain ruled notebook, and set a dime-store Biro next to it.

The discovery that a great many of the earlier documents were virtually indecipherable came as a rude shock. Tybalt looked across at Dr Adair in panic.

Dr Adair, sorting their booty, said tranquilly, 'Some of these are Latin, Tybalt. I'll take those and you take the later stuff.'

Tybalt took a deep breath and reached for a wodge of stuff

that did not look as if it was in any kind of Latin. It still looked as incomprehensible as Holy Writ in its original form, but by dint of concentrating and trying to clamber inside the mind of the people who had written these faded pages, he eventually began to make out some of the wording.

Dr Adair said, softly, 'The more you read it, the easier it will get, Tybalt. It's a matter of tuning in,' and Tybalt remembered all over again Dr Adair's own uncanny trick of tuning in to a thought.

From there, he plunged fathoms down into the past – not in a grand sweeping tumble which was what he would have liked, but gradually and gently, like sinking into a huge feather bed. He thought he would not give a damn if they had to spend an entire month here, as Dr Adair had half-warned. Hell, from the mountain of documents that were piling up on the table, it looked as if a lifetime might be nearer the mark.

But in the event, although it was not quite the month that Dr Adair had prophesied, it was certainly over two weeks before Tybalt came across the unremarkable booklet on the history of some place Tybalt had never heard of. It had been brought to the table along with a pile of accounts for somewhere in the County of Derbyshire – Tybalt had been painstakingly working through them for the last two days without the least hint of a Foljambe name anywhere.

The booklet was the kind of thing that libraries sometimes had on display or for sale, so that people could read about local history; Tybalt had often seen them back home. The addenda and corrigenda were awesome, and the footnotes took up more space than the pages of text. The date of its publication was 1920, and it announced itself as being *An account of the war of 1296, when his Majesty King Edward I – 'Hammer of the Scots' – captured the great Stone of Destiny.*

It was as dry as dust and about as romantic as dyspepsia. But he soldiered on through the turgid prose, his mind managing to absorb the story of how Edward had seized the ancient, legendary Stone of Destiny from Scone Abbey. He had then beat it back to England, bearing the Stone with him, which Tybalt thought was probably one of Edward's wiser decisions, since you did not liberate a practically-sacred artefact from a bunch of warlike Picts without stirring up a whole heap of resentment.

Tybalt read the closing pages, in which the unknown author had descended from the merely insipid to the downright boring, with a list of the names entered on the tax and homage list of a papal legate named Ragimunde.

A third of the way down were the names Alain and Robin Foljambe. Tybalt stared at the page, hardly daring to blink in case the names might suddenly vanish. He revised his previous opinion of the unknown author, and pulling himself together read with delight how Alain and Robin Foljambe – described as having led His Majesty's archery division in a battle at Berwick – had apparently made homage to the king on the battlefield, and with a dozen or so others had then formed part of the select guard of honour chosen to bring the Stone of Destiny to Westminster.

This was all so good that Tybalt had to make a conscious effort not to let out a war whoop of joy. He turned the page and read diligently through the remainder of the text which told him, in stultifying minutiae, the exact number of caparisoned horses Edward had taken as outriders and the arrangements made for the dead and injured after the Berwick battle.

But at the very end, the booklet's compiler had included a brief report of a curious event that had occurred when the king's party and the guard of honour had rested for a night in Derbyshire. According to local legend it was here that the Stone had, in some never-explained way, been damaged during the night watches. King Edward's men had stowed it in somebody's buttery or cellar for safety during the night, but the next morning, they discovered with horror that the great Stone of Destiny, the symbol of their recent triumphs, had been defaced.

The prosaic author gave it as his opinion that this story was nothing more than a snippet of romanticised legend. However, he said, sombrely, the evidence did seem to indicate that something unexpected had happened in the wilds of twelfth century Derbyshire:

For if you travel to Westminster and view St Edward's Chair, to this very day you may see for yourself the mark on the Coronation Stone. It is as if a small fragment – scarcely larger than a man's thumbnail – has been chipped away.

Chapter Eighteen

'So the Foljambes got it back after all,' said Nina, leaning her chin on her cupped hands, as Tybalt, scarlet-cheeked with achievement, finished recounting his discovery.

'They got its equivalent back,' corrected Priscilla.

'And,' put in Toby, 'you all realize, do you, that if you do travel to Westminster and view St Edward's Chair, you won't even see the Stone, never mind the scratch, because we gave it back to the Scots a couple of years ago.'

The team was seated in Piers's study, pooling the results of their various lines of exploration. It was an untidy, friendly room, strewn with books which had spilled out of the shelves and lay on the floor, and furnished with comfortably worn chairs. Piers and the two girls were drinking wine; Tybalt and Toby were drinking lager, and Dietfreid was ensconced in a large armchair with a large tankard of German beer.

'Imagine finding all that,' said Nina to Tybalt who had put down his notes.

'Me, I support the return of the Stone of Scone to its people,' declared Dietfreid. 'I am a believer in restoring a country's treasures to it. And no one must now make impolite remarks about Nazi looting in World War II,' he added with ponderous wit. 'I am not a Nazi. I am a good German citizen and a Christian person and I was not born until 1962 anyway.' He beamed gigantically upon the assembly in general and Nina in particular, and Tybalt felt embarrassed at the clumsy attempt at a joke.

Dr Adair, who had probably never been clumsy in his life, said, 'It's the first bit of outside proof we've got that the family really existed.'

'Or that a family of the name existed,' muttered Toby. 'Let's not get carried away, chaps.'

'Toby's right,' said Piers. 'More wine, anyone? Oh – there's coffee as well, wait a bit, I'll switch on the percolator.'

He went out to the kitchen and when he came back, Nina and Priscilla were arranging their own notes on the table.

'Now,' said Priscilla, adopting a businesslike air, 'Nina and I went out to Richmond, to the Public Records Office, and we found Foljambes listed there as well.'

'In fact,' said Nina, who was not letting Priscilla grab all the glory, 'we tracked down a reference in the Pipe Rolls of— Sorry, Toby, did you say something?'

'I groaned. It's likely that when I die, you'll find "Pipe Rolls" engraved on my heart.'

'The only thing engraved on your heart will be the address of the nearest branch of Threshers.'

'Nina should finish her story,' decreed Dietfreid, glaring at Toby.

'In the Pipe Rolls—' began Nina, and then said, 'Oh – does everybody know what Pipe Rolls are, because—'

'We all know,' said Piers, grinning. 'Go on, Nina.'

'In the Pipe Rolls there are actually three mentions of Foljambes.' Nina pretended to consult her notes, just as if the information was not indelibly printed on her brain. 'One entry was for Thomas Foljambe who was knighted in 1214 – he got a grant of £2.2s a year for that – but two other entries were for payments to the family for a certain service.' She paused and looked round the table, her eyes shining. 'Guess what the service was?'

'Wolf-hunting!' said several voices, with Dietfreid's rumble a syllable behind everybody else.

'Yes. *Yes*. And it was jolly eerie to see it there as well. But in 1160 and 1161 a sum of 25/- was paid as an extra fee—'

'With which they doubtless went on a riotous night of merry-making—'

'The third entry,' said Priscilla, repressively, 'was another payment, this time for two Foljambe men – it didn't give first names – but they were sent to Normandy to help the French king rid his dominions of wolves. That was in – wait, it's in my notes—'

Piers leaned forward, his eyes glowing. 'Did you manage to find a location for any of the wolfhunters?'

'Yes,' said Nina, breathlessly. 'Yes, we did.' She paused, and looked round the table. She was remarkably pretty when she

170

was excited like this. Piers was not surprised that Dietfreid was enamoured.

With the air of laying the victor's spoils at the feet of the emperor, Nina said, 'It was in Derbyshire.'

'Derbyshire?' said Toby. 'Derbyshire again?'

'But that's where—' Tybalt stopped, and looked across at Piers. 'That's where Alain and Robin and the king's men stopped with the Stone of Destiny in 1297 – when somebody chipped a bit of it off.'

'So it is,' said Piers. 'And that means—'

It was at this point that Priscilla said, 'I don't want to be boringly domestic or anything, but isn't something burning in the kitchen?'

It was the coffee percolator. It had burnt out because Piers had been so interested in the discussion that he had forgotten to put water in. He consigned the percolator crossly to the dustbin and opened a jar of instant coffee. He had trawled the supermarket earlier in the day, and there was a platter of cheese and paté, and French bread. Nina carried the tray into the study and Dietfreid instantly plunged across the room to help her, upsetting a side table bearing Toby's lager glass en route. When Toby had been mopped up and the table set to rights, and the food had been distributed, the team sat back and eyed their leader hopefully.

Piers said, lightly, 'So. The common denominator. All roads lead back to Derbyshire. I wonder if that's where the Wolf Clan had another settlement at some point.'

'You don't sound very surprised about it being Derbyshire,' observed Toby, returning from the kitchen where he had been liberating the rest of the lager from the fridge.

'Don't I?' said Piers, absently. 'More wine, anyone? Dietfreid, something else to eat?'

Dietfreid helped himself to a formidable wedge of paté, buttered a large chunk of bread, and said, 'You think that it is to this place – Derbyshire – that Karabas will find himself? To search out the descendants?'

'Yes, Dietfreid, that is what we think. In fact, he's probably found himself there already,' said Toby. 'Particularly when you consider he's been at large for weeks.'

Everyone fell silent at this, with the exception of Dietfreid

171

who was explaining to Nina that two separate problems had now revealed themselves. 'There is the problem of finding Karabas who may well commit some harms,' he said. 'But also there is the original aim, which is for us to learn about his people.'

'Dietfreid's summed it up accurately, of course,' said Piers, taking back the reins effortlessly, and Tybalt gazed at him and wondered whether he had acquired this easy air of authority which never seemed to put anybody's back up, or whether, like the sexual glamour over females, it was something you had to be born with.

Piers was not thinking about sexual glamour or about being authoritative. He was pleased to see the team again, and delighted at the results of their delvings. The discovery that they were being drawn so inexorably back to Derbyshire had shaken him, but he thought no one had realized this.

He said, 'Toby, how likely is it that you can stay with the wolf-hunt for a bit longer?'

'Accompanying you into darkest Derbyshire? I'd like to if I can.'

'I'd like you to as well,' said Piers. 'For one thing, you've got the edge on the rest of us when it comes to ferreting out stories and extracting information. And for another, you'd have the back-up of the BBC if necessary, as well.'

'And I was thinking it was for my scintillating wit and mesmerizing charm. I'll have to report to my masters to find out,' said Toby, thoughtfully. 'But what'll probably happen is that I'll be told to monitor your investigations for a while longer – they're keen on that kind of thing in my department, in fact most of us usually work with at least half a dozen strands at a time. That's partly because the heads of department think we've got nothing else to do, but partly so that leads that peter out can be dropped without too much grief. We're at the mercy of the ratings, dear boy. Were you thinking about funding?'

'Yes.'

'Well, as things stand, making the documentary now might prick the balloon that lays the golden eggs,' said Toby. 'But if you can trace Karabas and the Foljambe descendants it would make a much better programme than the original one, in fact it would be a cracker, and in that case I should be able to coast with it for a month or two.' He added, 'And the end should justify the means, which means the expenses can be justified as well – especially if there are any Foljambe descendants still living and if they'd agree to be interviewed.'

'I remember seeing an interview with somebody who claimed to be the last surviving descendant of Dracula,' said Nina. 'I mean the real one – Vlad the Impaler.'

'How quaint,' drawled Priscilla.

'No, but it made for fascinating viewing. There were family trees and things, proving the descent.'

'Oh yes?'

'Are we all going to Derbyshire?' said Tybalt, hopefully.

'I don't see why not. It'll probably be ages before we can return to the island, and it would mean we'd still be pursuing the original project. We'll get somewhere to stay as a base in Derbyshire—'

Piers stopped and Dietfreid said, 'That is a problem, perhaps?'

'No, it isn't a problem at all.' Damn, thought Piers, I don't want this to happen. I don't want to go back. Aloud, he said, 'I do know of a house we can have for a month or two.' And then, before anyone could ask about this, he said, 'And so, Nina, you might start looking up archivists' offices and record offices to give us a starting point – it's a large county, Derbyshire. It includes the whole of the Peak District – you'll like that, Tybalt,' he added. 'There're dozens of little villages all over the place, very English, very unspoilt.'

'Great.'

'Do you know the area then?' asked Priscilla.

'I used to,' said Piers vaguely. 'It's pretty lonely in parts.'

'Should we alert the police? About Karabas?' asked Nina.

'We could probably say we think a potentially dangerous character might be heading their way,' said Piers. 'But I don't think we can expect them to swallow our Wolf Clan story. Not until we've got things under way on Cruithin Island, and there's a lot more evidence.'

'Piers, you said something about a house,' began Toby.

Piers said at once, 'Yes, there's a house on the edge of a village called Kings Thane. It's near a National Park forest – it would be a good central base for us.'

'Who owns it?'

'I do,' said Piers, carelessly.

He had deliberately been off-hand about the house because he had no idea yet whether he would be able to enter it, or whether the memories would still be lying in wait.

And he had deliberately used the word 'wolf' during the discussion, because he had become increasingly aware that the whole of the team were still flinching from it. It was almost certainly due to a lingering atavism, of course, but it was extraordinary to witness such evidence of race-memory.

Race-memory. How much was genuine atavism, and how much was residue from childhood memories? And how reliable was it? How reliable were his own memories of his curious childhood, and of that dark secret-ridden house in Kings Thane?

The aunts had never once referred to the house, any more than they had used the word wolf. It had not been until the night before Piers's fourteenth birthday, midsummer's eve, that he had finally discovered the truth about his family.

He had not been thinking about wolves, and he had not really been thinking about his father either. He had been lying in bed, facing the door more from habit than anything else, thinking with pleasure about his birthday tomorrow. There had been rumours of a new bike, and the aunts, in an unprecedented break with tradition, had said he could invite some school friends to supper. They would play records and have fruit cup or cider to drink. By most people's standards this was quite tame, but to anyone brought up by Aunt Vera and Aunt Monica it was practically a Bacchanalian revel.

Piers had issued careful invitations to the supper, which had all been accepted with enthusiasm. Several girls were coming: most of them had wanted to know if Piers's father would be there, because they had all seen him at the last speech day when Piers had won the essay-writing prize and he was gorgeous, a knock-out, and imagine having a father like that. At least two had looked speculatively at Piers himself and remarked that they could see a likeness. Piers thought that most of the time his father was almost ordinary, but he was not as completely ordinary as other people's fathers. He knew that his father looked raffish and faintly exotic next to everyone else's parents.

The aunts had been a-twitter about the modest party for days; yesterday Piers had heard them talking about his mother – Poor Dear Helen, who would so have enjoyed to see her only son growing up like this – and then about That Man who had arrogantly walked into their lives all those years ago and brought grief and ruination. However much the aunts disliked his father, they always seized on the chance to talk about him.

It was about ten o'clock, and Piers had been reading for a while and had just switched off the light, although it was still so bright outside that he had barely needed it. He was just drifting in the pleasant half-awake, half-asleep stage, when a sound outside brought him sitting bolt upright in bed. There was the soft pad of footsteps crossing the landing and then going quietly down the stair. His father, going out on one of his strange nocturnal prowls.

Piers had long since grown out of fairy stories. He knew perfectly well that the creatures of those stories did not exist and that they had probably never existed. But he did know that there were evil and warped men and women in the world. He knew about sex, half from whispered giggles in the playground, half from biology classes at school, and from there he knew about rape, and even, in a vague way, about incest. He certainly knew about twisted people who tortured young boys and girls for kicks and then buried their bodies on lonely moors. And most of his mind knew that his father was not capable of any of these things.

But there was another part of his mind that did not wholly trust his father and it was this part that reared up tonight, and said wasn't it better to know the truth, once and for all? He pushed the bedclothes back and scrambled into his clothes.

Within minutes he was tiptoeing through the night after him.

Piers had often thought since that it had been on that night that he entered the darkling dreamworld that existed, unsuspected, alongside the ordinary everyday world, and in the years that were to follow, he had occasionally wondered whether he had ever really come out of it.

The seldom-heard, seldom-acknowledged underside of his nature came uppermost on that night: the side that knew quite well that there was a thin invisible wall in the world – a curtain separating that other world and shutting it safely out. But at certain times – when the moon was low in the sky and there was a scent of woodbine and honeysuckle, or on heady summer nights when you leaned out of your bedroom window and heard a thrumming anticipation in the air as if someone was drawing a finger round and round an immense glass bowl – on those nights the curtain was so thin that it was practically transparent, and anything might slip through.

I'm sounding like Peter Pan, thought Piers, crossly. But what I'll do, I'll just follow my father very warily and see where he goes. And then once I do know, I'll beat it back to bed and burrow down under the sheets and he'll never know I followed him.

His father had reached the old brick wall that bounded the gardens, and had gone to the small door that was hidden from the house by a group of old apple and pear trees – too few to accurately be described as an orchard although both the aunts did so. He leaned down to unlock it and Piers hesitated, looking about him. Dare he follow? Would he be heard or seen? Almost definitely his father would have locked the door from the other side, because this was a door that always was kept locked on account of straying vandals and tramps coming from the scrublands beyond. If it's locked, then I won't have to make a decision, Piers thought, half relieved, half disappointed.

The door was not locked. It swung smoothly open, as if it was often used, and as if it was kept oiled so that no one would hear it. Piers took a deep breath and, glancing over his shoulder again, stepped through.

Tonight was one of those nights when the moon was low and when nothing seemed to move in the vast old greenwood. Piers had the uncomfortable feeling that he was finally entering the half-world that lay beyond the curtain. He thought it might be a dangerous place, but he knew there was no turning back.

He could see his father very clearly in the moonlight: he could see his father's thin intelligent face, darkly good-looking, with high cheekbones and narrow eyes. He had dark, slightly curly hair which grew over his collar at the back, and sideburns.

Someone had once said to Aunt Vera that Poor Helen's husband was tremendously sexy, and Aunt Vera had looked icily down her nose and said disdainfully that it was not something she had ever thought about.

The deeper they went into the forest the less safe Piers felt. His father was padding ahead of him, going unhesitatingly through the trees. Wherever he was going, he knew the way very well indeed.

After a time the trees thinned, and gave way to a small clearing with fallen logs and well-trodden bracken. Piers dodged back at once, but his father went without pausing across the clearing. Piers waited, scanning the trees, trying to see where his father might have gone. There was a patch of denser blackness over to his left, but it did not seem to offer any clues—

It was not a patch of blackness at all. It was a house. It was a grim, grey house, with barred and shuttered windows. A cold hand closed over his heart, because who would build a house at the centre of a forest? And who would live in it?

Piers was not, he most emphatically was *not* going to give way to the whisperings of his mind and go up to the house. To go up to a sinister old house at the heart of an equally sinister old forest in the middle of the night was the absolute last thing you did.

But supposing that was where his father was? And supposing it would solve, once and for all, the mystery that surrounded his father?

I won't do it, said Piers, firmly.

Chapter Nineteen

But of course, he did. He knew perfectly well that he was out of Peter Pan territory now, and into Hansel and Gretel land, but he went, as if pulled by a thread, towards the forest house.

As he got nearer, he saw that it was a four-square redbrick house, not built of grey stone like so many houses in Derbyshire, and that it was much larger than it had looked from the trees. A brick wall surrounded it: not so high that it completely screened the house, but high enough to create privacy. It would be awkward to climb over it although it would not be impossible. In front of the front door was a strong wrought-iron gate with a thick black padlock.

The thread that had tugged him this far continued to tug him, and he saw his hand reach out to push wide the iron gate. A small hopeful voice within his mind said that of course the gate would be locked, but it was not. Piers drew in a shaky breath and went through. Everywhere looked well cared for, but the house had a lowering, frowning look and the downstairs windows all looked as if they were shuttered or as if thick heavy curtains had been drawn across them as soon as darkness fell.

He had no idea what to do next. There was a polished brass knocker on the door, but it would be the height of madness to even think about lifting it and letting it fall on the thick oak door. He was just thinking he might creep around the sides of the house and see if a chink of light showed anywhere, when he heard footsteps on the other side of the door.

It was a very bad moment indeed. The footsteps were slow but they were firm. Piers stayed where he was, suspended between panic-stricken flight and mounting curiosity.

The footsteps came right up to the door, and there was a fumbling sound as if the owner of the footsteps was having difficulty with a lock. Piers did not quite hear a voice say, Oh drat this lock, but he sensed it. There was the screech of a bolt being drawn.

Despite his resolve, he was still so deep inside the half-world of dark myth that he would not have been in the least surprised to hear a scratchy voice say, 'Come inside, you are expected.' What he actually saw was an apple-cheeked female, plump and middle-aged with salt-and-pepper hair, wearing an unremarkable tweed skirt and V-necked sweater. What he heard was a friendly voice telling him to come inside, and then calling over her shoulder that the boy was here, just as she had always predicted.

For a dreadful minute the scene teetered on the brink of outright nightmare again, and then a door opened at the far end of the hall, and Piers saw his father standing watching him.

The unknown woman led the way into a small room at the far end of the hall.

'Warmer in here,' she said.

Thick dark curtains were drawn against the night, and a fire burned in a small hearth. The room was comfortable, but the furniture was old-fashioned and oddly-matched; it felt impersonal, in the way that hotel rooms or weekend cottages felt impersonal. There were two deep wing chairs, one on each side of the fire; his father gestured Piers to one and then took the other himself. Piers saw that a decanter of golden liquid stood at his father's hand.

After the woman had gone out neither of them spoke for quite a long time. This was one of the strange things about Piers's father: he could convey a feeling or a mood without needing to say anything and sometimes he could sense the feeling or mood of another person as well. Once or twice Piers had experimented with this himself, and several times he had got quite near to understanding what other people were thinking or feeling. But he had absolutely no idea what his father was thinking now.

After a while, his father said, 'I'm glad you've come, Piers. I thought you would one day. Emma always insisted you would.' He leaned his head back against the chair, and Piers saw lines of tiredness around his father's eyes.

He said, 'Is Emma the woman who let me in?' This was just about the last thing he wanted to know, but he had to find out how his voice sounded. It was a bit shrill but it was not bad.

'Yes, that was Emma.' There was the chink of glass as his father poured a measure of brandy. He looked at Piers over the rim as he drank it, and Piers suddenly saw the darkness that he had always believed surrounded his father shift and subtly alter.

'Piers, you must listen very carefully to what I'm going to tell you,' said his father, and Piers caught his breath, because there it was at last, the *different* look. His heart began to race. I'm about to hear something extraordinary, he thought. I'm about to hear a huge secret. Do I want to hear it?

'I'm going to tell you about your mother,' said his father, carefully. 'I'm fed up with those two acidulated virgins casting me as the villain of the piece. I've fallen out with them a hundred times over the years about whether or not you should know the truth. But you're fourteen tomorrow and you're old enough to be told.'

Piers said, half-defiantly, 'My mother's dead. I know all about her.'

'Oh no you don't,' said his father. 'Oh no you don't, Piers.' He paused, but his next words were the absolute last ones Piers had been expecting. He said, 'Your mother's alive, Piers.'

The strange room with its clumsy furniture spun around him, whirling into a dizzy humming-top in which the firelight and the worn hearthrug blurred. Piers felt sick; he felt as if he was being sucked into the centre of a whirlpool. He gripped the arms of his chair to keep himself from falling over, and after a moment the spinning gradually slowed and then stopped. He could feel his father waiting for him to give a response. 'I don't believe you,' he said at length.

'Whether you believe it or not doesn't alter the truth of it.'

'She's in this house, isn't she? That's why you come here.'

'Yes. She's been shut away for the past thirteen years.'

So he had had thirteen years of stealing out of the house at night. He had had thirteen years of creeping through the dark, old forest. Piers shut the thought off abruptly, and said, 'Why? I mean, why is she shut away?'

'Because – she's not completely sane.'

'You mean she's mad?'

There was a pause. That's hurt him, thought Piers. Well, good. Because this is hurting me.

'Mad is a harsh word,' said his father. 'She can be perfectly all right for quite long stretches of time. But then she changes and becomes – disturbed. Fortunately,' he added, sounding and looking sardonic, 'your family has sufficient money to ensure she is looked after. There are a couple of women who live in the house with her. One is a nurse trained in the care of the mentally sick.'

'Emma.'

'Yes, Emma is one of them. She's a very good, kind soul, and what we would have done without her all these years I can't begin to imagine.' He set down his empty glass and leaned forward.

Piers stared at him. I'm going to remember this night for a very long time, he thought suddenly. It's going to stay with me for most of my life. And every time I remember it, it'll be all mixed up with the sound of a fire crackling in a hearth and those awful Victorian tiles framing it, and the scents of an unfamiliar house. And with feeling sorry for my father, and realizing that he isn't sinister or mysterious at all, he's thin and worried and sad, because once upon a time something dreadful happened to him, and whatever it was it's still happening.

And then his father said, 'What you have to understand, Piers, is that I'm not the villain of your family's tragedy. I didn't ruin Helen and spoil her life. It was Helen who spoiled mine.

'Your aunts got it nearly right about me,' he said. 'But they also got it very wrong. They got it right when they said I was a gypsy. I was. But I wasn't the kind of gypsy who lived in a scruffy caravan and sold pegs or told fortunes – that's the part they got wrong.

'I was the best kind of gypsy: the real kind who had turned his back on the conventional life and the conventional people, and roamed the world. My family were Irish – landed but impoverished. And they were arrogant – Jesus God, they were the most arrogant creatures on God's earth, my family. They never admitted that they were the last dying flicker of an outmoded way of life – I'm not sure if they even realized it – and they certainly never admitted that the money had long since melted away, and that we all should have been out in the world earning a living like most of the human race.

181

'They lived on in the house where the family had lived for nearly four hundred years – except that by the time I was born the place was crumbling into the ground. It was a huge decaying old house, Piers, and although there wasn't a whole brick in its walls or a sound tile on its roof, there were times when I understood why they clung to it. Even when it was falling down around our ears, it was the most beautiful place in Ireland – and Ireland's a very beautiful place indeed, Piers. The sunshine used to pour through the windows – they were latticed windows and the latticing was peeling away and the glass had become wavy with age, but that never deterred the sunshine. It streamed in, showing up the worn patches on the carpets and rotting the curtains until they were practically in strings.' He paused, staring into the fire.

'But when you walked through the rooms,' he said, softly, 'there was the scent of beeswax where generations of housemaids had polished the furniture, and when you walked in the gardens there was a scent of lilac and of the honeysuckle that had been there since the house was built in the days of Henry VIII. The Irish never much liked Henry VIII, but my family prospered under him,' said Piers's father thoughtfully, and Piers saw that he had gone back into that distant past, and that he was no longer aware of the impersonal firelit room.

'There were moss roses in part of the gardens that had grown there since the sixteenth century. And there were ancient trees with wild primroses beneath them, and broken stone statues crusted with lichen in little unexpected corners. It was a wilderness, but it was a romantic wilderness, and if you stood on the terrace and looked to the west, in the distance you could see the purple smudge of mountains. My mother – your grandmother, Piers – used to walk in the gardens as if she had all the time and money in Christendom and as if the entire world was arranged solely for her pleasure. She wore a white dress with a huge shady hat, and picked primroses and harebells or great sheaves of lilac, and arranged them in the house in huge copper jugs.

'And when I was sixteen I couldn't bear it any longer. I couldn't bear the unworldliness and the refusal to look reality in the face – by that time we were staving off bankruptcy and the bailiffs were practically camping out in the kitchen.'

He paused and reached for the brandy decanter. Piers said, carefully, 'You – walked out?'

'I did. I worked my way to England and from there to other countries. Once or twice I signed on with ships trading with the East. I worked in bars in different cities. Most of the time I was quite wild and fairly unprincipled. Several times I slept with ladies a little older than myself for money – you understand what I mean by that?'

'Yes.' By this time Piers was too deep inside the spell that was being spun to feel any embarrassment at this.

His father looked over the rim of his brandy glass. 'Do I go on?'

'Yes – please.'

'Somehow I made enough money to live on. And then I came to a large house in a remote Derbyshire village – for no other reason than that it was a part of England I had never before visited – and there I met a girl.'

'My mother.'

'Yes.' He studied Piers for a moment, and then said, 'She was the most fascinating, most beautiful creature I had ever seen, and I wanted her at once.'

Piers could not have spoken now if his life had depended on it. He could feel the sick tension building up inside him and inside the room. One half of him was thinking: I don't want to hear this. I don't want to hear some dusty love-story – I'll find it upsetting and I might find it embarrassing. But the other half knew the embarrassment did not matter and that being upset did not matter either.

His father was no longer looking at Piers; he was staring into the fire, his eyes far away. 'I've said she was fascinating and beautiful,' he said. 'But I haven't said that it was the evil beauty in the ivory setting that the poets write about. I haven't said that it was the treacherous beckoning lamp and the siren witchery of every romance ever penned.

'In those days she had a mass of cloudy dark hair and dark eyes and skin as pale as buttermilk. She was like an enchanted heroine out of an ancient romance, and she was absolutely irresistible.' The lines of tiredness smoothed out for a moment. 'And despite my way of life, I was still a bit of a romantic at heart,' he said, and when he smiled, Piers felt the tug of charm again. 'I saw myself as the knight who claimed her from her enchanted castle, or maybe woke her from her bewitched slumber,' he said, and looked across at Piers, as if saying: is that something you can relate to? Piers half-nodded, indicating understanding.

'And of course, Helen, in turn, was going to be the pure-hearted lady who rescued me from my dissolute way of life,' said his father. 'What neither of us recognized,' he added, wryly, 'was that I had really rather enjoyed being dissolute.

'Helen's parents – your grandparents, Piers – had died when she was sixteen, and since then she had been more or less brought up by her sisters. Your two aunts,' he said, tight-lipped, and Piers saw that he did not like the aunts any more than they liked him.

'But they couldn't prevent the marriage; Helen was only three weeks short of her twenty-first birthday – in those days that was the age of majority – and there was nothing they could do.'

'Did they try to stop it?' said Piers, fascinated.

'Oh God, yes, they did. They put forward a dozen different arguments a day. I didn't listen to any of them, of course, any more than Helen did. In fact,' he said, 'the only person I had any time for in the whole set-up was the village priest – Father Stephen Berry.' The sudden smile showed again. 'Wouldn't you know that an Irishman would have time for a priest, though?'

'A Catholic priest?' This was surprising.

'A Catholic priest. "Martin Adair," he used to say to me, quite fiercely; "Martin Adair, are you sure you know what it is you're taking on?" And I was arrogant enough to think I did know,' said Piers's father.

He stopped speaking, and for what seemed to be a very long time neither of them spoke. When a log broke and fell apart in the hearth, sending a cascade of red sparks shooting upwards, Piers jumped.

But the small sound had broken the spell; he was able to say, 'What happens now? I mean – now that I know she's alive? Could I see her?' He discovered that he could not quite say 'my mother' yet. He said, 'Would you take me to her?'

'Are you sure you want to see her?'

'No, I'm not sure at all. But I think I have to see her, don't I?'

184

For answer his father went to the door and called to the woman, Emma, in a low voice. Piers stayed where he was, trying to hear what was being said. They spoke quietly and he missed the first few words but he had the impression that they were disagreeing. Then Emma said, 'Remember she hasn't seen a child for a great many years.' For some reason this struck a chill.

At last his father came back into the room. 'Emma thinks you shouldn't see your mother,' he said, without preamble. 'She thinks there might be danger.'

'To me?'

'Well, possibly. Also it might be upsetting for you.'

Piers said slowly, 'But if I go away without seeing her, I'll always wonder. I'll know that she's here, and that one day I'll have to see her.' And then, as his father did not reply, he said, 'I'd much rather see what there is to see now, instead of imagining things.'

His father glanced at the clock ticking on the mantel, and then stood up, 'Let's do it now,' he said.

Piers did not really want to see his mother, resurrected for him in this bizarre way, but he followed his father out of the room that suddenly seemed to represent safety, and up a narrow stairway with polished oak boards and an elaborate carved banister.

The rooms were at the back of the house – 'Overlooking the forest,' said his father as they went along a narrow passageway where the floors creaked and in places sloped alarmingly. They passed two or three doors: the doors were closed but the frames were out-of-true and light showed beyond them. It was very quiet and there was a scent of lavender and sadness.

We're going back, thought Piers. We're going back into that past that my father unwrapped and spread out earlier on. It's quite close to us, that past – I can feel it. I feel as if I might see the characters walking towards me at any minute as well: my mother with her evil siren beauty; my aunts, perhaps softer, because they were younger; my father as a wild romantic young man . . .

'This is the original part of the house,' said his father. 'Your Weston ancestors built it – that's your maternal grandfather's family. Odd, isn't it, to think that when my family was building

185

their marvellous house with the rose gardens and the statuary, your family was also building a house – this house. Parts of the original Tudor structure are still apparent, as well: when the Tudors built, they built to last.'

'What happened to the house?'

'It burned down. It was probably quite a big house once, because the Westons were quite a prominent family.'

'Who burned it?'

'I don't know. I don't know that anyone burned it; it might have been an accident. But the fire destroyed everything except the foundations and the servants' rooms. That's the part we're going into now.'

He spoke as if this might be of interest, but Piers heard the indifference beneath, and he understood that although his father knew it was correct to admire Tudor houses, he had no real interest in possessions or houses. He really is a gypsy, thought Piers. He had absolutely no idea whether he trusted his father, or how much of that intriguing background he believed, but when his father led the way down a short flight of twisty steps to a small door with a big black iron lock, Piers followed without hesitating.

'On the other side of the door is a set of rooms with locked doors and barred windows,' said his father. He produced a key, and looked down at Piers.

'You don't have to do this—'

'I know. And I don't want to do it. But,' said Piers, trying to still the wild beating of his heart, 'I'm not going to run away.'

'Of course you're not,' said his father, and reaching down, unlocked the door and pushed it open.

Chapter Twenty

The first thing he saw was the silver moonlight lying in bars across the floor, and when he looked across to the uncurtained window he saw the bars themselves: thick iron staves set closely together, shutting out the wilderness of the night forest. Shutting in the room's occupant.

The room's occupant . . .

She had seen him long before he finally turned his head to look at her. She was seated in a corner of the room, in a large, old-fashioned rocking chair; there was a scarlet plaid cover over it and the chair was rocking gently to and fro. Even in the half-light Piers saw that his father had spoken the truth; once upon a time Helen Adair, who had been Helen Weston, had been extremely beautiful.

Traces of that beauty remained. The cloud of hair was no longer there, but the hair itself was still dark – it was short and clipped close to her head, but little tendrils curled around her cheeks and over her pale forehead. The ivory-pale skin was still the most noticeable thing about her; the flesh firm and smooth over the bone structure. Piers realized with a start of surprise that his mother would only be around the same age as the mothers of most of his schoolfriends. If she had married his father when she was twenty-one she must still be under forty.

And she was smiling at him and holding out her hands.

Piers had absolutely no idea whether he should go forward to greet her, or even whether she knew who he was. He glanced at his father for guidance, but his father was watching the gently rocking figure with such infinite sadness that Piers looked quickly away.

The rocking slowed and eventually stopped altogether. No one spoke and no one moved, and the silence seemed to gather in strength until Piers could feel it pressing down stiflingly.

And then without warning the silence changed and the whole mood of the room changed with it, and the lady in the chair clapped her hands in delight and said, 'Martin, you've brought him to see me at last!' To Piers, she said, 'I've asked him so many times – you wouldn't believe how many times I've asked him to let me see you!'

'I thought he was old enough to understand.'

'Oh yes, of course he is. How very good-looking you are, Piers,' she said. 'A little like my father, I think.' She studied him, her head to one side, considering. 'Yes, there is a particular likeness to my father.'

Piers was beginning to think that after all he had not fallen into Peter Pan land; he had fallen into Lewis Carroll, because this was unquestionably Looking-Glass World where nothing was quite what it seemed, and where ordinary things distorted as you looked at them.

His mother said, 'You will stay and talk to me for a while, won't you, Piers? There's so much I want to know – about your school and your friends, and all the things you like to do, and what you're going to be when you're grown up. Martin, can't he stay for a while?'

She had the trick of speaking in breathless little rushes as if she was perpetually trying to catch up with herself. Piers found this attractive. He thought she had a slight foreign intonation or perhaps it was only an unusual way of stringing sentences together, which might be the result of living in such isolation. And she was lovely and tragic, and she was looking at them both with such wistful hope that the pity of it slammed into his heart. He remembered that his father had said something about her having long stretches of normality and he thought this was certainly one of those stretches. Even so, it was with a shock that he heard his own voice say, 'Of course I'll stay.'

'Oh, I knew you would! How wonderful! Now, you shall sit here opposite me where I can see you, and Martin shall ask Emma to bring up some ginger beer or cider or whatever you like. Martin, will you do that?'

Piers felt his father hesitate. He glanced at Piers, and Piers thought he caught the thought: be careful! But then he only said, 'Yes, why not?' and went from the room. Piers heard the key turn in the lock on the other side, and then his father's footsteps going away down the hall.

'That's a bad sound, isn't it?' said his mother. 'The sound of a key turning in the lock?'

'Well, yes.'

'Sit opposite me,' she said again. 'You must be almost fourteen now, mustn't you?'

Piers, seating himself in the chair facing the rocker, said carefully that he was actually fourteen tomorrow.

'A good age to be,' said Helen Adair, nodding. 'Especially for a boy. Boys are very beautiful at fourteen.'

This was a curious word to use. Piers felt a faint prickle of unease, but he doused it, reminding himself that she had been shut away here for a long time. But when she said, with sudden urgency, 'Piers, quickly, you must listen to what I'm going to tell you,' the unease returned.

'What—'

'Before Martin comes back – before Emma comes back – I'll tell you the truth. You should know the truth, Piers.'

Piers sprang out of the chair and tried to back away, but she had the swiftness of the cunning, and one hand darted out to grasp his wrist. He said, 'I don't understand—'

She pulled him nearer. 'The truth is very different to the story they'll tell you,' she said, and Piers registered with growing horror that her voice was changing; it was becoming slurred and blurry.

'He'll try to tell you that I once killed a child,' said Helen. 'And that it was mindless murder. That's what they've all pretended, all these years, you know.'

As Piers struggled to release his hand, glancing frantically over his shoulder to the locked door, he knew that his earlier instinct about distortion had been right: if there ever had been any ordinariness in here it was disintegrating fast, and something so utterly insane was pouring into the room that he felt as if he might drown in it. The impossibly strong hand was still snaked about his wrist and he could only get free by using extreme violence. The thought of using violence against her was impossible.

She released his hand suddenly, so that Piers half fell backwards onto the floor. 'Here's the truth, Piers,' she said. 'I really did kill a child, but it wasn't like they said, and it certainly wasn't mindless—'

She began to rock the chair again, to and fro; it creaked as it rocked, rhythmically and hypnotically and it ought to have been a soothing, comforting sound but it was not.

The chair cast its own shadow on the wall – Piers could see it clearly, and he could feel the madness becoming mingled with horror. And the horror was a very familiar one indeed.

It was then that he knew for sure that the dark fears of his younger self had been real, and that there truly were people in the world who were not quite what they seemed. He stared at the figure rocking in the patch of moonlight, and his mind looped backwards: to all those dreadful stories of creatures who rocked by their firesides pretending to be normal, but who, when they turned their heads to look at you, were not normal at all and who were certainly not human. They had slanting eyes, those creatures, and they had grinning lips and a muzzle – a great, wide, dripping maw that was waiting to devour little children . . .

Whatever the creature in the chair was, it was no longer his mother. It leaned forward then, and its thick smeary voice said, 'He was your brother, Piers – didn't you know that? Didn't they ever tell you about that other little boy – the one who never lived to grow up? Didn't you know you once had a brother?'

The hairs were lifting on the back of Piers's neck, and he was frantically listening for his father to return, but he forced his voice to sound calm, and he said, 'I don't believe you.'

'Oh, it's perfectly true. You had a brother – he was born three years before you. Martin and those two grim virgins will tell you I killed him,' she said.

And then, as Piers tried to think of something to say, Helen Adair smiled, and then said, 'And I did kill him, of course—' She paused, and Piers saw that she was picking over the memory. 'Martin and my sisters thought it was a temporary insanity,' she said. 'They hushed it up because they thought I was mad. But I wasn't mad, Piers, I wasn't mad in the least. I'm not mad now, am I? *Am I?*'

Piers stole a quick look towards the door. But even if he could bound across the room, the door was locked, and she would surely be after him. And she had killed one boy, she had killed his brother.

He managed to say, 'Why? Why did you kill him?'

'Because he had the taint, Piers. Didn't you know about that? It came into this family four hundred years ago, and it's still here. It skips generations sometimes – four or five at a time, it skips. But then it appears again. I knew as soon as your brother was born that he had it. He couldn't be allowed to live.'

She half-turned in the chair, and pointed to a carved oak chest standing beneath the window. 'You see that, Piers?' she said, and Piers thought: Oh God. Oh God, she's going to tell me she killed him and hid the body in there! *And that he's still there . . .*

'Look in the chest, my dear,' said his mother. 'Open it up, and see what you find there.'

Look in the chest, my dear, because you might find the body of your brother, melting into decay and dripping with corruption . . .

With a kind of helpless disgust, Piers discovered that he had crossed the room, and that he was standing before the window, in the spot where the bars of moonlight cast the thickest shadows. He saw his hand reach down to the chest lid to lift it. There would be nothing inside – *of course* there would be nothing inside! – except maybe ordinary household things. There was an almost identical chest in the hall at home; the aunts used it to store blankets and sheets, and Aunt Monica always laid sprigs of dried lavender in the corners so that there was a pleasant scent if anyone opened it.

The oak chest in Helen Adair's room did not hold blankets and it did not smell of dried lavender. Piers took a deep breath and, half-closing his eyes, lifted the lid. It came up smoothly, as if it was often raised, or as if somebody might frequently creep over here and lift the lid and stand there gloating. A faint stench reached his nostrils and he shuddered and then forced himself to look down, because the reality could not possibly be worse than the imagining.

There was no body there, of course. All that the chest contained were two large earthenware jars, standing side by side. They were rather like the flour jars that Aunt Vera kept in the larder at home. Old-fashioned, with brown rims. But Piers stared at them and his heart began to race.

'They're blood jars,' said his mother, softly. 'They've been handed down in my family for over four hundred years. I've kept them hidden,' she said. 'Because I was afraid that if I didn't manage to kill your brother – if I had bungled his murder – they would have shut me away so that I couldn't get to him a second time. And then, Piers, once he had grown up, he would have used these jars.'

'What for?' whispered Piers.

'He would have killed me or one of your aunts and then he would have drunk the blood,' said Helen Adair. 'He might have waited until he had a son of his own to do it, and then he would have made the son drink it. That's what they believe has to happen, you see. They believe they have to drink the blood of their ancestors to pass the line down. Martin and my sisters never understood that, but I understood it.'

She stood up and began to move towards him. 'I wonder if you understand it, Piers?' she said, and incredibly the slurry voice had vanished and in its place were the soft beckoning tones of the temptress. To his utter horror, Piers felt a twitch of sexual arousal. It was gone almost as soon as it happened, but he knew it had happened and he knew he would remember it for ever and that he would feel ashamed and sickened for ever.

She was standing very close to him now; he could feel her breath warm on his neck.

'I wonder if you have the taint,' said his mother, softly in his ear. 'They took you away from me when you were born, of course: they said I couldn't be trusted with another child. Shall we see if you have it, Piers? Reach down and lift the jars.'

I'll have to humour her, thought Piers, appalled.

The stone jars felt cold and smooth under his hands. He lifted one out carefully, using both hands; it was heavy and dead-feeling. As he set it on the floor, he saw for the first time that the inside was stained from something dark.

'Lift it up,' said the terrible voice. 'You can still smell the blood.'

As she said this, a faint sour taint seemed to gust into Piers's face. He shuddered and looked up at the mad glaring eyes, and knew the nightmare had tricked him: the nightmare in which his father had crept up the stairs, his shadow not quite matching his physical body, had been wrong. It was not his father who was the slinking snarling wolf-creature, and it never had been.

It was his mother.

As he bent over the jar, he heard the door unlock behind

him, and his mother's howl of fury as his father crossed the room to restrain her.

'I honestly don't think she would have harmed you,' said Piers's father as they walked back together. 'But I'm glad I got back when I did.'

'So am I.'

'It's like a sick nightmare to have to tie her up like that. Every time I think it will be easier, but every time it's worse.'

'Yes.'

The forest seemed to have subtly altered, and as they walked along the narrow woodland path Piers thought it was pressing in on them as if the trees were trying to hear what the two intruders into their world were saying. Several times they heard the high-pitched sonic squeaking of bats, and once an owl swooped with predatory grace through the night in pursuit of its supper.

Piers was still not sure if any of this was really happening. He was still half-expecting to find that it was a dream, and that at any minute he would wake up.

After a moment, he said, 'Was it true, what she told me? Did I really have a brother?'

'Oh yes.'

'And did she really kill him?'

'Yes. We managed to keep it quiet – there was a doctor who was supposed to have been in love with your Aunt Monica for years – we got him to write out a death certificate and there was a normal funeral and burial. Father Berry helped – he knew the truth. In fact,' said Martin Adair, thoughtfully, 'I always suspected that Father Berry knew more about the Westons than he ever let on.'

Piers thought that later on – maybe when he was about ninety-two – he might find it intriguing to focus on the extraordinary idea of someone being in love with Aunt Monica. He thought at some stage in his life he might want to know more about the unknown Father Berry as well. But for the moment he had no mental energy to spare for anything other than what had happened tonight.

He said, 'She – my mother – talked about an inheritance.'

'Call her Helen if you jib at calling her mother.'

Piers thought this was perceptive of his father. He said, 'Well,

OK. Thanks. Uh – Helen talked about handing down an inheritance. She said that something came into my family four hundred years ago and that it was still there. What did she mean?'

Their eyes met. 'I don't know,' said Martin Adair, coolly. 'You do.'

They stopped walking and looked at one another. Piers saw how the lines of tiredness around his father's mouth and eyes had deepened into lines of exhaustion in the last few hours.

But at last he said, 'I know a very little. And all it is, is an old legend. It's one of those ridiculous tales that people pounce on and make a great deal of. And it seems to have come into existence around the time the house burned down, so it probably made a strong imprint on people's minds.'

'What is it, this legend?'

'I only know bits,' said his father. 'And what I know is probably not very accurate. But I do know that your mother knew about the legend – and I think it preyed on her mind. Father Berry thought so certainly and Dr Blundell agreed – oh, that was Monica's swain.'

There did not seem to be anything to say to this. Piers waited.

'Whatever it was that Helen found or heard,' said his father, 'it caused her to believe that a long time ago something . . .' he paused, as if searching for the right word, and then said, 'something odd came into your family. Something that had cropped out over the years, and that would continue to crop out in succeeding generations. Like a flaw in the weave of a length of cloth. She thought your brother had inherited that flaw – she genuinely believed she had done the right thing in killing him.'

'That's why you hushed it up?'

'Yes.'

'Is it real, this flaw?' said Piers after a moment, and then, as his father did not reply, he said, 'You think it is, don't you? Have I got it?'

'I don't know,' said his father, and Piers felt something cold and sick turn over at the pit of his stomach.

As they neared the edge of the forest, and saw the lights of their own house in the distance, his father said, 'I've never been able to find the whole story – I've never really wanted to – but the belief is that in fifteen hundred and something, a

Weston lady was raped by what the whole village – and also the adjoining villages – believed to be a werewolf, and that a child was born somewhere in extreme secrecy nine months later.'

Piers was surprised at how unsurprising he found this. He thought about it for a moment, and then said, 'That couldn't really have happened, could it?'

'Of course not. Life's not a horror film. But it was a time when superstition was rife,' said his father. 'There were witch hunts in every village in the land about once a month on average – people had nothing else to do for most of the time. So of course Kings Thane would have its own witch or its own—'

Piers said abruptly, 'What happened to him? The – the werewolf creature?'

'I don't know,' said his father, meeting Piers's eyes very straightly.

After a moment Piers said carefully, 'And that's what my – what Helen believes? That there's a – werewolf taint in the Weston family from four hundred years back?' He looked at his father. 'I don't believe I said that.'

'I don't believe you did, either.' They exchanged uncertain smiles.

'It's like something out of a nightmare,' said Piers at last.

'Oh yes. I've been in the nightmare for years. We all have – Helen not least of all. And your aunts, of course. They always blamed me for what happened.'

'I don't see why.'

'Oh, they thought Helen's madness was something to do with being married,' said Martin Adair vaguely. 'The exigences of childbirth,' he added, off-handedly, and Piers heard the withdrawal and understood that there were still forbidden areas in all this. After a moment he said, 'I had the nightmare as well.'

'That's because you're sensitive to other people's feelings.'

'Well, I wish I wasn't.' Piers hesitated, and then said, 'When I was small I thought you were part of it. I mean, really part of it. I used to watch you creeping up the stairs after you had been into the forest – and I used to imagine that I was seeing wolf-images.'

'Perhaps you were. Perhaps I brought something back with me – some aura.'

'Is that possible?'

'Listen, Piers, I don't believe in werewolves who rape human females, but where I grew up they used to put milk and bread out for leprechauns and even today, on certain nights in the year, they still double-lock their doors and hang crucifixes over the windows. There are a whole lot of things in the world we don't know about and it's probably better that we shouldn't know them. But,' he said, in a totally different voice, 'I'm sorry you had all that fear and didn't think you could tell any of us.'

'I got over it,' said Piers, knowing he had not.

'Good. Keep getting over it. Or tell me about it the next time and if there's a solution we'll look for it. Knowing the answer often helps.' Martin looked at Piers. The trees cast branchy patterns over his face; Piers could not decide if it made him look extremely old or extremely young.

'None of this has anything to do with your life, Piers. It's a tragedy, but it isn't your tragedy – it mustn't affect anything you decide to do. And what you must not do, is see it as some kind of crazy romantic crusade, and decide to make it your life's work to track down the truth.'

'No, of course I won't,' said Piers, thinking: but I suspect I might. Because once upon a time, in the days of the Tudors, something immensely evil came into that house in the forest. And I don't think it ever left.

Chapter Twenty-One

'Not much of the original house remains,' said Piers, as they drove towards Derbyshire. 'But there is still a small portion that's intact.'

Toby, who was seated beside him, said, 'And how old is the original house?'

'Tudor,' said Piers. 'Fifteen twenty or so. But the main house was built much later – the early eighteen hundreds, I think.'

From the back seat Tybalt gave a happy sigh.

'Landed gentry,' remarked Toby. 'We're not about to find out that you're some kind of feudal squire, are we?'

'God, no. This is just a house that's been in my family for ages,' said Piers. 'It's normally rented on a long lease, but the last tenants left and the agents haven't found a replacement yet.' He paused, and then said, 'It isn't everybody's ideal, the house. So it isn't always easy to find tenants.'

'Why not?'

'Oh, it's an isolated spot,' said Piers, vaguely. 'A little cluster of villages – the local name for them is the Thanes, although Kings Thane is the largest. But there are no shops or supermarkets very near. You get power-cuts in bad weather. And the house is a peculiar size – too big for today's average family, but too small for any kind of business set-up.' *And very few people can cope with its atmosphere*, he thought.

'Did you ever live there?' asked Tybalt, hopefully.

'No, I don't think I've spent more than an hour in it since I was fourteen.'

'Oh.' Tybalt sounded so gloomy that Piers said, 'What's the matter?'

'I guess I was thinking you might know some of the local folklore. Like – stories about the families who lived there.'

'"Families who lived there" being the Foljambes?'

'Uh, I guess so.'

197

'No, I don't,' said Piers, rather shortly. 'I'd have said so at the start if I did.'

He instantly wished he had not said this, because Tybalt turned brick red and said he hoped that Dr Adair had not taken any offence, because none had been intended. He looked so miserable that Piers said, 'It's all right, Tybalt, I know what you meant.' He paused, and then said, 'I lived in Kings Thane until I was eighteen, but I had a rather peculiar— I was brought up by two elderly aunts who were very strict. We didn't mix with the local community at all. For all I know there could have been Foljambes all over the place.'

His tone was studiedly light, but he was already wishing he had not offered the house for their base. It would have been easy enough to have found a holiday cottage or even a good-sized pub for the team to rent for a month. But in London, with the memories safely banked down, it had seemed the ideal solution. Now, driving along the forest road, he began to wonder whether he would be able to cope. It would be interesting to see if any of the team were affected by the house's atmosphere: Tybalt might be, and also Nina, who was arriving with Priscilla tomorrow. Dietfreid was coming by train next week. Piers thought he would watch for their reactions.

He swung the Range Rover off the road and drove it up the track that had been made ten years ago after both his parents had died, and which wound up to what Piers always thought of as the back of the house. Approaching it from this direction meant it was not necessary to go through the forest, for which he was profoundly thankful. But the forest was there all the same, dark and forbidding, and Piers felt the undercurrents reach out strongly to him as soon as he swung off the main road. He felt the shiver of unease as he glimpsed the house with its glowering roofline and the glowering windows like lidless eyes just beneath the eaves.

The track was rough and a bit bumpy, and the Range Rover jolted and bounced its way up to the house. Piers parked it on the oblong of hardcore at the side.

'I haven't been here for years,' he said, switching off the engine and studiedly avoiding looking directly at the house. 'In fact I've only been back three or four times in the last fifteen years, just briefly to check in with the agents. But the house should be in reasonable repair – the last tenants only left about a month ago. There was a requirement written into the lease that they maintained the inside, and the agents inspect the outside pretty regularly.'

And I don't want to be here, he thought. I don't want to be here, and I certainly don't want to go back into that house. Because anything might be lying in wait for me in there . . .

He produced the keys and handed them to Tybalt. 'Open the front door, will you, Tybalt?' he said, and heard with gratitude that his voice sounded perfectly ordinary. 'Toby and I will unload the provisions and carry them in.'

'OK.'

Tybalt was loving every minute of this. He was loving knowing that this was one of those ancient pockets of England that tourists hardly ever got to see, and that the English themselves hardly ever admitted existed, and he was loving the knowledge that they would be staying in a house where parts dated from the sixteenth century. That surely was extremely old. He was secretly grateful to Dr Adair for living up to Tybalt's private image of him; it was exactly right that Dr Adair belonged to a family who owned this incredible old house.

The forest lived up to his image of it, as well. It reared up behind the house, and it was just about the spookiest place Tybalt had ever seen. It was late afternoon when they got there: day was sliding down into night, and a thin rain had been falling for hours so that the forest was shrouded in mist when they drew up at the house. Tybalt gave a sigh of pure ecstasy.

But he had not been inside the house for more than five minutes when he realized that it was the worst house he had ever encountered, and if he could politely have left he would have done so, at the speed of a bat escaping hell.

He had absolutely no idea why he should feel like this because the interior was pretty ordinary. There were a couple of sitting rooms and a small study, all with solid, old-fashioned furniture and the kind of garish tiles around the fireplaces that until twenty years ago had been called ugly but that were now considered collectable. And there was a big kitchen and a scullery and something that Dr Adair said absently had probably once been a flower room. There were four or five bedrooms upstairs, and the plumbing was pretty OK, which was one good thing.

But while Tybalt could deeply appreciate the house's antiquity and become light-headed on the forest scenery which you could see from just about every window, what he found practically unbearable was the crushing weight of pain and desolation that lingered here.

This was worst in the Tudor part. Dr Adair showed them over the house, and when he said, in a bored voice, 'Oh, this is the Tudor part,' as if it couldn't have mattered less, Tybalt felt as if something had grabbed him by the throat and shaken him. He had been expecting to be entranced by that part of the house, but all he felt was huge relief when they left those rooms and went back downstairs. He felt even more relieved when they began to plan their research.

Concentrating on tracing the Foljambe family and eventually finding Karabas would surely serve to chase the ghosts away. Not that he believed in ghosts.

Felicity had found that concentrating on Bracken Hall's bicentenary week helped to chase the ghosts away.

There had been further interviews with the police; the inspector had gone on being kindly and fatherly. They would continue the hunt for the man the school had known as Brother Karabas, of course, and they would let her know if there were any developments.

Felicity said, 'Don't count on me to identify him, inspector, or give evidence at a trial.' The inspector had looked at her for a long moment, and then said, 'Is it the publicity you're fearing?'

'Yes, of course.' The thought of Bryony being exposed to the kind of media coverage that would inevitably accompany a kidnapping trial was not to be considered.

'If you catch him and I can do anything anonymously,' said Felicity, after a moment, 'I will. But I mean really anonymously, not a Miss or Mrs X thing with photographs splashed across the papers so that everyone knows.' She paused, and said, 'And if I have any more contact from him I'll let you know.'

'You think he might contact you again, do you?'

'Not really, but anything's possible.'

Because Karabas wants Bryony and he might try to get her again . . .

She said, 'He's clearly mad. Sometimes mad people get fixations, don't they? Obsessions?'

200

'Sometimes. We'll be in touch, Mrs Stafford,' said the police inspector, after another of his shrewd looks. 'In the meantime, try to remember that life goes on.'

And life went on, even when you were pulverized by guilt at a blameless monk's dreadful death, even when you wanted to lock Bryony up somewhere safe and never let her out of your sight, and when you realized that you had taken to checking every room in the stable house before you felt it was safe to lock the door.

'And even then I get up four or five times during the night to make sure it's really locked,' confessed Felicity to Morag Mackenzie.

'You don't think he'll come back, for goodness' sake, do you?' demanded Morag.

'Not logically, but I keep imagining him crouching in dark corners, ready to leap out. I keep wanting to rush into classrooms to make sure that Bryony's where she should be.'

Morag said, 'You can trust us to watch Bryony, Felicity. Listen, you will get over this. Life truly does go on – yes, I know that's a cliché, but that doesn't stop it being a truism as well. You still look a bit frayed, if you don't mind my saying so.'

'I still feel a bit frayed.' Felicity did not want to admit to the spells of sick horror that still engulfed her regularly. She said, 'I'll take some vitamin pills or something.'

'Oh blow vitamin pills, let's have a large gin each,' said Morag. 'I brought some with me, and a bottle of tonic.' Felicity found this extraordinarily helpful, not so much for the gin's restorative qualities (which were probably questionable) as for Morag's brusque gesture of support in bringing it. It was noticeable that most of the staff had taken to dropping in to the stable house after supper, nearly always with a carefully prepared reason. John Lucas, the music master, would bring a tape of something that they might want to use for one of the bicentenary events, or one of the brothers would have discovered a piece of information about the school. Brother Andrew had proofs for the commemoration booklet which had to be checked, or photographs that had to be approved. One of the senior school teachers had a birthday and Felicity was invited to her house for drinks and supper. John Lucas drove her and Morag there and back, and two of the sixth formers spent the evening in the stable house with Bryony. Felicity had nearly forgotten how it felt to dress up and spend the evening with adults. She was intensely touched by all these examples of community life in its truest sense.

Brother Andrew had talked to her for a long time about Dominic.

'We can't know the whole of God's plan,' he said. 'We can only act on the little corner that God permits us to know at the time. It's all any of us can do. None of us could possibly have foreseen what that creature would do. You can't blame yourself for what happened, Felicity – you did what you thought was necessary under the prevailing circumstances – and so did Dominic. Remember that Dominic elected to come with you.'

Father Abbot addressed the whole school after the tragedy, saying that the loss of Brother Dominic was a grievous sadness, but that they should all remember that he had gone home to God and that was all any devout man or woman could wish for. Felicity, sitting at the back with the rest of the lay teachers, thought that this was rather a nice way of putting it: it was sufficiently homely for even the smallest children to relate to.

How good they all are, thought Felicity, sitting in her tiny friendly study, forcing her mind to the work she was here to do. How good and gentle, and how *enviable* they are, able to see violent death as going home to God, and believing devoutly in Divine plans and the inscrutable benevolence of Providence. But how unarmoured they really are against the world.

Because how could any of them possibly understand how it felt to be dragged, mentally and physically, down into a seething half-world where there were sinister byways and evil-drenched blind alleys into which mankind occasionally stumbled by mistake – byways and alleys from which there sometimes emerged macabre creatures who had never been intended to be born.

And then she wondered with sick horror whether she would ever be able to forget how, for a terrible treacherous few moments, she had actually responded to one of those creatures. But for a moment he brought Connor back to me! pleaded her mind as if seeking justification. I was frantic with fear for Bryony, and it was as if Connor – the real Connor, the Connor I married – had come back to be with me for a time.

The sick horror stayed with her. It stayed all through the Christmas festivities – Bracken Hall, it transpired, celebrated

Christmas in practically Dickensian manner – and although the pupils were not there, most of the lay teachers turned up for a truly sumptuous Christmas dinner.

'What about your family?' asked Felicity of Morag.

'This is my family,' said Morag, with an abrupt gesture to the monks ranged round the long table.

Four pupils whose parents were working in the Far East stayed at the school for the holiday; Felicity felt sorry for them, unable to be with their parents, but they joined forces with Bryony, and when Bryony's cronies, the O'Callaghan twins, came to stay for three nights, the seven of them formed a gang, amiably intentioned but so lively that Brother Joseph said they might as well have the entire school back, for all the noise that was being made. The O'Callaghan twins thought Bracken was a great place, a terrific place, and entered with energetic enthusiasm into Morag Mackenzie's scheme for a pageant to help celebrate the bicentenary. They made gleeful forays into the attics where trunkfuls of costumes and properties for school plays were kept, and said they would ask if they could come to stay at Easter, because they wanted to see as much as possible of the celebrations.

Morag and John Lucas were planning that the entire junior school would stage a pageant showing the whole history of the school, right back from the original land grant in 1540. Bryony's all right, thought Felicity, listening to the tumble of details she was giving the O'Callaghan twins about the costumes and the pageant. She's filed the entire thing into one of her fantasy worlds, and I think, I really do think, that's the best thing for her to do.

She turned with relief to the progress of the qualifying heats for the choral competition. The heats had been held just before Christmas, and eight schools were through to the quarter-finals. The monks had been delighted at the number of schools which had entered the contest.

Felicity had worked out the details of accommodation for the finalists. Brother Stephen, who had been appointed as Bursar in Dominic's place, had said there were a couple of quite good youth hostels nearby, and although Felicity had not yet driven over to see them, she thought they sounded as if they would fit the bill. The trouble was that most of the schools would be sending teachers, and parents of finalists would probably want to come as well. They might have to restrict numbers, or ask parents to make their own arrangements.

She heard the lunch bell ring out down in the main hall, but she thought she would work through lunch today. She actually felt a bit sick, so it would not hurt to give lunch a miss. She was drafting out a letter to be sent to the semi-finalist schools, when the sickness suddenly mounted, and she had to dash to the loo and bend over the basin, retching miserably.

It was not until she was swilling cold water onto her face afterwards, that a sudden terrible realization broke against her mind like a choking tidal wave.

The unknown doctor in Caldbeck was kindly and definite. The test was positive, he said. There was absolutely no doubt at all. Felicity saw him start to frame a sentence in which some kind of standard congratulation was included.

She said, in a rush, 'This isn't straightforward. I'm a – my husband died last year, and this is the result of a rape a couple of months ago.'

He studied her for a moment and then said, 'That's a very bad thing indeed. There are a couple of roads we could take, of course.'

'Abortion,' said Felicity, staring at him. And thought, wouldn't that be the best way out for everyone?

'Yes, that's one of them. You can talk to one of our counsellors about it, of course. There's a week or two before the decision gets urgent.' He made a brief entry on a medical card. It was unexpectedly soothing to find that doctors still did this, instead of tapping information into a computer.

'Were the police involved?'

'Yes.' This seemed an odd question to ask.

'It's just that sometimes where it's a case of the rapist being known – someone in the family, even – the police aren't always called in.'

'Oh, I see. Well, they were certainly called in,' said Felicity. 'But it was kept pretty much low-key. There was a question of my small daughter being kidnapped for a few hours— The man simply vanished when it was all over.'

Again he seemed either to understand or at least sympathize. But he said, 'Did the police ask you to take a blood test after the rape, Mrs Stafford?'

The unexpectedness of this nearly threw Felicity off-balance. After a moment, she said, 'No. Should they have done?'

'It's usual,' said the doctor, non-committally. 'Routine procedure, just to be sure that nothing's been transmitted.'

'Oh God,' said Felicity, staring at him. 'Oh dear God, you mean AIDS, don't you? But that's the last thing—'

'That occurred to you? Of course it would be. But it would be routine to make sure you aren't HIV positive.' He made it sound as if it was the most minor thing in the world. 'I can take a blood sample now if you like and we'll send it off to the lab.'

'Yes, all right.' After the initial reaction, Felicity had calmed down. She thought it was a safe bet that Karabas was not an AIDS sufferer in any form, but the explanations were so exhaustingly complex that it would be simpler to go along with the blood test.

As she was rolling her sleeve down again, he said, 'Let me know about a termination. And do remember that we have trained people you can talk to. On all subjects.'

Rape, unwanted pregnancy and AIDS. Felicity forced her voice to normality. She said, 'You've been very kind. I'll think about all those things for a day or two and come back to see you.'

The nightmare had assumed a far more menacing aspect now. The night when Karabas had taken Bryony and had raped Felicity was no longer something that could be pushed into the past while life went on; it was something that was about to thrust its macabre hands deeply into the future.

Only I don't believe I can go through with an abortion, thought Felicity, curled up miserably in a corner of the comfortable worn sofa in the stable house, watching the grey wintry rain slide down the windows. I know it's legal and easy, and I know that a great many people don't see it as much more than a visit to the dentist, but I don't think that's how I see it. What had Polonius said in *Hamlet*? 'To thine own self be true.' It's a question of your innermost beliefs, thought Felicity, and of being true to those beliefs. And my innermost belief tells me it's something I can't do.

But how am I going to live when this interval with the monks is over? It's going to be hard enough as it is to get a job and juggle Bryony's school hours with child-minders or after-school groups— And that's another thing you'll have to cope with. Because unless you can drop on another job in a school – which isn't very likely – you'll have to leave Bryony with strangers for part of the day; with people who don't know about Karabas and what happened up here. People who don't know and probably shouldn't be told that a watch will have to be kept for a charming, sinister man who claims to be her uncle – and who may even be her uncle, for all I know – but who wants to spirit her away to some God-forsaken tribe of freaks! And the fact that it's melodramatic doesn't prevent it from being real.

Finding work and fitting it around Bryony would have been difficult, but Felicity thought she could have managed it. Finding work and fitting it around Bryony and a tiny baby would be virtually impossible. Felicity could not think how she would begin to do it.

She could not begin to imagine how she would feel towards the child, either.

Chapter Twenty-Two

'**I** don't know how I'll cope with the child,' said Felicity, facing Brother Andrew across the desk. 'I don't know whether I'll be able to cope. But I'm going to try.'

She thought the word 'abortion' hung perilously on the air, just out of hearing, and so she said, 'Let's clear the air on this once and for all, shall we? I do know that abortion isn't an option within your Church – or any Church, probably. Well, it isn't an option for me, either.'

'I'm extremely glad to hear you say that, Felicity,' said Brother Andrew, and for the first time Felicity caught a glimpse of the iron codes that ruled these men. It was like unexpectedly hitting something solid and safe, and it was extraordinarily strengthening; it was a reminder that there was still integrity and faith in the world. Felicity took a deep breath and plunged on.

'I'm hating what I'm about to say,' she said. 'But I've thought and thought; I've looked at the situation from every aspect I can, and the only way I can see is to ask you for financial help.'

'Ah,' said Brother Andrew. It was impossible to tell from this what he was thinking.

'It isn't an attempt at extortion,' said Felicity. 'And it won't ever be – I'd like to clear the air on that one as well. If for any reason at all help isn't possible, then the matter will be closed and it needn't ever be referred to again. I certainly won't ever make it public. However—' She stopped. This was the difficult part, the part she had rehearsed in the stable house, even writing down a rough and ready dialogue for herself.

'However,' said Felicity, willing herself to go on, 'once I leave Bracken after the bicentenary week, I'm going to be in an extremely difficult financial situation, in fact unless I'm very lucky, I'll be virtually homeless.'

Had that sounded all right? She thought it had. She had

deliberately not said 'Bryony and I will be homeless' in case they thought she was playing it for sympathy.

'It seems that my husband and the man we knew as Brother Karabas both belonged to some slightly peculiar sect that come from the back of beyond,' said Felicity, who had spent a long time before coming up with this fairly acceptable description. 'Karabas told me a bit about it on the night – on the night he took Bryony.'

'You didn't get any clue as to where he actually came from?'

'No. I don't understand all of it,' said Felicity, 'and I don't think he told me more than a small part of it, although it certainly explained a few odd things about my husband – in particular the fact that he apparently never paid any kind of pension contributions or National Insurance. That means that for starters I don't get a widow's pension. So as well as not having a home, I haven't got any income whatsoever.'

'I see,' said Brother Andrew, and made a brief note on his notepad.

'Connor also left me with a huge amount of debt,' said Felicity, managing not to grind her teeth at the sheer bloody embarrassment of having to talk about this. 'The house had to be sold and when that was done, I was left with a small amount of capital – seventeen thousand pounds, in fact.' Hateful, said her mind angrily. Hateful to have to drag all this out and lay it before strangers. She said, quickly, 'I'm not telling you this to get sympathy or anything. I'm telling you so that you understand the exact nature of the dilemma.'

'To understand a dilemma is sometimes to go halfway to solving it,' said Brother Andrew, and Felicity felt the first inkling of optimism.

But she said, 'Unfortunately seventeen thousand doesn't solve anything, in fact it compounds the difficulty, because it's both too much and too little.'

'Could you explain that?' said Andrew. 'We like to think we're fairly well in touch with the world, but—'

'Yes, I'm sorry. It's too little because it won't buy a house, even in the cheapest parts of the country. It would provide a hefty deposit towards a mortgage, but to be given a mortgage I'd need to be in reasonable employment. So that knocks buying on the head. But renting's as much of a problem, because most landlords want some assurance of regular income.'

She leaned forward. 'Either way I'd have to work. That's all right – I want to work and I want to be independent. Fitting a job round Bryony would be difficult but it wouldn't be insurmountable. But I can't see how I can fit it round a small baby – at least not for two or three years. I don't have any family – at least, not any that I know. My parents are both dead. My mother was brought up by a distant cousin, and she lost touch with the cousin when she got married. So I never knew my family – only through my mother's tales about them.'

She paused, assembling her thoughts again, and then said, 'I know that there are various Government allowances for single mothers and people in genuine need, and I don't think I'd be too proud to apply for them. The trouble is that the seventeen thousand pounds will be a stumbling block. Until most of it's gone, I won't be eligible for any help, financial or housing or otherwise.'

Brother Andrew said, 'But you think you might be eligible for help from us?'

There was still absolutely nothing in his tone to indicate how he was reacting to what she had said. Felicity met his eyes levelly, and said, 'I don't know. But I can't think of anyone else to ask.'

'We think we've come up with a solution,' said Brother Andrew, three days later.

'As quickly as all that?' Felicity had expected the Roman Catholic Church to work roughly at the same speed as the mills of God.

'Well, we might have been a bit quicker, only it was a question of reaching the Abbot General,' said Brother Andrew. 'And then we have to at least make a show of consulting our own Father Abbot.' His thin Scottish face broke into a conspiratorial smile.

'Yes, of course.' Felicity pressed her hands tightly together. She would not show any panic, she absolutely would not. She took a few deep breaths.

'It's not altogether easy for the Church to just write out a cheque,' said Andrew. 'Although of course, that would be the simplest thing as far as you're concerned.'

Felicity wondered if the Abbot General had suspected her

209

of milking the Church of its riches in order to go on a luxury cruise or buy a villa in the South of France.

'But,' said Brother Andrew, 'there are certain private funds on deposit to deal with – transgressions by members of the Church.' He sent her another conspiratorial look, and then with the air of saying, Oh to hell with all this pussy-footing, said, 'Mostly for priests who become entangled with ladies or succumb to drink, you understand?'

'Oh, I see.'

'I have heard it referred to as the Punch and Judy fund,' said Brother Andrew, with caustic wit. 'But that's neither here nor there.'

'Well, no.' If Brother Andrew was being this light-hearted, surely it must mean the decision was favourable?

'So what we're going to suggest,' said Andrew, flicking open a page of his ubiquitous notebook, 'is that we make a capital investment to buy a house, giving you a secure tenancy but at a peppercorn rent – something ridiculous like five pounds a year that would be. You'd have the tenure for as long as you wanted it, but if you did leave, the property would revert to the Church.'

'Yes, I understand that.' This was sounding better than Felicity had dared hope.

'We take long-term views of investments, you see,' said Brother Andrew. 'And although we wouldn't get any returns on this one for a while, eventually – even if it was seventy or eighty years on – we'd have the house at whatever it was worth by then. Property,' said Brother Andrew, suddenly looking more like a shrewd stockbroker than a devout Scottish monk, 'is still one of the best long-term investments. And land, of course, is the finest thing of all. Land can't get burned down or vandalized. It can't get up and walk away.'

'Would I have a say in the house?' asked Felicity.

'Oh yes. I haven't got the exact amount we can spend yet but you can be sure it will be a realistic sum for today's prices. Not a mansion, but not a hovel either. And although we'd have to make a few stipulations, we'd give you a reasonably free hand.'

Felicity wondered if she could ask what sort of stipulations but just as she was framing a polite question, Andrew said, 'We'd want to be sure that whatever you chose was sound in wind and limb, of course, and not due to be knocked down to make way for a new motorway or anything like that.'

'How about the location?'

'Well, we'd probably ask you to avoid houses miles from civilization, in case we wanted to house a Church dependent in the future – oh, and also houses smack in the middle of large modern estates or inner cities, which might be difficult if we came to sell. They can be a bit of a drag on the market, those types of property,' said Andrew, dropping the stockbroker look and assuming the manner of an estate agent. 'But other than that, you could probably have a free hand.'

Felicity said, 'I understand all that.'

'You wouldn't stay in this area?'

'No,' said Felicity, after a moment. 'I'd like to, and I do know that it would be the most sensible option – especially if it meant that Bryony could stay on here. But I certainly couldn't afford the fees, even if she was a day pupil.' She had no idea what she would say if the monks' solution included some kind of arrangement for Bryony's schooling. But Andrew merely nodded.

'Bryony understands that this is just an interval for us,' said Felicity. 'I think that's one reason she coped so well with the abduction – none of this is wholly real for her. So I'd rather move before she's started to see Bracken as permanent.'

'Yes, I see all that,' said Andrew. He paused, and then said, very gently, 'And you're afraid that he might come back. Karabas.'

'Yes,' said Felicity, in a whisper. 'Yes, I am.'

She half-expected him to say, in a forcedly bright voice, Oh, he won't do that, but he did not. He looked at her thoughtfully for a moment, and then said, 'There's more to this than meets the eye, isn't there?'

'Yes.'

'I thought there was. Well, we don't pry, but we're always here if you want to talk about it.' And then, without giving her time to respond, said, 'Now then, since you've been so open about your finances, can I ask how long you think you can live on the money from your own house sale?'

'If you're going to be helping me to this extent I should think you're entitled to ask all the questions you want,' said Felicity, gratefully. She thought for a moment, and then said,

211

'If there's no rent or mortgage to come out of it, I should think it would last about three or four years.'

'That's about what we thought. So for the first five years of your occupancy, we'll make you what we're going to call a caretaker's allowance,' said Brother Andrew. 'In effect that's what you'll be because you'll be looking after a piece of Church property. That's a legitimate debit on the balance sheets, and it's a post that commands an annual stipend of £3,500.' He glanced up from his notes and said, 'I know that's a pittance, but put alongside the house and the interest from your own bit of capital—'

'You might call it a pittance, but I'd call it security,' said Felicity. 'At least until I'm able to get work. I can't begin to tell you how grateful I am.'

'Good. Well now, there's a small *quid pro quo* here. We'd expect you to keep the property in good repair – inside and out, including the gardens.'

'Yes, of course.'

'And day-to-day maintenance would have to come out of the caretaker's salary, I'm afraid. Redecorating and blocked gutters and new washers on taps and that kind of thing.'

'Fair enough.' Felicity thought that providing she was careful about what she bought this need not be a major concern. Small modern houses did not need much maintenance.

'And on top of that,' said Brother Andrew, turning to a new page of his notebook, 'I've told the Abbot General how delighted we are with what you're doing to mark Bracken's bicentenary, and I suggested that we might recommend you if a fund-raising situation arose in any of the other dioceses. You've probably heard or read about the various appeals and restoration funds that get launched when a cathedral starts to fall down?'

'Yes.'

'We have our own fund-raising boards and committees, of course, but quite often an outside professional is co-opted for a spell, just to set things up. It's not something that's likely to happen with any regularity, but there'll probably be times when you could be of help with the publicity for the kick-off. In that situation we wouldn't exactly expect you to work for nothing, but—'

'You wouldn't expect to pay full whack either,' said Felicity,

212

and smiled at him. 'Of course not. I hope it happens, however; I like the sound of it very much.'

'I should tell you that the Abbot General was quite taken with the idea,' said Brother Andrew. 'He's coming for the celebrations, of course, and he'd like to meet you.'

Felicity said carefully, 'You're being more than generous about this. I don't just mean the house purchase and the caretaker's salary.'

'We have a large degree of responsibility for what happened,' said Brother Andrew, seriously. 'Bryony came immensely close to the most extreme danger. And you were brutally attacked by someone you had every right to trust, because you thought he was one of our Order. To be fair, we thought so as well, but we shouldn't have been so casual about accepting him into Bracken. We should have made sure who it was we were inviting into our house.'

Felicity managed not to shiver at this, and Andrew closed his notebook, and said, 'You were right to ask us for help, Felicity; I'm only glad that we can provide it,' and smiled at her in a way that made her think he might have fluttered a few hearts in the outside world in his time.

'So,' said Andrew, 'you'd better start house-hunting.'

After supper, Felicity dug out an AA book, and closing her eyes, held it between her flattened palms and then let it fall open at random. It was not quite as ridiculous as sticking a pin in the map of England, but it was not far off.

It was somehow no real surprise to discover that the book had fallen open on Derbyshire and the Peak District. There was even a feeling of inevitability about it. You've known all along that that's where you wanted to go, she thought. Back to where it started, back to where your own grandparents lived – maybe still live – and back to the genesis of all those stories, handed down and handed on. They were most probably embroidered out of all recognition, those stories, but for all that they were evocative and bewitching and they reminded you that once upon a time there had been other worlds and other manners. They were threaded with history and adventure and with the kind of rose romance poetry that had gone out of fashion about six hundred years ago, but Felicity had loved them as a child, just as Bryony loved them now.

Here on the map were the places in those stories, so familiar that they were like a litany.

Tissington and Ilam and Thorpe. Scarcely more than dots on the map, and from the look of it untouched by sprawling modern housing estates, and still surrounded by farmlands and dales and fells. Farther north was Buxton with its famous caves and spring water, and a little farther east was the market town of Bakewell, where, if you drove through it, you could guarantee that somebody would make the joke about it being the town where the tarts came from. If she and Bryony went to live in this area, Bryony should have Bakewell tart for afternoon tea, and delicious sage Derby cheese. Felicity let her gaze move across the page, because in another minute she would find what she was looking for.

And then they were there, lightly marked as befitted their lowly position in the hierarchy of such things, but clearly marked all the same. They lay in a fold of the hills, near to the ancient Thor's Cave and within sighting distance of the Manifold River, in a slightly untidy heap as if they had been flung down by a careless hand and not tidied up: the cluster of tiny villages called collectively the Thanes. The names struck deep down into Felicity's mind and dragged up myriad childhood stories.

Thane St Mary with the ancient beautiful church of Mary the Virgin, where the graves dated as far back as 1535. Felicity had always visualized the churchyard as a haunted Gothic place, perpetually wreathed in pale mist, with rearing Saxon crosses looming out of the gloom.

And there was Croyse Thane, which was a corruption of the French *croix*, from which came the word crusade. Croyse Thane had been named for the unknown twins who had gone with Edward Plantagenet to one of the Crusades.

Slightly farther south lay Kings Thane, where the Tudor Foljambe, Francis, had presided over some kind of local witch trial. The cousins who had brought her up had vaguely thought that somebody in the village – the local priest, perhaps? – had considered it worth recording the trial and Kings Thane's modest claim to a place in history. They thought the account probably no longer existed, but if Felicity ever went to the area it might be interesting to try to find it.

What about Karabas? Supposing he comes after me? But even as the thought formed, another one was nudging it aside.

Surely this was the one place that Karabas would never look for her and Bryony? And the area was large enough for one solitary female and one small girl to blend unnoticed into the landscape. Felicity looked down at the map again. The village names looked back at her: the twins' Croyse Thane. Kings Thane. Thane St Mary.

And there, just on the edge, a little removed, was the place where once upon a time the great Foljambe estate had stood, and where the long-ago Richard Foljambe had built his modest little house – later to grow into a rich sprawling estate – and had hunted wolves for the Norman king.

Bishops Thane.

Chapter Twenty-Three

Felicity had managed to steer reasonably clear of the industrial areas of the north-west, but part of the journey looped unavoidably around the outskirts of Manchester, and from the motorway she could see grey-roofed factories silhouetted against the skies. It was just approaching one o'clock, and the grey January day was misted with a sleety rain. As the motorway curved, she could look across to one of the factories and see the workers starting to stream out for their lunch hour. There was a moment when, peering through the misty windscreen of Morag's Mini, it was like looking into a painting by Lowry.

She stopped at the next motorway service station for a sandwich lunch, and to consult the map once more. It was not a terribly difficult journey, but without a car it would have been a nightmare. Felicity was unutterably grateful to Morag who had practically thrust her into the driving seat and handed over the keys.

'House hunting will be impossible without a car,' Morag had said. 'I'll put you on my insurance for the weekend – yes, I know you'll reimburse me for it, you don't even need to say so. And although it's a bit elderly as cars go, it's good for a few thousand miles yet. It's never let me down, and it's just been serviced so you should be all right.'

Felicity made a mental note to bring a really nice thank-you present back for Morag. Something local, perhaps, maybe a piece of pottery or something like that. Just as she was setting off, she had said, trying to sound off-hand, 'Morag, you will keep an eye on Bryony, won't you?'

'Of course I will. We all will. She's sleeping in one of Primary Two's bedrooms for both nights – she's thrilled to pieces about that. There's the netball match on Saturday morning, and then I'm taking a bunch of them into Keswick afterwards. She'll be with people all the time, in fact I even hear on the grapevine that there's a midnight feast planned for Saturday. The little monsters are smuggling in pizzas and jam doughnuts, can you imagine the state the room will be in in the morning? But I'm turning a blind eye for once,' said Morag.

'It's just – if he should come back for her—'

Morag, like Brother Andrew, did not offer any false reassurances. She said, 'It's understandable you should think that. But he was no fool, that one, and I should think he'd be far too canny to even think about returning. But we know the concern, and one or the other of us will be permanently on watch – without Bryony realizing, of course. And we've got the phone number of that place where you're staying – the Prior's Arms.'

As Felicity crossed the Derbyshire border the signs of human habitation grew less, and the landscape gave way to gently undulating countryside with rolling farmlands on both sides of the road. If the earlier, inner-city view had been Lowry, this was surely like stepping into something from a Roland Hilder landscape, with layers of aerial perspective like a 3-D pop-up in a child's book. And here, as well, were the tiny B-roads leading off the main highway, like little capillaries branching with determined independence from a parent stem. They had place-names that could not possibly have existed anywhere other than the heartlands of Midland England – Wincle and Danebridge and Ramshorn.

The traffic had thinned out and Felicity was glad because she was able to spare some of her attention for the countryside. She had discovered that she was still absurdly jumpy at the sight of motorbikes; there had been several on the motorway, and then, just after leaving the motorway and heading down through Cheshire, one had seemed almost to be following her. She watched it nervously in the driving mirror, berating herself angrily while she did so, because, for heaven's sake, there were thousands of motorbikes on the road today! But she was still thankful to see it turn off just as they crossed from Cheshire into Derbyshire.

The past was tugging her on far more strongly, drawing her down to its heart, and Felicity felt delighted anticipation welling up. I'm about to see it all, she thought; all the places of all the stories.

But beneath the anticipation was still the dark undertow of fear. Would she and Bryony really be safe here? Would Karabas find out that they had left Bracken, and would he, with his uncanny intuition, guess where they had gone? Because if he knew so much about the family history, he would surely know that this was where they had lived; he would know that once upon a time the Foljambe estate had sprawled with feudal arrogance half across Bishops Thane. Would he then calculate that Felicity would come here, or would he have the understanding of bluff and double-bluff, and think it would be the last place she would flee to?

But there was no reason for him to come here; it was not as if any of the family were still living here. Felicity, driving more slowly and looking out for signposts to Bishops Thane, suspected that wherever she and Bryony went, she would worry about Karabas. And they had to find somewhere to live.

The Prior's Arms was midway between Bishops Thane and Thane St Mary, and Felicity found it without too much difficulty. She drove through Kings Thane – larger and more prosperous-looking than she had thought – and after a couple of wrong turnings eventually came upon it.

It was set back from the main road, and from the outside it might have been built any time during the last two hundred years. But inside the floors sloped and the ceilings were so low that you had to duck when you went through doorways. Felicity had a quick wash-and-brush-up after the journey, drank a cup of tea in the small reception lounge which had a pleasing scent of woodsmoke, and set off on a tour of the local estate agents. The afternoon would be devoted to gathering details of suitable properties, which she would study this evening. She had allotted as much of Saturday as possible for actually viewing likely houses.

The sleety rain had stopped and the countryside was spangled with thin dewy moisture. In the far distance were the forests of the National Park; here and there were white sprinklings of frost, just touching little patches of grass and tops of trees, as if quicksilver had leaked from the sky. It was the kind of day when you might very well imagine that ghosts were walking with you, but Felicity determined to ignore the ghosts, because this was a day for being sternly practical. It was a day for finding a sensible house that the monks would approve of, and that would be comfortable to live in and easy to maintain.

It ought to be easy enough to find a modern house with two or maybe three bedrooms and a bit of garden, not too far from buses and shops and a good school.

The house was the fourth one she looked at. It was on the edge of Bishops Thane, standing by itself at the end of a narrow farm track. Huge old trees formed a backdrop for it. It was called Charect Cottage and it was the most beautiful house Felicity had ever seen.

It was also the most derelict.

She suspected that she was hooked as soon as she stopped the car, and by the time she inserted the key into the lock and pushed the main front door open, she knew it for certain.

There were two rooms on the ground floor, one on each side of the door; the larger one had an inglenook fireplace and a bow window jutting out over a wildly overgrown garden at the house's rear. Behind the smaller room was a square, rather gloomy place with a deep, old-fashioned sink and a single rusting tap that looked as if it had spent the last ten years dripping. There was absolutely nothing else in the room to suggest that it might be intended for use as a kitchen. It was a rather dark room because of backing onto the start of National Park forestland.

But modern sinks could be fitted and antiquated plumbing could be brought up-to-date. Felicity's beautiful old Welsh dresser would look terrific in here – and the large oak table with the lovely graining. You would want proper quarry tiles on the floor and a rush mat or maybe even a rag rug . . .

The stairs creaked ominously, but at least the treads did not actually give way and she reached the upper floor safely. There was a big L-shaped landing, with two large bedrooms and a smaller one, and on the half-landing a smaller door opened onto a large boxroom. It was a bit small for a bedroom, but Felicity thought it would convert into a bathroom.

To even consider this as a possible home for herself and Bryony was the outside of madness. Even supposing the monks would finance it, it was still madness. Felicity, trying to hold on to a vestige of practicality, went carefully through the bedrooms, looking for signs of damp on the ceilings. There was nothing. With luck, then, the roof was sound. She went back downstairs, trying to decide if she would be able to recognize the smell of dry rot.

But the only scents downstairs were the ghosts of dried herbs in the kitchen and a faint drift of lavender in the room with the inglenook. It was immensely quiet, and Felicity had the feeling that she had slipped through a crack in time, and that she was in a place where all the clocks had slowed down and stopped. Or as if they were about to start going backwards . . .

She sat on the square window seat and stared into the tanglewood gardens. The light was draining from the day and there was a feeling of immense peace. I could live in this house, thought Felicity, leaning her head back against the wall. I feel immensely safe here – as if something's spun a protective shell around the house. I think that it might be slightly haunted, but I don't think I'd mind, because if anything walks here it's something gentle and a bit sad.

She was succumbing to the wildest madness, of course: what she ought to be doing was making an offer on the neat modern semi she had looked at earlier; two and a half bedrooms, living room, dining-kitchen, bathroom, and a briskly efficient central heating system.

She prowled through the rooms again. I'll find something terrible, she thought, half-hopefully. At any minute I'll come upon something – some huge fault – that makes this absolutely and once-and-for-all impractical.

But there was nothing. There were traces of damp around a couple of the windows, but that seemed to be due to rotting window frames. The only plumbing was the rusty cold-water tap in the sink, but when Felicity turned it the water ran out at once; brownish for a few minutes, but then clear. There was electricity, and although from the look of the switches it had been installed around the time of the Second World War, Felicity thought that to rewire a small house like this one would not be too costly.

She came back to the sitting room with the inglenook, and stood looking at the soft mellow brick of the fireplace, at the oak ceiling beams, and at the untrimmed lavender bush pushing against the bow window. The feeling of immense security came back, and with it old-fashioned words: haven. Sanctuary.

This isn't going to happen, said Felicity, firmly. It truly isn't. The monks won't play; they want something easy and modern; something that won't be any bother to them, and something that will re-sell easily at some unspecified time in the future. And so the sooner I put this beautiful derelict house out of my mind the better.

It was not until she was carefully locking the door that she at last looked with more attention at the surrounding countryside and at the forest itself.

'The estate agent says the original Charect Cottage was built in 1520,' said Felicity. 'In fact one of the rooms still has traces of the original structure – there's a beautiful old inglenook fireplace with panelling on each side. It used to be called Charect House when it was bigger and the name's been carried on.'

'I rather think that *charect* is an obsolete word for a charm,' said Brother Andrew, thoughtfully. 'A spell set down in writing – literally in characters – to ward off evil.'

Then that's it! Felicity thought. That's why there's that feeling of complete safety – that sensation of nothing-can-touch-me. It's had a charm woven around it and nothing evil can ever get inside – that's why I knew we'd be safe from Karabas there! Rot! said her cynical half. Medieval superstition.

She said aloud, 'That's rather interesting. If we take this any farther I'll try to find out a bit more.' And then, because it was important to remain wholly businesslike, she said, 'The first house was partly burned, but it was built up about a hundred years later, I think. They managed to save some of the original features, like the inglenook. Oh, and there're some ceiling beams that look pretty old. But most of the present cottage was built in 1740 for a gamekeeper or a steward attached to some large estate.' She thought her voice sounded acceptably off-hand about this last part. Because you don't know that the estate it was built for was the old Foljambe estate.

Brother Andrew said, 'It sounds a fascinating place.'

'Yes, it is.' Felicity looked at him very straightly. 'It isn't in the least the house I set out to find,' she said. 'The cottage itself is two hundred and fifty years old and parts – certainly the foundations – are another two hundred and fifty on top.

It's derelict, virtually unmodernized, and the forest's almost on the back doorstep.'

Brother Andrew waited.

'It's being auctioned in a couple of months,' said Felicity, 'along with four or five other smallish properties. They haven't set a reserve price yet, but the agent hinted at a figure which is about half the amount you're allowing. It might go for treble that sum, of course – country cottages are generally snapped up very smartly indeed.'

She leaned forward. 'I do realize all this sounds totally impractical, Brother Andrew. But would you just consider this: if the cottage really could be bought for that figure, then the other half of the money could be spent on modernizing it—' She stopped, and he finished the sentence, exactly as she had hoped.

'And we would end up owning a property worth at least twice as much as we'd spent,' said Brother Andrew, thoughtfully. 'Yes, I do see that.'

'And they say the Church is not venal,' murmured Felicity, and he gave her the sudden sweet smile.

'What's the area like? I mean, is this place – Bishops Thane – is it within practical reach of shops and roads and a railway station?'

'You'd be a bit stuck without a car,' said Felicity. 'But you wouldn't be entirely stranded. There's a village shop and post office, and there's a bus service. I think the nearest school would be in Ashbourne – that's about six miles away. And the house feels more isolated than it actually is, because it stands in about half an acre of land, and you can't see any other houses once you're inside – it's off the main road, along a little road that's not much more than a farm track.'

Andrew said thoughtfully, 'So it would be necessary to find out about rights-of-way on that.' He paused, and Felicity waited. 'As you say, it's almost certain to be out of the question,' he said, at last. 'But it might be a much better long-term investment for us. It might just be worth getting a few estimates for the major work. Could you do that? I mean, could you get them in time for the auction?'

'Oh yes,' said Felicity, who had no idea whether she could or not.

'Local builders would be best,' he said. 'See what you can

222

do, and we'll at least get our Finance Division to take a look at the figures. If they're even halfway possible I'll see if we can get somebody from the Church Architects to take a look in time for the auction. When is it? – oh, the twenty-eighth. That's a couple of weeks after our bicentenary celebration, isn't it? But listen, don't build your hopes up too high.'

'No, of course not.'

'It sounds an alluring part of the world.'

'It is,' said Felicity.

Bryony was pleased at being chosen to be part of the pageant telling how King Henry VIII had given Bracken Fields away as a present in 1540. The whole junior school was going to act out Henry presenting a scroll to the court gentleman – they were using the hockey field and the rest of the school and quite a lot of visitors would sit on chairs carried out there for the afternoon. A lot of other things would be happening all through the week, but this was going to be the first thing of all.

'You'll be opening the celebrations,' said Miss Mackenzie to them when they got the giggles at a rehearsal. 'And so it's important to get it right. People who don't concentrate won't be allowed to take part on the day.'

The senior school art classes had made the scroll which had spiky writing on it and coloured decorations at the start of each sentence, and the school orchestra was going to dress up as troubadours and play music that had been played in those days.

'It's *not* "Greensleeves",' said Mr Lucas, distractedly. 'If anyone else asks me if we're having "Greensleeves", I won't be responsible for my actions.'

Bryony was being a court lady for the afternoon, in a long green velvet gown with her hair in a kind of a hairnet with sparkly bits in it. She did not have any words to say, but she had to stand at the front and smile when the scroll was given and then join in a song.

It was all lavishly good. Everyone was starting to get hugely excited, and people were constantly called out of classes for rehearsals for the pageant or the orchestra, and then Father Abbot had to draw a name out of a hat to see who would present a bouquet to the Countess of Beck after the finals of the singing competition at Beck Old Hall.

Brother Stephen was telling everyone that it would probably rain for the whole Easter weekend, and people who were dressing up as troubadours looked worried in case the feathers in their hats got soggy or the rain spoiled violin strings and recorders. That was the trouble with open-air things, you worried in case the weather spoiled them.

'They're all in a shocking state of disruption,' said Brother Andrew in the common room.

'It's only for a few days,' said Brother Joseph, cosily.

'I still think it will rain,' said Brother Stephen, gloomily.

Chapter Twenty-Four

It did not rain. Felicity thought it would not have dared after so many people had put in so much work, and when so many local dignitaries were flocking to Bracken.

She was still feeling a bit sick in the mornings but she had managed to hide this from Morag and the staff. She would probably tell Morag about the child just before leaving Bracken. She was not going to tell Bryony until after they were settled in Charect Cottage. If they managed to buy Charect Cottage. It was important to keep saying this, like invoking a charm. In the meantime, it was nice that she was still slim enough to be able to wear ordinary clothes, which was one mercy, because this was a time for appearing businesslike and in control.

After some thought, she disinterred from the wardrobe a navy linen suit which had been bought for a friend's wedding in London, in another world and in another life. She could wear it for all the events, but for the daytime ones she could have a plain white shirt under the jacket, and for the slightly more formal events, like the choral finals at Beck Old Hall, she could swap to the cyclamen silk blouse or the saffron one. She thought she could allow herself something a bit more dressed-up for the Earl's supper, however; she still had the wine-coloured devoré two-piece or the Jasper Conran amber silk.

Having reached these sartorial decisions, she put on the suit, added shoes which were low-heeled enough for comfort, brushed her hair and surveyed herself in the mirror.

Cool and efficient navy-and-white elegance looked back. She had had her hair re-styled in Keswick last month, and it fell in a smooth chestnut bob. It's not bad, thought Felicity, critically. There was a sudden, delicious prickle of anticipation; half excitement, half stage-fright, because the next four days were the culmination of four months of hard work and careful planning, and nothing must be allowed to go wrong. For the next four days she was going to be on show, on call from dawn to dusk, and she would have to think on her feet because however much you planned things, there was always the unforeseen. Terrific, thought Felicity, and grinned at her reflection. She had forgotten how much she enjoyed this kind of thing.

She thrust the keys of the stable house into the jacket pocket, picked up the clip-board with the various lists of events and people and who was doing what, and who should be where and at what times, and set off for the fray.

With the disconcerting way that young children often have, the junior school's pageant illustrating Bracken Hall's history looked set to steal the entire show.

Felicity sat with Morag Mackenzie, who had been dashing between classrooms and the hockey field all morning, shepherding children and searching for last-minute items. She had, however, managed to scramble into the outfit which, after much anxious consultation with Felicity, she had bought for the celebrations. Felicity had guided the homely-featured, camel-haired Morag away from the beiges and fawns which made her practically vanish, and had got her into a bronze-green trouser suit which Morag thought outrageously daring, but which did good things for her figure and complexion.

'They're on their own now,' she said, sinking gratefully into the seat Felicity had kept for her, and studying the massed junior school who were being efficiently assembled by John Lucas. 'If they get anything wrong there'll be nothing I can do.'

'They'll be terrific, you know they will.'

'Revolting little monsters,' said Morag, with exasperated affection.

'In any case, it's a captive audience. Have you seen how many parents have come?'

Quite a lot of parents had come, which had pleased the monks greatly, and quite a large proportion had asked if there could be seats for younger or older brothers and sisters, or cousins, which had pleased Felicity because it indicated that the programme was attractive enough to draw in people other than doting mothers and fathers. Parents who lived near enough were coming just for a single event in which their offspring were performing, but a surprisingly large number were staying in the area for the whole weekend. Felicity had helped book hotels for some of them, and she and Morag, with John Lucas, had had three free lunches and two free dinners which had been the hotel managers' method of expressing their gratitude to Bracken.

'Father Abbot's arrived,' said Morag, turning round to scan the audience.

'Is Brother Joseph here?' said Felicity, grinning.

'Oh dear, poor Joseph.'

Father Abbot had unexpectedly decided to remember the medieval tradition of monasteries providing hospitality to all travellers, and had issued a firm edict that parents and visitors to Bracken on the day of the pageant must be fed by their own kitchens, which had catapulted Brother Joseph, never the most tranquil of monks, into a state of agitated activity. In the end the matter had been solved by the simple expedient of doubling up the domestic science classes for the run-up week to the celebrations, commandeering the results for the refectory's new and capacious deep freeze, and squeezing in an extra event to be called a senior school cocktail party.

'They can hand round drinks and food, and we can set up a display of some of their work,' said Brother Andrew, firmly. 'There's really no problem about any of it.'

'It isn't the work that's the problem, it's the *cooking*,' said Brother Joseph, distractedly, and was later heard bewailing the lower fourth's endeavours in the way of spinach quiche.

The upper fifth were all for boycotting the genteel buffet scheme and setting up a barbecue on the tennis courts for hamburgers and spare ribs, and a rumour of spiced rum punch being illicitly brewed in one of the sixth form bedrooms reached the monks' common room, but other than this the exercise had worked quite well.

The pageant was a triumph. The younger children were solemn and absorbed; the older ones had been gently dragooned by Morag and then ruthlessly dragooned by John Lucas and Brother Stephen so that they did not resort to squirm-making precocity, and the tale of how Henry VIII had made the Deed of Gift to the unknown gentleman was attractively unfolded.

The school orchestra painstakingly worked its way through appropriate music, starting with Palestrina madrigals, moving on to folk songs for the building of the first manor house in 1590, and ending with the conversion to the first school premises two hundred years earlier. For this last, the choir monks joined in, wearing the brown and white robes that were reserved for Sundays and feast days, and walking in procession across the outskirts of the field, singing an unaccompanied Gregorian plainchant as they came. They assembled without fuss at the southern end of the hockey field where the old oak trees made a natural frame for the grey stone house in the near distance, and as their voices mingled in seamless practised silkiness, and as the children's lighter voices blended in, absolute stillness descended on the audience.

Felicity felt a sudden lump in her throat, because this was all so unutterably beautiful – it was so *Englishly* beautiful – and so filled with happiness and with the uncomplicated delight of the monks themselves. She found herself wishing she could reach out and take hold of the moment and the feeling, and that she could fold it away so that at some future time she could unwrap it, and relive the rural beauty of the English afternoon and the singing of ancient sweet music, and the shining unworldly goodness of the monks.

The afternoon ended with everyone joining in a rousing rendition of the school song and with a standing ovation from the delighted parents and visitors. Felicity's gravity was severely upset by John Lucas's look of indignant outrage when one parent was heard to querulously ask why they had not had 'Greensleeves' for the Tudor section, and to demand of her neighbours that surely they could have done 'Greensleeves'?

She was walking across the main quadrangle in the slightly flat period between the ending of the pageant and the start of the much-debated senior school supper, when a flicker of movement caught her eye and made her turn sharply and look back over her shoulder. There was absolutely no reason to feel suddenly uneasy; it was half-past six and although the sun was beginning to sink and to shower its red and gold glow over the countryside, it was nowhere near being dark or even dusk yet. And it was not as if she was alone because people were scurrying about all over the school buildings and the grounds.

228

But nothing seemed to stir within the quadrangle, sun-drenched from the warm afternoon and surrounded on three sides by grey stone walls, half-covered with Virginia creeper. The setting sun was just touching the latticed windows of the first and second floors and it would be easy to persuade herself that this glinting light had tricked her vision. But she knew it had not. The movement, whatever it was, had not come from within the school, it had come from the quadrangle itself. She stood very still, and the feeling that she was being watched stole unmistakably over her. She turned slowly, scanning the corners of the courtyard, and as she did so the movement came again, and Felicity's heart gave a huge bound.

It seemed as if one minute he was not there, and the next minute, he was standing only a couple of yards away, the eyes that were so uncannily not his own watching her unblinkingly, the lithe muscular grace that was neither completely human nor wholly bestial more noticeable than she remembered.

He had grown a beard since the night he had stolen Bryony away; it made him look darker and wilder. But when he spoke, his voice was the same.

'I've been waiting for you, Felicity,' he said, softly, and Felicity hesitated, and then glanced over her shoulder again. No one was in sight and probably no one was in hearing either. She looked back at him, her mind in tumult, trying to decide whether to run or raise the alarm, or whether to keep him talking in the hope that someone would come along.

'There's no point in shouting for help,' said Karabas. 'No one's near. I made sure of that.'

Felicity said, 'So you still calculate your moment, do you?' and heard with astonished relief that her voice came out coldly and without the smallest tremor.

'I wanted to make sure you were still here,' he said.

'I am still here.' Felicity dredged up an edge of bitterness. 'I don't have anywhere else to go.'

'You don't, do you? Connor left you without any money or any home, didn't he?' said Karabas. 'You see, we know about all that, Felicity.'

'Well, good for you,' said Felicity sarcastically, but a tiny spiral of triumph had uncurled, because he had not guessed her plans to leave Bracken; he had been assuming she would have to stay. She looked at him and thought: you've learned a lot about the modern world, Karabas, you and your strange people, but you haven't learned quite enough! You haven't learned that people help one another when there's trouble. I'm going to outwit you, Karabas, thought Felicity, exultantly. You and your freakish people!

She said, 'Did you come here to gloat? Or only to check on me?'

'I came here to remind you that I still want Bryony,' he said.

'Well, you won't have her – you won't ever have her.'

'Oh yes I will,' said Karabas. He took a step towards her.

'Stay there,' said Felicity, backing away, and for the first time her voice sounded shrill with panic. 'Don't come any nearer. If you do I'll yell the place down!'

'Scream away. Before anyone gets here I'll be out of reach. To scream would do you no good at all, my dear.'

My dear . . . Oh God, there it was again – the lick of sensuous macabre sexuality.

'You'd be caught,' said Felicity.

'I wasn't caught last time, was I? Even though you broke our bargain, Felicity.'

'We didn't have a bargain!' said Felicity, angrily. 'I'd rather bargain with the devil than with you!'

Unexpectedly he smiled. The dark beard made his teeth look very white and very strong. 'Even without bargains, we still want Bryony,' he said. 'We still want to find out if her conception was simply one of Nature's quirks, or whether it really does mark the start of a new path in mankind's development.' He considered her for a moment, his eyes sliding over her body, and without warning intimacy flared in his eyes.

'So,' he said at last, 'it happened, did it? I gave you a child. That's very intriguing.'

'I'm going to have it aborted,' said Felicity at once.

'Oh Felicity,' said Karabas. His voice was low and silky. 'Would you really kill our baby?'

'I wish I could kill the memory of its conception!' said Felicity, furiously.

He looked at her for a moment, and then said, very softly, 'No, you don't.'

'Oh God, I do, I do! I hated it. I hated every second of it. I loathe you!'

'Oh no, you don't,' he said again.

They stared at one another, and suddenly and shamefully, the memory of the fire-washed night when he had raped her with that mixture of ferocity and sensuality scalded through her mind.

'You see?' said Karabas, and smiled with what Felicity could have almost believed was genuine affection. 'And now I will be watching you even more closely,' he said.

At once a wholly different fear gripped her. She said, in a voice of extreme horror, 'You want them both. You want Bryony and now you want the unborn child.'

'Yes, of course.'

Of course he would want them both. 'Then,' said Felicity, with an asperity she was not feeling, 'I expect that means that I've got a stay of execution until after the birth. But you'll never get away with it. You do know that? You do know that the police are still looking for you.'

'Oh Felicity,' he said, in a soft caressing voice that made her skin tingle. (With fear—? Yes, of course it's with fear!) 'You of all people should remember how good I am at assuming protective coloration.'

The sun was sinking fast, but as he said this the dying glow seemed to wash over him, giving him the eerie seductive beauty that Felicity remembered so well – too well – from that appalling night.

'I'm going to be near to you all the time,' said Karabas, coming a step closer. 'You'll never be quite sure where I am. You'll imagine that you see me in the shadowy corners of gardens, or stealing along behind you if you walk down a lonely road.' He paused. 'And sometimes you'll think I'm there inside the house with you,' he said. 'Because I'm very good at getting into houses without being seen. I creep in during the day, and I hide until it's dark – until all the doors are locked against intruders. Remember that, Felicity, when you lock your doors at night. Remember that you might not be locking me out, you might be locking me in with you . . .'

For a dreadful moment Felicity thought his lips and the lower part of his jaw narrowed and took on the aspect of a pointed muzzle. She took an involuntary step backwards, but before she could speak he turned and went swiftly across the darkening courtyard, and was lost in the thickening shadows of the encroaching twilight.

Felicity was left a prey to a jumble of conflicting emotions and agonizing indecision. The first, reflex reaction was to dash to the nearest phone and summon the police, but Felicity discarded this almost at once. To call the police now would not be a great deal of practical use: for one thing by the time they got here – by the time they had managed to get through the crush of people inside Bracken's grounds – it would be too late. Because he would be over the hills and far away. Because he's the traveller who travels light and by the dark of the night, and no one sees him or even suspects he's there ... And I have absolutely no idea where he might have gone.

But even more powerful an argument was that churning it all up again might cause irreparable damage to Bryony. Felicity was never going to forget Bryony's white, determinedly courageous little face on the night Karabas took her. She thought Bryony had just about managed to banish the entire thing and she thought she would do absolutely anything in the world to make sure it stayed banished.

And we're safe for the time being, thought Felicity. He said we were safe until the other child was born. And by that time I'll be miles away; I'll be in Charect Cottage, the sanctuary place – oh please let it happen! – and I'll have left Bracken so stealthily and so secretively that Karabas won't know until it's too late. And in the meantime, as everyone had kept telling her, life went on and the bicentenary celebrations went on, and there was a job to cope with.

Felicity dragged out the amber silk for the supper at Beck Old Hall, doing so more or less at random. Disconcertingly, a flicker of memory came with it – herself and Connor attending a more than usually grand dinner at the Dorchester; Connor dressed in the sharp black and white formality of evening dress; Felicity in the amber silk. That had been the night he had turned up with a half-pint flagon of *Je Reviens*, and the extravagantly costly brown velvet cloak. 'You look like something out of a woodland fable in those colours,' he had said when she was dressed. 'A tree nymph or a naiad.'

Felicity had enjoyed sweeping into the foyer in the velvet cloak, and she had enjoyed seeing the females flock round Con, because in those days she had still trusted him. At this distance, she could not decide whether she had been smug or simply naive.

When she had packed up the London house the velvet cloak was nowhere to be found, but she had put the amber dress in one of the suitcases. When she put it on tonight, it still smelled of *Je Reviens*. Felicity sat down suddenly on the bed, the memories crowding in. *Je Reviens* . . . *I will return* . . .

Oh damn! thought Felicity, angrily blinking back tears. Connor, I don't want to feel like this! I don't *want* to keep remembering you, and above all, I don't want you to keep looking at me out of that evil creature's eyes! She snatched up her coat and went swiftly out of the stable house.

By the time she had reached Beck Old Hall, with everyone assembling in the ballroom for the choral contest final, it was too late to do anything other than sort out the last-minute panics, and then watch John Lucas lead the three finalists through their performances. It had been decided to have three rather than just two finalists, because, as Morag had pointed out, two sets of losers could commiserate with one another, whereas a sole loser would feel it more acutely. For this reason, they were awarding a joint runner-up prize, which was a block of tickets to both schools for Halle Orchestra and BBC Philharmonic concerts that summer.

'The artless little grubs will probably say they'd rather go to a pop concert,' John Lucas had said, gloomily. 'But we'll do it anyway.'

Felicity thought she managed to behave as if nothing in the least untoward had happened. She responded normally to everything that people said to her; she listened with apparent absorption and seamless patience to visiting teachers who were determined to sing the praises of their own entrants, and she helped shepherd the smallest and most nervous performers to the lavatories and found tissues for those who had forgotten handkerchiefs.

She dealt efficiently with the bishop who had benignly turned up for tomorrow's High Mass half a day before anyone was expecting him; remembered that the correct method of address for a bishop was My Lord, and detailed an enthusiastic fifth former, who was acting as runner, to stand guard on the front steps so that the Bracken Hall party could be apprised of their prelate's premature arrival.

After this, she warded off the Earl's rather heavy-handed advances and hoped she had done so tactfully – Morag was right about the Earl having been a bit of a lad at one time – and finally sank gratefully into a seat halfway down the hall.

Chapter Twenty-Five

'There's only one thing to be done,' said Felicity, once again seated opposite Brother Andrew in the quiet, book-lined room. 'And that's to get away as unobtrusively as possible.'

For answer, Brother Andrew said, 'Why on earth didn't you tell somebody at the time?' And then, almost in the same breath, 'No, all right, I understand your reasons.' He frowned, thinking, and then said, 'I think you're right about leaving Bracken inconspicuously.'

'The job here's over anyway. I wish it wasn't,' said Felicity.

'So do we. We've liked having you here. We've liked having Bryony as well. But you'll come back to see us?'

'Of course I will,' said Felicity, hoping this would be possible. 'But I think we should wait until I'm safely fixed far away from Bracken before telling the police about Karabas's reappearance. Until then, absolute secrecy.'

'I agree,' said Andrew, after a moment. 'No one in the school knows where you're going, anyway – apart from Morag Mackenzie, that is, and you can trust Morag with your life.' He paused, and then said, 'We'd better talk about Charect Cottage, hadn't we?'

'Yes.' Felicity leaned forward, pressing her hands together, annoyed to find that her heart was suddenly beating faster. She said, 'The surveys and building estimates are all coming in more or less satisfactorily.'

'Yes. I see,' said Brother Andrew, 'that the surveyors are cautiously optimistic and the builders are subtly pessimistic.'

'Yes, but surely that's the right way round; you don't want your own surveyor being gloomy,' said Felicity, 'any more than you want the builder telling you cheerfully that nothing much needs doing – and then finding a whole raft of things once he starts work.'

'True.' Andrew went on studying the reports that Felicity

had put in a file for him the previous day. She knew them practically by heart now, and what they effectively and collectively said was that the house was in a shockingly dilapidated state; that wiring, plumbing, damp-proofing and timber treatment were needed; that a bathroom and kitchen had to be provided; that anyone taking all this on would have to be slightly mad or very rich or possibly both, but that providing all this was understood, the fabric and foundations – not to mention the roof – were a whole lot sounder than any house that age had any right to be. And finally, that if the work was done to an acceptable standard, the present negligible value would very probably increase five-fold.

'What do you think?' said Felicity, at last. 'Can I do it? I mean – if I can get it at the reserve figure, and if I mastermind the work and promise not to trouble anybody with that part of it, is the Church prepared to fund it?'

'Could you cope with it? There's a great deal of work here.' He looked back at the sheaf of reports.

'Yes,' said Felicity, quelling a sudden spiral of excitement. 'Yes, I could.'

'What about getting to and from places? Bryony's school and so on? The cottage sounds a bit isolated.'

'I've thought about that and I think that if I'm careful I could squeeze enough money for a small second-hand car. In fact,' said Felicity, wondering how far she should go, 'Morag is thinking of up-grading her Mini. I haven't talked to her yet, but it would be a good possibility.'

'Yes, I see. You'd probably have to move in before some of the work was completed, wouldn't you? Would that be a problem?'

'No. I don't care if it means camping on the floor in sleeping bags while the house is rebuilt around us—'

'We'll lend you a primus stove,' said Brother Andrew, and there, again, was the sudden sweet smile.

Bryony was pretty sad about leaving Bracken, even though she had known, really, that they were only here for a short time. She had thought they would go back to London, but mother said no, they were going somewhere quite different, and then had smiled the special smile which Bryony thought made mother look the most absolutely beautiful person in the world.

It was then that mother had asked how Bryony would feel about going to live near to the wildwood – the real true wildwood where Richard Foljambe and the twins and Thomas who had been Sir Thomas had all lived.

This was just about the most lavishly perfect thing that had ever happened in the whole of Bryony's life and probably in the whole of anybody's life anywhere in the world. Bryony listened carefully, even though her insides were doing delighted somersaults, and mother explained that there might be a house they could live in right on the edge of the wildwood.

And it was the dearest little house ever, said mother, and Bryony saw that mother had what Bryony called the *shining* look that she hardly ever had these days, on account of father having died and there not being very much money. But she had the shining look now, as she explained that there were going to be builders and plumbers looking at the house this very Friday and on Saturday was the auction which was when the house was being sold. Miss Mackenzie had said that Bryony could have a special half-day holiday and they could borrow her car, which meant that mother could take Bryony to see the house in the wildwood. And if Bryony liked it, and if all the builders and people liked it they were going to try to buy it at the auction.

Bryony was enchanted with the village called Bishops Thane, and she had been enchanted with the other places as well. Mother had pointed the signposts out as they drove along; there was Thane St Mary, and there was Croyse Thane which was named for Alain and Robin, and which had an iron cross at the centre of the village in memory of them going off on a Crusade.

'And down that road just there is Kings Thane – that's the biggest of the villages,' said mother, pointing.

'Gosh. Have you been there?'

'Not yet.' Mother frowned into the driving mirror. 'Wretched traffic,' she said, half to herself. 'Wretched motorbikes hogging the centre of the road.' And then, just as Bryony was starting to remember about Karabas and the growling motorbike at Bracken, mother suddenly said, 'Look, we're here – this is the Prior's Arms where we'll be staying,' and Bryony was so delighted at the thought of staying in a real, grown-up hotel, and at knowing they would be seeing the wildwood very soon, that she forgot all about people who rode on black motorbikes that looked like snarling wolves.

Mother turned off the road and parked carefully at the side of the building. 'We'll unpack, have a cup of tea, and then it'll be time to meet the builders.'

As they drove towards the house Bryony could see the forest from the road; it was a huge, sprawly, green and gold mass, and she knew at once that it was the wildwood – the real wildwood, where the Foljambes had hunted wolves, and where Richard and Madeleine had built the house, and where Edmund had lived, and where the twins and all the other people of the stories had lived. This was so absolutely lavishly good that she did not want to speak at all, and mother seemed to understand, because she did not speak either.

The wildwood was green and gold on account of it being nearly spring. Bits of sunlight glinted through the leaves and even from the road Bryony could see that there were little twisting paths going in and out of the trees, and she knew exactly how it would feel to tread on those paths. They would be very soft and very quiet because of all the leaves and bracken that had fallen onto them in the autumn, and you would be able to pad silently along with no one hearing you and no one knowing you were there. And as you went padding along, you would hear birds singing and you might hear little scufflings of rabbits and squirrels as well. And the really curious thing – the really extraordinarily peculiar thing – was that ever since Bryony had known the stories, ever since she had known about the wildwood and all the people who had lived there, she had secretly thought it might be a scary, spooky old place. It might very well turn out to be a place that you would like to walk into when it was day, but that you would not want to walk in after it was dark and never *ever* on your own.

But Bryony knew at once that the wildwood was not the least bit frightening. It was beautiful and friendly and it was not a place that she would ever be afraid of, certainly not in the way she had been afraid of the wildwood at Bracken. She thought if they came to live here she would walk in the wildwood quite a lot, and she would know that Edmund and the twins and all the others had walked there.

The house was the best house she had ever seen. It was

right on the edge of the wildwood, just as mother had said, and it did not matter in the least that it was tumbly-down. Mother said Bryony could have the bedroom that looked onto the forest at the back: she could have whatever colours she liked in it. Bryony thought she would like to have green, so that it would look as if the forest was inside the room. That would be pretty good.

Mother met two men who talked about making a bathroom and a kitchen, and who drew diagrams to show how it could be done. There was something called a soakaway and something else called a septic tank. People at Bracken said that if things were utterly dreadful they were *septic*, like having double maths with Mr Bryant or Latin with Brother Andrew. Bryony thought this was a different kind of septic, however.

In one of the downstairs rooms was a brick fireplace that went all the way up to the ceiling and had alcoves on each side. She sat for a long time by the brick chimney breast while mother was talking about kitchens and bathrooms, and after a little while she began to have the feeling that once upon a time somebody had lived here who had liked to sit in this seat and enjoy the firelight in the evenings. It had been somebody who was sad and lonely and frightened – although it was not a frightening thing to know this, it only made you feel sorry for the person.

Bryony thought it had been a lady who might have been called Isobel and that she had lived in the house that had been here before this one was built. Mother had said that there had been another house on the site hundreds of years ago. Isobel could have lived in that. Bryony did not see why this could not have happened. She thought there would have been a servant who lived with her on account of Isobel's family being quite rich.

What Bryony decided had happened all those hundreds of years ago, was that Isobel had fallen in love with a man who had come to the village unexpectedly – it had been really seriously falling in love, not like people in pop songs or TV adverts. It had been more like people in sad films or books. The man had been very good-looking and very charming so that to start with everyone had liked him, but in the end he had done something so lavishly bad that everyone had seen that actually he was evil and cruel. This was something that might very easily happen; Bryony knew that because of Karabas. She was not absolutely certain what it was that this man had done, but she thought the people living in Isobel's village had punished him. They had wanted to punish Isobel as well, only she had been smuggled away to Charect Cottage.

Mother had said Brother Andrew thought the word *charect* meant a charm that somebody had written down to keep evil away, or perhaps illness. It was rather nice, said mother, sounding pleased, to think that they might live in a house that had a charm to keep all the bad things away.

But Bryony, curled up in the chimney corner, knew that the charm that had once been spun inside Charect Cottage and around its gardens had had nothing to do with illness and she knew it had not just been a vague spell meant to keep away bad things in general.

It was a very firm, very definite charm, and it had been written for the sad, frightened lady called Isobel who had been so terrified of the villagers and of the man she had fallen in love with, that her servant had got the charm to protect her. Then she had felt safe.

Felicity had been expecting the euphoria of the last twenty-four hours to evaporate once she got to the auction, but it did not.

She was not precisely nervous about bidding for Charect Cottage, but she was strongly aware of being on unfamiliar territory. It was ridiculous to remember all the jokes about people at auctions sneezing or waving to a friend and ending up owning tumbling-down stately homes with thirty bedrooms, no roof and a cesspit, but she did remember them.

The auction took place in an upstairs room of the Prior's Arms which was highly convenient. Felicity explained to Bryony about sitting very quietly while all the houses were being sold, and gave her a catalogue with the six house lots listed. Charect Cottage was number four which was good because it meant that Felicity could watch what other people did, and see how bids were made and what the correct procedures were. In her hand was a small square of card with the number twenty-one written in large, thick characters, which would identify her to the auctioneer, and in her handbag was the name and address of the diocesan solicitors for this area.

While they waited for the auction to start she and Bryony studied their catalogue and tried to guess which of the people present were interested in which house. This fascinated Bryony, who loved looking at people.

The catalogue showed a photograph of each house, but whoever had been detailed to photograph Charect Cottage had clearly not thought it worth waiting for a sunny day because if you went by the photo you would imagine it to be the bleakest hovel ever built. Felicity pointed this out to Bryony, and said that with any luck it would put everybody else off, and no one would try to outbid them.

'Once it wasn't so small,' said Bryony thoughtfully, tracing the dark lowering house with the tip of her finger. 'Once it was quite a big house.'

'Yes, there was another house on the site before this one. In fact I think there've been two.'

'The first house of all was quite big,' said Bryony. 'It had timbers nailed onto the outside and there was a secret hidey-hole behind the chimney.'

Felicity looked at her carefully, and then said, 'Darling, is this one of your tales or have you heard someone talking about Charect since we got here?'

'No, it's all true, there was a hidey-hole and you had to slide a panel back and people who went to the wrong church, or sometimes monks, had to hide there.' Bryony wondered whether to explain about Isobel, but mother was wearing the concerned look she sometimes got if Bryony tried to explain about the mind-pictures, and so Bryony said, 'The man with the glasses is going onto the stage. Does that mean the auction is going to begin?'

'It looks like it. Hush now, because I want to see how people bid for the other houses, so I'll know what to do when it's our turn.'

The auctioneer walked to the table set out for him and reached for a gavel. Felicity watched and listened carefully and wished her heart would stop beating so fast.

But when Lot Four was called her heart gave a huge bound of excitement, and she understood for the first time why people got so carried away at auctions.

The auctioneer suggested that bidding might respectably start at twenty-five thousand, and Felicity raised the cardboard square and saw him nod. The sudden rush of excitement increased. This is it.

Chapter Twenty-Six

Felicity and Bryony had a special supper at the Prior's Arms that night, to celebrate buying Charect Cottage so easily.

Mother telephoned Bracken Hall and Bryony heard her talking to Brother Andrew, and saying, 'Twenty-five thousand. Yes, truly! No, I couldn't believe it either! No, there were absolutely no other bids.' There was a pause, and then mother said, 'No, of course there's nothing wrong with the house. It's been examined so thoroughly that it's practically been taken apart and each brick checked before putting it back together!' And then, slowly, as if a new idea had occurred to her, 'Well, yes, I suppose there could be some kind of local superstition about it – especially with the name. No, it wouldn't worry me in the least, of course it wouldn't.' She hung up, looked at Bryony as if she might be deciding whether to say something or not, and then said, 'Are you ready to go downstairs?'

The supper was in the dining room, and it was a proper grown-up supper with soup first, and then a chicken dish and chocolate pudding to finish. Mother had a glass of wine and Bryony had ginger beer.

'You'll get hiccups and you won't be able to sleep,' said mother.

'If I won't be able to sleep, it'll be on account of being 'cited about the house. Could we go back to look at it?'

'Tonight?'

'Well, because I'd like to see what it looks like at night.' Bryony finished the last spoonful of chocolate pudding, and laid her spoon down regretfully. It was always a pity when you came to the end of any chocolate pudding and this had been a specially good one.

'You're crazy,' said mother, but her eyes had the shining look. 'If we did drive out there we wouldn't be able to go inside.

I shan't be given the keys until Monday when the deposit cheque's cleared by the bank.'

Bryony only vaguely followed this. She said, 'I don't want to go inside. I'd just like to see the forest and the house again.'

Felicity glanced at the window where shadows were already pressing against the panes. Go out to that tanglewood desolate place in this gathering dusk? But it's a sanctuary place, she thought. And maybe it would lay the ghosts for both of them. She looked back at Bryony.

'All right,' said Felicity, and grinned. 'If I'm driving again tonight it's a good thing I only had one glass of wine.'

Charect Cottage was just as good as Bryony remembered, and the wildwood was terrific. It was filled with mysterious shadows and although the little paths were still there, they looked different now. She remembered that, after all, this was the real wildwood where the wolves had lived, and that somewhere in this massive sprawly forest was the house where Richard Foljambe's servant, Edmund, had been killed by the thing in the cellar, and that the house and the cellar might still be there. This ought to have been frightening, but it was toe-curlingly exciting.

Even though it was on the edge of the wildwood, Charect Cottage was a good place. Isobel had known that she was safe in Charect Cottage, which had been Charect House then. Bryony thought she and mother would be safe here as well.

On the way back they had to pull Miss Mackenzie's Mini onto the grass verge to let a Range Rover get past. There were two men in the front; and as the Range Rover inched past and drew level with them, the man who was driving put up a hand to mother.

'Did he know you?' asked Bryony, turning round to look through the window.

'No, he was just saying thank you to me for letting him get by. At least—' Mother slowed down and looked in the driving mirror to watch the Range Rover as it drove away into the night.

'What?'

Mother said slowly, 'It's odd you should say that, because I did think he looked vaguely familiar for a moment.' She frowned, as if she was thinking hard about something, and then said, 'No, it's absurd. Of course it isn't anyone I know. Here's the Prior's Arms again.'

It was exciting to be going back into the Prior's Arms which felt quite different at this time of night. It was practically as late as ten o'clock. People were still drinking in the little bar, and Bryony was allowed to ask for their key at the desk.

Piers knew it was the height of absurdity to have this growing sense of Karabas's closeness, but he had it very strongly indeed.

They had been in Kings Thane for several weeks, exploring the area carefully, working on the south and east sides of the village first, for no other reason than that they had to start somewhere. They had quartered the area, and Nina and Priscilla had spent some time in the library headquarters at Matlock, compiling lists of record offices and archivists' departments and of small branch libraries in which they could search for references to the Foljambes.

But so far there had been nothing at all, and several times Piers was on the point of calling the whole project off. What am I doing here? he thought. What am I doing returning to this house?

Every night brought appalling nightmares, from which he woke drenched in sweat and gasping. They were the nightmares of his childhood: swift, vivid glimpses of the horrors that lay in wait in the ancient eternal world that walked alongside this one: macabre things that occasionally crawled up out of the nightmare into a too-imaginative child's bedroom . . .

His mother was there, of course, walking through the nightmare landscapes, reaching down to the bed to caress him with curving, greedy hands that dripped with the blood of his own dead brother. But when she smiled the dreadful seductive smile that had stayed with Piers for twenty years, there was still the shameful hardening between his legs. Go away! cried Piers to the terrible thing that beckoned with such evil allure. Go away, I've done with you!

It was Tybalt who found the old print of the house. He had been detailed to ransack libraries for locally-printed books on the area, and had become extremely glum at his lack of headway. He had turned his attention to the house one dull, rainy morning, saying with owlish solemnity that a house whose

245

foundations went back to Tudor times might have a few clues to be uncovered.

'Oh God, he'll start ransacking the attics if you don't watch him,' said Toby, who was by now working on two other projects, but travelled to Kings Thane once every ten days or so.

'Listen, I wouldn't do anything like that without Dr Adair's permission—' began Tybalt indignantly.

Piers said, 'Tybalt, I don't care where you go – you can climb up the inside of the chimneys if you think there's anything worth finding.'

Tybalt did not climb up the chimneys, nor did he go up to the attics. 'Not yet, anyhow,' he said. But in a dimly lit alcove near the top of a back stair which none of them used, somebody had hung a faded, framed print of the original Weston House. Tybalt brought it to the supper table, the cowlick of hair tumbling over his forehead in excitement, making him look even younger than he actually was.

By tacit consent the team had adopted the kitchen as their meeting room; as Nina said, it was rather cosy to sit drinking a cup of coffee after supper with the percolator within reach for refills, and share the day's gleanings. Piers thought the truth was that the kitchen was the only room that had fully escaped the creeping menace of the rest of the house, but he had not said anything.

The wooden frame was dry and cracked and the surface of the print itself was spotted with damp, but Tybalt displayed it with glee.

'See, it's the house as it was in 1535,' he explained earnestly. 'Well, I guess it's an artist's impression, really. But it was pretty large, and there're all these cute twisty chimneys and things.'

'Tudor chimneys,' said Priscilla, leaning over to see.

'Never speak ill of a Tudor chimney or its pot,' remarked Toby. 'They were masters of pot and chimney, the Tudors.'

'What happened to the house, Piers?' asked Priscilla. 'Do you know?'

'It burned down,' said Piers. 'Fifteen-forty, or thereabouts, I think.'

'Well, that's absolutely right, because if you look right here there's a label on the back that says, "Weston House before the fire of fifteen-forty."'

Piers said, before he realized, 'My mother's maiden name was Weston.'

'Really?'

'Yes, really.'

Tybalt digested this with deep pleasure, and then said, 'This print was made in – uh – 1780. I guess that would be from some sketch somebody found somewhere, wouldn't it?'

Why did the house burn down?' asked Nina. 'I mean – what caused the fire?'

'No idea. But I think it was quite extensive. Only the foundations escaped. Oh, and the servants' rooms.'

Tybalt was charmed to hear his idol referring to family servants in this throwaway fashion.

'Even if you allow for the artist getting carried away, it was a lovely house, wasn't it?' said Nina, sighing romantically over the print.

'I do hate to pour cold water on these transports,' said Priscilla, 'but does this actually get us nearer to the Foljambes? Or to Karabas?'

'I'm afraid not,' said Piers. 'It's very interesting, but I do think, Tybalt, that you'd better carry on with ransacking the libraries. Sorry it's a bit of a dry task and all that.'

Tybalt instantly became afflicted with preternatural solemnity and said it was not dry at all, in fact it was an honour to be allowed to do it.

It was Toby who said, 'I tell you what Tybalt might do, Piers, and it might be more productive—'

'Yes?' said Piers, as Tybalt looked up hopefully.

'Churches,' said Toby. 'Didn't Nina get a list of local ones from the library headquarters in Matlock?'

'Oh yes, I did.'

Toby said, 'It's astonishing the information you can get from graveyards and parish records. If Tybalt could tour round the older ones and see if there're any Foljambes lurking in the graveyards or listed on memorial tablets—'

'Good idea,' said Piers. 'Tybalt, how about it?'

'I'd *love* to!' said Tybalt, pink-cheeked.

Piers said, 'There's one in Thane St Mary that's quite old. I remember being taken there a few times. You might start there.'

It had been a very good idea of Toby's to check the churches, and it was truly exhilarating to be driving through the English countryside like this. Tybalt had borrowed Dr Adair's Range Rover and Dietfreid's map, and had charted himself a careful route right after breakfast.

He was following Dr Adair's suggestion, and starting with the Church of St Mary the Virgin. The printed list that Nina had obtained gave helpful potted backgrounds, and it appeared that at the time of the Reformation St Mary's had been one of the stubbornest strongholds of Papist England, although by great good luck it had escaped Cromwell's vandals during the Civil War. Tybalt read this and thought it was an absolute knock-out the way you kept tripping over these fragments of history.

But to start with the Thane St Mary church was kind of disappointing. It was a whole lot smaller than Tybalt had been expecting, although he guessed that there would not have been terrifically big congregations in a place like this. He peered respectfully inside and thought that about sixty people could probably be housed. There was the immense hush you got in most churches along with faint scents of damp and cold stone and polish. Tybalt tiptoed reverently around the interior, conscientiously searching for monuments or tombs or memorial tablets.

There was a really beautiful rose window in the western wall which would look spectacular with the setting sun behind it, and there were curiously carved gargoyles and a deep old font with a practically indecipherable date of 1420 carved into its underside. There was even a dusty, half-disintegrated paper garland draped over a stone boss, with a little hand-written card beneath explaining that it had been the custom to put these paper garlands on the coffins of unmarried ladies, and that it was called a Virgin Crant. Tybalt found this faintly grisly.

But of Foljambes there were no traces at all.

He retraced his steps a bit despondently, closing the massive oak door, and then going back to put some money into the collecting boxes that stood just inside. It would be the height of discourtesy to tramp round a church without so much as a by-your-leave, and not make some kind of contribution. After thought he put two pounds each in the boxes labelled 'Church Restoration' and 'Almshouses'.

The churchyard was a rather dismal place, but Tybalt felt a strong empathy with it. It was still quite early in the day and there was a thin mist everywhere. The graves were scattered around: they looked a bit haphazard to Tybalt who was accustomed to the neat lawns of his own country's Gardens of Rest, and the ground was certainly very uneven. But it thrilled him to the depths of his romantic soul to see ancient elaborate Saxon crosses marking some of the graves.

He was not expecting to find anything, of course. He was, truth to tell, becoming a bit discouraged about the search, although it had been great to find that old print of Weston House. The mist was dissolving into a thin chilly rain – the kind that drenched you to the skin before you realized it was there. Tybalt shivered, turned up his coat collar, and went doggedly on. Narrow, badly tended paths wound in and out of the graves, and the trees dipped their boughs, their leaves dark green and dripping with moisture.

He was among the oldest of the graves now, and there was a feeling of immense desolation and silence as if anyone hardly ever came here. Tybalt was not surprised.

And then without warning it was there. Set at the farthest end, practically hidden by several elaborate headstones of later graves, some of which had winged angels holding up scrolled Books of Judgement. There were no stone angels or Books of Judgement on the little solitary grave under the old cedars; grass had grown thickly over the mound, and Tybalt would probably have missed it altogether if it had not been for the small headstone marking it. The headstone had slipped with the settlement of the ground, so that it toppled drunkenly to one side, but at some time during the centuries somebody had planted a little bush of rosemary at the grave's centre.

Carved into the skewed headstone was the usual Latin memorial: Tybalt was not very fluent in Latin but he had had to learn a smattering of it. He did not for the minute bother to try translating.

Because there at the centre, the letters eroded and pitted by time and the elements but still readable, was the information that here lay the body of Sir Francis Foljambe, 1515 to 1560, who had died without issue or wife, and upon whose soul it was requested that God had mercy.

Nina said, 'So they really were here.'

'It looks like it. It was pretty creepy finding the grave,' said

Tybalt. 'Uh, I took a couple of Polaroid shots of it.' He put these on the table with the air of a pleased retriever.

'You're right, it is creepy,' said Nina, looking at the photographs and passing them to Dietfreid. 'I don't know about the rest of you, but it gives me the oddest feeling to know that we're right, and they really did live here.'

'And that they were living around here as recently as 1560,' said Tybalt, who understood by this time that 1560 was practically like yesterday to the British.

Dietfreid, poring over the photographs, said, 'This is very good. I do not know where we should go from here, however.'

'Well don't look at me for help, dearie, I'm just a downtrodden researcher.'

'We're getting closer to Karabas's people,' said Nina, suddenly. 'Piers, aren't we getting closer?'

Piers said, softly, 'Either we're getting closer to them, Nina, or—'

'Or?'

'Or they're getting closer to us.'

There was a rather unpleasant silence, and then Priscilla said briskly, 'Never mind who's getting close to whom. At least we know we're in the right part of the country. All we've got to do now is find the exact place.'

'I suppose you think that once we find where they lived we'll automatically find Karabas, cosily holed up in the ruins of the ancestral home, with the welcome mat hung out,' remarked Toby.

'Isn't that why we came to Derbyshire?' said Priscilla, at once. 'Didn't we agree he'd head out here?'

'Yes, because he took a vow to seek out and destroy the accursed Foljambe line,' murmured Toby.

'Will you *stop* that!'

Piers grinned, but said, 'Listen, now that we know we've hit the target we'd better alter the angle of attack. We'll draw up a list of all the large houses hereabouts and try to find out who owned them or lived in them. Some might be nothing more than ruins and some will have been taken over by the National Trust or English Heritage. But we can't afford to miss a single one.'

'We could talk to local people, as well,' said Nina eagerly. 'I know you didn't hear anything when you lived here, Piers, but

I don't believe that the Foljambes could have lived here for any length of time and left no mark at all.'

'And the grave I found was *Sir* Francis,' put in Tybalt eagerly. 'You'd remember a sir, wouldn't you?'

'Well, not necessarily.'

'Um, there was a rosemary bush on the grave.'

'So?'

'Well it's – uh, rosemary for remembrance.'

'Oh I see. So somebody wanted him remembered,' said Toby. 'Piers, you said you went to the church in Thane St Mary a couple of times? Didn't you see the grave?'

Piers said, 'I never walked round the churchyard,' and Tybalt looked up at him and thought: oh my! that's his hands-off voice if ever I heard it!

He said at once, 'The grave's a long way from the church. You could go there every Sunday for a year and never know it was there.' He saw Dr Adair flick him a quick glance and thought there might have been gratitude in it.

'Well anyway,' said Toby, 'I'll bet that if we started to really pry and probe we'd pick up all kinds of tales.'

'I do not like pry and probe,' stated Dietfreid, frigidly. 'That would give us gossip. I do not like gossip and handed-up stories.'

'Dietfreid, it's handed-*down* stories.'

'Whatever it is, I do not like it and we do not want it.'

'Yes, we do, it's exactly what we do want,' disagreed Toby. 'Gossip's the stuff that documentaries are made on, Dietfreid. Where would history be without the gossips? Sam Pepys and the Paston Letters and—'

'I had not seen that side of it,' said Dietfreid. 'Here are my apologies, please.'

'Thank you very much,' said Toby, solemnly.

'Where does the map find itself?'

The map, it appeared, found itself on the floor, whither it had fallen during supper. Dietfreid crawled under the table to rescue it, patting Nina's ankle with elephantine coquettishness on the way. He spread the map frowningly over the table, and decreed that they should divide the area and spread the net wider. 'We make to our search,' he announced. 'And I will go west,' he added, stabbing the map with a chubby finger, and speaking with all the fervour of a frontier pioneer in the nineteenth century. 'Because it is my belief that there in the forests we will find Karabas.'

'The wildwoods,' said Piers, softly. 'Yes, if Karabas really is here, he'll probably head for a forest.'

'I, too, think this.' Dietfreid was pleased to find his reasoning appreciated. 'So I will go to these places here – Miller's Dale and Monyash which are found on the boundaries of the National Park areas. It is not a long journey, but I will need a car.' He added, rather wistfully, 'Also, I should like to have a companion, since I am not good for driving on the left.'

With horror, Nina heard her own voice say, 'If we can have Priscilla's car I'll come with you,' and Dietfreid beamed at her, and then with Germanic precision began to plan the exact route they would take and the villages they would visit.

'I have read that at Miller's Dale there is a legend of how a werewolf haunts a particular stretch of road,' he said. 'We shall look into that and also we shall go to this place here, called Ilam, where there is a story about a saint who battled with a wolf.' He assumed his rimless spectacles and regarded his companions severely. 'His name was Bertelin and he bears looking at more closely,' he said. 'But the threads of our legend, they are there, yes?'

'Wolves all over the place,' agreed Toby. 'Piers, are you going to help with the stately home search? Because if you are, we might need to sort out cars—'

Piers said thoughtfully, 'Not for a couple of days, Toby. There's an old friend I have to call on.'

Chapter Twenty-Seven

Father Stephen Berry waved Piers to a chair, and seated himself opposite, studying Piers with interest.

'I'm so glad you came,' he said. 'D'you know, I never thought I'd see you again.'

The years had stripped the surplus flesh from Stephen Berry. Piers remembered him as plump-faced and genial; now he was thin and spare, and his skin had the frail, papery look of extreme age. Piers made a quick calculation. Father Berry could surely not be much more than sixty-five, but ensconced in his warm little house on the north side of Ashbourne he looked more like eighty-five. We did that to him, thought Piers. The Westons turned him into an old man.

Piers had been given the warmest of welcomes the minute the door was opened, and taken into a small room at the back of the house that appeared to do double duty as dining room and study. There were books everywhere, and on the gate-leg dining table was a slightly battered typewriter, and a sheaf of papers with what might be the draft of a sermon. Father Berry no longer had a parish of his own but he helped out with several parishes in the county; filling in when the incumbents were ill or away or simply overloaded with work.

'So now,' said Father Berry, suddenly fixing Piers with a very searching stare, 'you're here to learn the truth about your family, are you?'

'Do you know the truth?'

'I doubt anyone will ever know the whole truth,' said Father Berry. 'Your father uncovered a part of it when he married Helen Weston. And I uncovered yet another part when I first came to Kings Thane. You uncovered a little of both those parts, of course,' he said. 'But unfortunately you did so while you were too young to have any real sense of proportion.' He leaned his head back, studying Piers from beneath half-closed eyes. 'Has something happened – something recent – that's made you start delving again?'

It was inconceivable to Piers that he should lie to this man who knew more about him than any living soul. He said, 'My work has – rather unexpectedly – brought me up against the legend again.' He paused, and then said, 'No, that's not absolutely true. It isn't unexpected.'

'Tell me.'

Piers assembled his thoughts. 'About six months ago I began work on a study project involving a curious tribe of people on a remote Scottish island,' he said. 'The tribe's history is believed to have bizarre echoes with wolf-pack rituals, and the university asked me to head the team because it was an area of anthropology I was fairly knowledgeable about.'

He paused, and then said, 'I admit that I manipulated the situation.'

'Yes?'

'I always intended to go there,' said Piers. 'With or without a team. As it turned out, I got the university to fund part of it, and the university got the BBC to fund another part of it. That made the whole project much easier. I was able to do the thing openly and comfortably, under the umbrella of scholarly research and television documentaries.'

'It's Cruithin Island, isn't it?'

'Yes.'

Father Berry looked at Piers thoughtfully, and then turned his attention to the tray of tea before him. He made rather a long business of pouring out two cups of tea, and it was only when he had done this that he said, in a neutral voice, 'You remembered the name all these years?'

'I never forgot it.'

'No, of course not. And you got permission to stay on the island from the agents?'

'Yes. They're the same agents that handle the letting of Weston House, which made it a lot easier.' Piers drank the hot tea gratefully. 'They let me have an old farmhouse as a base – heaven knows how old it was or when it was last lived in.'

'Did they tell you the owner's name?'

'No. Client confidentiality. Cheques and so on were payable to the agents themselves. But I did get the impression—'

'Yes?'

'That they acted for someone who was elderly, and that after his – or her – death, the estate would probably revert to the Crown.'

'Someone expected to die without issue,' said Father Berry, thoughtfully.

'Yes.'

'Piers, you'll forgive me if I'm prying, but when you say you were known to be knowledgeable—'

'Yes?'

'Did you deliberately choose to follow that path, that career? As a way of dispelling what happened when you were a child?'

'I don't know,' said Piers, after a moment. 'But I do know that there were too many links between the Cruithin Island project and the Kings Thane legend for me to ignore it.' He leaned forward, his eyes intent. 'All we know about this tribe on Cruithin came from hints. There were whispers about their way of life and their appearance – there's a strong physical resemblance to wolves, although that might just be generations of in-breeding. It's not unattractive, in fact. But I thought the whole thing would turn out to be some form of lycanthropy – the actual medical condition, not the horror-film shape-changer stuff. I thought if I could prove that it was inherited lycanthropy—'

'You could put Helen's insanity into an acceptable category?'

'Yes. I would have found an explanation for her behaviour – I mean an explanation I could live with.' He sat back in his chair. 'But I'm not so sure that it is lycanthropy at all. We kept coming up against freak-ish coincidences. And then we found stone jars in the tribe's caves—'

'Ah yes,' said Father Berry. And then, very gently, 'They have the same belief that a lineage can be passed down by drinking the blood of ancestors?'

'Yes.' Piers was grateful for Father Berry's intuition. He said, 'And now a thread of our research has led us here – to the Thane villages, and I have the increasing feeling that I'm about to find the connection between this tribe and the Weston legend.'

'You believe there is a connection?'

'I don't know. But if you remember what – Helen said that night—'

'Yes,' said Stephen Berry, softly. 'Yes, I remember.' He

paused, frowning, and then said, 'By "Weston legend" you mean the sixteenth-century werewolf fable?'

'You can't think how glad I am to hear you use that word, Father.'

'"Werewolf"?'

'"Fable".'

Father Berry smiled.

'The problem is that I don't know if I can go on without knowing what might be ahead,' said Piers.

'You do have to go on, do you?'

Piers stared at him. 'It's not a mission carved in stone,' he said, after a moment. 'But it would be awkward to abandon it now. A lot of questions would be asked. It would certainly mean giving very good reasons to the university and the BBC – they think it might turn out to be a good subject for a documentary.'

'I should think it would be riveting,' said Father Berry, with the gentle irony that Piers remembered.

He smiled, and then, choosing his words carefully, said, 'I think I need to know what I might uncover. So that I'm at least prepared. I don't know exactly how much you know about that – fable,' he said. 'I've never been sure of that. But I thought you might tell me what you do know. There are so many gaps,' he said, drinking the tea, grateful for the little core of warmth it set up. 'And I've never known how much was fact and how much was just legend.'

'Well, the legend of a werewolf has certainly persisted,' said Father Berry, stirring his own tea. 'In fact I've come across mention of a werewolf who haunts the area around Miller's Dale.'

Piers remembered Dietfreid saying he had found something about this as well.

'But you'll find these quirky bits of folklore in practically every village in Europe,' said Father Berry. 'In your work you know that better than I do.' He paused, and then said, 'Piers, your family closed ranks against the world four hundred years ago. Whatever happened then, they kept it from the world. I don't know the truth, I only know the legend.' He paused, and then said, 'But don't you think you should try to come to terms with what happened twenty years ago, before you start worrying what happened four hundred years ago?'

* * *

In those days – the days of twenty years ago – Father Berry
had been the energetic priest of Kings Thane and Thane St
Mary, and Piers's father, ruefully picking up the threads of his
religion, had taken the young Piers to Mass several times.

'It'll either click for you or it won't,' he had said. 'And you
can believe or not, just as you like. But at least you'll know
what the choices are.'

Piers had liked the old church in Thane St Mary; he had
liked the rise and fall of Father Berry's voice mingling with the
music and the feeling that here was something solid and
enduring: generations handing down to generations. But he
had seen it as little more than a group of people gathered
together to chant meaningless words by rote.

'Ah. That's a pity, now,' Martin had said when Piers admitted
this. 'But then I was exactly the same at your age. We'll keep at
it for a couple of years, however; it won't hurt you and it'll give
you a few basic values. And if you turn into a hardened old
sinner like me, one day you might be glad to remember the
church is there.'

Piers, who was by now much more comfortable with his
father, had grinned and said, 'You aren't repenting in your old
age, are you?'

'We'll say I'm hedging my bets. But listen, always remember
that Steve Berry's a good and reliable man in a tight situation.
Don't ever forget that, Piers, because it's something else you
might be glad of some time.'

Piers, at fourteen, and then at fifteen, had not forgotten it,
even though he had not been able to imagine the kind of tight
situation in which the only possible solution was to turn to a
priest for help. But by a curious twist of fate, it had been the
night before his sixteenth birthday, midsummer's eve again,
when he had fallen, nightmare-deep, into precisely that
situation.

And he had understood then what his father meant. He
had known that Father Berry was the only man who could
help him.

The house in the forest had never ceased to tug at his mind. It
was two years since the night he had stalked his father through
the trees, but the macabre pull did not lessen.

257

He had no idea how much he believed of what he had been told, and for a long time he was not sure whether his father, exerting his own brand of charm, had simply spun a tale that would allow an impressionable fourteen-year-old boy to come to terms with his own mother's insanity.

The insanity was never in question, of course; Piers had witnessed it for himself and he knew it quite surely. At times he saw his mother as a tragic victim: a doomed Lady of the Lake heroine, fated to bear the burden of her curious ancestry. But at other times he saw her as a dreadful, hungering thing; a grisly villainess bound by a grim enchantment that lay slavering behind her eyes, and occasionally cast its own dripping-fanged shadow on a moonwashed wall . . .

They believe they have to drink the blood of their ancestors, she had said. *They believe that's how the line is passed down . . .*

It was so utterly unbelievable in the modern world that it did not merit dwelling on. But he did dwell on it, and to his horror a treacherous little voice began to whisper to him at night when he was in bed. Supposing it's all true? Supposing there really is an ancient, unguessed-at species in the world, not quite human and not quite wolf, but somewhere in between the two? And supposing that this wolf-line has to be passed down and passed on, and that the way to do it is by drinking the blood of your own forebears?

And supposing it would be *good* to do that, said the voice, and now it held a low sexual purr that seemed almost to caress his inner thighs with a velvet finger, causing a violent and instant physical response. Supposing it would be the most intensely exciting thing ever? Piers, torn between helpless arousal and scalding self-disgust on those nights, fought to shut the voice out, but it slithered under his defences every time.

Worst of all were the nights when the voice said: *Supposing Helen Adair is sane . . . ? Supposing what afflicts her isn't madness sparked off by a fragment of local legend at all . . . ? Supposing it's all real!*

In the end, he had gone back to the house, just as he had always known he would. He had stolen out of his bedroom, pausing in the silent, shadowy kitchen, looking about him. The memory of how his mother's madness had so swiftly reared up had never left him, and he thought: supposing she really attacks me this time? Supposing she leaps on me and there isn't time to shout for help? I need a weapon, he thought. Something small but effective.

He glanced at the large old-fashioned butcher's block in the corner, where the kitchen knives were kept, but he flinched from taking something so potentially lethal. In the end he selected a small but heavy-headed meat mallet, which he thought was heavy enough to inflict a telling, but not fatal blow. He stuffed it into a pocket and let himself out through the garden door.

It was midsummer's eve once more, with the pale midnight moon low over the trees and the forest seeming as if it was poised on the brink of something enchanted and pagan. As he went through the forest he was aware, all over again, that he was drawing near to that other hidden world; that he was pushing aside the invisible veils and approaching the fabled low door in the wall: the door through which poets and philosophers claim to step with frequency, but which ordinary mortals seldom even encounter, and from which they certainly never return to tell of their adventures on the other side . . .

He was again taken into the house by Emma, and again, there seemed to be no surprise.

'She's been looking for you,' Emma said. 'All day she's been looking out into the forest. "He'll come tonight, Emma," she's been saying. "He'll come because I *know* he'll come."'

The feeling of unreality increased. Piers said, 'How would she know that?'

'That I can't tell. But I'll take you to her room if that's what you want. You understand that it's necessary to be wary of her?'

'Yes, I understand.' And this time I am armed . . . Aloud, he said, 'It's all right, Emma. I only want to sit and talk to her for a while.'

As they went down the same corridor that led into the old part of the house, Emma said, unexpectedly, 'It's your birthday tomorrow, isn't it? Sixteen?'

'Yes.'

'Perhaps that's how she knew you would come tonight,' said Emma, and Piers suddenly understood why he had waited, not for his birthday, but for midsummer's eve, when dark enchantments might be stirring and ancestral voices might be woken, exactly as they had been woken on a night two years

259

earlier, when Helen Adair had looked at her son with eyes that were not human. *I need to see if that night can be recreated,* he thought.

The room with the barred window overlooking the tangled forest was exactly the same. The figure sat quietly in its corner and moonlight trickled through the trees and lay in feathery patterns across the floor. Piers had no idea what he would do if Emma insisted on remaining in the room, but to his relief she only hesitated and then said, 'I'll be within call.' As she closed the door Piers heard the key turn in the lock.

He was once again alone with his mother. He drew in a deep breath and walked forward to sit opposite her.

To begin with he thought it was not going to happen. He thought he had miscalculated – or perhaps only misunderstood – and he thought there was nothing in her eyes save the blank bleak stare of the mentally flawed. He thought: she doesn't recognise me this time! and had no idea whether he was relieved or disappointed.

And then she began to rock the chair, slowly at first, almost imperceptibly, but then faster, until the shadow on the wall was flickering again, and Piers felt himself being pulled back into that other night.

'Why are you here again, Piers?' said Helen Adair, and Piers jumped because after all she knew who he was.

He paused, and said carefully, 'To talk to you. To try to under-stand—'

'Yes?'

'The things you told me last time.'

'About how I killed your brother?'

'Yes.' Piers was strenuously avoiding looking at the shadow on the wall. It was not changing, of course it was not, any more than his mother was changing. He said, 'Please tell me. I need to understand.'

'About the young man who came to Kings Thane four hundred and fifty years ago? He was not a man at all, of course.' She leaned forward, her eyes glowing. 'His name was Marcus Fitzglen and he came from a place called Cruithin Island. But while he was here,' said Helen Weston, 'he sired a child onto this family.'

Piers heard the sudden craftiness in her voice, and drew

back instantly, but her face was so close to him now that he could feel her warm breath on his cheek, and he could smell her body-odour: faintly sickish.

'You've inherited the taint, haven't you?' she said suddenly. 'I can see it – just as I saw it in your brother.' Her words were faintly slurred, and Piers saw with a mixture of relief and panic that there could be no possible doubt about her madness: it shone redly from her eyes. He made to get out of the chair, but her hand came out to him, imprisoning his wrist.

He jerked his hand free and stood up, one hand going to his pocket for the mallet, but she was swifter. She moved out of the chair in a single upwards bound, and one hand, clenched into a fist, slammed against his throat, cutting off his breath. He choked and struggled and fought to call for Emma, but the thing that was his mother was already pressing against him, winding her arms around him.

'You're Marcus Fitzglen's descendant,' said the smeary voice. 'And you'll have to die because of that.' Madness poured into the room in a red roaring tide, exactly as it had done on this night a year ago. Piers struggled again, and felt the grip tighten.

'If I don't kill you,' said Helen, 'you'll do all the things he did. One day you'll drink the blood, Piers, and you'll *enjoy* it— You're so beautiful,' she said, her voice clotted with madness. 'It's such a shame to kill you, because you're so beautiful.' One hand came up to caress his throat.

To Piers's utter horror his body reacted in exactly the way it had reacted on all those nights when he had lain awake, and helpless crude arousal surged through him. Dreadful! Disgusting! But in another minute I'll break free. I'll wait until she's off guard and then I'll push her aside and get to the door. Now? Yes! He tensed his muscles but instantly the hard thin fingers curled around his throat. Piers struggled and at once the hands tightened their grip. Oh God, she's going to strangle me! He reached up to prise her fingers away, struggling to reach the heavy-headed mallet with the other hand.

The room was spinning into a sick blackness, and the blackness was becoming shot with crimson lights. Piers could feel his strength ebbing away. After what seemed an eternity his hand finally closed around the mallet and he dragged it out of his pocket.

With the last shred of his strength he raised the mallet and smashed it across the clutching strangling fingers. The iron grip on his throat loosened at once and he pushed her away. His throat felt as if it had been scorched and he was trembling violently, but he could breathe again. He moved to the door, keeping a firm grasp on the mallet. In another minute – in just a few seconds – he would regain enough breath to shout for Emma, but if he could get to the door he could bang on it to attract her attention.

Helen Adair was standing at the centre of the room, staring at him in bewilderment. There was the hurt, uncomprehending look of an animal in her eyes, and she held out her bruised hands.

'You hit me, Piers,' she said. 'Why did you hit me?'

Piers felt the pity of it scythe through him. But he said, 'Don't – don't come any nearer.' His voice came out in a husky whisper, but he was thinking: it's all right. I've fought her off and I don't think I've done anything worse than bruise her fingers. If I can just get to the door—

And then she moved without warning: launching herself through the air, screeching with laughter as she did so and knocking him flat to the ground. Her fingers, curved into claws, raked at his face, and he felt her nails draw blood.

There was a moment when he hesitated, the mallet still clutched in his hand, his imagination too easily able to conjure up the feeling of bone crunching beneath the blow. And then his mother's words washed scaldingly against his mind once more. *You've got the eyes and the lips and the face of Marcus Fitzglen . . . You've inherited the taint, haven't you . . . HAVEN'T YOU? . . .*

'*No!*' cried Piers, fear and rage rushing into him, and without hesitating he raised the mallet and this time brought it smashing down on her head.

This time she crumpled and fell helplessly to the ground, unmistakably unconscious, and Piers scrambled to his feet and stood looking down at her. His mind was still boiling with fear and disgust, and drumming against his brain was the uncontrollable need to destroy all visible evidence of the grisly, impossible taint.

The mallet was a light-weight weapon, but with murderous rage and wild passion driving it, it was lethal. Piers, sobbing with disgust but unable to help himself, brought it down again

262

and again on the crushed, bleeding skull, and it was only when Emma came running into the room that he realized that his hands and his face were spattered with Helen Adair's blood and brains.

And that his mother was dead.

'Of course you acted in self-defence,' said Stephen Berry, pouring tea for Piers in the cluttered little study-cum-dining-room.

'Yes, of course.' But the mallet, thought Piers. Supposing I took the mallet intending all the time to kill her? And why didn't I stop after the first blow?

Father Berry was saying, 'I knew it was self-defence, Piers, and your father knew it as well. Otherwise we would never have helped you.' He raised his eyes from the tea things and sent Piers a very direct look.

Piers accepted the cup of tea and sat back, his eyes shadowed. After a moment, he said, 'Helen talked of Marcus Fitzglen as if he was some sort of supernatural being. As if he came out of the night, charmed everyone into a false sense of security, sired a child on some long-ago Weston lady, and then vanished. She talked of Cruithin Island as if it was a place where demi-gods walked.'

'Do they?' said Father Berry, lightly.

Piers smiled reluctantly. 'I didn't see any,' he said. 'But, Father Berry, surely there was more to it than my mother told me?'

Father Berry stirred his tea thoughtfully. 'I've never come across a direct reference to Marcus Fitzglen in local folklore,' he said at last. 'And, as you know, I've been in this part of Derbyshire for a good many years. What I have come across are vague contemporary references to a witch-trial that took place in Kings Thane in 1540.' He looked at Piers very intently. 'Now I know the witch-hunts didn't get going in this country until a lot later—'

'Seventeenth century,' said Piers, mechanically. 'James I was paranoid about them.'

'Yes. And there were any number of witch-hunts long before James's time. But I've always wondered whether the Kings Thane witch-trial wasn't really something a bit more sinister.'

'Marcus Fitzglen's trial? On what charge? And aren't you

making rather a big leap of supposition?'

'The charge could even have been witchcraft,' said Father Berry, thoughtfully. 'As for the leap of supposition—Well, the official Court records for the whole of 1540 were destroyed in a fire at the start of 1541. Highly convenient for the Westons, don't you think?'

Piers felt an acute stab of disappointment. He said, 'So that cuts off a line of research we might have followed up.'

Father Berry said, 'Well now, there's another possibility, but it's a very slender one.'

'Yes?'

'A long time ago it was a tradition in my family that third sons went into the Church. In the year Marcus Fitzglen came to Kings Thane, the third son of the day was called Simeon. He was my several-times great-uncle – quite a lot of "greats" I should think, and by all accounts he was a bit of a renegade. But he obeyed his father and entered the Church.' Father Berry paused and smiled. 'I, of course, entered it simply because I wanted to,' he said.

'But Simeon is my family's small claim to posterity. He came to Kings Thane as its parish priest, and while he was here he wrote one or two books on local lore. He even tried his hand at poetry. Parts of some of the books have survived and they were quite good. The poetry, on the other hand, was very bad.'

He stopped again, and Piers leaned forward eagerly. 'You think Simeon wrote down the story of Marcus Fitzglen?'

'In the fifteen hundreds it would have been quite acceptable for the parish priest to act as Court scribe, wouldn't it?'

'Yes, the priest was often the only one who could read or write. But you said the records were all burnt?'

'The official records were,' said Father Berry, reaching for the teapot. 'But Simeon liked writing. He liked putting his own stamp on events – he wouldn't have been able to do that in the official records.'

Piers stared at him. 'You think he wrote a private account?'

'I think he might have done. He wrote quite a lot about the Thane villages and the day-to-day life of the people.'

'Diary of a Country Parson,' said Piers, thoughtfully. 'But listen, if he wrote anything about Marcus would it still be in existence?'

'I don't know,' said Father Berry. 'It isn't in any of the places you'd expect – archivist's office, local library – because I've looked. I don't know if that was the Westons covering their secret again, or simply that there was nothing to find.'

'Oh,' said Piers, slightly nonplussed.

'But there is one place I haven't looked,' said Father Berry. 'And it's worth trying.'

'Where?'

'Weston House,' said Father Berry. 'The old attics. Another cup of tea, Piers?'

Chapter Twenty-Eight

Peers waited until everyone had gone out before going up to the attics.

Nina and Dietfreid set off on their exploratory expedition for Miller's Dale after breakfast, apparently on good terms with one another, although looking somewhat mismatched. Nina was wearing a long Indian-print skirt with a vest-type top and laced half-boots. She had crammed a black, velour, Twenties-flapper hat over her fair hair and she looked, Piers thought, ingenuously pretty. Dietfreid, who took field research seriously, had donned a peculiar tweed suit with a khaki shirt and knitted tie. Piers tried to visualize them eating lunch together in some country pub, and failed entirely.

Tybalt partook of a huge breakfast and confided, in a burst of well-being and candour, that he saw what people meant when they said England specialized in spring. It was going to be a great day, said Tybalt, and he just loved this country to bits. He consulted the rota; discovered that he was on dishwashing duty that day, and crashed the crockery happily about in the sink, after which he and Priscilla drove Toby to the railway station for the London train. From there they were going on to scour as many churches as they could fit in, in quest of other Foljambes lying beneath the greensward. Piers hoped the two of them would not fall out too much.

Even so, it was late afternoon before he finally went through to the old part of the house, forcing himself not to look at the closed door that had once led to his mother's room, making his way cautiously to the small, half-hidden stair at the end of the narrow corridor. The floor was uneven here and black with age, and Piers paused, looking at the steps twisting upwards. There was a small door at the top, wreathed in shadows, but he could see that it was half-door and half-hatch. On the other side were the ancient attics of the original house.

He stood there for a long time, trying to make up his mind to go on. His emotions were so tangled that it was impossible to extricate any one feeling from the morass and identify it; there was certainly fear and disgust, but in addition there was a growing curiosity, and there was a sense of possessiveness as well, because whatever he might find in the attics – if, indeed, there was anything to find – it was his own family's history and his own family's legend.

The house was cool and very quiet, although through a half-open window somewhere came the soft liquid notes of a wood pigeon, pouring its song into the golden afternoon. The old beams creaked gently from the warmth of the day, and there was a warm powdery scent from the sun-drenched timbers. Piers had the sense of the past reaching out to pull him in, and taking a deep breath he went up the narrow stair and pushed the attic door open.

The attics stretched for almost the entire length of the house; they were straggling chambers, opening one out of another, rather roughly joined where the newer part of the house started, but with low cross-beams and black timbers showing where the original structure still existed. The floors were reasonably level and sturdy-looking, but in places the height between floor and roof joists was so low that Piers saw he would have to bend almost double to get under them.

There were piles of household junk – Piers made out an ancient mangle, along with a number of broken-backed dining chairs and oddments of furniture, most of it late Victorian from the look of it. There were tea-chests and large packing cases, and boxes of books and old gramophone records and newspapers and magazines tied up with twine.

Late-afternoon sunlight slanted in from several places in the roof, probably where tiles had lifted – Piers made a mental note to have a word with the agents – and dust motes danced in and out of the soft golden rays.

There was a stillness and a silence in the attics, but it was not a very good silence. There was a brooding, watching quality to it. Piers felt his skin prickle, and in the same moment thought that there was a flicker of movement in the shadows – almost as if a half-glimpsed figure had darted out of sight. Helen! Was she crouching in the shadows, watching him as he delved into the ancient legend? With her smashed-to-pulp skull and her evil beauty in its ivory setting?

He cut off the images before they could take root in his mind. There was absolutely nothing up here save the discarded household junk of decades. He looked about him again. If anyone had been up here, he or she must needs have walked across the floor, and the thick dust had plainly not been disturbed for years, maybe even centuries.

But dead creatures do not leave footprints when they walk, my dear . . .

Piers shivered and looked round for light switches. He could hear the scratching of house martins under the eaves, flying in and out and twittering to one another as they made their nests. Or was it house martins? Was it really someone concealed in here, laughing, not-quite-silently? Whispering: *You've inherited Marcus Fitzglen's legacy, Piers . . . You're so beautiful, and you've got the eyes and the face . . . Haven't you admitted it yet, Piers?* Stop it!

He found a light switch at the juncture of the Tudor and Victorian part, and switched it down with a brisk click. Glad yellow light flooded the attics, and Piers felt instantly better. He surveyed the attics thoughtfully and walked across to the oldest of the tea-chests.

The shadows lengthened and the house martins had long since stopped scrabbling in the eaves when Piers straightened up from sorting through the tea-chests. He stretched his aching neck and back muscles, and glanced at his watch, remembering that he had promised he would have supper ready. He went reluctantly back down to the kitchen.

Somebody had disinterred a large pack of chicken portions from the freezer earlier on, which was at least one blessing. Piers put them into a casserole dish, added wine and stock, sliced up some mushrooms, and put the dish into the oven. He washed several large potatoes and placed them on the oven floor to bake in their jackets.

As he retraced his steps, he knew that what he sought was very near. He reminded himself that it could take several weeks to sort through the attic and that Simeon Berry's trial account had probably never even existed. And even if it had, it would have been long since destroyed.

But it was with a sense of inevitability that he saw, near the

268

bottom of the third tea-chest he opened, the thin inconspicuous book, bound in what was probably calf – once green or brown, but faded now to an indeterminate grey. The binding was dry and cracked and the lettering was rubbed and indistinct. Piers felt his heart begin to beat faster. He opened the book carefully, creating a shower of tiny dry snowflakes from the crumbling paper. The unmistakable smell of foxed paper and scholarship drifted upwards. Nice. Like opening up the sealed centuries of the past.

There was a scrawled inscription on the flyleaf – an indecipherable signature, and some kind of dedication. There was a date – September 1541 – and the title was clearly printed on the right-hand page. It announced the subject of the pages as being '*An account of the dread trial of Marcus Fitzglen, assembled and written by Father Simeon Berry, from courthouse records, from his own observations and also from the many legends surrounding the creature*'.

This is it, thought Piers, staring down at the book. In here is the truth, the legend, the genesis of that sinister mystery that came into my family all those centuries ago. All I've got to do to unlock that past and solve the mystery is to open the covers. Am I going to do it? God yes, of course I am!

For some reason he could not analyse he did not take the book down to his own room where he could read in comfort. Was it because Berry's book was so much a part of the silent, cobweb-shrouded attics? Was it because he felt Helen's presence quite strongly, and because he thought this was as much her discovery as his?

He seated himself on an old chaise longue, and opening the covers with great care, began to read.

Stephen Berry's ancestor set his scene with unexpectedly vivid imagery. Piers had half-expected to have to wade through florid, turgid prose and to find his attention wandering, but once he had caught the rhythm of style and attuned his eye to the slightly crabbed writing, this was not the case.

Simeon Berry was eloquent about the local people gathering for the trial; he described how they had walked down from their small farms and cottages, crowding into the low-ceilinged, wooden-floored room, bringing with them the stench of unwashed bodies and hot eager anticipation. Piers could almost see the stuffy room with the solemn-visaged judge and the avid faces; he could smell the sweaty flesh of the watchers. Berry recorded the month of the trial as having been June and said it was suffocatingly hot, which gave him a suddenly friendly aspect. Piers visualized him as a stouter version of his descendant, perpetually a bit out-of-breath because he was too plump. He thought Berry might have been one of the round-faced, chubby species of *religieux* of the day, the kind who enjoyed a tipple of wine and had a liking for cosy gossip.

Berry had the knack of painting word-pictures, and his description of Marcus Fitzglen being brought into the courtroom was startlingly vivid.

'He fought,' said Berry, 'like the wild thing we all by that time knew him to be, snarling at his captors so that his teeth showed wetly glistening, and clawing at their eyes with his thin hands. Eventually they manacled him and fastened gyves about his ankles, but they had to drag him, fighting and cursing, to stand before the judge seated at his high table. A murmur of terror went through the watchers and several people, glancing round furtively, sketched the sign of the cross on their bodies.'

Piers, reading this, remembered the religious turmoil that had boiled in England at that time. There was no indication as to which side of the episcopal fence Berry ranged himself, but Piers would have staked money that the good father had trimmed his sails to the prevailing wind.

Berry described Marcus Fitzglen as being ragged and unshaven, and with dark hair that was unkempt and sweat-soaked from the days in the cells below the courthouse. He was so thin, said Berry, in another of his energetic flights of rhetoric, that the hard pointed bones of the evil he harboured showed through, and the glowing eyes glared at the watchers with hatred.

'Thin, with narrow glowing eyes, and dark hair.' Piers stared at the words, and for a moment was back in the catacombs on Cruithin Island, watching the strange wild people form a circle to chant their eerie ancient ritual. Simeon Berry might have been describing any one of them. He forced himself to adopt a proper scholarly detachment, but even though he repeated the words, 'sixteenth-century peasant superstition' several times, they did not have much effect.

The conscientious Berry, having finished his scene-setting,

turned his attention to the reading of the charge.

There was half a page of preliminaries – Berry must have scribbled at the speed of light if he had got all this *verbatim* – but Piers was by now so well adjusted to the writing that he could skim this. The charge, read by the scarlet-robed bewigged justice, was given the full weight and awe and pageantry of the day. Piers was so deep inside the account now that he could almost feel the hush that would have fallen on the courtroom, and he could hear the ringing tones of the judge.

'Marcus Fitzglen, you are charged with the crimes of having raped and put to death more than twelve girls, in an inhumane and cruel manner, and of conspiring to practise witchcraft.'

Multiple murderer and serial rapist, thought Piers. With a dash of black magic. Well, it was no more than I expected. And after the build-up it couldn't have been anything less.

'And specifically,' ended the charge, 'with the rape of Mistress Isobel Weston.'

Isobel Weston. Piers stared at the page, and although he had never seen or heard the name before, his mind curled around it with familiarity. He thought: Isobel Weston, yes, of course, that was her name.

The first witness to be called had apparently been a servant of Marcus's, and his name was simply given as Walter. He was questioned about his master's way of life, and about his relationship with Mistress Weston. Berry had the knack of bringing his characters strongly to life, and Piers had the sense that Walter had enjoyed his brief notoriety.

His master had always had a liking for pretty young girls, he had said, and Piers could hear the slyness rising up from the printed page. Walter sounded like the kind of weasel-faced youth who stood too close to young females on the underground and pressed his repulsive crotch against them. He said that Mistress Weston had taken the Master's eye soon after they came to the village, and there had been a great many visits. Yes, quite often the visits had been at night, and sometimes when it was known that her father would not be there. He did not think, said Walter, that it was specifically to meet Mistress Weston that his master had come to Kings Thane; he thought it was all to do with some kind of vow that had been handed down in his master's family, and he had once told Walter how a forebear had lived for a time in Ilam. But that had been hundreds of years earlier, said Walter.

Questioned further, he had finally admitted that at times his master had moods when he was not quite as other men. When the hunger was upon him, he liked the taste of blood, said Walter, and Piers could almost hear the wet lick in his tone.

'He *liked* the taste of blood?' said the judge.

Yes, it was something handed down to him from long ago.

Piers could almost see the crafty-eyed Walter standing boastfully in the hot sweaty room, glorifying in the brief notoriety, but so stupid that he did not see he was probably talking himself into a punishment of his own, and he could hear the gasps, half of shock, half of prurient delight, that would have gone through the room.

Walter was led away, and Hugo Weston was called. Isobel's father, thought Piers.

Master Weston had apparently informed the court, with what sounded like a good deal of belligerence, that he had at first offered no objection to the courtship of his daughter by the stranger, Marcus Fitzglen. Quite the reverse, he said, for it was a hard thing for a man to be forced to rear a motherless daughter, and to find a good honest man to wed her. But Fitzglen had come to the village and he had taken a liking to Isobel – and why should he not? Piers could see him, bull-necked, red-faced, glaring pugnaciously at his auditors.

No reason at all. So there had been a courtship?

It appeared that there had. It further appeared that Isobel Weston had quite often been alone with Fitzglen, since, said Master Weston challengingly, there had been no reason against it. Only then had come the night – Father Berry would bear him out, he said, and Berry had here set down a small footnote, explaining to his reader that he did indeed bear out Master Weston's statement – when Hugo had been returning from an evening spent drinking ale with a few friends. There was no reason why a man could not enjoy a convivial evening with his neighbours, was there?

There was no reason in the world.

There had been no candles burning in any of the downstairs rooms when he approached his house, he said, but he had not thought this particularly unusual, thinking that Isobel had probably retired. There had been a bit of a light in Isobel's room, said Hugo. It had prompted him to just look in to bid her a goodnight – and well that he had, for a sight such as he had never witnessed had met his eyes, in fact he doubted but that it was a sight no Christian person had ever witnessed before – setting aside the Bible, that was!

He was persuaded to give the court a description of what he had seen. 'My daughter was lying on the bed, mother-naked, legs a-sprawl in a manner more suited to a harlot than a decent woman. Standing over her was the creature who calls himself Marcus Fitzglen.'

He paused. The judge said, 'Yes? He was – was he in a state of nature?' With unexpected delicacy, he added, 'Perhaps even a state of nature's arousal?'

'Arousal!' said Master Weston. 'By God, you might call it arousal! He had a stalk on him like an autumn crocus and he was in the very act of thrusting it in between her thighs!' Here he was interrupted by the assembled villagers, most of whom had apparently descended to ribald comment at this newest revelation. Master Weston waited righteously until the judge had succeeded in quelling the unseemly outbreak, and then unleashed his next piece of evidence.

'Furthermore, your honour, I'll swear before the king himself that the creature's face was no longer that of a human soul, but that of a snarling wolf.'

This had had the effect of instantly switching the mood of the court from bawdiness to consternation, and several people were forcibly ejected from the court, with the threat of a day in the stocks held over the rest by way of intimidation.

The judge finally asked what Master Weston, faced with this extraordinary sight, had done. What Master Weston had done, it seemed, was what any decent God-fearing father would have done in his place. He had stridden angrily across the floor, tapped the monstrous thing on its unnatural shoulder and requested that it leave his house at once.

He might have saved his breath. For answer, Marcus Fitzglen had rounded on him, snarling and spitting, and, said Hugo, had proceeded to smite him across the face and then knock him to the ground with as little effort and less heed than if he had been no more than a babe!

And then?

And then, by God, he had carried on with his devil's work,

said the outraged Master Weston. He had padded back to the bed with his soft-footed devil's prowl, and had taken his wicked pleasure there and then!

He – had carnal knowledge of your daughter in front of you?

That he did, by God! said Hugo. Shafted her with his great swollen battering ram, and his accursed buttocks pumping in and out for all the world like a flailer with Old Clootie driving him! *And*, said Hugo, with her own father a helpless witness to it all, his face streaming from the blood of a broken nose and his ribs cracked, for sure!

The judge, caught, Piers suspected, between establishing the precise facts and a certain inescapable prurience, had then posed a question as to the culmination of the episode. And no matter how the beleaguered member of the judiciary had phrased his question, and no matter how the faithful Berry had tried to temper it for posterity, Hugo Weston's reply had been uncompromisingly down-to-earth.

'Shot its seed straight into her and then threw back its head and howled its triumph like a wolf baying at the full moon.'

It was at this point in the narrative that Piers heard, with real fury, the sounds of a car drawing up outside and of doors being banged and Priscilla calling to Tybalt to park nearer to the side of the house.

The spell of the sixteenth century splintered at once, and the present came pouring in. Down below, Piers could hear doors opening and closing, and then the sound of crockery from the kitchen. He remembered with sudden guilt the casserole consigned to the oven an unknown time earlier, and hoped it was still eatable.

Impossible to finish reading Simeon Berry's half-macabre, half-Rabelaisian account now. Piers closed the book carefully, slid it into his pocket, and went down into the kitchen to discover the fate of the casserole.

Chapter Twenty-Nine

Nina and Dietfreid had had a very good day. Dietfreid had unexpectedly revealed an old-fashioned streak to his nature, and had treated Nina as if she was a delicate piece of Dresden china. She found this rather endearing.

They began by driving to Ilam, where the curious legend of St Bertelin had its roots. Nina dutifully followed Dietfreid through the village, which was a picturebook place with a stone monument at the centre. When they found the church, which was the Church of the Holy Cross, Dietfreid waxed loquacious on Saxon, Norman, Early English and Decorated styles. He planted himself in the centre of the church, and read aloud the entire contents of a leaflet left out for the edification of visitors, which traced the legend of Bertelin, Prince of Stafford, and his ill-fated journey through the ancient Kingdom of Mercia, during which his young wife and new-born baby had been attacked and devoured by wolves.

'And here is Bertelin's very tomb!' Dietfreid declared, galloping down the aisle in high excitement. 'With a carving of a giant wolf devouring a human head!' His feet clattered on the stone floor and his voice echoed boomingly around the small church, and Nina wondered what on earth she would do if anyone came in.

They had lunch in a country pub, and Dietfreid became very solemn and described to Nina how privileged and honoured he had felt when Dr Adair had asked him to join this team. 'He has twice lectured at the university where I studied, and he is regarded as very eminent.'

'He's regarded as very eminent here, as well, Dietfreid.' Nina picked up her shoulder bag. 'Are you ready to set off again, or are you having pudding?'

'It would be better if I do not,' said Dietfreid, indicating his girth sadly. 'Although I see that on the menu there is fudge cake.'

Nina put her bag down again resignedly, as Dietfreid went happily back to the bar. 'With cream,' he said anxiously to the barmaid.

Nina hoped he would not be sick in the car.

He was not sick, of course; in fact by four o'clock, when they had gathered a few disappointing notes about several rather unlikely ruined manor houses, he thought that afternoon tea was called for.

'To cheer us up,' he said, as they drove along a road like a switchback with forest sprawling out on both sides of them. 'For we have found nothing of contribution, and it is a good institution, the English afternoon tea.'

'I think we turn left down here,' said Nina, who had folded the unwieldy map into a small square and was reading it as they went.

'Scones and jam with cream—'

'No, *left*, Dietfreid—'

'And perhaps the egg and cress sandwiches, or ham, very pink and juicy—'

They both stopped speaking at the same time and stared through the trees. Dietfreid rolled the car onto the grass verge and switched off the ignition. They peered into the trees.

'It is the ruins of a very large building,' stated Dietfreid after a moment.

'It certainly looks like it.' Nina wrestled with the map again. 'There isn't anything marked. I mean, there isn't one of those little symbols that tell you there's a place of historic interest or anything in this spot.'

'We should not leave unturned any stone, however.'

'You're right,' said Nina. 'Where's my notebook? And your camera?'

As they went deeper into the forest, the light seemed to drain from the afternoon. The trees twined their highest branches together over their heads, forming a roof that even on the brightest of summer's days would admit only the occasional watery spear of sunlight. There were thick patches of undergrowth everywhere, so that in places Dietfreid had to trample them flat in order to get through. He did this in the manner of a medieval knight hacking at a dragon-infested wilderness so that his lady might walk through in safety. It was a pity he was too podgy to convincingly support this role.

The trees thinned out as they approached the ruins; Nina thought it looked like a cultivated thinning out, as if long ago someone had cleared a very large section of the forest to build a house. The forest had grown up since that time, but it was easy to identify the new trees that had sprung up since.

The ruins seen so clearly from the road were much farther into the forest than either Nina or Dietfreid had realized, and when they finally reached them, at first sight they were not much more than a random jumble of stones.

'It's a kind of optical illusion,' said Nina, as Dietfreid showed signs of succumbing to gloom. 'Like when you view an oil painting or a watercolour. Close to it looks peculiar; it's only when you stand back you get the full picture. We got the full picture from the road.'

'And now we are getting the peculiar.' Dietfreid began rather glumly to inspect the broken pieces of stone.

It was Nina who discovered the lichen-crusted archway half hidden by the trees, covered with tangling mats of bracken and brier.

'It looks like an entrance to a courtyard,' she said, pointing it out, realizing that she had instinctively lowered her voice.

'We will explore,' decided Dietfreid, brightening up at once, and plunging forward. 'Come, my *Liebling*.'

Nina was not at all sure that she liked being suddenly addressed as Dietfreid's *Liebling*, and she was even less sure that she wanted to explore beyond the stone arch, but Dietfreid was already well ahead and anything was preferable to being left by herself in this increasingly sinister part of the forest. In any case, the whole point was to check all large houses – ruined or otherwise – in case they might provide another piece of the jigsaw. Nina thought of how Piers's eyes would light up if they could carry home the knowledge that they had found the old Foljambe estates, and allowed herself a moment of pleasurable anticipation before catching Dietfreid up.

The sun was already sinking below the horizon, sending low-lying spears of fire through the trees. They could no longer see the road, and they certainly could no longer hear the occasional roar of a passing car. As they passed under the crumbling stone archway the brooding silence seemed to intensify, as if the entire forest was waiting and watching.

'I think perhaps this was once the front of a very large house,' offered Dietfreid, planting himself before the main part of the ruins. 'With a garden. You see that there in front of us are the walls of what would have been the house.'

'Yes.'

Dietfreid moved amongst the stones, his large face absorbed. Once he stopped and looked at what appeared to be a fragment of an immense stone chimney-piece, and this seemed to absorb him so completely that Nina went up to see what it was. The sun had vanished by now, and shadows were starting to creep between the trees. She quelled the desire to scuttle back to the safety of the car.

'Here we find a crest of some kind,' announced Dietfreid, and delving into a capacious pocket, produced a torch which he shone onto the section of stone. It was roughly six or seven feet high but it had clearly once formed part of a much higher wall. There was an immense slightly curved horizontal lintel about four feet from the ground; it was blackened from thousands of fires.

'Tsk. I cannot make this out with any clarity,' said Dietfreid, crossly. 'It is very worn away and it is too dark to see for me. But,' he said, his nose practically touching the worn surface, 'it is possible that it could be a wolf. And it is also possible that it could be very like the emblem we saw on Bertelin's tomb in the church in Ilam. The wolf devouring the human head.'

Nina said, 'I don't think it's a wolf devouring a human, Dietfreid. I think it's a human devouring a wolf.'

They looked at one another. 'The Foljambe crest?' said Dietfreid.

'I don't know. But if they had one, don't you think it would have had a wolf in it somewhere?'

'We should search further,' said Dietfreid, firmly. 'To see if there is anywhere other evidence. Perhaps the crest appears in other places more readable.'

'Tonight?' The forest was becoming bathed in an eerie green twilight and the birdsong was dying away.

'We will take only a brief look,' said Dietfreid, comfortingly. 'And then we will return home.'

They retraced their steps to the outer sections again. It gave Nina a curious and not very comfortable feeling to be walking through the tumbled broken stones like this. She was glad of Dietfreid's large presence.

'I am thinking it might be possible to sketch out a ground plan of what the house would once have been,' he said. 'Then we can show the others.'

'That's quite a good idea,' said Nina, and then, glancing about her, 'only – would it take long? Because I have the feeling that we aren't very welcome here.'

'It is not a very friendly place,' conceded Dietfreid. 'And so I will make the plan speedily, and tomorrow we will return to take photographs. The light is not good now for photographs.'

'The light is not good now for anything, Dietfreid.'

'No, so the diagram I make by itself.'

'OK.'

As he commenced to sketch a workmanlike outline of the ruins, Nina found she was imagining the people who would have lived here. It was easy to visualize the original modest little house – perhaps a tied cottage originally, for foresters or bailiffs to some feudal estate. There might have been a small family with perhaps a son – yes, she could see a young son growing up out here, learning his father's trade, whatever that trade might have been, whatever the family's name might have been . . .

Had the name been Foljambe, and had the trade been wolf-hunting?

Have we really found the wildwood? she thought. And are the family who once lived here the ones we've been looking for?

She glanced about her and shivered, because if ever a forest qualified to be called a wildwood, and if ever a forest bore the ancient imprint of wolves, this one did.

She got up and wandered around to the left-hand side of the ruins, where there was a jumble of stones and pieces of rotting timber that seemed to stand a little apart from the main building.

'Servants' quarters,' said Nina, as Dietfreid, his sketch almost complete, came over to her. 'Or maybe a dairy house or buttery.'

'We take a look,' suggested Dietfreid. Night was beginning to creep through the forest in earnest now, and the green twilight was giving way to a soft violet dusk. Nothing stirred, and Nina shivered and then wished she had not, because Dietfreid instantly offered her his jacket.

'My coat's fairly warm, thanks,' said Nina. 'But it's nice of you to offer.'

The smaller ruins were not nearly as dilapidated as the main house. 'In fact, there's practically a complete building still standing,' said Nina. 'D'you see, under all that ivy? It looks like some kind of outhouse. I think there's even a door.'

They looked at one another. The forest was very dark and very silent now. 'Take the torch, please,' said Dietfried. 'I see first if it is a door in very truth. Then we decide whether to look inside.' He stepped forward and as he began to industriously clear away the thick mat of ivy, Nina directed the torch.

They both saw almost at once that there was a door: it was a small oak door, black with age, the timbers at the top rotting where the ivy had not covered them, but apart from this reasonably sound. There was an immense ring handle, made of black iron.

Dietfried surveyed it doubtfully. 'You wish us to take a look inside?' he enquired.

'Er – well, not really. Not in the dark.'

The ivy had fallen in a huge pile in front of the ancient door, partially blocking its lower half. To get to the door it would be necessary to crawl across it. But it was possible now to see that the door was set at an unusual angle, tipping inwards and down. This might be because the whole structure had simply fallen in with the passing of time, or it might be that the door itself opened downwards, in the manner of a cellar trapdoor. Seeing this door gave Nina the same uneasy feeling she had had in the ruins earlier. But instead of being able to imagine a family living here and growing up here, happy and normal, this cellar door provoked a much darker feeling. It made her think of old, old evil, and of all the cruel things that had once walked the world, and that still did walk it.

She grabbed Dietfried's arm and said, urgently, 'No – let's go back. *Please* let's go back.'

'Tsk, there is no need for panics,' said Dietfried, grabbing her hand and patting it. 'I shall allow nothing to hurt you.'

'Um, well, thank you.' Nina withdrew her hand and hoped she had done so politely.

They walked slowly back through the dark forest, discussing their find. Dietfried was inclined to be distrustful of jumping to wild conclusions; he reminded Nina that there might be any number of wolf-head crests in Derbyshire, and pointed out that it was the duty of any scholar to verify data.

'Oh, blow being scholarly and blow verification,' said Nina. 'Of course it's the Foljambe estate – I feel it in my bones.'

'I am only saying there should be many more checks before we make any supposition, and—' Here Dietfreid broke off as Nina suddenly stopped walking and looked about her. 'What is wrong?'

Nina said, 'I think we're lost.'

Chapter Thirty

There was absolutely no need for panic. All that had happened was that they had lost their bearings amongst the ruins, and had turned left instead of right, or perhaps right instead of left, and come deeper into the forest. This was not some wild primeval forest that stretched on and on for miles before you came to civilization; it was a National Park forest in the English countryside, for goodness' sake. All they needed to do was walk along, leaving themselves markers so that they did not go round in circles, and eventually they would come upon signposts directing them to the road.

Nina and Dietfreid told one another all these things very firmly indeed. Dietfreid said there was absolutely no cause for worry, apart, that was, from the imminence of the supper hour at Weston House, and suggested several plans for marking their progress. As these ranged from pinning fragments of his notebook on trees to unwinding a ball of twine, rather in the manner of Theseus trying to penetrate to the minotaur's lair, Nina felt he was parting company with reality.

'Why don't we just make a little nick on the tree-trunks as we go?'

'If we were ancient Druids we would not dare to damage sacred trees by making a little nick on them,' observed Dietfreid. 'We would be nailed to the tree by our navels, in fact, and then driven round and round the trunk to unravel our intestines by the yard.'

'Well, we aren't ancient Druids. We can use the ignition key to scratch the trees, and we've got the torch to see our way. And,' said Nina, with emphasis, 'if you so much as *think* about saying the torch battery is low, I'll nail your navel to a tree and unravel your intestines by the yard myself!'

'So. Can you,' enquired Dietfreid, 'see the lights from the road?'

'No,' said Nina after a moment.

'Nor can I. We will go in this direction,' said Dietfreid, with decision. 'And we will not think about our dinners.'

'It's the last thing I'm thinking about.'

They had been walking carefully forward for about fifteen minutes, when Dietfreid stopped, and said, in a suddenly hushed voice, 'There is a light through the trees.'

'Where? What sort of light?' Nina peered through the trees, trying to see.

'A moving light.'

'Oh for heaven's sake—' And then Nina saw it as well. It was a rather dim, bobbing light. Exactly as if someone was walking through the forest carrying a lantern.

'Whatever it is, it's coming towards us,' said Nina, a bit uncertainly.

'I will protect you, my *Liebling*,' announced Dietfreid. There was probably no need for Dietfreid's protection because there was no reason to think that the light was anything other than someone about his – or her – perfectly lawful occasions. There was the obvious possibility that it might turn out to be a poacher or tramp or a New Age traveller or a brace of disturbed lovers, and that any one of these people might not be best pleased at being interrupted at whatever they had been doing. But even then there was no need for Nina to feel scared, or to have the ridiculous feeling that they were being drawn into a macabre fairytale world where evil-intentioned people stalked darkling forests, holding aloft old-fashioned lanterns, ready to lure unsuspecting human travellers into gingerbread houses . . . Stop it! said Nina to herself, firmly.

After this build-up it was slightly disconcerting to realize that the light – which turned out to be a large torch – was being carried by a lady, and to further realize that the lady was quite elderly.

She hailed them cheerfully, coming right up to them as fearlessly, thought Nina, as if she might never have heard of modern-day evils like violence, or mugging and rape. Dietfreid had politely dipped their own torch beam, rather in the manner of a courteous motorist trying not to dazzle oncoming traffic, and Nina saw that the lady was tall and spare and vigorous-looking. She was probably about seventy, but she was an energetic-looking seventy. Age had dried and sharpened her, and she had a slightly weather-beaten face as if she spent a good deal of time out of doors. She was carrying a shooting stick and wearing a green weatherproof jacket with a battered felt hat.

'Hello there!' said this lady, raising the shooting stick and switching off the torch in order to transfer it to a pocket. 'Are you lost?'

Nina was suddenly very glad to be with Dietfreid, who, whatever his other shortcomings, exuded an unshakable air of calm authority blended with a courteous amiability. He said in a robust voice, 'Good evening to you. Yes, we are lost certainly.'

'We took a wrong turning at the ruins back there,' put in Nina, pointing vaguely.

'Oh, no, did you really? How *very* tiresome for you. But perhaps I can help. Tell me, where did you leave your car? Or are you walkers?' she added, with a doubtful glance at Dietfreid's girth.

'No, we were driving. And the car's on the Kings Thane road,' said Nina, before Dietfreid could launch into one of his Baedeker-style descriptions of their journey.

The weather-beaten lady looked at them more closely. 'Are you from Kings Thane, or just travelling through?'

'We are staying in Kings Thane,' began Dietfreid.

'Only very temporarily, though,' Nina cut in.

'Now, that *is* interesting. Not many people come to Kings Thane.'

Dietfreid opened his mouth to explain why they were in Kings Thane and what they were doing there, and gave a grunt of surprise as Nina trod hard on his foot. You did not, unless you were completely witless, tell your entire life story to strangers whom you met in a dark forest. She said, 'If you could direct us back onto the road we'd be extremely grateful.'

'No names, no pack drill, is that it?' said the lady disconcertingly, and gave a short bark of laughter. 'Quite right too. For all you know I'm an IRA terrorist or the head of a coven of witches or the brains behind a drug-dealing ring. I'm not, of course,' she added as Dietfreid tsk-ed at the very idea.

'But you're a long way from your road, I'm afraid, my dears.' The 'my dears' came out quite naturally, in the country fashion. 'You're much nearer to what we call the upper road – that's the road overlooking Bishops Thane – than to the Kings Thane

284

road,' said their companion, and gestured vaguely with her shooting stick. 'It would take you the best part of an hour to get back to your car, but it's no more than fifteen minutes' walk to the upper road. That would be your best plan. Especially now it's dark.'

'So,' said Dietfreid.

'I'll tell you what we could do,' said the lady. 'My house is just over yonder—' she waved the stick again. 'You come back with me, and we can phone to wherever you're staying and ask your friends there to pick you up. Or,' she added, resourcefully, 'we could phone the taxi people in Thane St Mary. They'd come out at once and take you back around to your car. It's not far by road.'

'We wouldn't want to impose—' began Nina.

'No imposition,' said their companion. 'And I can see you're neither of you muggers or vagrants.'

Nina and Dietfreid exchanged a quick look. Then Nina said, 'Thank you very much. We'll phone for a taxi if we may.'

'Certainly. This way.'

As she led them through the trees, Nina said, 'I hope you don't mind me asking this—'

'Ask away.'

'But aren't you a bit afraid to walk in the forest like this on your own? At night?'

'Goodness me, not at all,' said the lady with a chuckle. 'I've lived here all my life; the forest's my friend. And I'm armed in a sense,' she added, raising the shooting stick. There was a click and a wicked-looking blade shot from the bottom. She brandished it, smiling. 'It's a useful thing for cutting back the pesky undergrowth, *or* for putting rout to attackers,' she said.

'We should introduce ourselves,' said Dietfreid. 'I am Dr Dietfreid Valk, and this is Miss Scott.'

'Nina,' said Nina, putting out a hand.

'Hello Nina and Doctor,' said the lady. 'I'm Madeleine – just Madeleine, no fuss no frills. And here's my house, and as you see, there're lights left burning in the windows and a lamp over the front door.' She smiled at them again. 'Just like in the best fairy stories. It used to be the gatehouse to the estate – when there was an estate, which was a very long time ago. But I don't like a lot of fuss and pomp, so this suits me very nicely.'

The house was a grey stone building, with windows on each

side of the door. A spiral of smoke rose up from a central chimney and there was a wisteria growing over one wall. In the daylight it would be a glowing splash of vibrant colour against the grey walls.

'It's a beautiful house,' said Nina, sincerely.

'Yes it is. A bit too near to that road now, of course: they built *that* fifteen years ago, despite all the local protests. I helped protest about that,' she said. 'We stormed the local MP's office and got up a petition and had a march. They still built the road, but I never enjoyed anything so much for years. Now protesters camp out in trees and build tunnels. Going a bit far that, I'd say. Or maybe I'm just getting old.'

'So you've lived here all your life?' Nina hoped that this abrupt, likeable old lady had a nice matching husband waiting for her inside the house, and that there were grown-up children who came to visit.

'Yes,' said Madeleine. 'The people regard me as the local eccentric – Mad by name and Mad by nature, they say. I don't pay them any attention.' She transferred her stick to her left hand and fumbled with the lock. 'Right hand's a bit weak,' she said, brusquely. 'Bit of a stroke last year. Nothing much, but it's a nuisance at times.'

'Can I help—'

'No, it's all right, I've got it.' The door swung open, and Nina caught a pleasing scent of lavender and beeswax.

'The phone's on the hall table, there. Sing out if you want the taxi people's number – tell them it's for me and they won't overcharge. They know me,' said Madeleine. 'And I expect you'd like a cup of tea, wouldn't you, or a glass of something a bit stronger?'

'A cup of tea would be lovely,' said Nina, who was feeling cold from tramping about the forest. 'Shall I help you while Dietfreid makes the phone calls?'

It was while they drank the tea in the chintzy sitting room behind one of the leaded-light windows, and waited for the taxi that would take them back around to the Kings Thane road and their abandoned car, that Nina began to carefully work the conversation back to the ruins.

'If you've lived here for so long, I expect you know a bit about the area, Madeleine.'

'I should think I do. I've lived here for close on seventy-one years. My family have lived in these parts for generations. Hundreds of years. I was born in this house and I expect to die in it, although not for a long time.'

'You have clearly a great many years yet,' said Dietfreid with one of his sudden smiles, and Nina was grateful to him, because although she would have liked to say this it was the kind of remark that sounded better from a man. Even when the man was only bumbly Dietfreid.

She said, 'You live by yourself?'

'Best way to live. I have a girl who comes in to help with a bit of cleaning a couple of times a week. Nice girl. She keeps me in touch with modern ways. They make good listening, her tales, but they make me glad I'm not eighteen any more,' said Madeleine. 'I suspect she's what they call a bit of a goer with the men – is that the expression?'

She grinned engagingly, and Nina said, 'Well, probably.'

Dietfreid looked disapproving.

'Have you any family?'

Nina put this a bit hesitantly in case it sounded as if they were prying, or – even worse – casing the joint, but Madeleine said, 'Parents are dead – well, you'd expect that at my age. Neither of them had brothers or sisters, and neither did I.'

'Oh, I see.'

'And I never married either, if that's what you're about to ask, my dear.' She poured Nina a second cup of tea. 'But,' said Madeleine, her puckered-apple face suddenly crinkling into a mischievous and rather engaging grin, 'I did have a daughter. A shocking scandal it was at the time – we hadn't reached the permissive society in those days, and there's some that would say the permissive society still hasn't reached us in the Thanes. But I had a daughter outside of wedlock which was a fate worse than death in the nineteen forties, and so it was hushed up and she was taken to live with a distant cousin.'

Nina said, 'How – sad.'

Madeleine gave another of her abrupt hoots of laughter. 'It was more than fifty years ago, and the only really sad part was that I was deceived by a rogue,' she said. 'He was *very* charming, but he was a rogue. We attract rogues in this part of the world and my family attract them worse than anyone, in fact there's a story about how we imprisoned one for witchcraft back in the sixteenth century. Still, my rogue wasn't a witch, I do know

287

that.' She patted Nina's hand. 'It's old history, my dear – I was seventeen and I thought I knew it all, which nobody at seventeen ever does, of course. And she was still with the family, my daughter. I liked to know that. And at least, as Jane Eyre once said, I was not unsought. Was that Jane Eyre?'

'I don't recall,' said Nina.

'Tiresome female, I always thought.'

Nina saw Dietfreid draw breath, preparatory to sailing in with a turgid dissertation on Victorian literature, and to prevent him, said hurriedly, 'Did you never have any news of your daughter?'

'Oh yes, quite a few times,' said Madeleine. 'She went to live in London, and got married – 1967, that was – my cousin wrote to tell me. Nice of her. But she died quite young – my daughter, that is. My cousin wrote to me about that as well.'

'Oh, I'm so sorry—'

'She left a daughter of her own,' said Madeleine. 'My granddaughter. Imagine having a grown-up granddaughter and never having met her. She was married a few years ago. My cousin sent me a cutting about the wedding. Lovely-looking girl and she married the most striking-looking man I've ever seen – not that you can trust newspaper photographs. I hope she's happy with him.'

'Perhaps you'll meet your granddaughter, some day,' said Nina, hopefully.

'Perhaps I will. I'm talking too much about myself. Comes of living on your own. Tell me about you: are you on holiday here?'

'We are interested, my friends and I, in local history,' said Dietfreid.

Nina thought that for Dietfreid, this was tactful as well as rather clever, since it gave her the chance to say, quite naturally, 'We were exploring the ruins when we lost our way.'

'They are perhaps belonging once to some wealthy family of landowners, those ruins?' enquired Dietfreid, and Nina repressed a compulsion to tell him not to gild the lily. He added, hopefully, 'Would you know about them?'

'Of course I know about the ruins,' said Madeleine. 'They're what's left of my own family's estates.'

'Oh, I didn't realize—'

Madeleine set down her teacup. 'Oh, it's a good many years

since any of it was intact. Couple of hundred at least. None of it means a thing to me, my dear.'

With the sensation that she was walking across very thin ice, Nina said, 'We've been delving into some of the history of the area. I wonder if we might have come across your family?'

'Not unless you've delved very far back,' said Madeleine. 'But once they were what people called a leading family in this area.'

Nina felt as if she had been plunged, neck-deep, into a churning cauldron. She said, 'How interesting. And how remarkable to be able to know your own family history so far back. That's something that people lose today, isn't it?'

'I don't know that it makes a great deal of difference in the end,' said Madeleine. 'And in any case, I should think the original family name is lost by this time.'

Nina said, 'What was the original family name?'

'Once upon a time it was Foleschamp,' said Madeleine. 'French, of course. My branch always spelled it as Foulsham.'

Nina started to say something and stopped.

'But,' said Madeleine, 'for a great many years in these parts, the family was known as Foljambe.'

Dietfreid said in a voice totally devoid of all expression, 'Here is the taxi.'

Lights were showing at most of the windows of Weston House when they eventually got back, and in two of them the curtains had not been drawn.

As she and Dietfreid came up the path, Nina looked up to the first floor. In the large bedroom overlooking the front of the house, a soft yellow table lamp had been switched on, casting pools of light. Piers's dark head was bent over a small desk and even from here Nina could see that it was piled with papers.

She smiled. It was remarkably good to think she was going into this house where Piers was, and absolutely marvellous to know that they would be able to tell him that they had done what they had come to Derbyshire to do. They had found the Foljambe house and its living descendant.

Chapter Thirty-One

Piers had escaped to his own room as soon as decently possible after supper.

The casserole, put together in what seemed to be another time and a different world, had not been ruined, but it had been a close thing. Piers had rescued it from the oven, and with a feeling that he was separated from Tybalt and Priscilla by a glass partition, had eaten his share, trying to listen with appropriate interest to Tybalt, who had not had a very fruitful day, but was already bouncing with energy for tomorrow.

When Priscilla answered the phone halfway through the meal, and came back to report that Nina and Dietfreid had apparently lost their way, but would be back sometime in the next hour, he said, 'Oh. Oh, good,' rather absently, and helped carry the dishes to the sink.

It was not until almost nine o'clock that he murmured an excuse, poured himself a hefty measure of whisky, and stole half-guiltily up to his own bedroom. There was a curious feeling of familiarity in sitting at the desk and in opening Father Simeon Berry's book once more.

Berry's own evidence came next; he told the court how, to start with, nobody had thought to question anything about Marcus Fitzglen who had come to the village earlier that year. He had appeared to be a wealthy gentleman – he had been staying at the Black Bull with his servant – and he had been charming and good-looking and it had been nobody's business to enquire into his background. People had been glad to welcome him into their houses, and Berry had added, with what Piers recognized as half-horror, half-relief, that Berry had himself wondered whether he should invite the man to stay at the manse for a week or two. He had the trick of interesting conversation, said Berry, as if by way of mitigation, and people had enjoyed his company. Well, his honour the judge knew that for himself.

His honour the judge had apparently nodded gloomily at this.

It had only been recently, explained Berry, that the whispers had started. Some of the village girls had apparently disappeared, and Berry, listening to Hugo Weston's tale, had realized with horror that it was incumbent on him to confront Marcus Fitzglen.

In the end, there had been quite a party of them, said Berry, because as well as a couple of farmers from Thane St Mary who had both lost daughters, Berry had taken with him the gentleman from Bishops Thane.

Sir Francis Foljambe, eldest son of the ancient house of His Majesty's wolfhunters.

Piers had been half-expecting it, but the sight of the name, black script outlining it on the pale page, still gave him a shock. He stared at it, his mind a seething tumult of emotions. It's real, he thought. The legends are coming together – they're intertwining and they're real.

The four men had gone along to the Black Bull at the after-supper hour; Berry had been wearing the good woollen cloak, which had been a present from a wealthy parishioner, since the nights were chilly, even at this time of year. The farmers carried a horn lantern each, and Sir Francis, as befitted a gentleman of his standing, had been leading a chestnut horse, although he had not mounted it but had walked with Berry, talking in the friendliest of fashions.

The Black Bull was at the village centre, and they had gone inside, intending to ask if they might have a friendly word with Master Fitzglen. No one at that stage, explained Berry, had had any idea of being other than friendly; all of them had wanted to believe there was some ordinary, natural explanation.

Just as they had been about to step through the door, Mistress Ablepiece, who kept the Black Bull (and very well too, observed Berry parenthetically), had stepped out and said that if it was Master Fitzglen they were looking for, he had gone out after eating his supper.

Well, said Berry, for a moment he had not known what to do. His honour the judge doubtless knew how it was when you

291

had summoned up your courage to an unpleasant task, and then found the task snatched from you. Berry had suspected Marcus Fitzglen of deliberately avoiding them, and Sir Francis, it seemed, had been sure of it.

'The creature is up to no good,' he had said. 'We should try to find him.'

'But where—'

'The forest,' said Sir Francis, his eyes gleaming. 'He will head for the forest, like all his kind.'

'Do we go after him?'

'We do,' said Sir Francis, and he had set off there and then, Berry and the two farmers in his wake, puffing a bit as they went, what with Sir Francis being a slenderly built gentleman and able to set a sharp pace, and Berry and the two farmers being what you might call stout.

Piers repressed a smile and read on.

The forest by night was a disturbing place, and the men were glad of the two lanterns. Sir Francis had stridden forward, his eyes scanning the dark trees and the undergrowth. Here, Father Berry added a sentence or two explaining that Francis had the slender whipcord strength of all his family, along with the russet hair and clear grey eyes.

Sir Francis had walked alongside Berry, and after a time Berry had plucked up his courage to ask whether they might be mistaken in their quest and whether Marcus Fitzglen might not have come into the forest at all.

But Sir Francis at once said, 'The creature is very near to us, Father. My family have hunted these monsters for so many generations that we have a great understanding of them. Marcus Fitzglen's kind have returned to these parts over and over, ever since the time when St Bertelin of Ilam slaughtered one of them.'

Berry looked about him nervously. 'And – you are sure he is here, are you, Sir Francis?'

'I am very sure.' Sir Francis had paused, and then had said, 'My grandfather believed that there always came a time in any hunt when the hunter sensed his victim's presence. Tonight I am the hunter and I can sense our victim's presence. He is in this forest.'

They had padded on, listening as they went, the two farmers glancing worriedly about them, wondering how far their priest and Sir Francis would be able to protect them. Even Berry, who had hoped to find himself intrepid, was aware of a burgeoning fear.

The forest was eerily quiet, and the feeling that they were drawing near to something dark and cruel began to grow on Berry. The lantern he carried cast a thin yellow light on the path, the dark trees looming ghostlike outside of it. Sir Francis said, very softly, 'Look there. Lights – can you see?'

'Yes.'

Sir Francis tilted his head, listening very intently, and said, 'Listen.'

One of the farmers started to say, 'I can't hear—' And then stopped, because they could all hear it.

The rhythmic scrape of spade or trowel on wet earth.

In the heart of the dark forest, someone was digging.

Piers could not help thinking that if the good Father had lived today he would have made a bomb from writing schlock horror. He topped up his whisky glass and read on.

Going forward towards the dull flickering lights was like going forward to hell's portals, said Berry. Sir Francis led the way, and if he felt fear he did not show it. Berry himself came next, holding aloft a crucifix. The two farmers brought up the rear.

The light was coming from a small clearing, from pointed sticks thrust into the ground, their upper tips burning brightly. The flames twisted upwards, crimson and scarlet, so that Berry's earlier feeling about approaching hell seemed not in the least far-fetched.

As they drew closer they heard laboured breathing as if someone was struggling with an immensely heavy task. Marcus Fitzglen stood at the centre of the clearing. He was naked, and there was a moment when Berry saw – unmistakably and unquestionably – that he was a nightmare blend of human and beast: his limbs were normal human limbs but here and there were patches of sable fur. He saw with horror swollen sex organs rearing up from between fur-covered thighs.

And then Marcus turned his head and the macabre image vanished and he was nothing more, nothing less, than a madman about to assault his victim.

His victim was Isobel Weston.

She was naked and she was tied to a tree. Her hands were bound over her head, the ropes looped around a high branch, and her legs were stretched wide, each ankle secured to a tree root. Her dark hair streamed loose over her shoulders, and she was bleeding from a dozen different places. As Marcus turned to glare at the intruders, they saw with sick horror that the lower part of his face was slicked with blood. Berry took this in, and then took in as well that the sly-eyed Walter was here and that he held a large spade in his hands. On the far side of the clearing was a large trench, half-dug.

Sir Francis did not hesitate. He flung his horse's bridle over a low branch and went forward at once, and Marcus Fitzglen stood very still, eyeing him. They were much of a height, and they were both slenderly built, but each gave the impression of immense inner power. Berry had the strange impression that although they had never met until this moment, they knew and recognized one another, as if they were communing at some level beyond human speech and outside of human hearing.

And then Marcus smiled and spread his hands in a travesty of greeting as if saying, welcome to my lair, humans, and with that gesture and that smile, Berry's fear increased a hundredfold, and he found himself remembering a dozen tangled tumbled fragments of ancient myth. The forest gods and demons who prowled through the night with cloven hoofs and three-cornered faces . . . The half-female, half-beast things who combed their eldritch hair with the sharpened bones of their victims, and who lived within the night tempests and keened into the wind . . . The wolves who could walk the world in the guise of humans, but who left dark and bloody imprints in their wake.

'His eyes were like slits as he watched Sir Francis,' wrote Berry, 'but they glowed red and his lips drew back from his teeth in a snarl. We all knew it was imperative to reach Mistress Weston and untie her, but I truly think that for a moment we were caught and held helpless by the sheer power that blazed from the creature's eyes.'

Piers felt for the whisky glass with his hand, and read on.

Sir Francis Foljambe looked at Fitzglen for a long moment, and then he said, very softly, 'I see your wretched catspaw servant is preparing a grave for your newest victim, werewolf.'

Marcus Fitzglen laughed, and leapt at Sir Francis in a single snarling bound, knocking him to the ground. The two of them went down in a whirling tangle of russet hair and glaring red eyes and teeth and claws and fists.

The farmers started forward at once, but the servant, Walter, lunged across the clearing, snatching a burning torch out of the ground as he came, and jabbing it hard into their faces. The younger of the farmers fell backwards with a scream of pain, his hands flying upwards to his eyes. Berry caught the dreadful stench of hair burning, and stood in agonized indecision, not knowing whether he should go to the man's assistance, or whether he should help Sir Francis.

'And my moment of indecision cost us dearly,' he said, soberly. 'For in that moment Walter had turned on the other farmer and myself, threatening us with the flaring wood, and holding aloft the spade. It was two of us against his one, and we ought to have overcome him with ease, but he had already felled our companion, burning his eyes out, and we were both wary.'

The two against one had suddenly become two against two. Marcus Fitzglen leapt up from his own fray, leaving Sir Francis half-conscious on the ground. He cried, 'Walter! Keep the humans there, while I finish my night's work!' and Berry had remembered with a start how attractive – how *cultured* – Marcus Fitzglen's voice was.

His night's work? asked the judge, and Piers conjured up a swift image of him leaning forward, the better to hear every nuance.

Father Berry confided to the pages of his journal that he had found it difficult to describe to the court the exact nature of what had happened next. 'For,' he said, 'I was a man of God and moreover celibate.'

Piers thought, with a wry inward twist, that the good Father had in reality probably had no difficulty at all in unfolding the next part.

Fitzglen had paid the intruders no further attention. He had turned his back on them with supreme insolence, and padded across the forest floor to where Mistress Weston was still tied helplessly to the tree. Berry had seen her lift her head and watch him approach; he had seen the expression of frightened fascination in her face.

295

'She feared him greatly, but she was also in his thrall,' stated Berry. 'And although she was tied so tightly, it was noticeable that she did not struggle against her bonds.'

Marcus had stood before her, reaching his hands out to caress her body. As he slid his hands between her upper thighs a low moan broke from her – Berry, the celibate, was not prepared to offer an opinion as to whether this was from fear or sexual arousal.

Marcus Fitzglen placed both his hands flat on the tree trunk, and then exactly as he had done before Isobel Weston's outraged father, he thrust easily and smoothly into his victim's body. And the curious thing, wrote Berry, descending into confidential mode once more: the thing he had not dared or even attempted to describe to the court, was that quite suddenly there was nothing repulsive or bestial or even particularly cruel about any of it. The flickering torchlights showered over the two naked bodies – Fitzglen was slender but he was well-formed and his skin gleamed like satin, and Isobel was a fragile figure, the cloud of dark hair framing her little white face, her body like ivory against the darkling background of the trees.

Fitzglen's movements had been rhythmic and smooth – the word *silken* had slid unasked into Berry's horrified and fascinated mind. He was powerless to do anything to stop Fitzglen, and he was powerless to drag his eyes away from the two figures locked in the most deeply intimate embrace imaginable.

When Fitzglen's thrustings quickened, Berry even had the wild thought that at least the creature was not about to commit the sin of Onan and spill his seed on the ground. And still he had not been able to look away. Shamefully aware of his own hitherto sternly repressed manhood stirring, he watched Fitzglen's strong thighs and lean hips moving faster; he saw, in the final seconds, two bodies shudder uncontrollably in simultaneous culmination.

The judge, presumably left in happy ignorance of Father Berry's response, both mental and physical, had asked whether any of them had made any attempt to intervene?

Piers was glad the judge had asked this, because he had been wondering it himself. Berry explained that they had wanted to: they had been concerned for the young farmer, writhing on the ground, his eyes scorched, and they had also been concerned for Sir Francis, bleeding from Fitzglen's teeth wounds. But the servant, Walter, had kept them at bay all the time, thrusting the burning torch at them if they so much as attempted to take a step forward.

'We could do nothing,' said Berry.

Marcus Fitzglen, having taken his strange, beautiful pleasure, had finally turned on the two men, 'Snarling and lashing out,' wrote Berry. 'Excitement, raw and fierce, blazed from him, and I thought my last hour had come,' admitted Berry. 'We all thought it.'

It was then that sounds from within the forest had alerted them, and they turned and looked into the black and green denseness of the trees.

'It should have been our chance to overpower the wretched Walter and his evil master,' said Berry. 'But what we saw filled us with such dread.'

What they had seen were pinpoints of light coming through the forest, so that for a heart-stopping moment it seemed that dozens of red-eyed creatures were marching through the night towards them. Even Berry had succumbed to panic, for if Marcus Fitzglen had in truth traded with the dark powers for that fearsome wolfish self they had glimpsed earlier, what might not be coming to his aid through the night now? His mind filled with visions of demons, summoned from the fiery caverns of hell and accoutred with red-hot pitchforks, or grinning devils brandishing affidavits that demanded Berry's instant presence in the deepest and hottest of their furnaces.

For a moment he had stared in frozen terror, and then the fiery lights had resolved themselves into the lit torches of a procession, and after all there were no dancing demons; there was nothing more sinister than the villagers of the Thanes, seeking out Marcus Fitzglen, just as Berry and Sir Francis had sought him, intent on forging their own rough justice.

He had seized his chance then, and had darted across the clearing, first throwing his own good warm cloak around Mistress Weston, and then going to Sir Francis. As he helped him to his feet, the procession burst into the clearing, Hugo Weston at its head.

'We've come for the wolf!' he cried, stepping out in front of the others, his jaw thrust pugnaciously forward. 'We want the wolf, and we're going to see he suffers what's due to him!'

The cry was taken up by the men and women standing with him.

'The wolf! The wolf!'

'Burn the wolf!'

'Keep our women safe!'

The garish torchlight fell across Marcus Fitzglen, and in that moment Berry saw clearly the wolf-mask overlying the human face. The villagers saw it as well; a gasp of horror rippled through them and they surged forward, and Berry thought that Fitzglen was about to be burned alive where he stood. His mind churned with indecision, but then Sir Francis, his face pale and streaked with blood, held up his hand. Berry noted with a very human pang of envy that immediate silence fell on the villagers.

'You shall have your wolf,' he said. 'But first you must let us try him according to the law of the land.'

'He's guilty of rape and murder!' cried several of the villagers.

'And witchcraft!' shouted several more.

'If he is, then we shall find him so,' said Sir Francis. 'And you have my word that he will be punished.'

'Hanging?' cried Master Weston scornfully. 'That's too good for the creature!'

'Burn him!' shouted the villagers. 'Burn him and send him down to Hell where he comes from!'

A curious and not very pleasant smile had curved Francis Foljambe's lips then; Berry had looked at him with surprise, because he had never before seen any evidence of cruelty in the man.

But Sir Francis was speaking again, and although his voice was soft his words were audible to every person present. 'We shall not burn him,' said Sir Francis. 'We shall deal with him as my family have dealt with his kind for five hundred years.'

'How?' demanded several truculent voices.

'You will see. For now, take him and throw him into the cells of the courthouse!'

To start with, the villagers had apparently been more or less appeased. They had muttered amongst themselves for a few minutes, but the majority appeared to agree that if you could not trust the word of Sir Francis and Father Berry you could not trust the word of anyone.

It had taken six strong men – the blacksmith and his son

among them – to overpower Fitzglen and two more to subdue Walter. But eventually they had managed to tie Marcus's hands behind his back and pass a makeshift rope halter around his neck so that if he tried to escape he would half-throttle. In this way they had half-carried, half-dragged him and the now-cringing Walter through the forest, and only then had Francis Foljambe and Berry been able to untie Isobel Weston.

But unfortunately, said Berry, suddenly descending to the sententious, in every majority there was a minority and where there were human emotions, there were human jealousies. From the back of the crowd came a voice that was filled with angry jealousy and hard with resentment.

'That's the wolf's paramour!' it shouted. 'Isobel Weston! What are we going to do with her? Is she to escape?' and Berry had recognized, with a sinking heart, the muscular figure of a young man from Croyse Thane who had been hopeful of wedding Isobel.

His cry had been taken up.

'The wolf's paramour! Isobel Weston who lay with the wolf!'
'Isobel Weston!'

'There she is!' cried the spurned lover, and Berry had seen the jowly countenance of Master Weston turn pasty white.

'Burn her for a wolf-lover!' cried the villagers.
'Hang her for a witch!'

The little lick of anger took hold and tore through the crowd, firing their animosity anew. They surged forward once more, their faces red and avid in the torchlight, that of the erstwhile suitor at their head. Berry was sorry to report that he had taken one look at the ravening crowd and stepped hastily backwards, but Hugo Weston, fearful for his daughter's safety, had stood his ground and tried to prevent them. He was pushed summarily aside as the villagers made for Isobel.

And once again, Sir Francis did not hesitate. Before anyone had realized what he was about, he had snatched Mistress Weston to him, and half thrown her into the saddle of his horse, springing up behind her. Before any of them could get to him, he turned his mount's head about, and galloped off into the darkness.

And although, said Berry, some of the villagers had made to follow, the horse with its two riders had swiftly been eaten up by the night. The crowd had been cheated of its prey and the rejected lover had been cheated of his revenge, and, said Father Berry, remembering his calling twice in the space of two paragraphs, men who were made to look fools were frequently inclined to give way to unwise actions.

This time, it was not just a lone voice that called for Mistress Weston to be brought to justice; it was the entire population of the Thanes.

Piers turned the page, prepared to read the good Father's colourful description of Isobel Weston's eventual fate. But either Berry was bound by the confessional – Piers tried to remember whether the Romish practice of confession had been outlawed by 1540 and could not – or more likely, knowing Berry, he was saving up the tale in order to treat his readers to a dramatic *dénouement* in the closing chapter.

It did not really matter which it was, because unless a great many people had told a great many elaborate lies in the succeeding four hundred years, Piers knew that Isobel Weston had given birth to Marcus Fitzglen's child – a child who had survived to pass the story of its curious ancestry down.

The only thing Piers did not know was whether the enraged villagers and the resentful lover had finally found and punished Isobel. Nor did he know where Francis Foljambe had taken her.

Chapter Thirty-Two

After mother and Bryony had been in Charect Cottage for a time, Bryony thought she knew how Isobel's house had looked and where the rooms had been. The house had been a lot different then, but the rooms had all been pretty much in the same places.

The garden had been in the same place as well of course, although Bryony thought there would have been different things in it. Mother had said that once they got the cottage straight they could try to make an old-fashioned garden. They could have what was called a knot garden and a herb garden. Bryony thought this would be lavishly good. She had walked around the garden, thinking where they would have the flowers and trying to visualize what a knot garden might look like. Isobel had had plants with wonderful names like gillyflowers and love-in-a-mist and heartsease. Bryony had been thinking about them when she had found the invisible line where Isobel's servant had sprinkled the charm.

It was a hugely secret charm and if the servant had been caught with it she would have been burned alive on account of having bought it from a witch. Isobel had been scared ever since she had been brought to this house, but she would have been a whole lot more scared without the charm. The servant said it would make them safe and not to be frightened, but Isobel spent a lot of time in her room, sitting on the padded window seat and looking out into the forest. Bryony thought that part of Isobel was watching to make sure that the people of the villages did not come through the forest to burn her for being a witch, but another, secret part, was wishing the man who looked like Karabas would come to take her away. Bryony was not sure about this man's name, but she thought he had been dark-haired and very good-looking and that Isobel had loved him a whole lot. It was only when he had turned out to be evil and cruel, and when he had done the thing to Isobel that made her have a baby, that she had had to hide. Bryony was not too clear on this matter of having babies, except that whatever it was that you did, you should not do it unless you loved somebody very much and only then if you were absolutely certain. It was not something you should do with somebody like Karabas, and it was not something that Isobel ought to have done with the man who looked like Karabas.

The day after they came to the house, the servant had gone out, wearing a cloak with a hood to hide her face; she went to the village green, and into bakeshops and pieshops, and listened secretly to what people were saying. She heard how the Karabas-man was in prison and how he was probably going to die and that people thought Isobel should die as well.

This was alarming and so the servant had got the charm at once. It had to be half-said and half-sung all the way around the garden so that it made a kind of circle around the house. It was not a circle you could see: Bryony thought probably it was not meant to be seen. But if you walked slowly and concentrated extra hard, you could feel it. It kind of sizzled very softly along the ground, and when it was the time that the Foljambes had called the Purple Hour you could just hear it very faintly, as if it was singing to itself. This was how Bryony had discovered it – she had felt it sizzling and heard it singing when she was exploring the garden. It was lavishly good to live in a house where there was a charm that sang to itself. Bryony was pretty pleased about that. She was pretty pleased to think how Isobel had lived here with the charm as well, all through the months she had stayed here with the servant. Bryony expected that Isobel would have thrown open the windows in the warm nights, and listened to the charm softly singing to itself, and felt safe.

But even with the charm, Isobel had thought the people would find her in the end. She had felt them getting closer and closer, and she knew that one night they would come through the forest, and they would see the house and they would guess that she was hiding there. Perhaps they would break the windows or batter the door down to get in, and then they would drag her out to die.

Bryony thought it was pretty strange that the villagers had to look for such a long time because Bishops Thane was not very far from the other Thane villages. But in those days you could not just get into a car and drive somewhere.

Bryony had just started to wonder whether one of the Foljambe family might have had anything to do with all this, and if so which one and why, when something absolutely extraordinary happened.

It started off by being an ordinary Saturday afternoon; they had had lunch and they were putting up the curtains in Bryony's bedroom. It was a really good bedroom now; there was the green and white wallpaper and there was fresh white paintwork everywhere. The carpenters who were making cupboards and things in the kitchen had built her a window seat under one window and a desk under the other one.

So the bedroom was a very good room by this time, and it only had to have the curtains, which they had bought from a market last week. Bryony had liked the market, and they had stayed out almost all day and had lunch in a bakeshop where you could smell the bread and cakes being baked in the back. They could drive to places by themselves, because mother had bought Miss Mackenzie's Mini; she said they would have to look after it very carefully, but it had been a good thing to have done.

Mother was standing on the stepladder hooking the curtains across the window and Bryony was holding the stepladder because you should never get on a stepladder without someone to hold the foot. It was then that they heard the door knocker rat-a-tatting and mother said, 'Oh drat, that'll probably be some boring old salesman or a Jehovah's Witness or something. But I suppose we'd better find out. Listen, if it's Jehovah's Witnesses we'll say we're Plymouth Brethren and if it's a salesman we'll say we're bank robbers, hiding out, OK?'

'OK,' said Bryony and giggled, because mother was great when she was like this.

It was not a salesman or a Jehovah's Witness at the door at all. It was a tall old lady with a battered felt hat and a shooting stick. She looked very intently at mother for a moment, and then said, 'You'll forgive me if I'm intruding, but I rather think, my dear, that we might be related.'

And as mother stared at her, the lady said, 'I'm Madeleine Foulsham, and if your mama was called Serena then I think I'm your grandmother.'

It was just about the most lavishly good thing Bryony had ever known. This was not Richard's Madeleine from all those hundreds of years ago, of course; Bryony knew this practically at once, but there was a moment, just at first, when she did not know it, and when she stared round-eyed at this tall old lady and thought she might be a ghost.

But ghosts did not knock politely on your door in the middle of the afternoon and wait for you to invite them in, and they did not wear green waxed jackets and lean a bit on walking sticks and smile like a slightly weather-beaten, rosy-cheeked apple. They did not apologize for having to be helped to sit in the deep armchair and say it was a nuisance being lame but too tiresome to talk about and anyhow it was only getting in and out of chairs that was a problem.

Madeleine Foulsham sat in the armchair and looked at mother with a look that was not quite like any look Bryony had ever seen on anyone's face before. It was how you might look if you had been longing and longing all your life to see something extra doubly precious, and as if – just when you had given up ever seeing it – you suddenly found it there in front of you.

Bryony curled into the chimney seat which was the best place in all the house, and listened carefully to what was being said, and understood pretty well that this lady had once had a daughter called Serena but that she had not seen Serena since she was a very little baby. Serena was not a name Bryony had ever heard before, but she thought it was beautiful.

'It means serene,' said Madeleine. 'Calm and untroubled. I don't know if she was any of those things, but I've always hoped so.'

'She was,' said mother at once. 'She was very tranquil. Her voice was restful as well.'

'Ah. Yes, good. You'll tell me a bit about her perhaps? When we've got to know one another better?'

'Oh yes, of course. I've got some photographs somewhere as well. I'll look them out for you.'

Bryony looked up at this because it was surprising that mother did not find the photographs there and then, but then she saw Madeleine nod and smile as if this pleased her. Bryony understood then that Madeleine did not want to hear about

Serena all in a lump this afternoon; she wanted mother to sort the memories out first and then to hear them a bit at a time. Bryony was glad that mother had understood this.

Madeleine looked across at Bryony then. 'Serena would have been your grandmother, Bryony,' she said. 'Which makes me your great-grandmother. That's pretty good, isn't it?'

Bryony said in her best voice that it was extremely good; it was lavishly good, in fact. She glanced at mother a bit uneasily and hoped there was not going to be any embarrassing slopping and kissing and crying about any of this.

But Madeleine was not embarrassing. She just kept looking at mother as if she wanted to memorize her, and as if she could not bear to let go with her eyes, and after a few minutes she put out a hand and closed it about mother's hand, and said, 'This is a very great happiness – I'm so glad I found you, my dear.'

And mother clasped her hand back and said, 'Yes. So am I.'

That was all either of them said. Bryony was hugely relieved, because although it was going to be extra doubly good to have a great-grandmother, it would not be good if there had to be a lot of slop over it.

'How did you find us?' mother asked, while they were drinking cups of tea, and Bryony caught a note of wariness in mother's voice, and looked up. But then mother said, 'I mean, how did you know who we were?' and Madeleine smiled.

'My dear,' she said, 'it's easy to see you've never lived in the country before.'

'People gossiped?'

'People always have gossiped about this cottage,' said Madeleine. 'It's got a bit of a past, you know. And I have a girl to help me with the cleaning who doesn't miss much. She's a bit of a bright spark with the men, I'm afraid, and she knows your builders and one of the assistants in the auctioneers' office. She was full of the news about the romantic young widow, Mrs Stafford, who had come to live at Charect with her small daughter.' She smiled. 'I recognized the name and wondered. Stafford isn't such an unusual name, of course, but then I saw you in the village one day— Well, you were unmistakable, Felicity.'

'You . . . recognized me?'

'Yes, I knew about you, even though you didn't know about

305

me,' said Madeleine. 'I had news of your mother over the years; I knew she had died, and then my cousin sent me a cutting of your wedding. He was very good-looking, your husband. I'm so sorry to hear he died.'

'Yes, it was very bad. But Bryony and I always promised ourselves we'd come here one day. We know a lot of the stories about the family, as well. Bryony loves them,' said mother, sending Bryony their private grin.

'So the tales still get spun, do they? Well, it's good to know that. I know some stories about the family as well,' said Madeleine. 'You must both come to visit me very soon, and Bryony can hear them.'

'We'd like that very much,' said mother. 'Wouldn't we, Bryony?'

Bryony, gazing at Madeleine Foulsham entranced, said oh yes, and remembered to say thank you.

'Well, I shan't be a nuisance, or forever on your doorstep, in case you were worrying about that,' said Madeleine, setting down her teacup and getting up out of the chair. 'But my house is quite near – you can drive around the lower road in about fifteen minutes if you have a car, and if you haven't, you can walk through the forest. You'll be very well come if you visit me.'

She did not say 'welcome' like most people; she made it two words.

'And you must come to tea on your own one afternoon, Bryony. We'll make fudge in my kitchen if you'd like to – I've got an old family recipe and it's the best fudge in the world – and then we can swap stories about our ancestors.'

This was just about the best thing that had ever happened to anyone in the entire world. Bryony wondered what she ought to call this astonishing lady, because if she had to keep saying great-grandmother it was going to slow up the conversation, but then Madeleine said, 'I hope you aren't going to be calling me grandmother or great-grandmother, either of you. I can't be saddled with that kind of title at my time of life, it's far too ageing.'

And as mother smiled, Madeleine said, 'Call me Mad. It's what everyone else does.'

Bryony thought this was a lavishly good name for a great-grandmother.

They walked part of the way back to Mad's house with her. Mother said the curtain-hanging could easily wait another hour and they would like to see the house and know where the forest path was.

'I actually live in what was the old gatehouse to the Foljambe estate,' said Mad as they went along. 'It's a bit big just for one, but I like the garden, and there's Sonja who comes in twice a week to help with the cleaning.'

'The one who's a bright spark with the men?'

'That's Sonja.'

The forest was lit by sunshine this afternoon; it poured down through the branches making patterns on the bracken at their feet. Bryony thought you might very easily see squirrels on an afternoon like this. She skipped once or twice as they went along because of it being such a happy forest today.

Mad said to mother, 'The estate fell down bit by bit around our ears. I never saw it of course, but my grandfather remembered his grandfather telling stories about it. George Foljambe was the one who let it go to rack and ruin. Victorian profligate, from the sound of it, that George. Better at spending money than at making it. He gambled most of it away. Bad, that. Don't approve of gambling. My grandfather said that was when the place started to go downhill. Francis Foljambe was the one that brought it to its greatest prosperity – bit fond of the ladies, he was, but I always rather liked the sound of him. I don't know what he'd have thought of George's carryings-on.'

She jabbed at a narrow path leading away on their left. 'The ruins are along there – if you've got time we can walk through to see them now. It isn't very far.'

Bryony would really have liked to see the ruins on her own, or with just herself and mother. But this would have been rude, and so she said, 'Yes, I'd like to see them, please.'

'All right. But listen, you must promise never *ever* to come into the forest by yourself. Isn't that right, Felicity?'

'Yes, it is. But she's already promised that, haven't you, Bryony?'

'Um.' Even good grown-ups could sometimes be absolutely septic about the really important things. But mother had been very firm and now Mad was being firm as well, so she said, 'OK, I promise again. I *doubly* promise.'

'Down this path here,' said Mad, and Bryony's heart did a flip-flop of excitement because this was really truly the house where the Foljambes had once lived.

But the ruins were disappointing. Bryony stared at them, and felt a sick lump of disappointment rise up in her throat, so that there was a bad moment when she thought she might cry.

Where were the five doors on the house's front, two at the front and one with a church-like door and a twisty iron ring for a handle? Where were the splendid grey stone walls with the glossy green ivy, and where were the windows – rows and rows of them – that caught the setting sun so that if you came up the carriageway at sunset the house looked as if it was on fire?

This was just a heap of old mouldy stones lying on the ground in between the trees. It was not even an *interesting* heap of stones. Bryony stood at the centre of the tumbly old bits of stones and stared about her.

She managed not to cry in the end, which was good. She said it was all lavishly interesting, and then Mad said she had an old drawing of how the house had looked around George the gambler's time, and they would look at it together one day very soon, and try to work out where all the rooms had been. Bryony felt a bit better then, because it would actually be pretty good to see the drawing. She wondered if it would show the small secret door that led down to the cellars with all the wolf-snares and the ogre-teeth traps.

She waited to see if Mad would say about the black door and the cellar but Mad did not, and so after a little while Bryony asked very carefully about it. Hadn't there been a little house with a cellar where the Foljambes had kept all their wolf-hunting things? Did Mad know where that might have been?

Mad gave a sudden chuckle, and said, 'Ho, so you've got a bloodthirsty streak, have you, my little one? Well, there *are* traces of what was probably once a cellar, and they say that that was where all the traps and snares were kept. You shall see it if you really want to and if your mother says it's all right.' She glanced at Felicity and Bryony looked up hopefully because mother hated cellars and underground places worse than anything in the world.

But mother grinned and said, 'What a revolting little ghoul you are, Bryony. Yes, do show her if you can spare the time,

Mad. But I'm not wild about poking around in disused cellars. I'll sit on this bit of stone here and commune with the forest.'

'Off we go then, Bryony. We'd better tread carefully, because it's the oldest part of the ruins. Do you know, it might even be almost a thousand years old?'

They trod carefully. It was getting a bit dark in the forest by this time: it had been a beautiful sunny afternoon, but as they went through the ruins the sun was starting to go down. It was a good thing, after all, that Mad and mother were here, because quite suddenly Bryony did not like the forest very much: it made her remember Karabas and the night he had carried her into the forest. She had pretty much managed to forget about that, but now it came back and she felt as if something might be creeping along after them, dodging behind trees as it came so that it kept out of sight. It would not be Karabas, of course, but it might be that bad old wolf that had eaten Edmund up on that long-ago Wolf Night. You could never be sure about wolves; you could not be absolutely sure that they ever really died.

And then Mad was saying, 'Here we are, my dear,' and there they were. Straight ahead of them was the dark, bad-smelling place where Edmund had been eaten up by the wolf.

And somebody had torn aside the ivy covering and somebody had broken down the door. A black gaping hole yawned wide into the ancient foundations of the forest house that Richard Foljambe had built nearly a thousand years earlier.

Felicity was surprised at how unsurprised she had been to meet Madeleine Foulsham and how easy it had been to slip into an instant comfortable rapport.

Madeleine – Mad. It was easier to think of her by that name, just as it was difficult to think of her as a grandmother. Felicity thought this might be because she had never had a grandmother. I'm not used to family and relations, she thought, as she leaned back against the trunk of an old tree. It had soaked up the afternoon sun so that it was warm against her back, and the sunlight filtered through the leaves, casting dappled patterns on the ground. From somewhere overhead wood pigeons poured their liquid song into the quiet afternoon. Nice. She could just make out the green-hatted figure of Mad waving her stick as she pointed out bits of the ruins to Bryony, and she could see Bryony's small figure trotting at Mad's side.

It had been nice of Madeleine Foulsham to seek them out and pay that carefully understated visit. Felicity had noted how Mad had stayed for half an hour only, drunk one cup of tea and refused offers of biscuits. Nice of her to make the point about not intending to intrude, as well. And she had been extraordinarily good with Bryony; she had displayed the instinctive immediate empathy that elderly unmarried ladies so often and so unexpectedly had with children. Felicity thought they would go to the gatehouse quite soon. They would keep a few polite barriers in place, but they would certainly get to know Mad much better. She was pleased to think she had photographs of Serena to show to Mad.

It was peaceful in the forest, although it felt slightly odd to know that they were on the site of the old estate where their ancestors had lived and served the king with that curious profession. If I was fanciful, thought Felicity, lulled by the warmth of the old tree, I might even start seeing ghosts. She considered the forest drowsily. The sun was just starting to set; the shadows were lengthening on the ground, and the birdsong had stopped. There was a feeling of immense stillness.

It's as if time's slowed down for a few moments, thought Felicity. And as if I could look across to the past, if only I knew where to look and if only I knew how to see. If I could do that, and if I was very lucky, I might just catch a glimpse of those ghosts . . .

Bryony's beloved Richard, perhaps, building that first little forest house under the aegis of William the Conqueror. Or the elusive, attractive twins who had fought in a Crusade . . . And Francis. Felicity and Bryony had not known about Francis until today. Felicity rather liked the sound of him.

I believe I can almost see him, she thought, drowsily. Dark hair with reddish lights in it and very clear eyes. Yes, he's there, standing under that low branch. I can see him watching me. Odd he should look so familiar. Or is it? He belongs here, after all . . . A ghost between the trees. It seemed entirely natural that Francis Foljambe, who had brought the estate to its greatest prosperity and been fond of the ladies, should sometimes walk in the forest he would once have known so well.

And then between one heartbeat and the next the sun-drenched tranquillity fled, and Felicity sat bolt upright, her

310

mind instantly alert. There was something wrong somewhere. Something menacing was nearby. Something to do with that feeling she had had of brushing against the past, was it? Or something to do with glimpsing the slight, clear-eyed figure of Francis moving between the trees?

Or was it Francis? thought Felicity, the hairs prickling on the back of her neck. No, of course it wasn't, you fool, you were half asleep and you dreamt that. There are no such things as ghosts. But there are other things. There are creatures who make frightening promises about watching you . . .

Ridiculous to think that Karabas or his people could have followed her here. Ridiculous to think he had been standing watching her. Yes, but there's *something* in the trees, thought Felicity, I *know* there is. She stared into the thickening shadows. Nothing. Or was there? In just another moment she would call out to Madeleine and Bryony – panic for Bryony surged upwards instantly, because supposing Karabas really was here—?

Directly in front of her, the undergrowth moved and there was the soft, stealthy sound of footsteps padding away from her.

She thought she maintained a reasonably calm front as they prepared to return to Charect Cottage, and Mad prepared to return to her own house.

Felicity toyed briefly with the idea of mentioning to Mad that she thought she had heard someone in the undergrowth, and then dismissed it. It had almost certainly been nothing more than her imagination, or, at worst, an animal, and Mad was apparently very used to walking by herself in the forest. She showed Felicity the wicked-looking knife that slid from the bottom of her walking stick. 'I'm a switchblade kid,' she said, grinning. 'And I have a police whistle in my pocket as well – one of those really high-pitched things that practically bursts your eardrums. Oh, and a can of that chemical gas spray they use in riots – here, look.'

'Er – isn't that illegal?'

'Oh yes,' said Mad. 'But I'd rather be illegal than mugged. I'll get you both one – it doesn't hurt to carry a bit of an arsenal around.'

So Felicity thought that Mad would probably be all right

walking home. She listened to Bryony explaining how they had found the really old part of the house, and about it being where all the wolf-traps were kept, and felt reality blur a bit, because it was difficult to know if Bryony was spinning one of her eerily fey stories again, or whether she and Mad had actually found something among the ruins.

But when Bryony had wandered a few feet away to inspect a clump of scarlet toadstools growing in the deep shadow of an ancient tree, Mad suddenly said, 'Felicity – better to keep Bryony away from these ruins for a while.' She did not exactly whisper, but she lowered her voice.

'Any particular reason?' Felicity glanced at the apparently absorbed Bryony.

'Well, it rather looked as if someone had broken into the old part where the cellars used to be,' said Mad. 'Quite recently, I mean. We didn't go very near to it – best not tempt providence.' She regarded Felicity kindly, her head to one side. 'I'm sure there's no cause for alarm – it'll only be tramps, or those New Age traveller people. They're always camping out in the forest. But best to steer clear of the forest for a time.'

It was probably only coincidence that it was at this precise moment that the sun sank beneath the horizon.

Chapter Thirty-Three

Renovating Charect Cottage was turning out to be amazingly therapeutic. It was a well-worn cliché that hard work was the cure-all for heartbreak, but Felicity had discovered at Bracken Hall that it was a truism as well. If you worked hard at something and concentrated fiercely on it, you succeeded in blotting out practically everything else. It did not work all the time but it worked for some of the time, which was the best anyone could hope for. Immersing herself in Bracken Hall's bicentenary, Felicity had managed to push away most of the bitter-sweet memories of Connor, and now, focusing on renovating Charect Cottage, she was pushing away the nightmare of so nearly losing Bryony and of Karabas's violence.

Karabas . . . It would not have been him in the forest that afternoon, of course, although it was curious how several times lately she had felt that he was quite near to her. This was nothing more than nerves; a delayed shock reaction to the rape – yes, and also to that sinister sunlit afternoon at Bracken when he had reappeared and when he had told her he would be watching to see the child born. Felicity thought only one of those things would be more than enough to spook you.

It would be this that was making her imagine that Charect Cottage was becoming host to something dark and very frightening. At the beginning, when they had practically been camping out on the floor and cooking over a primus stove, the little house had been welcoming and sympathetic. Felicity had remembered her first feeling that if a ghost did walk here it was a gentle and rather poignant ghost.

The house was still welcoming and it was still sympathetic and Felicity thought the wistful little ghost still occasionally flitted unseen through the rooms. But something else had crept into the cottage: something that was malevolent and sly, and whatever it was, it stalked the darkened house every night when

Felicity was in bed, and it peered out from the cracks in cupboards or behind doors.

You'll never be quite sure where I am . . . Karabas had said. *Sometimes you'll think I'm inside the house with you . . .*

Felicity caught herself looking over her shoulder in the evenings after Bryony was in bed and everywhere was quiet, just in case the sitting room door was being stealthily pushed open. Several times she got up to check the locks on the doors, and make sure the downstairs windows were safely closed.

Remember, when you lock your doors at night . . . remember that you might not be locking me out, you might be locking me in with you . . .

At this rate, thought Felicity crossly, I'll find myself looking under the bed every night, like a frustrated Victorian spinster! I don't believe that Karabas could have found us and I don't believe it was him I saw in the forest. I don't believe I saw anything in the forest! She fought the absurd nervous fears down and concentrated on drawing Charect Cottage's gentle reassuring aura about her again.

She was determined to be thrifty but practical with the Church's money and her own modest nest-egg; she was trying to strike a compromise between the unnecessarily luxurious and the downright penny-pinching. Most of the furniture from the London house fitted into the rooms, although some of the larger pieces had to be sold. Felicity watched the dining table being loaded onto a trailer, and experienced a sharp, wholly illogical pang of loss. She and Con had given so many dinner parties on that table – not elaborate five-course banquet affairs, but riotous, relaxed evenings, with people eating huge platefuls of curry and fluffy rice, or unpretentious garlicky casseroles with mounds of French bread to mop up the sauce, continental-style, or even just Chinese take-aways. Oh, go *quickly*, said Felicity in silent anguish to the table. Go quickly, and take the memories with you, because I can't bear them!

But if the table and the wardrobes were gone, the Welsh dresser looked terrific in the kitchen, and the small sofa – appropriately chintzy – and the rosewood desk were just right in the inglenook room. Carpets had to be bought new – the price was truly alarming – but Felicity had tried to economize by leaving the beautiful oak stair uncovered except for a narrow red strip down the centre. Good curtain material could be bought in markets for a quarter of its original price, and wallpaper did not have to be expensive to be attractive.

The kitchen and bathroom were blessedly complete now: the kitchen cupboards were plain but they were solid, made from creamy ash wood. The floor had been tiled with brick-coloured tiles and Felicity had found some really good rush mats in the local market. There were unbleached open-weave linen curtains at the windows, and later there would be a scarlet geranium in a pot on the sill. She had shown Mad the kitchen, and Mad had said, Bless your heart, my dear, I've got any number of bedding plants in my garden shed; you shall have as many as you want.

Her own bedroom was not quite finished yet. The builders had left fireplaces in each of the bedrooms, small Victorian hearths, and there had been a hilarious afternoon when the chimneys had been swept. But it would be blissfully soothing to lie in bed with the firelight washing over the walls, and listen to the shushing of the leaves in the trees outside her window.

And of course there were no ghosts in Charect. They were going to be very happy here, she and Bryony and the new baby.

Felicity was gradually starting to think about this baby as a normal entity; a dark-haired, soft-headed little scrap of humanity who might look a bit like Bryony, but who would not look in the least like Karabas. She had registered with a doctor in Ashbourne who had been friendly and practical, and shortly there would be regular ante-natal clinics to attend. She had even begun to think about names. She considered calling a boy after her father, who had been Peter, but with the thought came the jarring memory of the Prokofiev music, *Peter and the Wolf.* Oh God, no, not that. It might be rather nice to name the child for one of the Bracken Hall people who had been so extremely kind. Morag, perhaps, for a girl – or maybe the Irish version, Maura. Maura was nice. And there was Andrew or Dominic for a boy. Dominic Stafford sounded rather good.

With so much to think about and so much work to focus on, it was relatively easy to shrug off the creeping sense of unease. During the daytime Felicity could even laugh at herself. When Bryony started at the new school there was the flurry of new school friends and a new routine to get used to. There had been an interview with the headmistress and one of the teachers, and it seemed a small, friendly place. There was a school bus that collected the children; Felicity got into the way of walking to meet it each afternoon. It was a nice walk, just long enough to be enjoyable. She wondered about getting a dog. Bryony would love a puppy and they could train it together. She might ask Mad about that.

She began to exchange good-mornings with one or two other parents as they waited for the morning or afternoon school bus, and she was invited to coffee with two or three of the mothers. There were murmurs about a casual lunch club – once a month, trying a different pub each time – and there were suggestions about the PTA and the local amateur dramatic group and the history society. It was all very friendly and undemanding and rather pleasant. I'm putting down roots, she thought. This is going to work. Bryony was asked to tea parties and included in an outing to the stalactite caverns at Matlock. This had apparently been brilliant.

She's all right, thought Felicity. We're both all right. Little by little, she began to relax.

And then the builders discovered the original foundations of the first Charect House, and the cottage that had been such a refuge and a sanctuary finally and irrevocably crossed over into its haunted state, and the darkness that Felicity had sensed came streaming out in a huge choking torrent.

It happened by accident. Charect had a small half-cellar that led off the kitchen, and that was going to house the small central heating boiler, along with extra plumbing for a washing machine. Felicity had gone into it once, and found it a rather gloomy, vaguely damp-feeling place. There was an ancient behemoth of a boiler against one wall, which would have to be dismantled and disposed of. But once that had been done, a modern boiler could be installed, the walls plastered and whitewashed, and some bright tiles laid on the floor. But the plumber said, and Felicity agreed, that the half-cellar would make a good laundry. It was a pity to let all that space go to waste.

The dismantling of the old cast iron boiler took the best part of a day, and it was only when the final section was pulled clear of the wall that the bricked-up doorway was revealed. It was a small area, barely five feet in height, and the bricks were dry-looking and so thickly veiled in cobwebs that for a moment Felicity thought that a grey curtain hung there.

'Will you absolutely have to break through that?' asked Felicity, eyeing the ancient brickwork distastefully.

"Fraid so, Mrs Stafford. This cellar you've got is only about a quarter the size of the present house. There's probably another room on the other side of that wall – it looks as if it was bricked up a long time ago. It looks as if the original foundations were never filled in. And you'd want to know what was in there, wouldn't you?'

Felicity resisted the compulsion to say, Not in a thousand years. 'Yes, of course.'

'Only take an hour or two,' said the plumber, cheerfully. 'I'll get the boy to fetch a pickaxe.'

Bryony knew not to go into the half-cellar while the builders and the plumbers were working there and especially not to go in today when they were breaking up a wall, or something. It was a crumbly, mouldy old place, that cellar, and a person would not go into it from choice anyhow. There was a badness in it – not a frightening *evil* badness but a sad lonely badness.

Bryony thought it might be because of Isobel. She had been frightened all the time, even with the charm sprinkled round the house. You could feel her fear in parts of the house: Bryony had felt it in several places, but worst of all was in the kitchen, by the door that led down to the cellar. That was where Isobel had been when the servant had come running in to say that the villagers had burned down Isobel's home – her real home where she had lived with her father – and that he had only just got out in time to avoid being burned up. Isobel was very upset about her home being burned and about her father. Anyone would be sad at all that, but Isobel was frightened as well, because she knew that tonight the villagers would come to Charect House and that they might try to burn it down as well.

They had been packing their things, panicking but trying to be quick, and trying to think where they would go and what they would do. Bryony could easily imagine Isobel snatching clothes and shawls and a woollen cloak and stuffing them into a bag. And then Isobel had suddenly stopped, her hands full of garments, and lifted her head to listen. After a moment she had stared at the servant, her eyes huge with terror.

From beyond the windows, from within the dark forest, came the sounds of shouts. And, as the servant ran to the window to peer into the night, they both saw the lights of blazing torches coming through the trees towards them.

They crouched together beneath the window so that they would not be seen, and prayed to escape. The servant kept reminding Isobel about the charm, but Isobel knew the charm would no longer protect them. It had done so at the very beginning, but it would not do so now. Perhaps it had grown weaker over the months they had been here – perhaps you had to renew charms to keep them working and the servant had not known it – or perhaps the hatred of the villagers had finally become stronger than the charm.

It was too late to escape into the night and run away somewhere to safety. The villagers had reached the house and they formed a circle all round it, chanting and shouting. Isobel peeped over the edge of the window and then dodged down again, because that one quick glimpse had shown her the crowd of people: it had shown her their faces, and they were red and shiny, their eyes glittering as if they were hugely excited. It was pretty horrid when people got excited about cruel things like burning somebody alive. Isobel had felt sick seeing it and Bryony felt sick as well, just thinking about it.

But then the servant had thought of a way Isobel might escape. There was the slidy panel at one side of the fireplace – it had been built to hide a priest – and the servant said that if Isobel hid in there, there was just a chance that the villagers would not find her.

It was dark behind the panel and there was a smell of mice and dead things. Isobel could not breathe very well once the panel was back in place, but it was a great deal better to be uncomfortable for a short while than to be dragged out by the angry villagers and burned alive. She stayed crammed into the horrid dark hole, listening and waiting, and very soon she heard the sound she had been dreading. The villagers were pounding on the door. They had found her.

They pounded and they shouted all in a rhythm, so that it came through to Isobel as, *Find the witch, Find the witch . . .*

She began to shiver all over, and then the shouting got faster;

it changed to *Burn-the-witch, Burn-the-witch* . . . and there was a crashing and a splintering, and she knew they were inside the house.

She shrank into the tiniest little huddle possible, but her heart was beating so violently that she was afraid the villagers would hear and tear the panel open. She tried very hard to be brave. She tried to think about the priests who had hidden from the king's men in here, and she remembered that priests were brave men and that they might have left a bit of their courage behind. Courage was not something you could see, but it might be something you could feel. Isobel had thought if she could feel somebody else's courage, she might manage to be brave herself.

But the village people were running all over the house – she could hear their heavy footsteps thundering up and down the stairs and in and out of the rooms, and she could hear them shouting what they would do to her if they found her. She was trembling with fear and now there was something about a pain as well – Bryony did not absolutely understand this, except that it was something to do with the baby and that it was an extremely bad pain. But after a while Isobel had to bend over and clutch her stomach, and then she had to tear off a piece of her gown and stuff it into her mouth because the pain was becoming so terrible that she would have cried out and they would have heard her.

There was a smell of burning wood now, and for a dreadful minute Isobel thought the house was going to be burned down and that she would burn with it. And then she understood that the people had found the room, and that they were on the other side of the sliding wooden panel and it was their burning torches she could smell.

She huddled into her corner, hunched over the dreadful pain, and then there was a scrape of sound, and light – hot, dry, burning light that hurt her eyes – flooded the cramped space, and she looked up to see the glittery-eyed men staring down at her. Behind them the servant was crying and wringing her hands, and she could hear the poor woman screaming to the men to have mercy, could they not see that her mistress was about to give birth.

But they reached down into the hiding place to drag her out: they had horrid scratchy hands with dirty broken nails that scraped her skin, and they smelt of onions and woodsmoke and unwashed flesh. Isobel felt sick and dizzy with the smell and the panic and the tearing pain.

They pulled her out of the hiding place and tried to make her walk out to the forest, but she could not stand up because of the pain.

'She's giving birth,' cried one of the men, and the big red faces swam into her vision as they leaned over her.

'She's faking,' said another voice, scornfully. 'That's an old trick, that is. I say we kick the bitch and make her stand up.'

There was a jumble of voices arguing loudly, and then somebody said, 'No, she's not faking. Look – the head's half out,' and then the voice that had said about kicking her, said, 'Good! We can kill the bitch and her wolf-whelp with her!'

'Bring her to stand trial!' cried a different voice.

'No!' said another one. 'Not another trial with people talking on and on all the day! Let's deal with her now! Let's do to her what they're going to do to her wolf-lover tonight!'

It had been as the men said this that Isobel had stopped fighting. She had known, just as Bryony knew, that they were going to kill her, but she had not fought them any more. Bryony found this difficult to understand.

What she found hardest of all to understand was that from that moment, Isobel Weston had shown no fear.

Chapter Thirty-Four

What Piers found hardest of all to understand was that apparently Marcus Fitzglen had not shown the least trace of fear.

There was not a great deal left of Father Berry's remarkable account, and he was reading it more slowly now, giving each word his full attention. If I didn't know better, thought Piers, angrily, I should almost think I wanted to find that the creature had gone free.

The clinching evidence had been that of Sir Francis Foljambe. He had taken the stand in a cool, unruffled way, and told the court how, after Fitzglen had been taken to the cells beneath the court-house, they had turned their attention to the trench half-dug by the hapless Walter.

'The werewolf's poor wretched victims were all there,' he said. 'Branding him unmistakably as the murderous thing we knew him to be. He had thrown them into the makeshift grave, and they lay as they had fallen. Some of them were incomplete, but we knew some of them by the jewellery they had been wearing.'

Piers read this with a mixture of nausea and pity. Berry had shown surprising restraint, but the word *incomplete* was dreadfully evocative, and the half-buried bodies must surely have been in different stages of decomposition. The reference to jewellery was heart-breaking: whoever the poor little village girls had been, they had decked themselves out in their pitiful little bits of tawdry finery for their assignations with the fascinating gentleman who had come to Bishops Thane.

It had taken the jury of twelve good men and true precisely half an hour to return an unequivocal verdict that Marcus Fitzglen was guilty of rape, murder and the practice of witchcraft. He was certainly destined to die, but the court had deliberated for a long time before pronouncing sentence, retiring to a private room to do so. Berry had been admitted to the discussion, partly as the official scribe, but also because of his position as cleric. Piers guessed that this harked back to the days when the priest had a certain standing in every community, generally because he was the only literate person there.

'He is not to be burned,' Sir Francis had said, eyeing the small group around the table. 'Burning does not put an end to the unnatural line he springs from.'

The judge, carefully polite, had asked about that, and Sir Francis had said, 'He is one of a line of freaks. Neither quite beast nor quite human. My family have encountered his kind several times over the centuries, and we have always dealt with the creatures in the same way.'

'By beheading?' asked the judge. 'By hanging?'

'No. Listen.' Sir Francis had leaned forward over the table, his grey eyes shining, an Berry had looked at him and thought that if he had not himself renounced such worldly things as physical attraction, he might very well have been a little envious of Sir Francis.

Francis Foljambe had his way, of course, and Berry faithfully set down the exact wording of the sentence:

Whereas the confessions and testimonies have demonstrated to this court your guilt . . . Whereas, Marcus Fitzglen, you are guilty of terrible crimes against humanity and also of the extreme sin of consorting with demonic forces, and shall shortly be brought to sentence . . .

Your servant, Walter, shall suffer the punishment decreed by our laws, which is to say he will be chained to a stake and burned until he is dead, so that his soul may be purged and cleansed.

Burned alive. Piers felt his skin crawl, and he turned over the page, aware of a mounting sense of anticipation. He realized he was gripping the book's edges so hard that his knuckles had whitened. And then, without warning, Marcus's fate was there.

Marcus Fitzglen, by the power vested in me, I condemn you to perpetual imprisonment. You will be immured in the cellars of Sir Francis Foljambe's house, which is at his express request and is in accordance with the authority vested in him by the King's Grace, which comes unbroken across nearly five centuries.

And so that you shall never wreak your terrible vengeance on another living soul while you still live, iron spikes will be driven through your jaws before the bricking up is done.

'In the dawn of the day of execution of both sentences,' wrote Berry, in the closing chapter, 'which executions I was in duty bound to attend, I rose from my bed with the feeling that leaden weights lay at the pit of my stomach, and that a huge dark weight pressed down on my head.'

It had been a rose and gold dawn, with a faint shimmering haze everywhere which would burn off with the day's heat. Berry noted this with immense sadness. It was too beautiful a day to die, he said.

He gave only a cursory account of Walter's death, which still managed to be a pretty graphic thumbnail sketch. Piers, reading of how Walter's skin turned shiny and red and then began to split in the fire, and of how his hair caught light and his eyes burst, was not surprised to also read that Father Berry had not fancied his dinner afterwards, even though it had been the Feast of the Ascension, when he normally allowed himself a little indulgence by way of a well-cooked duckling with a glass of the local wine.

And then, said Berry, with the air of one arriving at the main event, as night fell, all their attention had turned to the beast Fitzglen.

The sentence had been carried out at midnight, but there had been a feeling of unrest in all of the Thane villages throughout the entire day. Berry had heard some of the men gathering together in furtive little groups as darkness fell, and he had felt a twinge of unease. Ordinarily, he wrote, I would have approached them to make sure that no devilry was afoot, but as it was I was too taken up with the coming night.

As midnight approached, the judge, along with the executioner and Sir Francis Foljambe, walked in solemn, torchlit procession to the courthouse, where Fitzglen was held. Berry had been with them, unhappy and uneasy but intoning prayers as he went. He confided to his readers that he had

323

chosen the lines of the Ninety-first Psalm as being most appropriate to the macabre night.

Whoso dwelleth under the defence of the most High, shall abide under the shadow of the Almighty.

I will say unto the Lord, Thou art my hope and my stronghold; my God in Him will I trust.

For he shall deliver thee from the snare of the hunter, and from the noisome pestilence.

Piers read this prayer three times, because its power seemed almost to leap off the page. It was frighteningly easy to visualize the determined, grim-faced men walking through the village towards their prisoner, entering the courthouse and descending to the underground cells.

When they unlocked the cell door, Marcus Fitzglen was entirely composed, and apparently received his executioners with no sign of interest. As they led him through the forest to Sir Francis's house, he looked neither to right nor left, and the only time he had shown any emotion was when Berry had tried to give him a silver crucifix, blessed, he wrote, by the Cardinal himself. Marcus had dashed it from Berry's hands with a snarling oath, and then snatched his hand back as if burnt.

Piers, reading this part, could not decide how much credence to give to it. It was bordering on vampire territory and also on werewolf country, of course: the crucifix, the silver bullet, both of them lethal to the possessed creature, both of them with the power to burn and destroy. He tried to remember whether the myth had been born out of genuine mid-European folklore, or whether the films and the books had started the myth, and could not.

The local blacksmith and his two brawny sons had set up a makeshift, but serviceable anvil in the cellars of Sir Francis's house, wheeling it through the forest on a small cart after dark, and as the macabre group went down the steps they heard the sound of hammering and caught the scent of burning metal.

Iron spikes through his jaws, thought Piers, turning a page, still trying to suspend credence, but reading every word as if it was Holy Writ or the Koran. They were going to drive iron

324

spikes through his jaws so that he could never savage anything again.

The spikes were already forged and cooling: two long, narrow, glinting spears, evil and black. The blacksmith had confided to Berry that even with Sir Francis and the judge present, as well as Berry himself, they would be glad when tomorrow's dawn broke.

The executioner's assistants made to bring Marcus forward to the anvil, but he shook them off impatiently, and brushed his sleeve where they had touched him as if to wipe away a contagion. He was arrogant to the last, thought Piers, conscious of unwilling admiration.

The blacksmith had brought steel clamps with him, and his sons adjusted them so that Marcus could not move his head. He lay facing upwards, his head hanging back down over the anvil's edge, his hair brushing the floor. His wrists were bound tightly together and iron gyves were looped around his ankles. There was a moment when the candles burned up more brightly, casting curious shadows on the strange scene, casting a three-cornered illumination across the prisoner's face, giving it the aspect of a wolf's mask, triangular and sneering. Berry was dreadfully reminded of how Fitzglen had looked in the forest glade that night.

Marcus Fitzglen fixed his eyes on Sir Francis and without warning spoke. He said, softly, 'You think you have destroyed me, Francis Foljambe, but you have not destroyed my people. Remember that. They still live – a line of them will live through Isobel Weston, and my descendants will return over and over to vanquish you and your line until nothing remains.'

And then, almost as if losing interest, he closed his eyes as if saying, Well? Shall we get on with it?

But as the first spike was positioned beneath his jawbone, the sharp point denting into the flesh, his eyes opened again and throughout what followed he kept them fixed on the motionless, watching figure of Sir Francis.

The blacksmith wiped sweat from his forehead with the back of his hand and reached for the large, heavy-headed hammer.

The first blow of the hammer sent a shuddering agony through Berry's body, and there was the sickening crunch of bone splintering. The prisoner's eyes darkened and a low moan broke from him. His hands clenched in spasm, but then he

325

was still. Blood was welling up from the deep wound beneath his jaw, and dripping onto the floor, and Berry had the absurd inconsequential thought that somebody would have to scrub it very hard to remove the stain. He thought for a moment that Marcus had passed into merciful unconsciousness – 'Though why I should wish him any mercy when he had shown none at all to his victims I cannot tell,' he wrote. But then Sir Francis, standing next to him, had said very softly, 'The creature is still conscious, Father.'

Marcus's eyes were still on Sir Francis, and even though he was barely able to move for the gyves around his wrists and ankles and the tight clamp in which his head was held, such blazing vengeance streamed from his eyes that the blacksmith – six feet of bone and muscle – was unable to go on and his elder son had to take the hammer from his trembling hands.

As the boy resumed his father's work, striking a second blow, there was a sound from overhead, and everyone glanced upwards uneasily. From above their heads came the low growl of thunder.

Sir Francis motioned to the boy to finish his father's work, and the third blow brought the tip of the spike bursting through the prisoner's face. Blood and colourless fluid ran down his face, trickling into his eyes, and Berry had to master an impulse to step forward and wipe it away.

With the preparation for emplacing the second spike, the storm rolled nearer, and the candles flickered wildly and then, as one, went out. The pungent scent of candlewax drifted across the dark cellar and it was several minutes before the executioner's assistants were sufficiently master of themselves to re-light them. Afterwards, they said with bluff embarrassment that they had half-expected that when the lights flared again, they would find their prisoner had vanished. 'Taken by his dread Master,' they said, so that the very next Sunday Berry had taken his text from Ephesians: 'We wrestle not against flesh and blood, but against principalities, against powers, against the rulers of darkness of this world, and against spiritual wickedness in his places.'

The storm was growling menacingly as, by the light of the newly-lit candles, they drove the second spike through the prisoner's jaws, spattering the ground with his blood. As the black point burst through Marcus Fitzglen's cheekbone, there was a crash of thunder so tremendous that everyone jumped. The candles failed again at this point, and it was several minutes before they could be got to burn again.

As the executioner brought the prisoner to an upright position once more, the storm was raging in earnest, and even in the cellars the lightning penetrated in sharp erratic flickers, setting everyone's nerves on edge. As the candles burned up, the cruel iron spikes driven through Fitzglen's jaws caught the uncertain glow. His face was smeared with sweat and with his own blood, but although his eyes were glazed with agony, malevolence for Francis Foljambe still blazed from them.

As the thunder crashed over their heads they led him forward to the prison they had made that day, and as one of the men held the candle aloft, Berry saw it for the first time and his heart misgave him, for it was a truly terrible place. It was little more than an oblong box, a dank, dark tomb. There was the smell of new mortar from the hastily-laid bricks and stones, and propped against the wall was a set of thick iron bars which the blacksmith had forged to the exact measurements of the opening. Once in place the bars would form a grille within the new brickwork and the remainder of the bricks would be laid over the grille.

Marcus sat straight-backed on the wooden chair, his mutilated face so swollen and distorted that Berry, who had been trying to think of him as an ordinary human being, suddenly saw that the distortion was the real creature: that what was chained down here was something truly monstrous: something out of one of the ancient fables of the world's dark ages . . .

As the blacksmith and his sons dragged the grille into place Marcus's demeanour was impassive. The grille filled the space very precisely. And then they began to haul the bricks into place, and Berry understood that the iron bars were for extra security. Newly-built walls could be dislodged; mortar could be scraped out while it was still damp, and desperate prisoners could squeeze out through the smallest of apertures. The grille was reinforcement.

The blacksmith's sons worked quickly at the bricking up, anxious to be finished, resolutely avoiding looking at the prisoner. Berry began to pray again but the storm crashed overhead, drowning his words, and after a moment he faltered into silence.

But as the last row of bricks was laid in place, his compassion almost overwhelmed him, and he started the prayer a second time, raising his voice against the moaning wind and the deafening thunderclaps. Because whatever else he could or could not do, he could at least try to ensure that the last thing this evil being heard was the Word of God.

He shall defend thee under his wings, and thou shalt be safe under his feathers;
His faithfulness and truth shall be thy shield and buckler.

Thou shalt not be afraid for any terror by night, nor for the arrow that flieth by day;
For the pestilence that walketh in darkness; nor for the sickness that destroyeth in the noon-day sun.

The power and the comfort of the prayer seemed to sing all around the cellars, but as the final brick was laid in place, there was a tremendous, earth-shattering explosion of thunder, and fiery crackles of lightning streaked through the cellars, sizzling in and out of the corners.

And even though Marcus Fitzglen could no longer speak; even though he was muzzled like the wild savage beast he was; even though he was bricked up and behind an iron grille, his voice seemed to reverberate through the flickering darkness.

You think you have destroyed me, Francis Foljambe, but my people still live – a line of them will live through Isobel Weston, and my descendants will return over and over to vanquish you and your line until nothing remains.

Piers, his ears deaf to the outer world, his eyes blind to the twentieth century, felt his skin prickle with the horror and the agony with which the long-ago Father Berry had painted his story.

Berry had been faithful to the end, but Piers suspected that the priest had no longer been objective in his recording. In the last few pages he had recorded his own torment at the imprisonment of the creature.

'He was more alone than any creature in the world could

ever have been,' said Berry. 'I prayed for him night and day; spending hours on my knees, beseeching God and his saints to give me a sign that the creature had repented, and that we might bring him back into the world, marred and branded, but whole in God's sight.'

It had not happened. The sign had not come and the young, once-dazzling man who had charmed a forest community had died alone, in the dark silence of his terrible prison.

'It was a terrible punishment,' wrote Berry on the last page. 'They would have done better to execute him outright – even to burn him with his wretched servant – and have done.'

And then he added, 'But despite my prayers for him – and I prayed long after he must have been dead – I have never managed to believe that God has had mercy on the soul of Marcus Fitzglen.'

Piers laid Berry's book down. He did not believe it, he simply did *not*, and that was all there was to it.

It was every ridiculous horror film ever made: it was the evil entity from the past, vanquished and cornered, clawing out at its assailants and flinging out its last defiant curse: *My people still live – a line of them will live through Isobel Weston, and they will return over and over . . .*

But Marcus's people did still live; Piers had seen them on Cruithin Island, and he had seen them behind his own mother's eyes.

He stared out of his bedroom window, frowning. It was completely dark now; the ancient forest was shrouded in impenetrable shadows. Had the creature that had been Marcus Fitzglen truly walked through those shadows four hundred and fifty years ago? Or was this whole thing some kind of hyped local legend? What I need, thought Piers, is another opinion on Father Berry's book.

After a moment he stood up, and slipping the book into a pocket, went along the corridor to Tybalt's room.

Chapter Thirty-Five

It was almost supper time of the next day when Tybalt took the chair under Piers's bedroom window, and silently put Father Berry's book down.

For a moment neither of them spoke, and then Tybalt said, 'Why did you choose me to read it? Why not let everyone in on it?'

'God knows.'

'Are we going to tell the others?'

'Not yet.'

'Why not?'

'Well,' said Piers, 'you've read Berry's book.' And waited to see if the boy had the sensitivity he had hoped.

'It's because it's your family,' said Tybalt, after a moment. 'That girl, Isobel Weston, who was – um – with Marcus in the forest; she was your ancestor, wasn't she? You said when I found that old print that your mother's name had been Weston—'

'Yes.'

'And that means— Oh wow,' said Tybalt, as he suddenly realized exactly what it did mean. 'It means that if there was a child, this Marcus – this weird werewolf character – could have been your ancestor.'

'Possibly.'

'And,' went on Tybalt, 'if Marcus was one of Karabas's people—' He broke off and stared at his mentor, torn between fascination and a sudden horrified suspicion that he might have overstepped the mark. 'Uh – excuse me if that's kind of personal—'

But Dr Adair said, 'No, it isn't. It's what I wanted. I wanted to see if someone else made the connection without me pointing it out. That's why I gave it to you to read cold.'

'You thought you might have been jumping to the wrong suppositions.'

'Yes.'

'Well, if you did, I jumped to the same ones. The link – I mean the slight possibility of a link – with your family. And the link – not so slight – with the guys on Cruithin Island.'

'Admirably succinct,' said Dr Adair, and gave Tybalt the sudden smile that sent Nina and Priscilla into transports of bliss.

He said, 'Was there a child? I mean – do you know if there was?'

'I don't know,' said Piers, meeting Tybalt's ingenuous stare.

'No, I guess you wouldn't, what with it being so far back and all like that.' Tybalt frowned, chewing the problem over, and then said, 'Well, whatever the truth is or isn't, I surely wouldn't want to tell people a tale like this one. Even if it was only a legend.'

'I don't want to tell them. I suppose I might tell Toby when he gets here. I'd have to threaten him with dismembering if he ever made copy out of it, though.'

Tybalt thought it might be OK to tell Toby. He had unsuspected depths at times, that Toby. 'But not the others,' he said, firmly. 'They'd either laugh or not understand. Either way you'd be – you'd be *shrivelled*.'

Piers said dryly, 'Priscilla would almost certainly laugh. Dietfreid would be earnest and painstaking—'

'We don't want earnest and painstaking right now, we want a bit of imagination—'

'Precisely. Nina would be sympathetic, of course.'

'Yes, but sympathy's not what we want either. We want the truth. Well, that's what I'd want,' said Tybalt.

'It is what I want. Thank you, Tybalt.'

Tybalt blushed bright red, and Piers smiled a bit absently. 'We'll try to find out what happened to Isobel and where Sir Francis took her,' he said. He was staring ahead of him, and he had curled his hands around his mug of tea as if, thought Tybalt, he needed to draw warmth into his body. He guessed it would be pretty shattering to discover you had a werewolf in your family tree – hell, Dr Adair was entitled to feel as frozen as an iceberg for about a zillion years!

'Did you believe all of what Berry wrote, Tybalt?'

'To start with I thought I was going to dismiss it as hokum,' said Tybalt. 'I was pretty sceptical, you know? All that stuff about village maidens and the wolf-mask lying across Marcus Fitzglen's face. That was a lot to expect anyone to swallow.'

'Those parts could have been due to Father Berry's romantic soul,' said Piers, with a smile that Tybalt thought you could only describe as painful.

'Well yes. But by the time I got to the end I guess I did believe.'

'Because you had seen the creatures on Cruithin Island,' said Piers, softly.

'Yes. Yes, if I hadn't seen them I could have dismissed the whole thing. But as it is, it makes another thread in the pattern, doesn't it?'

'Oh yes. And we have to investigate it.'

'Uh, yes, I guess we do.' Tybalt knew he would never wholly understand Dr Adair – he guessed no one would ever wholly understand him – but what he did know was that Dr Adair was holding out on something somewhere.

Piers said, 'Have you seen Nina or Dietfreid since yesterday morning?'

'No, they were late back last night, and then they set off early this morning; Dietfreid wanted to look at a church in a place called Croyse Thane, I think. Anyhow, I was holed up in my room with Father Berry's sixteenth-century spine-chiller. Why?'

'They found the Foljambe estate yesterday,' said Piers, very softly. 'That's why they were so late back. It's in ruins, but it seems certain that it's the place all right.'

He looked at Tybalt and Tybalt said, 'That's terrific. That means—' He stopped. 'Oh God, that's where they put him.' He stared at Piers. 'Oh God, you're going to see if you can find that cellar, aren't you?'

'Yes.'

'And if you find it, you're going to break down the wall and see if Marcus Fitzglen's body is still there?'

'Yes.'

They looked at one another.

'You want me to come with you?' said Tybalt at length.

'Would you?'

'Oh, wow!'

'It's a simple question of physical strength,' said Piers. 'I can't do it by myself.'

332

'Well, all right. Yeah, OK.'

'It had better be done secretly. When the others are in bed.'

'When exactly—'

'I thought we might do it tonight,' said Dr Adair, his voice sounding as cool as if he was arranging to put the cat out or go out to the movies.

'What time?'

'Midnight.'

Tybalt supposed he should have known better than to ask.

'Do we know exactly where these ruins are?' demanded Tybalt as they free-wheeled the Range Rover down the track to avoid waking anyone.

'Oh yes.' Piers swung onto the road and turned on the ignition. The engine growled into life, and he switched on the headlights. 'Dietfreid showed me on the map. He and Nina found it by the sheerest piece of luck – they were over the moon about it. It's actually only about half an hour's drive along this lower road.'

The Range Rover's headlights picked out a faint ground mist, like the fake fog you sometimes saw in horror films. Tybalt thought you had to hand it to the British: they were kind of difficult to understand at times, but when it came to haunted backdrops they beat the rest of the world hands down.

'I think this is the place,' said Piers, presently, swerving onto the grass verge.

'Through those trees?'

'Yes. Let's break out the arsenal, shall we?' They had brought torches and hammers and chisels, and as they lifted these out, Piers said, 'If it looks like a sledgehammer job when we get down there we'll have to postpone it until daylight. I'm betting it won't be, though. I think we're going to be confronted with an old crumbling wall.'

'Almost like a drystone wall?'

'Let's hope so. Let's hope we can find it as well. Four hundred and fifty years is a long time. Ready? Let's get going, then.'

Tybalt had been hoping that the night on Cruithin when he and Dr Adair had gone down into the catacombs would have given him a veneer of courage. He discovered now that it had not. He was very unhappy about going into the forest by midnight, and he was plain downright scared of digging behind some old cellar wall to disinter a four-hundred-year-old werewolf.

He did not say this, of course. He plodded along at Dr Adair's side, and when Dr Adair commented dispassionately on the mist he even managed to make a joke about how no self-respecting grave-robber would dream of going about his work other than in spooky ghost-ridden fog.

Dr Adair said smoothly, 'No, of course not. But whatever we find, we shan't find any ghosts, Tybalt.'

Tybalt bit down a compulsion to say, Oh yeah? He was not admitting, even to himself, how very weird – how really *extremely* weird – it felt be walking through this ancient forest, knowing that your companion might just possibly, only just very slightly possibly, have a werewolf in his family tree.

He knew, of course he did, that outside fiction there were no such things as werewolves, but as they went through the silent forest, a sneaky little voice whispered: Are you absolutely sure about that? Supposing there are? He glanced at Dr Adair again, and when Dr Adair said, 'That looks like the ruins over there,' Tybalt felt a rush of relief, because Dr Adair's voice was absolutely ordinary, and of course there were no such things as werewolves or their descendants.

In other circumstances he would have found the ruins absorbing. He would have wanted to explore them in minute detail, trying to work out what room had been where, enjoying the feel of words like still-room and great hall and solar. As it was, he just wanted to get the hell out of here.

It took some time to find the cellar. Piers explored the ruins with all the absorption that Tybalt would have liked to feel; he shone his torch into cobwebby corners and found the chimney remains that Nina and Dietfreid had found and that might represent a wolf being devoured. At least the mist had dispersed a bit.

Tybalt was beginning to think they were not going to find the cellar, and he was even starting to think that the whole thing about Marcus and all the others had come from Berry's subconscious – always supposing that Papist priests had had subconscious minds, and always supposing that there had been a Father Berry in the first place. And then Dr Adair straightened up from examining the carved crest, and said, 'Tybalt – I think the cellar's over there to the left.'

Tybalt thought: oh *Jesus*! How does he know that? and saw that Dr Adair's eyes were shining brilliantly in the moonlight. He felt the crawl of fear all over again, and he said, 'Listen, are you sure you haven't been here before? Like in another life, or something?' And wondered if this was as ridiculous as it sounded.

Piers said, 'I studied the sketch Dietfreid made of the place,' and Tybalt said, 'Oh well, of course.'

The cellar door was exactly where Dietfreid's neat sketch indicated; it was tip-tilted with age, the timbers black and rotting, but the iron ring handle was still in place. The thick mat of ivy that Dietfreid had pulled away lay a little to one side.

'Will it be locked?' whispered Tybalt.

'After four hundred years?'

'No, I guess not. But we ought to be ready to – to get back to the car pretty quickly, in case anything's down there.' This sounded too stupidly childish for words, and so he added, 'I mean tramps or animals or anything like that.'

'You think I'm mad, don't you?' said Piers, and grinned. In the moonlight his teeth were very white.

'No—'

'Well, I think I am. Shine the torch, will you?' He dropped to his knees and began to crawl cautiously forward across the tangle of ivy. Tybalt watched, directing the torch, his heart thumping erratically. He had no idea whether it was from fright or excitement.

Dr Adair had reached the door, and he stood up, brushing bits of ivy from his knees. 'Horrid stuff,' he said.

'You should be glad it wasn't poison ivy.'

'So I should. Keep the torch steady, Tybalt, I'm going to see if the door will open.'

The door opened at once. It swung inwards at Piers's touch, with a shriek of protesting hinges reminiscent of a dozen dark fairy tales, and Piers and Tybalt froze. But nothing stirred, and after a moment Piers flicked on his own torch, showing up a narrow flight of stone steps leading down into the blackness. There was a drifting, rather sad odour that might have been something sinister and ancient. The mouldering bones of a walled-up werewolf? Don't be ridiculous! thought Piers. It might just as easily be dry rot.

And so when Tybalt picked his way across the ivy to join him, and said, 'It smells kind of menacing down there,' Piers said, at once, 'Yes, I know. But it's probably only damp and age.'

Tybalt guessed it was stupid to think that the gaping doorway was like a toothless mouth, waiting to devour foolhardy anthropologists. He asked, in a businesslike tone, what there was to see inside.

'Damn all so far. Wait a bit, let's shine both torches together.'

'Be careful,' said Tybalt, as Piers stepped onto the threshold and leaned inside. When he spoke again, his voice picked up a hollow resonance.

'The stone steps go all the way down, and there's some kind of large room at the bottom. Much larger than you'd expect from up here.'

The torch beams picked out the underground room, slicing through the darkness. The stone walls and the floor of the room were slimed with damp, and repulsive, pale, fungoid growths clung to the cracks in the walls. The stench of decaying vegetation was suffocating.

At the foot of the stair, to one side, was a large recess; it might once have been a large cupboard, and although the door had gone, rusting hinges hung drunkenly from one side. Tybalt manoeuvred the torch around to try to see inside it, but it was at a sharp angle to the stair and he could not. He moved the beam slowly across the floor, trying not to shudder at the dozens of black beetles and spiders that were scuttling away from the light.

There was nothing to be seen, of course, only piles of rotting leaves or vegetation. Decades of spiders' webs had formed over cracks in the stones, and grey strings of cobwebs stirred gently in the draught from the newly opened door.

'We have got the right place, haven't we?'

'Oh yes,' said Piers. 'We're in the ruins of the Foljambe house. Look there!'

Picked out in the beam of light, clear as a curse, was a section of wall where the bricks formed the unmistakable outline of a door. They were discoloured with the dirt of centuries, but they were very plainly different bricks to the rest of the walls.

'I think this is it, Tybalt,' said Piers. 'I think we're looking at Marcus Fitzglen's tomb.'

Piers's heart was beating uncomfortably fast, which annoyed him intensely, because he was not frightened or worried by any of this: it could not matter to anyone what was down here. Marcus Fitzglen was *dead*, he died four hundred years ago, said Piers to himself.

He took a firm grip on his torch, picked up the loose canvas bag with the hammers and chisels, and began to descend to the underground room.

The stench almost overwhelmed them, and mingling with it were layers upon layers of other emotions: some of which Piers could catch and identify as fear and pain; others which eluded him. The walls with their crusting of decades-old dirt closed suffocatingly around him so that for a moment he thought he would not be able to go on.

And then common sense reasserted itself, because this was only a crumbly old cellar, and he was a seasoned anthropologist, and for the sake of the project they were going to see if the bricked-up body of Marcus Fitzglen was—

Was what? Alive and well and slavering for a new victim? Magically preserved with a pious expression like a Catholic saint, or bloated and dribbling fresh blood over its vest like a Carpathian vampire? Or maybe caught in a grisly halfway metamorphosis stage, with a human body, but snarling, blood-smeared wolf-jowls? Oh, for heaven's sake!

As they reached the foot of the steps they caught a faint, far-off sound, and they paused and looked at one another.

'Midnight,' said Piers. 'It's the church clock in Thane St Mary striking midnight.'

'Well, sure it is. I didn't think we were going corpse-hunting at any other time of the day.'

Piers grinned, but said, 'Let's get this over with.'

'Wasn't it midnight when the sentence on Marcus was carried out?' said Tybalt.

'Yes, but I'm trying to forget about it.'

'I wish I could forget it.'

'The evidence bears out Berry's story so far, anyway,' said Piers. He surveyed the brick wall, and said, 'Chisel and hammer first, I think,' and hoped that by reference to down-to-earth implements, he had injected a little normality into a wildly abnormal situation. 'Tybalt, you insert the chisel into the seams of the brickwork and I'll see if I can knock it in far enough to dislodge them. If we put the torches on the ground about here they ought to shine directly onto the wall.'

'OK.'

'Hold it absolutely steady,' said Piers, raising the hammer.

The first blow made scant impact, but Piers swung the second blow with more force and this time a shower of brickdust poured out, loosening several bricks with it. Tybalt re-positioned the chisel, and Piers swung the hammer again, and this time at least a dozen bricks tumbled to the ground. He stepped back, his face white in the torchlight.

'I think we can scrabble the rest out.'

Between them they half-pulled, half-scraped at the opening they had made. The bricks came away easily; they were dried-out and crumbling with age. Piers bent for the torch, his heart racing. We're about to look on the thing that an entire community feared so much they dared not even execute it, he thought. This is the werewolf of all the legends, the inhuman creature whose kind we saw on Cruithin ... And if Father Berry's book can be believed, he died unrepentant and vowing to return. *And did you die with him, Isobel? Did the villagers kill you the same night, and can I be free of the taint?*

He pushed the clustering thoughts away and shone the torch into the opening, moving it slowly around.

And now there was no possible doubt; this was assuredly the dank, dark tomb of Berry's description, and it was dreadful beyond belief. It was a slit of a room, barely larger than a cupboard, and it stank of hatred and bitter agony. *Because he showed no fear, not then, not ever . . .* As Piers moved the torch around, Tybalt said, in a voice that was harsh with panic, 'He's not here. Piers, he's not here, he must have got out—' He stopped and drew in a shuddering breath. 'Sorry.' A detached part of Piers's mind registered that at least the boy had finally managed to drop the formality. He said, 'It's OK, Tybalt,' and reached for the chisel and hammer again, this time inserting the steel tip into a lower section of wall. And now the bricks from the lower part of the wall fell away, and they saw the glint of black behind them, and remembered how the blacksmith and his sons had constructed a set of iron bars so that the prisoner would not be able to demolish the newly built wall with its unset mortar.

'Oh,' said Tybalt, suddenly. 'Oh *Jesus*.'

He was there after all. He was lying in a huddle of bones directly beneath the opening, as if, in his last hours, he had tried to crawl to what had been the entrance to his prison. Shreds of cloth clung to the bones – scraps of rotting velvet and silk, and there were the remains of what were plainly leather boots with tarnished spurs. Tybalt had a swift, vivid glimpse of a young man with compelling eyes, riding through the forest glades, his hair lifted by the wind, the admiring glances of every female for miles following him . . . Because he must have had charisma, Marcus Fitzglen. He must have had charisma and magnetism and authority and plain downright sex appeal.

Piers said, 'Move the torch a bit, Tybalt, I can't see— *Oh my God*.'

They both froze in horror. The jumble of bones lay as it had lain for four centuries, as Marcus Fitzglen must have lain when he died. It was recognizable as a human skeleton: the legs and pelvis and ribs and shoulders were all familiar from dozens of photographs and reproductions. Piers, who had taken anatomy in his post-graduate year, could almost have taken a run at guessing how old Fitzglen had been when he died down here. Twenty-seven? Twenty-eight, maybe? Whatever age he had been, he had died with his face turned upwards, as if seeking a shred of light in his lonely death agonies.

His face.

It was the face of an animal: the skull of a thin, snarling wolf, incredibly growing up out of the human spine. The flashlight beam picked it out mercilessly; Piers could see the rounded occipital and parietal bones, and the complex sphenoid bones around the base. But the nasal bone was impossibly elongated and the cheekbones were flat and slanting. The jaw was thin and pointed.

Whatever Marcus Fitzglen had looked like in life, in death he had the skull of a snarling wolf.

'There'll be a perfectly logical explanation,' said Piers, at last. 'It might be something to do with the preservation process. Or even a trick of the light.'

'You think?'

'Yes. Because the alternative's unthinkable—' said Piers.

After a moment, Tybalt said, 'The iron staves that Berry

said they hammered into his jaw—'

'Yes, they're there,' said Piers, directing the torch. 'Can you see?'

'Yes I do. See, I was kind of hoping they wouldn't be. Because,' explained Tybalt, 'that could have meant the skull wasn't real.'

'How on earth— Oh, I see. You thought somebody might have sneaked down here after he was dead and substituted a wolf's skull. But why on earth would anyone do that?'

'As a warning,' said Tybalt. 'If he was a witch – excuse me, warlock – he could have had sympathizers in the area. Like, a coven. They might have tried to rescue him, or later on they might have tried to get his body. For – like – their rituals.'

'Or a lover might have tried to get it for different reasons entirely?' said Piers, lightly.

'Uh, well, maybe. Oh right, Christian burial.'

'Isobel,' said Piers, half to himself. 'The villagers tried to capture her that night in the forest, didn't they? Only Francis Foljambe rode off into the sunset after he'd thrown her across his pommel—'

'Excuse me?'

Piers grinned. 'Saddle. You know, if we could find out what happened to Isobel—'

'Oh, that's easy,' said a soft voice from behind them. 'She died in a house called Charect House.'

Piers and Tybalt spun round. Standing behind them, blocking their path to the steps, stood eight or ten young men with dark eyes and lean, sinuous bodies.

In front of them, plainly their leader, was a dark-eyed young man with slanting cheekbones. He surveyed Piers and Tybalt with his head to one side and, after a moment, he said, 'How do you do, Dr Adair. My name is Karabas and I think you have been wanting to meet me?'

Chapter Thirty-Six

Nina had been hovering on the borderlands of sleep when the scrape of sound below her window brought her fully awake. She sat up in bed listening.

There were any number of explanations for the noise, and the likeliest was simply a roof timber contracting as the place cooled down. Most buildings, and especially old buildings like this, were never entirely silent at night. They creaked and sighed; sometimes water trickled off channels in the roof, or pigeons scrabbled about in the attics. It was probably a pigeon I heard, thought Nina, listening carefully. Pigeons or starlings or house martins, that was all it would have been.

The sound might be one of the others, about some perfectly lawful occasion. Midnight hunger or thirst. Somebody going along to the loo at the end of the corridor, or searching for aspirin for a headache, or indigestion powder after too much supper. Priscilla had cooked a huge chicken curry that evening – it killed Nina to admit it, but it had been absolutely delicious. Dietfreid had thought so too; he had placidly eaten his way through two helpings, and then had had two platefuls of one of the large local Bakewell tarts that Tybalt had discovered on one of his forays and brought back.

It might even be somebody creeping along to keep an assignation; Priscilla stealing into a bedroom other than her own perhaps – *whose bedroom?* Nina's thoughts snapped onto a totally different track. She pushed back the sheets and padded barefoot to the window.

To begin with nothing seemed to be moving outside, although a thin ground mist had formed. Perhaps after all she had not heard anything. It was beginning to be cold by the window, and she was just managing to persuade herself that the sound had been nothing and she could get back into the warm bed, when she saw Piers Adair climbing into the Range

341

Rover and freewheeling it down the drive.

A conscience is sometimes an inconvenient thing to possess. Nina found it inconvenient now. She wanted very much to go after Dr Adair; she wanted to drive with him through that curiously intimate mist, and find out where he was going.

She stood irresolute, watching the tail lights of the Range Rover going down the road. Was there someone in the passenger seat? Nina leaned farther forward, but could not see whether there was or not. She heard the growl of the engine starting up when the vehicle reached the road, and she stepped back from the window. Dare she follow? Priscilla's car was parked beneath the window which meant that if there was anyone with Dr Adair, it was not Priscilla. Nina had clearance – Priscilla's and the insurance company's – to drive it, and the keys were hanging in the kitchen. The thought of Priscilla decided her. Priscilla would not hesitate; she would go hell-for-leather after Dr Adair.

Nina made up her mind. She dragged on a thick sweater and the long woollen skirt she had worn that evening; thrust her feet into the ankle boots standing by the bed, wound a scarf around her neck, and went stealthily down to the kitchen. The keys were there, and she slipped out through the house.

Priscilla's car fired at once, and Nina swung it over to the left as she reached the road. The Range Rover had turned left, and there was a very long stretch of main road before you had to turn off. She thought she would catch up with Piers fairly easily – Priscilla drove a sleek sports car which Nina thought flashy of her, but tonight she was glad of it. She was even glad about the automatic gear box; it was surprising how many seconds you trimmed off a drive when you did not have to think about changing gears.

The mist swirled in and out of the sports car's headlights, and there was a muffled feeling to the night. Shreds of white clung to the trees, so that they loomed up suddenly and rather threateningly. Nina found herself flinching from them, because driving along the dark road like this, it was suddenly very easy to start believing in every creepy ghost story ever written.

She had been looking out for the Range Rover, but it still came as a shock when she suddenly came upon it after about twelve miles, neatly parked on the grass verge on the roadside, the lights switched off. Nina braked sharply, and swung in behind it. For a moment she could not think what Piers could be doing out here, and then she recognized the road as the one that she and Dietfreid had driven along two days earlier. He's gone into the forest, thought Nina. He's gone to look at the ruins of the Foljambe estate. At *midnight*? But there might be any number of reasons for that, even though Nina could not, at the moment, think of any.

She was just deciding that after all it might be better to get into the car and scoot discreetly back to Weston House, when from within the forest she caught a flicker of light. The beam of a torch? She peered through the trees.

It was becoming more attractive to make that scoot back to the house and pretend she had never been here. If Piers Adair was out here, pursuing some plan of his own, he had every right to be left alone. Nina shivered, wrapping her arms about her body for warmth, and hated herself for being so irresolute. She remembered the strangeness of the creatures they were studying and the odd unsettling feeling she had had within the ruins – almost as if people were watching from a hiding place. She remembered how far from the road the ruins were as well.

It might be a good idea to make sure that if Piers was all alone out here, he was all right. If he was with Tybalt or Dietfreid, there would be no need to reveal her presence, but if he was on his own they could explore the ruins together. The thought of walking amidst the dark forest with Piers was so intensely alluring that Nina put her fears firmly in their place, looked quickly up and down the deserted highroad, and plunged into the dark forest.

She had managed to persuade herself that she was not frightened, but treading between the massive old trees was unnerving. The soft mist was snaking shiveringly around her ankles, but soon it cleared slightly and cold moonlight showered down. Nina began to realize that this whole thing was an enormous mistake. She had thought she was going towards the ruins and towards the elusive lights she had seen earlier, but now she was not so sure. She did not recognize the forest path as being the one she and Dietfreid had found, although she was by no means sure that she would recognize it. She sent an uneasy glance over her shoulder. Had that been a blurred movement on the far side? Her heart began to race. Dr Adair after all? Nina waited, and the movement came again, from a different direction this time.

Whoever it was, it was not Piers Adair. It was too slight, too darting. Nina received the impression of something – several somethings – slinking in and out of the shadows, occasionally pausing to glance over their shoulders.

She turned back at once, because clearly discretion was going to be the better part of valour now; if she was really worried about Piers it would be better to get back to the house and rouse the others, so that they could come back out here together. Yes, this would be the most sensible thing to do. And surely the road ought to be ahead of her now—

The road was not ahead of her. The trees and the undergrowth were denser than ever and there was a massive fallen oak half-blocking the path. Nina had most definitely not seen it before. She stood very still, staring at it in horror.

She was lost.

At least twenty of Karabas's people filed silently into the grim underground room. Piers and Tybalt, held firmly by four of them, both saw at once that there was no possible chance of overpowering them and escaping.

It was eerie in the extreme to be so close to these creatures they had studied for so long, but to Piers, eeriest of all was the realization that the figure at the centre of the room was the one they had left Cruithin Island to find, and the one they had come to regard as a symbol of the entire clan. Karabas, thought Piers, staring at the dark-haired figure.

Their captors tied their hands with brisk, silent efficiency, and pushed them into a corner against one wall. Two of the men looped cords around their ankles and knotted them tightly.

The rest were moving around the stone cellar, setting their torches into rusting wall sconces, but Karabas remained where he was, watching the others. Piers thought he was exactly like some eastern prince of ancient days holding court, leisurely considering poor wretched prisoners brought before him, while the serfs and vails scurried hither and thither to do his bidding.

He said, in a low voice, 'Tybalt – this isn't as bad as it looks.'

'I am truly glad to hear you say that.'

'No, listen. The car. We left it on the side of the road. When the others find out we're missing they'll come out to look for us. They'll see the car.'

Tybalt half turned his head. 'Don't look at me!' said Piers at once.

'Sorry. But you're right, you know that? Hey, that's terrific.'

'Hush, he's coming back over here.'

'Dr Adair,' said Karabas, coming to stand in front of them. His voice was exactly as Piers remembered from the tapes made on the island; silky and very faintly accented. 'So, we finally have a confrontation.'

'This isn't my idea of a confrontation,' said Piers, and his voice held the exact right note of cool anger. Tybalt, at his side, was overwhelmingly grateful to him: he could not have borne it if Dr Adair had been frightened or begged to be set free. He surreptitiously tried to work his wrists against the knotted cords. Were they the tiniest bit loose? No, but perhaps they could be made loose.

Piers was not thinking about being frightened, or even about getting free. He was furious with himself for getting so easily caught, and he was concerned for Tybalt. But beneath that he was aware of a surge of exultation and of a curiosity so intense that it was blotting out everything else. We're face to face at last, he thought.

He said, 'What do you intend to do with us?'

'You will take part in one of our ancient rituals,' said Karabas.

'The resurrection rite with the *Lia Fail* perhaps?' said Piers, sarcastically.

'You consider that primitive, perhaps?'

'It's the primitive superstition of savages.'

'Ah. And yet, you know, there is power behind the ritual. The fragment of the *Lia Fail* that we possess has a remarkable property.'

He glanced at Tybalt, who had not dared speak yet but who had been so encouraged by Piers's cold sarcasm that he said, scornfully, 'Life after death?' And even managed to add, 'Oh *really*.'

Karabas said, 'Because your brash young culture has dismissed the ancient religions and the old enchantments, it does not mean they do not exist.'

'In my culture,' said Piers, instantly, 'there is a theory that certain things can *not* exist unless there is belief in them.'

Karabas's lips curved into a smile that was so unmistakably wolfish that Tybalt felt as if someone had poured ice down his spine. 'But your culture and your century, Dr Adair, does not believe in humans with wolf-blood in them,' said Karabas. He looked at Piers intently. 'But you believe,' he said very softly. 'We both know it, and we both know why you believe.'

For a moment there was absolute silence. Tybalt could hear the faint sizzling of the torches as the wood burned down.

Then Piers said, 'Well? Is it the resurrection ritual, Karabas?'

The wolf-smile curved Karabas's lips again. 'Oh no,' he said. 'A much older ritual than that, Dr Adair.'

Before either of them could speak, he turned and went swiftly up the steps and out into the night.

Nina had carried on walking through the trees because there was nothing else to be done. Sooner or later she would come to the road – any road – and the worst that could happen was that she would have to spend the night here, and find her way out when it was morning. It was not a particularly nice thought, but it served her right for trying to follow Piers.

She remembered how she and Dietfried, half serious, half joking, had said they should mark the trees as they went, so that they would not go round in circles, and with this in mind she began to break off little pieces of branches, low down on the trees so that she would be able to recognize them. I'm coping with this, said Nina to herself very firmly. I'm in an unpleasant situation, but I'm being extremely sensible about it, and I'll be perfectly all right.

Snapping off the twigs made an astonishingly loud sound in the dark forest. Each time Nina did it she had to look quickly round to make sure she had not woken something that it might have been better not to wake. But nothing moved, and each time she went on again.

She thought she had been in the forest for about half an hour when she came into a small natural clearing. It ought to have been friendly, reminiscent of summer afternoon picnics, but it was not. Nina disliked it very much indeed, but she stopped there to take a breather, and to see if she could get her bearings. She heard a church clock somewhere in the distance. It was a rather lonely, rather chilling sound. I'm in the middle of an ancient forest and I'm on my own, thought Nina. And for all I know there might be creatures who are part-wolf prowling around. And I really don't like this clearing one little bit.

With the thought, she heard a sound – a half-rustling, half-snapping, as if someone had pushed aside the undergrowth to get through, and had trodden on a fallen twig. She spun round at once. Something out there? Something standing in the shadows, watching, waiting its chance to pounce . . . ? She stayed very still, and after a moment the sound came again. Nina scanned the edges of the clearing, trying to penetrate the darkness. Had it come from there? Or over there?

And then it came again, and a figure appeared, seeming almost to materialize out of the shadows. Slender, narrow-eyed, with dark silky hair like an animal's pelt. Nina caught her breath. He stood in front of the oldest tree on the clearing's edge, his eyes on her, and then he smiled. Nina felt her heart lurch and then resume a painful too-fast pace, because surely no one had ever conveyed so much by a smile. Strength and arrogance and ruthlessness, and a queer inverted beauty. He might have been saying: *come into my arms and let me steal you away to worlds you never dreamed existed* . . . Except that Nina was not going anywhere near him, of course. In a minute she was going to run as fast as she could, into the dark, safe shadows where he would never find her. In just another minute she would do that . . .

'Hello, Nina,' said Karabas, softly. 'Are you lost, my dear?'

He was across the clearing in a single bound, his arms pinioning her wrists together, his eyes shining with unnatural brilliance in the moonlight. Nina stared up at him, and saw with terror that Dietfried had described his eyes very exactly indeed: the pupils were slits of black, set at an angle in the irises. Wolf-eyes. Oh God.

She managed to say, 'How – do you know my name?' and Karabas smiled down at her. It was a dreadful smile, filled with the most inhuman greed Nina had ever seen, but filled as well with such alluring promise that a tiny pulse of excitement began to beat within her. This is *Karabas*, she thought, it has to be him; this is the strange startlingly attractive creature we've been trying to find. She did not think, I'm alone in the forest with the wolf; she thought, he's far better-looking than I expected.

Karabas said, 'Of course I know your name, Nina. I know all your names. Did you think you were watching my people all those nights without us knowing and watching you in turn?'

'Were you watching us?'

'Oh yes. The study of humans is a fascinating one,' he said, softly, and Nina stared at him and thought: now I'm *really* afraid.

But she managed to say, 'Let me go – if you don't let me go, I'll scream for help.'

The smile slid out again. Oh God, it was a dreadful smile. But it was incredibly seductive. 'Scream then,' he said. 'I'd like that. It would excite me even more.' His face was very close to her; Nina could feel his breath on her cheek. Warm. Sweet-smelling. Fresh masculine sweat and clean hair. Oh God, he ought to smell like the wild animal he was, not like this.

'Fear is exciting,' said Karabas. 'Human fear is *wildly* exciting, Nina.'

So he had picked up her thoughts and was pitching them back to her. Nina struggled and he pulled her against him, and then picked her up in his arms.

In his beautiful, dangerous voice he said, 'And now, Nina, I will take you to join your friends.'

She was dimly aware that after all they had not been so very far from the ruins of the Foljambe estate, but as Karabas took her around to where she and Dietfreid had found the opening to the sinister cellar, panic welled up once more.

I'm going into the wolves' lair, she thought. Oh God, this can't possibly be happening. She risked a glance at her captor's face, but his eyes were unreadable and his expression was remote as he carried her down a narrow flight of stone steps.

The underground room was unexpectedly large. There was a stone-flagged floor, and in places the walls were brick and in others stone, as if a newer house had at some time been built over a much older one, and the foundations had mingled. Part of one wall seemed to have been knocked down.

At least twenty of Karabas's people were in the room, and in the far corner, bound by ropes around their wrists and ankles, were Piers and Tybalt. Nina was appalled to see them like that, but a rather horrid part of her was grateful that she was not on her own.

Karabas carried her across the stone floor and put her down with Piers and Tybalt, and two of the men instantly tied her hands and ankles.

Piers said, 'Nina, what on earth— No, never mind, we'll worry about all that later. Are you all right? I mean – has Karabas hurt you in any way?'

'I'm OK,' said Nina, wondering if she was.

Karabas, having watched Nina being tied up, seated himself cross-legged on the floor in front of them.

'He's about to tell us what he thinks he's going to do to us,' remarked Piers, his voice coldly sarcastic. 'Remarkable, isn't it, how madmen like to talk?'

'It's their basic inadequacy,' offered Tybalt. 'Any analyst would tell you that.'

'This lot don't need analysts, they need shooting.'

'With silver bullets?' said Nina, hesitantly, and was rewarded by Piers's smile.

Karabas said, 'Your little beliefs and superstitions amuse me, Dr Adair.'

'I'm so pleased,' said Piers, sarcastically.

Karabas said, 'A few miles from here, in the old Foljambe gatehouse, lives an elderly lady.'

'Madeleine Foulsham,' said Nina, before she could stop herself.

'Yes. We have watched this lady for some time,' said Karabas. 'Mainly because she is one of the accursed Foljambe line. And now an interesting combination of circumstances has happened.' He paused, but neither Nina nor the two men spoke. 'There is a granddaughter of this lady,' said Karabas, 'who has come to live in a forest cottage. And there is a child: a little girl of perhaps seven years. It is the child who holds such interest for us, and she is the reason some of my people have left the island you knew as Cruithin Island and travelled here.'

'I'm surprised so many savages managed to reach Derbyshire without being taken up as vagrants,' said Piers, and Karabas regarded him thoughtfully.

'Normally we go out into the world singly, or in twos or threes,' he said. 'Not for many centuries has such a large group left Cruithin Island. But this place has a special meaning for us. This is the ancient wildwood where our ancestors fought their strongest battles with the accursed Foljambe.'

Piers, his eyes never leaving Karabas's slender figure, heard how the phrasing had a curious medieval battle-sound. So might the Saxon Harold have referred, with violent hatred, to 'the Norman invader'; so might Churchill have talked about 'the Nazi menace'.

Karabas said, 'This child was fathered onto a human female by one of our people. That is something that has only happened once before in our history.' He looked very intently at Piers, as if expecting a reaction. Piers stared at him coldly.

'I have deliberately sought out and befriended the grandmother's servant,' said Karabas, and Tybalt at once said, '"Servant"? You're a bit off-centre there, Karabas. I expect you mean a cleaning lady or an au pair.'

'If you want to pass unnoticed in the world of the humans, you ought to pay more attention to these details,' added Nina, encouraged by the cool contempt Tybalt and Dr Adair were displaying.

'It is of no account. The girl is a servant, and has been seduced. It was very easy to do so,' said Karabas, off-handedly, and Nina abruptly recalled Madeleine Foulsham saying that her cleaning girl was a bit of a goer.

'Two nights ago,' Karabas went on, 'while I was in the girl's bed, I stole from her the key to the Foljambe gatehouse. Tonight I shall get into the house, and there I shall kill the grandmother. My people will drain her blood into the ceremonial Stone Jars.' He paused, and then said, 'Once that is done we shall steal the child away and bring her here. And then we shall celebrate the oldest ritual of our people.' Silence closed down again, thick and charged with gathering menace.

'The drinking of the blood of ancestors,' said Piers, at last. 'My God, that's what you mean, isn't it?'

'Yes. We had intended to take the child to Cruithin and keep her there until she was thirteen. Then she would have been initiated as most of our people are initiated. But the grandmother is old and not well, and there is no certainty that she will live for another six years. Also, we are curious to know which of the two lineages is dominant in the child. That of her father or that of her mother. The ritual may tell us that.'

'How extremely fascinating,' said Piers, sarcastically.

Nina, remembering with sick fear the nice vigorous old lady she and Dietfreid had met, leaned forward. 'But Madeleine Foulsham isn't one of your people,' she said. 'You can't include her in this ritual. She's a . . . a human.' She registered briefly that down here, in this company, this did not sound as macabre as it ought to have done.

Karabas said, 'But that is the interest. Madeleine Foulsham is a human. So we shall try the child with the blood of the human ancestor first, and then with—'

'What?'

'With the blood of one of her wolf-ancestors.'

'One of your people?' Nina sent a wild glance around the room. Karabas's people seemed to be moving around, tidying up the partly demolished wall, coming and going by way of the narrow stair. 'One of those?' said Nina.

'No,' said Karabas. 'Not one of my people. One of yours.' He half-turned his head to look at Piers. 'Tomorrow night we shall kill you as well, Dr Adair, and then give your blood to the little girl to drink.' The cruel beautiful smile touched his lips. 'It was so helpful of you to seek us out,' he said. 'It saved us the trouble of coming to get you.'

Piers's brain was seething with half a dozen different fears, and the thought of the unknown child's fate sent icy horror coursing through him. He sought for some way to get them all out of this. What about the ritual itself? Could he throw enough doubt on it to deflect Karabas's intentions? After a moment, he said, 'You're wasting your time over the blood-drinking ritual, Karabas. I'm not one of your unnatural line.'

Karabas said, 'You are descended directly from Marcus Fitzglen, who came to these parts four centuries ago. He was one of our people, and although he was executed, before he died he gave a child to Isobel Weston.'

Piers was aware of Nina turning to look at him, and of Tybalt frowning, but he did not look at either of them. He said, in the coldest voice he could summon, 'Folklore. It's just a local legend.'

Karabas studied him for a moment. Then he said, 'It is not just a legend, Dr Adair. The child was born and against all the odds, it survived. The peasant villagers who executed Marcus would have killed his child as well, but they did not. The child was saved and brought up in the house of Hugo Weston.'

Piers said, 'Who saved it?'

'Francis Foljambe,' said Karabas.

Chapter Thirty-Seven

Felicity had determinedly kept away from the rather macabre work that was going on in the cellars of Charect Cottage. 'Better to leave us to get on anyway, Mrs Stafford,' said the plumber, who had roped in his builder colleague to help.

Felicity, who would have said she was the least squeamish, least fanciful female in Western Europe, had a particular dislike for the dank underground room. She was hoping very strenuously that once Charect's cellar was properly restored and brightly whitewashed, she would be able to enter it without the stomach-churning foreboding. To start with, she had thought the feeling was the feeling you would get if something was lying in wait for you, and she had identified this as the source of her earlier unease. But after a while, she knew that whatever was down there was not the source at all: the fear and the menace came not from within Charect Cottage, but from without. And what happened to the sanctuary?

She knew that the emotion printed so strongly onto the old cellar was not fear at all. It was despair. It was the deepest, most profound sense of despair Felicity had ever encountered. It was not anything that could be rationalized, but houses, like people, had memories, and it was entirely probable that there were sad old memories stored away in the walled-up foundations. If so, they would disperse once it was opened up. Felicity consoled herself with this thought, and went around to the front of the house with the idea of clearing some of the overgrown garden. She and Bryony had made it one of their projects to try to find the lovely old-fashioned cottage flowers: lupins and hollyhocks and moss roses. They had already uncovered a lavender bush; Bryony was going to take some of the seed heads to make lavender bags for her dressing table drawers.

* * *

Bryony liked working in the garden. She was making a wildflower garden. Mad had sent mother several cuttings which had included a really lovely honeysuckle, and she had given Bryony some clumps of earth with wild flowers growing, in case Bryony would like to start a small wild garden of her very own. There were celandines and primroses and harebells.

Bryony liked the feeling that lots of other people had worked in this garden before her. It was interesting to wonder who had planted the lavender bush. Could it have been Isobel? She thought that there had been lilac on the night that Isobel had been caught by the villagers, because Isobel had been able to smell it above the horrid, hot-breathed, smelly-clothed villagers who had dragged her out from her hiding place. One of them had broken a window so that they could get in, and there had been a huge bush of white lilac just outside. The scent had flooded into the room.

What had happened to Isobel in the end was pretty bad. It was just about the worst thing that could happen to anyone; Bryony was very glad indeed that it had all been such a long time ago.

Isobel had managed not to cry out when they dragged her through the house and down to the cellar. Bryony knew it had not been a cellar like today's cellar: it had been a horrid stone room, small and cold and bad-smelling. There was not much down there, except for some bottles of wine, which Isobel had on account of Sir Francis Foljambe who sometimes came to supper. The two of them would have eaten their supper at the front of the house – there had been a small round table that the servant had polished until it shone like silk, and there would have been candles burning.

Sir Francis had not been there on the night the villagers came. If he had he might have been able to do something to save Isobel. But nobody had been able to stop any of it, and Isobel had been half-carried, half-dragged down to the cold, cobwebby cellar, and two of the men had kept tight hold of her so that she could not run away, even though she could not stand up because of the terrible clawing pain in her stomach.

They had brought down a whole lot of stones and bricks, and then they had set to and walled off a small portion of the cellar. They had worked from right to left, building the wall from floor to ceiling as they went, laughing coarsely as they

354

did so, occasionally turning to jeer at Isobel, and saying things like, 'Naught but a whelping she-wolf,' And, 'Didn't we ought to muzzle the bitch?'

When there was only a bit of space to fill up with the bricks, they dragged Isobel across the floor and pushed her behind the wall they had made, and then finished bricking it up.

And then they went back upstairs, still laughing about what they had done, and when one of them said, Why shouldn't we eat at the she-wolf's expense? the rest cheered in agreement, and they all began to tumble food out of the cupboards. One of them scurried back down to the cellar to fetch some bottles of wine; when he got back he said you could just hear the she-wolf crying to be let out through the wall, but that once you were back up in the house you could not hear anything. He was a dreadful fat man with thick, coarse skin and little piggy-eyes, and Bryony hated him.

They tied the servant up while they ate Isobel's food and when she shouted to them to have pity, they tied a bit of rag over her mouth to stop her. They all ate horridly, slopping the wine and belching loudly, and talking with their mouths open, and spilling bits of pigeon pie. Bryony would not much have liked to eat pigeon pie, but in those days people had liked it a lot.

They had been eating and drinking for a long time and they were all a bit blurry with wine. The piggy-eyed man had found a cask of cider and they had drunk most of that. They were in a revolting half-asleep state all over Isobel's nice room with the polished table, when they were roused by the sound of hoofbeats coming through the forest towards the house.

There was no time for them to get out, and the piggy-eyed man said there was no need to. They were enjoying what was called the spoils of the victor. They would stand their ground against whoever might be outside.

But one or two of the men looked a bit frightened, and whispered to each other that Isobel Weston had loved the werewolf, and that werewolves had dark, evil powers. The werewolf had been put to death tonight, but supposing it had summoned a *something* to come galloping out of the forest and smite them all dead. Bryony was not sure what a smite was, but she knew about werewolves having evil powers, because anybody knew that.

The door of Charect House was flung open, and framed in the doorway was Sir Francis himself. Bryony thought he would have looked pretty splendid. His eyes would have been blazing with fury, and in his hand would have been a glitteringly sharp sword. He was just about ready to chop everybody's head off and Bryony did not blame him. She knew he had just helped to shut away the werewolf, and he had ridden straight from that to save Isobel and the baby. She could see the horse, tethered outside the house, and she could see the blue velvet cloak Sir Francis would have been wearing. It was a long cloak, and it swirled around his boots which were soft brown leather. He was so lavishly good-looking that Bryony might even consider putting him in as best favourite in place of Richard.

He had ignored the village people and he had snatched up a branched candlestick and walked through all of the rooms, flinging open the doors to find Isobel. The villagers had been huddling together by then, because Sir Francis was not somebody they wanted to upset.

Finally, he had gone down into the cellars, and seen the new wall. The younger ones who had wondered about the dying werewolf sending out a *something* exchanged glances, and then went down to the cellar to see what was happening.

Francis Foljambe was breaking down the wall with the flat of his sword. The stuff that held the bricks together had not set yet; it was still wet and squidgy, and the bricks came tumbling down almost at once. But it still took a long time, and when Sir Francis had made enough of a hole, he held the candlestick up and looked inside.

This was the part that Bryony knew she would have hated worst of all if she had been there. Isobel had been lying on the floor in a twisted heap, and there had been blood everywhere. It had not quite dried so that the flickering candlelight showed it as faintly glistening. It smelt dreadful.

Isobel's eyes were wide open and staring and her skin had a white marbly look. Bryony understood that this meant she was dead, and Sir Francis had understood it as well. He had stared down at her, and there had been a moment when he had thrust his clenched fist into his mouth and Bryony knew this was to stop him from showing any weakness to the horrid village people. But she knew as well that beneath it, his thoughts were scurrying this way and that – they were such clear thoughts that Bryony could practically see them.

Even though Sir Francis had sent the villagers away, he still did not dare arrange a proper funeral for Isobel. The villagers thought she was a witch and they would never allow her to be buried in the churchyard. Bryony knew you did not bury witches in churchyards. But it mattered very much to Sir Francis that Isobel had a proper funeral, and he was clever and brave. He decided to bring a priest to the house at night, and to give Isobel a secret funeral down here in the cellar. Nobody would ever know about it, because priests did not tell secrets and Sir Francis would not tell either.

And then Sir Francis saw the baby. It was lying at Isobel's side, and she had managed to tear off a piece of her skirt to wrap it up. It was small and covered with blood and its little eyes were shut tight. But it was alive, and after a moment, Sir Francis reached in and reached down, and scooped the poor little baby up in his arms.

The builder and the plumber were most apologetic. They stood in the half-wild garden of Charect Cottage, and explained it all to Felicity, keeping a wary eye on Bryony who was a few yards away, diligently digging a small patch of ground for her wildflower garden.

A very sad thing, said the builder. Part of some old tragedy, no doubt. Probably they would never know the story. The plumber said it was obvious that the body had been there for a very long time, hundreds of years, even. Part of the wall had been built in a much neater fashion than the rest – almost as if it had been torn down at some time and then rebuilt – although they would not swear to that. The plumber said that the cottage was on the site of a much older house, as Mrs Stafford doubtless knew. He added, sombrely, that it never ceased to amaze him, the things that turned up in people's cellars and sewers and cesspits.

Felicity, her mind tumbling, managed to edge them nearer to the house, away from Bryony. The child had far too many odd fantasies in her mind as it was. Felicity did not want her fastening on to the macabre discovery and building up one of her odd, evocative stories around it.

Keeping her voice carefully low, she said, 'Is there no indication of who the body might have been?'

The plumber was of the opinion that the pitiful little collection of bones had been that of a female. Small, he explained, earnestly. A young girl, maybe. The builder added that there had been the remains of what looked like a velvet cloak covering her. It had rotted almost to strings, but it might once have been blue, he added.

'Oh.' Felicity was not at all sure of the correct procedure for dealing with centuries-old bodies in cellars. She asked who they would have to inform. 'The coroner or the police?'

The builder thought they had better phone the local police station, where someone was bound to know what had to be done.

'Yes, of course.' Felicity wondered about reburial. The plumber said, comfortingly, 'Oh yes, of course she'll have that, but you know, Mrs Stafford, it looked to us as if the poor soul had already been given that at some time.'

'Really?' This did not square with being interred behind a cellar wall.

'Neatly laid out, she was, and covered with the cloak, as Bill's said.'

Bill nodded in a jowly and responsible fashion.

'And her arms crossed on her chest in proper Christian fashion,' said the plumber.

The builder added that at some time, someone – they would probably never know who – had placed a crucifix between her hands. The crucifix was tarnished black with age, but a glint of the good solid silver beneath still showed. Oh, and there was a withered spray of some flower or other clasped between her hands. Almost crumbled to dust, it had, but they'd seen its outline when they broke through the bricks.

'Lilac?' said Felicity involuntarily.

But neither the builder nor the plumber was able to say if the crumbled-to-dust flowers might have been lilac.

Chapter Thirty-Eight

The voice on the phone, when Felicity answered it, was apologetic and to the point.

'It's this wretched flu,' said Madeleine. 'I'm laid low, and I'm stuck. Now I said I wouldn't be a nuisance, and I won't. This is an absolute and all-time one-off. It's just that there's a question of a prescription to be collected from the chemist – antibiotics which I'd better take—'

'Of course I'll collect your prescription,' said Felicity at once. 'I'll do it right away. No, it's truly no problem.'

She had been intending to take Bryony into Ashbourne that morning, so that the child would not be there when the poor sad little bones were removed from the cellar. There was to be some kind of short memorial service later in the week; Felicity had thought she would go to that. She had been going to tell Mad about it and about the discovery of the little skeleton, and suggest they attend the service together.

Now she said, 'You've been more than kind to us since we moved in, I'm glad I can repay some of it. I don't mean I'm glad you've got flu.'

Mad had been very kind to them indeed. She had invited Bryony to the promised tea at the gatehouse and although the picnic in the forest had not yet materialized because Mad had still been concerned about tramps in the ruins, there had been an expedition to Hardwick Hall so that they could study the famous Elizabethan herb gardens of Bess of Hardwick, and see if they mightn't reproduce them in miniature at Charect. Bryony had loved that. There had been the cuttings for the garden, and then Mad had given them a beautiful little Victorian sewing table, which had an inlaid mahogany surface but a green silk pouch underneath and lots of tiny drawers for needles and cotton threads and embroidery silks.

'Surplus to requirements at the gatehouse,' she had said

brusquely, when Felicity had protested that they could not possibly accept anything so obviously valuable. 'I daresay you'll find it of more use for CDs or paper clips or video games, but use it for whatever you want.'

Felicity and Bryony had both exclaimed in delight over the elegant little table, and Mad had said, 'Well, I'm for ever tripping over it in my house, and since this pesky stroke it's a nuisance to have to polish all the fiddly bits. It belonged to a Mary Foulsham about a hundred and fifty years ago, so it's all in the family. And it'll look better here than in the gatehouse.'

It did not necessarily look better, but they put it in the inglenook room, where it looked terrific.

So Felicity was genuinely pleased to think she could return a little of Mad's generosity by fetching a prescription for her. She asked if there was anything else to be collected. 'Any shopping or anything like that?'

'There's nothing I need at all,' said Mad. 'I have a large freezer and I'm very well stocked up. The doctor was going to drop off the prescription at the chemist in Ashbourne – it's the one in the square—'

'I know it. Will the prescription be ready now?' asked Felicity. 'All right, we'll get it now and bring it over.'

'This is wonderfully kind of you,' said Mad when they arrived an hour later. 'I don't bother much with neighbours, you understand – not that there are many neighbours very near since they built that terrible main road. But those that there are think I'm the local eccentric, and I think most of them are fools. It's an attitude that works all right fifty-one weeks out of the year. But this is the fifty-second.'

Felicity unpacked her small shopping bag. 'You said no food and I don't suppose you feel like eating much anyway. But I brought you some fruit.' She put the bags of grapes and oranges on the table. 'Oh, and a bottle of Lucozade.' She had had no idea of Mad's taste in reading, but she had added a couple of paperbacks – a whodunit, and a bodice-ripper – along with a chatty magazine.

'How thoughtful of you.'

Mad was in the rocking chair by the old brick fireplace; there was not an open fire there any more, but there was one of the flame-effect gas fires which were practically indistinguishable from the real thing. 'Can't abide lying in bed,' she said, when Felicity asked if she was comfortable downstairs. 'I'll go to bed if I'm dying and not before. It's friendlier down here. And I'm near to the phone and there's the TV.'

Felicity glanced round. It was warm and comfortable in the room. She went into Mad's kitchen under pretext of fetching a dish for the fruit, and sneaked a quick look into the fridge and the freezer. Yes, there was plenty of food, and there were eggs and cheese and milk in the fridge.

Mad would not hear of either of them staying. 'No, not even for a cup of tea. There's no telling but that I might be infectious – in fact I shouldn't even have let you come into the house. I'm more than grateful for all this.' She managed a smile at Bryony. 'We don't kiss, do we,' she said. 'Lot of slop. But you're a good dear child and your mother's a good dear girl.'

'We'll make her some soup,' said Felicity to Bryony as they drove back. 'Properly simmered chicken broth. And maybe a casserole. I got a chicken and some mushrooms in Ashbourne. We could have a cooking afternoon, if you'd like that.' She paused, wondering whether that might be a good opportunity to tell Bryony about the baby. Some half-truths might be necessary which Felicity would hate, and which Bryony, with her queer fey perception, might pick up. She would try to sense Bryony's receptiveness while they were making the casserole. 'We can take Mad's over later this evening or first thing tomorrow,' she said. 'If she doesn't feel like eating it, it can go in the freezer.'

Bryony helped with the chicken soup making. It was nice in the kitchen now, with the warm-coloured tiles and the windows with the criss-cross of lead strips. It was nice to smell the good soup simmering in a huge saucepan, and to put the casserole ingredients into a huge pot. Bryony had the feeling that mother was trying to make up her mind to say something of immense importance; she waited hopefully, but mother seemed to change her mind, and concentrate on the cooking instead.

'Double portions,' she said, when the casserole was finally bubbling gently inside the oven. 'Some for Mad and some for us. Actually, it's nearer triple, I think.'

'It looks more like quadrupeddle.'

'Quadruple.'

'Sorry. Quadruple.' Bryony liked to get words right.

'We'll let it finish cooking and then it can cool overnight.

We'll take it over to Mad in the morning,' said Felicity.

'Not tonight?'

'Tonight you have weekend homework.'

'Couldn't I do that tomorrow? Tomorrow's Sunday,' said Bryony hopefully.

'No, because you'll enjoy Sunday much more if you've done your homework tonight. I suppose,' said Felicity, regarding Bryony with a mixture of amusement and exasperation, 'that it's arithmetic, is it?'

'Um, yes. I'm lavishly glum about it, actually.'

'I thought it might be. Well, get your books and we'll take a run at it together. And then just think how good you'll feel tomorrow if you've done it all tonight.'

Madeleine Foulsham thought she had not let Felicity see how genuinely wretched she was feeling. Flu did make people feel wretched, of course, and the doctor had said it was quite a nasty strain that was going the rounds just now.

Disgusting flu. Disgusting being ill and dependent on other people. She had deliberated for quite a long time before phoning Felicity; she had wondered whether it mightn't be better to phone the girl who came in two mornings a week to help with cleaning. Sonja was a nice cheerful girl – everyone referred to her as a home help or a carer, but Madeleine called her Sonja who helps me with the cleaning. This week she had been regaling Mad with the story of a new boyfriend; Mad enjoyed hearing about him, and if Sonja was to be believed, he was possessed of just about every virtue ever known. Mad, reading between the lines, thought he sounded rather a rascal and hoped Sonja was not going to get her heart broken.

But Sonja was a good-hearted soul and she would certainly have nipped out to collect the prescription in her ramshackle little car. The trouble was that this would not only mean that Mad had admitted to weakness, it would also mean she had admitted to having no one else to call on.

She had a lot of acquaintances – there was the gardening club and the Women's Institute; there were occasional charity events to help with, but no close friendships had ever formed. This was a little to do with being a lone female, of course, and a little more to do with Mad's own attitude of determined independence. But it was a lot to do with being part of a family who had been more or less feudal overlords in the area.

In a big town with a migrant population this last would long since have ceased to matter, but in the country people had long memories. As far as most of the local inhabitants were concerned, Madeleine Foulsham came from a branch of the Foljambe aristocrats, going back through George the profligate, to Francis who had exercised a kind of *droit de seigneur* over most of the female populace; all the way back to the first Foljambes, pursuing their curious profession under the aegis of William the Conqueror.

Madeleine knew the stories and she had been gratified and touched to find that Felicity knew some of them as well – that would have been from her own Serena, of course. Strange to think she had argued against Serena going to live with that distant cousin in Kent, but the cousin had handed the stories on as well. Serena had told them to Felicity, and Felicity had passed them on to Bryony. But Bryony, funny little scrap, seemed to be adding her own twist to them. Madeleine had no idea how the child had got to know so much about the family, but she either knew or was making up a great deal. She certainly knew about Richard and the twins, *and* she seemed to know something about that hussy Isobel Weston who had been one of Francis's little bits of fluff, or so Madeleine had always suspected.

She went up to bed earlier than usual, taking one of Felicity's paperbacks with her, and lay back on her pillows, sipping a glass of hot rum and water. There was nothing like hot rum to oil a wheezy chest back to normality!

It was to be hoped Felicity would manage to coax Bryony a bit away from those remarkable fantasies. Not too far – the child might well have the makings of a writer or a painter – but far enough to ensure she did not get reality and fairy tale mixed up. She considered mentioning this to Felicity, and decided against it. There was nothing so tiresome as an interfering old woman – a spinster as well! – and she would hate Felicity to think her tiresome.

Still, it was nice that they had come here. It was nice to think of them just on the other side of the forest, or on the other end of the phone, although Mad would hold by her lifelong independence. Seventy-one was not so very old by today's standards, and she had survived that mild stroke last year. It was only that her left hand had not quite the grip it had once had, and one leg was a bit unreliable if she put too much weight on it. But she might have had to put up with a lot worse than that.

The hot rum and the doctor's pills, whatever they had been, were finally having an effect. Her head had stopped aching and the grinding pains in her joints had stopped as well. She was feeling pleasantly sleepy, and it was warm in the bed and comfortable.

She was just crossing the borderlands into real sleep when something tugged at her mind – a sound? A movement where there should not have been any movement? She opened her eyes and looked round the room, but nothing stirred. She listened carefully. Had that been a scrape of sound from downstairs? No, she was imagining it. There was no whisper of movement anywhere in the house, and she knew quite definitely that all the doors were locked and bolted and all the windows were firmly latched.

Imagination. And it was to be hoped she was not going to turn into one of those irritating jittery females who thought burglars were forever breaking in. She closed her eyes again.

But sleep, so annoyingly broken into, refused to return. Madeleine lay on her pillows and considered switching on the bedside lamp again and reading another few pages of the paperback.

She was just reaching out for the lamp when she heard the sound again. And this time there was no mistake.

Someone was opening the garden door downstairs.

There was a blessed space of time when she thought it might be Felicity, perhaps returning with something for her, perhaps just looking in to see if she was all right. But Felicity did not have a key, and she would surely have phoned first.

It was just possible that it was Sonja, who certainly had a key. Mad considered this. But Sonja had never yet used her key without first knocking at the door to see if Mad was in.

Whoever this was, he was moving about quietly. It had to be a burglar. Mad began to reach stealthily for the bedside phone. Dial 999 and the police would come roaring out, lights blazing and sirens wailing.

It was disconcerting in the extreme to remember that the phone was on the left side of the bed, and to discover that her hand – the left, slightly weak one – was fumbling the clasp of the receiver. Madeleine felt a pulse of panic start up inside her head.

She could hear the intruder more clearly now; he – it had to be a 'he' – had opened the door to the inner hall. She had heard the characteristic squeak of the hinge quite clearly, and remembered with abrupt irrelevance that she had been saying to Sonja for a couple of weeks that they would have to oil those hinges, they shrieked like a banshee every time you opened the door.

The hinges shrieked now, betraying the intruder's presence. Madeleine, still scrabbling at the phone, pushing herself up in the bed so that she could reach for it with her other hand, felt him pause. He's listening, she thought. He's listening to see if he's disturbed me – I can *feel* him listening!

The blood was drumming in her head but beyond it she could hear soft padding footsteps. He was crossing the hall below – there was no carpet there because of the lovely old woodblock floor, and although he was moving quietly, there was absolutely no mistake about it.

He's heading for the stairs, thought Mad in panic. He's coming slowly and stealthily, but he's going to come up the stairs. The room began to spin, and with it came the terrifying *slipping* sensation inside her head that she recognized from the stroke last year. She forced the rising fear down, and this time managed to reach the bedside phone with her good hand. Relief shot through her. She would do it! She would reach the police – 999, the magic formula – and within minutes they would be here!

The intruder was coming up the stairs now: he had reached the half-landing and he had paused. There was the sound of something *sniffing* outside her bedroom door.

And now every fragment of her family's long, long history scudded through Madeleine's mind, and every snippet of legend and folklore and myth that had ever walked through her childhood nightmares reared up to taunt her. The humanized wolf that had stalked the ancient wildwoods of the Kingdom of Mercia . . . The evil hungering thing that had crouched below the old forest house, picking through the bloodied bones of its prey while its human adversaries slept . . . The wolves who knew how to stake out the houses of the humans – who learned human tricks and knew how to tap at the door and how to lift the latch and slide the bolt and slink inside.

An intolerable pressure was building up and up within her head. He was just outside the door, and if only she could stop shaking and if only she could force her flaccid left hand to obey her for just long enough to summon help . . . But by this time she was shaking too much and her weak left hand let her down. The phone slid from her nerveless fingers and crashed onto the floor. The sounds stopped at once. *He's listening to find out what I'll do next!* Madeleine drew in a shuddering breath and reached out again, and this time, by sheer blind chance, her right hand closed around the bedside lamp. She seized it eagerly. Would it serve as a weapon? It was attached to the wall by its length of flex but she thought there was enough play for her to lift it and deal a telling blow. In any case, it was better than nothing. She struggled to get a better grip on the lamp, her eyes still fixed on the door. The pressure was mounting inside her head, and at any minute her eyes might burst with it—

The old-fashioned door latch was depressed from the other side, and the bedroom door began slowly to open. Mad stared at it in mindless terror. *He's coming in. He's coming into the room and I'm trapped in the bed—* There was a warm animal scent in the room, and although her head was starting to crack under the unbearable pressure and although the left half of her whole body was being dragged down and down by leaden weights, she watched the door inch open.

A hand came around the door, grasping the edge firmly, and a dark shadow fell across the bedroom floor. For a moment nothing moved: the door remained as it was, partly ajar, the figure standing motionless.

And then the door swung wide open and there before her was the nightmare figure from all the old stories. The wolf who walked upright like men. The human mask hiding the slavering jaws and teeth . . . Black silky hair and hungry eyes . . . He was slavering over her already and he was eyeing her with the red glint of a meat-hungry animal . . .

She heard her voice cry out, and she heard with incredulous fear that it came out as an unintelligible babble of sound. Her vision began to blur, as if a thick crimson curtain was slowly being drawn down over her eyes. She did not feel the heavy lamp slip from her grasp, and she did not hear it crash to the floor, to lie there alongside the useless telephone receiver.

But she saw the wolf walk forward and she saw it sit on the bed and look at her with its head tilted to one side.

In a soft, cultured voice that was the most terrifyingly sinister thing Madeleine had ever heard, the wolf said, 'Did I frighten you, my dear?'

And smiled a dreadful, dripping-fanged wolf-smile as he bent over the bed . . .

Chapter Thirty-Nine

A worried conclave was being held in the kitchen of Weston House. It was a conclave that had been set in motion by Dietfreid, who had discovered with consternation that Nina was not in the house, and furthermore that it appeared she had gone out sometime before breakfast.

'Piers and Tybalt aren't here either,' said Priscilla, having checked the other rooms. 'And both the cars have gone. Bloody cheek, as a matter of fact, taking my car without asking.'

This had galvanized Dietfreid into immediate action, and he had made several plans, some of which were impossible, most of which were impractical, and all of which involved phoning the local police there and then, to report the three truants as missing people.

'Toby's coming on the twelve o'clock train,' Priscilla had said. 'Let's wait until he gets here.'

'Why?'

'Well, there might be a logical explanation.'

'And Toby will provide it?'

'No, but he might think of something we haven't.'

But Toby, arriving later, and pounced on by Dietfreid almost as soon as he got out of the taxi, could not think of anything that even remotely explained why Nina and the two men should have gone out some time during the night without telling anyone.

'They have fallen into the hands of the wolf people,' wailed Dietfreid. 'I know it. I have known it all along. There is a doom on this entire mission!'

'Oh God, Dietfreid, if you're going to start uttering Cassandra-like curses I'm heading back to London on the next train,' said Toby with an Englishman's revulsion for histrionics.

'But the *liebchen* Nina—'

'And Piers and Tybalt,' put in Priscilla.

'They have fallen on evil times. All of them! They are all at the mercy of that evil villain. I know it. I feel it *here*!' declaimed Dietfreid, thumping his middle. 'We call the cops,' he added, descending abruptly from Wagnerian melodramatics to drive-in movie-speak.

'No, hold on, I'm still thinking. They took the cars,' said Toby, frowning. 'The Range Rover and yours, Priscilla. Which indicates they went out of their own free will. Why would they take both vehicles?'

'I don't know, but if one of them prangs my car—'

'We go off to find them *now*—'

'No, hold on, I'm still thinking. If Nina and Piers had gone, or Nina and Tybalt, I'd take the cynic's view,' said Toby. 'But all three of them at once is a little hard to swallow—'

'So. I make the call.'

'Wait a *minute*. What if,' said Toby, still thinking, hard, 'one of them came upon a clue, and went off to investigate?'

'And the other two followed him?'

'Well, I can certainly believe that Piers took Tybalt off somewhere, and Nina got to hear of it and trailed them.'

'That would account for them taking both cars,' said Priscilla. 'So where are they now, then?'

'They might have crashed. Or sprained an ankle or something, somewhere out of reach of a phone. We don't even know how long they've been gone. You found out at breakfast time – what would that be?'

'Quarter to eight,' said Priscilla. 'But it's now half-past twelve.'

'I don't think the police would regard five hours as seriously missing. Not for an adult. But I think we'd better phone them anyway now.'

'I do it,' said Dietfreid, pleased at having some positive action.

'OK. But I'll take a bet they'll tell us to give it twenty-four hours,' said Toby. 'What I think we'd better do,' he added, as Dietfreid went plunging off, 'is take a look around the forest ourselves.'

'What do we do about transport? Both cars are gone. Can we get a taxi?'

'Not very easily if the turn-out at the station is anything to go by. I had to wait for nearly twenty minutes,' said Toby.

'We'll have to try and hire a car,' said Priscilla.

'Yes, on Sunday afternoon as well – that won't be easy. Oh *blast* Piers,' said Toby, 'why couldn't he disappear on a weekday?'

The light did not change much in the underground room, but Karabas's people had been coming and going all day – '*Slinking* in and out,' said Tybalt disgustedly – leaving open the half-rotted door at the head of the steps.

The morning was well advanced when Piers suddenly said, 'Listen to me, both of you. No – don't look at me; don't do anything to attract their attention or let them think we might be plotting something.'

'What is it? Have you thought of a plot?'

Nina's voice was so filled with sudden hope that Piers said quickly, 'Not exactly. But surely the car thing still applies? Nina, you took Priscilla's car, right?'

'Yes, I told you.'

'You parked it behind the Range Rover, didn't you?'

'Yes.'

'*Good*,' said Piers, and his eyes gleamed suddenly. 'So when Dietfreid and Priscilla start looking for us the first place they'll think of are the ruins. They'll take the road we all took, and they'll see the two cars.'

Tybalt sent a quick glance across the room. Karabas's people had been coming and going all morning, but there had never been less than six in the underground room at any time. He said, 'Won't those guys have moved them?'

'How? We've got the keys.'

'Well – they'd push them into the forest or something.'

'No, Piers is right!' Nina sat up excitedly, before she remembered about being unobtrusive and slumped down again. 'They're primitive creatures! Most of them are straight off Cruithin Island. They'd never have the – the human nous to even think about anything like hiding cars.'

'Karabas would think about it,' said Tybalt.

'But even if he did, he'd never move them,' said Piers. 'Priscilla's is an automatic and as long as Nina left it in "Park" with the handbrake on—'

'I did.'

'—then it wouldn't budge,' said Piers. 'And the Range Rover is too heavy to push anywhere with the handbrake on.'

'But they could break a window and get in to release the handbrakes.'

'They couldn't,' said Nina. 'Even if they knew about handbrakes – OK, Karabas might know: he seems to have been off the island for long enough to become very humanized – but both those cars have got automatic alarm systems. *Loud* automatic alarm systems. They'd alert the entire forest and no matter how humanized the others think they are, they'd be thrown into an absolute panic. You know how piercing any car alarm is!'

'Exactly.' Piers smiled at them both. 'And that means all we've got to do is sit it out and hope Dietfreid and Priscilla don't take too long about getting here.'

But even with this shred of encouragement, it was appallingly tedious. The day stretched out and out. Tybalt said he would never have believed he could have suffered from boredom while waiting to take part in an ancient grisly ritual, but bored was just what he was. He had been all for expecting their saviours within the hour, but Piers and Nina both agreed it would be much longer.

'They mightn't realize we've disappeared until after breakfast,' argued Nina.

'Even then they might not check this place first,' said Piers.

'Won't they call the cops?'

'Yes, but I don't think the cops would do anything yet. I don't think they'd regard us as missing until we've been gone for over twenty-four hours,' said Piers, thoughtfully.

'And remember they've got to get a car from somewhere,' put in Nina. 'We've got both vehicles.'

'Oh yeah, I'd forgotten that. But I guess they'll reach us before – uh, you know – before the action starts, won't they?'

'I'm praying so,' said Piers, softly, and Tybalt turned to look at him and thought he would never understand Dr Adair, not if he was in his company for a whole year without a break.

Bryony was having a very good day. It had started with the sun shining into her green and white bedroom, remembering that she had done that bad old arithmetic and that the entire day could be enjoyed as a result. They walked down to the village in the morning to buy a Sunday newspaper, and then stopped off at a farm, where there was a new litter of puppies. Mother said they could have one when the puppies were a bit older, and Bryony was practically speechless with delight. The puppies were spaniels: they were a tumbly, furry mass of golden fur and fat little bodies. They chose one who was just about the fattest and tumbliest of the lot and the farmer's wife said that Bryony could come to visit him once or twice a week so that he would get to know her, and when he was old enough to leave his mother he would not mind. She explained about looking after him and walking him and training him.

They discussed the puppy over lunch and thought about a name for him. That was an important decision; Bryony did not want to get it wrong. Mother wondered whether they could call him Bracken after the school. It had a golden-brown sound to it which would be just right.

Mother was going to spend the afternoon cleaning the cellar. She normally hated cellars to bits, but the men were coming on Monday to slosh whitewash everywhere. She said that now the rusting old boiler had been carried out and the old wall knocked through it was surprising how airy a place it was, and she would trundle the vacuum cleaner down the steps and have a grand spider hunt. Then it would be all ready for the whitewashing. Afterwards they would drive round to see Mad and take the casserole and the soup, but they would leave that until later, so that Mad could have a rest for most of the day. But Bryony could help with the vacuuming if she liked, said mother with a grin.

Bryony said, 'Spiders! Yuck!' and thought she would dig in her garden for a bit. She and Mad had bought some little pots of herbs at Hardwick Hall and she would plant them today.

'Don't go out of the garden,' said mother, dragging the vacuum out of its cupboard. 'And put on a jacket, it's quite cold today. Oh, and your old wellingtons – it's wet and muddy out there.'

It was very wet and muddy indeed. Bryony discovered this right away. The trouble with mud was that although it was nice to dig in, if it was extra-wet mud you got a *lot* of worms. There were a lot in the ground today. Worms were double-yuck – Bryony hated them even worse than spiders. It might be better to leave the herb-planting until the ground was a bit dryer.

She went back into the kitchen, taking off her wellingtons

by the door and padding across the floor in her socks. The casserole and the soup for Mad were standing on the table in the kitchen – mother had poured the casserole into a red earthenware pot with a tight-fitting lid, and the soup was in a plastic tub. Bryony eyed them thoughtfully. Mother was hoovering away like mad in the cellar; she had shouted up that it was horridly spidery down here, and she would not be much longer but she would have to wash her hair and shower before she could go anywhere. It seemed a bit silly to drive all the way round to Mad's house later on; Bryony knew the forest path very well by this time – she and Mad had walked through it together several times and it was the easiest thing in the world.

It would be lavishly good to walk through the forest on this sparkly afternoon and take Mad's food to her. It would be pretty helpful for mother as well who would be tired and grubby after all the vacuuming.

Bryony found the large basket from the pantry, and tucked a red and white checked teacloth in. It matched the dish and looked bright and cheerful. Then she went to the top of the cellar steps and shouted down, explaining what she was going to do. Mother was still tramping about with the vacuum, but Bryony thought she called back something that sounded like, 'Well, be careful.'

So that was all right. Mother did not mind her going. She remembered about it being cold, and went up to her room to get a jacket. It would be nice to wear the scarlet cloak that father had bought her. She took it out of her wardrobe.

Bryony, wearing the red cloak, carefully carrying the basket of food for great-grandmamma, set off through the forest.

Felicity was feeling better about the cottage. She was not feeling a great deal better about the cellar, but she thought the only way she would be able to cope with using it for a laundry room was to get used to it. Familiarity breeding contempt.

If I clean everything out, thought Felicity determinedly – really scour the entire place from tip to toe – then I shan't keep thinking about that poor little creature they found behind the wall. At least – I will think about it but it won't be frightening, it'll only be rather sad.

It was curious that Bryony had said there had once been a secret hiding place in the cottage. Felicity, dealing with cobwebs and the accumulated dirt of what looked like years and smelt like centuries, wondered if this cellar was where she had meant. The trouble with Bryony was that you could not always know when she was talking about reality and when she was talking about her own made-up stories. She had seemed to be caught up in one yesterday while they were preparing the food for Mad – something about a man in a velvet cloak who rode a horse through the forest – and Felicity had known it was the wrong time to tell her about the baby. She was trying to encourage the story-making without letting Bryony get too far into outright fantasy. It was sometimes quite difficult. But on the whole Felicity, who had listened to enough horror stories from other parents, could not believe her luck over Bryony. She was an oddity at times, but she was an agreeable, well-behaved oddity. Is that from me, Connor, or from you? But this was a thought that must instantly be pushed away, because Connor's curious ancestry must never be thought about. Always supposing, thought Felicity firmly, that I believed all that stuff in the first place.

Cleaning the cellar had taken longer than she had thought, but it looked much better already. When the helpful builder had painted the walls tomorrow and then laid the ceramic floor it would look very good indeed. I don't mind you at all now, said Felicity, to the corner where the poor, unknown little ghost had lain. I think you're the one who haunted the cottage; I don't know if you'll haunt it any longer, but if you do I shan't mind.

She went up to the kitchen. Bryony must still be digging in her garden – she had called something down a short while ago – something about getting on well with Mad's garden, and something about telling Mad all about it when they took the food over later on. Felicity had called back to be careful with the mud.

She headed for the bathroom to sluice away the dirt. It was half-past four. There was time to shower and shampoo her hair and rough-dry it before driving round to the gatehouse. When they got back they would heat up a portion of the casserole for supper; there were salad ingredients in the fridge and a nice crusty loaf. And although she was being very strict over alcohol because of being pregnant, she thought she might allow herself a modest glass of wine this evening.

374

Bryony was enjoying her walk through the forest. It was a spangly kind of afternoon on account of it having rained last night and the sun shining through the rainy bits. It did not shine in forests like it did in a field or on a road; it shone in trickly bits down through the leaves, so that you got splashy patterns on the ground. Bryony walked in and out of the patterns, enjoying them. There were a lot of birds singing today; she enjoyed that as well.

This was the first time she had been into the forest on her own, and it meant she could think about all the Foljambe people without anyone interrupting her. There were a lot of them to think about. She could pretend she was Richard's lady riding a white horse with a blue velvet bridle, or that she was walking with the twins, talking about archery and the Crusade with the golden-haired king, or that she was with Sir Francis who had tried to save Isobel. She thought she would be with Sir Francis this afternoon.

She was being extra doubly careful about the basket with the food in it; it would not be much good to Mad if half of it was spilt. Bryony was watching it to make sure it did not tip up. It was a bit heavy, actually, in fact it might have been better to wait for mother and the car after all. But she was quite near to the gatehouse now. Over to the right were the Foljambe ruins. Bryony was still a bit doubtful about those. They did not feel very good, which was odd when you remembered how much she had always wanted to see them. The bad feeling might be because one or two wicked Foljambes had lived there – there had been somebody called George who had not been very good; Mad often said he had brought the family to ruin. Bryony thought she would not have liked that George much.

She was starting to be a bit doubtful about the forest as well this afternoon. It was not quite as sparkly and as happy as it had been when she set off, in fact it was starting to be a bit spooky. The birds had stopped singing, and birds only did that when there was something dangerous prowling about. Bryony thought she would get to Mad's house quite quickly now. She would not run because of tipping up the basket with the casserole and the soup, but she would go as fast as she could.

The spookiness was getting worse. It was beginning to feel as though somebody was creeping along behind her – this was such a terrible thought that she risked a scared glance over her shoulder. There was nobody there. But Bryony thought that really there *was* somebody there; she thought there was somebody who was being so quiet and so clever that each time she stopped, this person stopped, and each time she turned round, this person dodged behind a tree. She began to remember about mother and Mad saying she must never – never *ever* – come into the forest on her own.

The thing to do was to get to Mad's house. Then she would be safe. She could see the house through the trees now, and she went towards it thankfully, still not quite running. It looked welcoming and very safe. There were the nice windows with the curtains all folded back so that the sun could get into the rooms, and she could see a figure in the downstairs window on the left-hand side of the front door, which was the window of Mad's dining room. This was very good because it meant that Mad was feeling better and was walking about the house. Bryony drew in a rather trembly breath of relief – it had been *frightening* in that old forest! – and went up the path to the front door.

For a moment she thought Mad had not heard her because she did not come to the door. But then Bryony was just lifting the knocker again when she heard someone cross the hall and walk towards the door. Bryony called out to let Mad know who it was and not to rush. Mad had to use a stick sometimes because of her bad leg; it would not be good if she tripped over on the way to answer the door. 'It's me – Bryony. I've brought a casserole and some soup. I'll wait till you to get to the door.'

She thought Mad's voice called out to her – it sounded hoarse and scratchy, which would be because of Mad having flu. She had had a sore throat yesterday.

The door swung open, and the voice that was not quite Mad's voice said, 'Come inside, Bryony. Come inside, my dear, and close the door.'

Bryony stepped into the hall.

She knew at once that something was wrong. Something was *different*. But it looked as if Mad was waiting for her in the sitting room, and so Bryony glanced round a bit doubtfully and then closed the door.

The curtains had been drawn in the sitting room, so that it

was not as sunshiny as the rest of the house. Perhaps that was why things felt wrong. Bryony paused in the doorway. It was dim and shadowy in the room, but she could see the chair where Mad usually sat; it was drawn up to the fire, and it was a nice deep chair with a flowery cover on it. Mad was sitting in it—

It was not Mad at all. It was a dark-haired man and he was looking at her and smiling. Fear began to fill Bryony up, as if somebody was pouring it into her from a huge jug. Because it was *him* – Karabas, who had shut her into the horrid hut in the forest, and who was really, secretly, the wolf.

There was a moment when she thought he might not be the wolf now; he might be the quite interesting person who had talked to her at Bracken about birds and wild flowers and who had known all about the Foljambes. But then he stood up and came towards her, and Bryony saw at once that of course he was the wolf.

She said, in a small scared voice, 'Where's Mad – I mean my great-grandmother?' and then the *really* scary thing happened.

The wolf said, 'She's dead, Bryony. I've killed her. But we're going to eat her up together.'

Felicity finished drying her hair, pulled on jeans and a loose shirt, and went downstairs to tell Bryony to put her gardening things away and come in to wash her hands before setting off for Mad's house.

She did not immediately see Bryony, who was probably at the side of the house, intent on her little herb garden. She was being very serious about it and she was going to write out proper labels for each plant so that they would know what everything was.

Bryony was not at the side of the house, and it did not look as if she had done much to the embryo herb garden. Felicity frowned slightly, and went around to the front. She was not there either. It was ridiculous in the extreme to feel the lurch of panic, because Bryony would not be far away at all. She might even be in the house – Felicity would probably not have heard her come in if the shower had still been running. Yes, that would be it. Felicity came back inside and went through to the inglenook room, and then, the little pulse of panic increasing, up to Bryony's room. And now she did panic. She tore open the wardrobe and searched along the rack of Bryony's clothes.

The red cloak was gone.

Chapter Forty

Felicity felt the strength drain from her whole body, and for a moment she half fell into the little chair by Bryony's desk. There would be a perfectly normal explanation to all this, *of course* there would! Bryony would turn up at any minute – she would certainly not be far away. Felicity forced herself to think calmly. Where could she have gone?

Madeleine's house! Of course. Felicity half ran downstairs to the kitchen. The casserole and the tub of soup had gone, and along with it, the large basket from the pantry. Relief, tinged with annoyance, flooded through her. Bryony was specifically forbidden to go into the forest by herself – in fact she was specifically forbidden to go anywhere by herself! – but at least Felicity almost certainly knew where she was. She would phone Mad at once and say that if Bryony had already arrived, she should stay put until Felicity got there. She reached for the phone, trying to think whether it would be quicker to walk through the forest or take the car round on the lower road.

It was infuriating to find that the phone was not working; Felicity jiggled the receiver rest but there was no dial tone at all, only dead silence. This was adding annoyance onto irritation. She would have to walk to Mad's house now, because she had no idea how long it was since Bryony had left. If she took the car, Bryony might be on her way back and they would miss one another. She reached for a jacket and went into the inglenook room to get the keys from her bag. She was crossing the room when she heard someone fumbling with a kind of soft stealthiness at the latch of the kitchen door.

Felicity stopped dead. She knew, instantly and unmistakably, with the curious extra sense that sometimes operated between her and Bryony – that probably operated between most mothers and their children – that it was not Bryony. In any case, Bryony

379

would not scrabble at the latch like that; if she found the door locked, she would go around to the front of the cottage and ring the doorbell.

Felicity moved warily to the doorway of the inglenook room, where there was a more or less direct sightline through to the kitchen. Terror poured into her at once, and her heart seemed to come up into her mouth.

The kitchen door was made of strong, thick oak, as befitted a door in a house with no near neighbours. But the aesthetically inclined builder had suggested the addition of an oblong of toughened glass in the upper half. 'Give you a bit more light,' he had said, 'and be just as secure – in fact securer than a plain door, because you'll be able to see who's there.'

Felicity could see who was there now. The glass was slightly opaque and there were strips of thin wire through it, but even from here she could see who it was.

Karabas. Karabas was outside the house, trying to get in.

Felicity's mind flew in three different directions at once. It flew to Bryony who might be out there in the forest, and who certainly might be in Karabas's hands all over again. And it flew to panic for her own safety, because although the door had a security lock, it was not on at the moment, and it would be child's play for him to get in. Lastly, it flew out onto a practical level: how was she going to get out and raise the alarm without him seeing?

The phone was no good, because the phone was dead. The fact of this broke against her mind with fresh horror, because this was all planned – Karabas had planned all this out; he had cut the phone line so that she would be unable to phone the police. She thought: *how very worldly wise you've become, Karabas!*

If she could get to the front door she might manage to scoot across to her Mini, parked outside, and be away down the road before he could do anything about it. But this would mean going out into the hall and he would almost definitely see her through the glass. It meant coping with bolts and with a complicated security lock as well, because they tended to keep the front door locked all the time, she and Bryony, and come and go by the kitchen door.

Still, if she was very quick she might just get through the

door and out to the car. The keys were in her hand, on the ring that held the house keys. She glanced out of the window, to where she could see the parked Mini. Could she do it? The Mini had never yet failed to start at first touch, and even if he caught her up she could lock the driver's door and simply drive away. And then she looked at it again, because there was something wrong about it – there was something she could not for a second or two identify— Oh God, he's worldly wise with a vengeance! The front of the Mini was sagging, it was wholly out of balance with the rear. He's cut the tyres, thought Felicity in panic. Or he's let the air out. It doesn't matter which, because either way it's not drivable, and I'm trapped— *He's inside the house!*

Extreme terror swept over her, and in its wake came again the memory of Bryony talking about the hiding place in the cottage. It wasn't the cellar at all. It was a sliding panel – a hiding-hole Bryony had said, for people who went to the wrong church. A priest's hole? Felicity was across the room before she knew it, her hands pressing against the glossy wood panels. Oh please, *please* let this not have been one of Bryony's flights of fantasy, and *please* let the hiding place still be here—

It was still there. The panel moved beneath her hands, and with barely a whisper of sound it slid to one side, revealing a black opening. Felicity gave a gasp of relief and stumbled in, pulling the panel back.

It was dark inside and it stank abominably. Felicity found it difficult to breathe, but when she did breathe she had the feeling that she was breathing in the dust and the dirt and the memories of a very long-ago time. She had the strong feeling that the sad unknown, little ghost was very near to her.

Karabas was in the inglenook room – Felicity could hear him walking around, opening a large cupboard set into the outer wall, drawing back the curtains to look into the window recess. He knows I'm here, she thought, her heart pounding. He knows I was in the house, and he knows I'm hiding. But he doesn't know where. She heard him go back into the kitchen and then his footsteps on the stone steps leading down into the cellar. Was there time to slide the panel back and get out? If she could only get out and find out what had happened to Bryony— But if Karabas grabbed her the instant she stepped out, it would be of no use to Bryony at all. She heard him come back and tears of frustration and anger stung her eyes. Too late. But supposing he went upstairs to look for her? Surely he would do that?

With the thought she heard the creak of the stair and hope bounded up. She would let him reach the top landing, and she would hear the loose stairboard creak as he went into her bedroom. Then she would move. Yes, there it went now. She would give it a count of twenty for him to cross to her room and then she would move. Ten – twelve – fifteen – get ready—

She had just grasped the ridge on the panel's edge, when she heard the creak of the stairs once more and knew he had been too quick for her. Despair swept in all over again because she had lost the moment.

The darkness inside the priest's hole was not absolute; Felicity could make out her own hands, and a thread of light formed an oblong where the outline of the panel was. But it was dreadfully cramped. It was necessary to half-kneel in a hunched-over position which was killingly uncomfortable after the first ten minutes. Felicity's muscles were starting to protest, and there was a heaviness at the pit of her stomach. But she did not dare to make even the smallest movement; the panel was fairly sturdy but anyone on the other side would hear a movement. Felicity half closed her eyes against the pain of protesting muscles, and it was then that Karabas spoke.

The sound of his voice made her heart jump violently, because it sounded impossibly near. He must be barely two feet away from her.

He said, 'Felicity, I know you're in the house – I can feel that you're here. And sooner or later I shall find you.'

A shiver of purest terror went through her, and with it this time there was a lancing pain, low down in her body.

'I've got Bryony,' said Karabas's voice. 'It was so easy, Felicity. I had a plan all made out but I didn't need to use it. For once the victim came to seek out the hunter.' A pause. He's listening for me, thought Felicity. Oh God, there's got to be a way of outwitting him!

'I've carried her to a place where my people are gathered,' said Karabas's voice. 'They've been gathering for several weeks now: coming from the place where they've lived to the place where it all began. They've been doing so slowly and gradually,

Felicity, so that they can become used to your ways – remember I told you that we learn the ways of the humans swiftly? But they're almost all here now, and tonight, once darkness falls, Bryony will take part in a ritual. You remember the one, Felicity? You remember the drinking of the blood of the ancestors?' Again the pause, and then, 'Only tonight it will be the ancestress,' said Karabas, and Felicity's mind instantly veered onto a different track, and she thought: Madeleine! Oh God, he's taken Madeleine as well! What do I do? The pain came again, stronger, like claws closing around the lower part of her stomach. Felicity dug her nails into the palms of her hands and waited for it to recede. It was nothing that needed to be given any attention; it would only be a twinge of panic. Yes, it had gone now, and she could focus on what was happening and what she could do.

There was a creak of the old floor as he moved to the window, and then a whisper of sound as he sat in the deep wing chair drawn up to the fire. Felicity had the ridiculous thought: I'll never want to sit in that chair again.

Karabas said, softly, 'I shall stay here until it's dark, Felicity. And when I leave, to preside over the ancient ritual of my people, one of my kind will take my place.'

Like a cat watching at a mousehole . . . Doing so in shifts . . .

'I do know you're somewhere in this house,' he said, raising his voice slightly this time, 'But I don't know where and I don't know how to look. You see, Felicity' – he almost sounded as if he was smiling now – 'we do know that you have sly little tricks in your houses, and we have still to learn about them. But we're very patient,' said Karabas, and his voice seemed suddenly nearer. 'And wherever you are in this house, remember that Bryony is alive at the moment.

'But after tonight she might not be.'

Around midday two of Karabas's people brought food to the three prisoners – bread and cheese and some fruit – and a mug of milk each. Afterwards they were taken, one at a time, and guarded by three of the men, to a secluded patch of the forest just behind the underground room.

Piers said this was considerate and boded well for their eventual fate, but Tybalt said it was disgusting and demeaning. 'I've plumbed the depths of humiliation,' he said when he came back from his turn. 'They stood and *watched*, can you believe that?'

'How do you think I felt?' demanded Nina.

'I wish Dietfreid and Priscilla would turn up,' said Tybalt, wistfully, and Piers remembered for the first time how extremely young Tybalt was.

'They will come,' he said. 'We can trust them to look for us.'

'Well, I hope so, Gee, I never thought I'd say it, but the best sight in the whole world right now would be to see Priscilla come down those stairs, with a load of cops.'

The shadows were just starting to lengthen when they heard footsteps outside once more, and Nina's heart leapt with hope.

But it was not Priscilla and Dietfreid; it was Karabas. He came lightly down the steps, and in his arms he was carrying a small girl with wide-apart scared eyes and hair the colour of beech leaves in autumn. He brought her across to the corner where Piers and the other two lay, and tied her up along with them.

Bryony was very frightened indeed. She knew now that she had been brought to the wolf's lair – the real lair where the wolf had hidden and where he had eaten Edmund – and she knew that something truly terrible was going to happen to her. She did not know if it would be eating up Mad, as Karabas had said, or whether it would be something even worse. It was difficult to know what would be worse, however.

The wolves were all there in the room: they were sitting or lying on the floor and they looked a lot like Karabas, but Bryony knew that they were really wolves, just as Karabas was really a wolf.

It was not quite dark outside, but it was very dark in the lair. The wolves set fire to pieces of wood and then wedged the wood in the walls so that the burning ends cast a red glow everywhere. Bryony did not like the red glow one bit.

But she was managing to be pretty brave, which was a good thing to be. This was mostly because of the three other people the wolves had captured. They were very nice to her. The lady was called Nina, and she was very pretty, with a lot of fluffy fair hair. She told Bryony not to worry because they would very soon be saved; there were friends who would be looking

384

for them this very minute, and although the wolf people did not know it, she and the two men had actually left several clues so that they would be found quite soon. The young man who spoke like Americans on TV said this was surely so; they would be out of here within the hour.

Bryony managed to say, in a frightened little voice, that her mother would have missed her as well, and would come to get her. So really, what with Nina's friends, and mother and the clues and everything, there was nothing to be specially worried about.

But it was only when the other man – the dark-haired one – leaned forward and looked at her very intently and said, 'Bryony, it's all right. We're going to be absolutely safe,' that Bryony really believed it.

It had given Piers an odd, painful feeling to see the white-faced Bryony struggling so valiantly not to cry, and he had felt his throat close up with emotion when she looked at him with sudden and overwhelming trust. He was deeply grateful to Nina, who talked gently to her, asking her name and where she lived; and then Tybalt explained how they had been studying these bad old people, and described exactly how they were going to deal with them when they got free.

Wherever she had come from and whyever Karabas wanted her, she was not conventionally pretty, this little girl, but Piers, studying her, thought she might well grow up to be a bit of a stunner. He found himself praying that she would live to grow up.

Nina told Bryony about Dietfreid and Toby and Priscilla. She described Dietfreid, making a story of it, caricaturing him a bit, so that he became a roly-poly person who bumped into things and got everything a bit wrong.

'He'll be here very soon,' said Nina. 'He'll be charging around outside somewhere, and he might trip over things a few times and bump into a few other things, but he's very, very dependable.'

'See, what we'll do,' said Tybalt, 'we'll beat these guys up and then we'll let Dietfreid roll on them.'

'Squash them flat?' asked Bryony, half doubtfully, half hopefully.

'Steam-roller them,' said Tybalt.

But he and Nina both glanced worriedly to the foot of the steps, to where the forest light was already changing from green to turquoise. Soon it would turn to the blue-grey of twilight, and then the ritual would commence.

Toby and Priscilla had phoned most of the car hire firms in the phone book but most of them appeared to be closed for Sunday, and the majority had answerphones on. After this, they had tried the garages and finally the taxi firms. It had taken an amazingly long time, but they finally hit on a small taxi company who would send out a taxi and a driver to be at their disposal for the next two hours. The cost made even Priscilla blink.

Dietfreid had vibrated nervously like a badly set blancmange between the door and the phone, occasionally wringing his hands. He had found the number of the elderly lady, Madeleine Foulsham, he and Nina had met in the forest, and he had tried to phone her to see if she had seen the absentees, but to no avail.

'There is a noise like a swarm of bumble bees on the line,' he said. 'The operator says there is a fault.'

After the taxi arrangement was made, he went down the track to the road to watch for it. 'Since it is possible they miss us,' he said, anxiously. 'I will flag them down to be sure.'

Priscilla stood at the window and watched Dietfreid position himself at the end of the track, waving at cars like a chubby windmill. 'Toby, I suppose we are right not to chivvy the police, are we?' she said. 'It's five o'clock now.'

'They told us to give it twenty-four hours,' said Toby. 'And I think they were stretching that a bit – I think it's usually forty-eight where it's an adult. Let's look around for ourselves first – it's not dark yet. Let's give ourselves until six, then we'll come back and start harassing them.'

Dietfreid had by now semaphored their taxi down, and had puffed his way back up to the house. 'We go first to the ruins,' he said. 'If they have gone anywhere, they have gone there. I show the way.'

'I hope you can show the driver the way,' said Toby, putting on his jacket. 'Last time you were there you got lost.'

'I shall not get lost! I shall not get lost when it is my *liebchen*.'

In the event, Dietfreid directed their driver very efficiently.

'Soon there finds itself a road-bend, and then a picked-up fence.'

'Picket,' said Toby, automatically.

'So. And then we are on a hump—'

'Bridge.' This time it was Priscilla.

'So. And then a pub called the Foresters Arms, and then a little way along we find the place we want—'

'Oh!' said Priscilla.

'What?'

'My car! Look! And Piers's Range Rover! Parked just where the trees start—'

'This where you want?' demanded the driver.

'Yes, thank you very much.'

'Shall I wait?'

'I don't think it's necessary now, is it? At least,' said Toby, 'providing we've got keys to one of the cars, it isn't. Priscilla, did you bring your spare keys?'

'Yes.'

'Thank heaven for that.' Toby paid the taxi driver, tipped him generously, and followed the other two to the grass verge that was the start of the forest proper. The taxi trundled back down the road. 'Are the cars all right?'

'No,' said Priscilla. 'Some bastard's cut all the tyres.'

'Oh God, and I've let the taxi go—' Toby spun round but it was already too late. 'Damn and hell! Well, at least we've got something concrete to tell the police now. Listen, we'll try to hitch a lift to a phone—'

'No, we should go *in*,' said Dietfried. 'Already it is growing dark, and we do not have the time. I have a panic about this.'

'Actually, so do I,' said Priscilla, glancing round a bit defiantly. 'How about if I do the hitching and phoning while you go into the forest?'

'Yes, it's likely we'd leave you on your own, isn't it?' said Toby, dryly. 'Especially with a madman around who slashes people's tyres. We'll have to stick together.'

'I do not like taking Priscilla where there might be danger,' said Dietfried. 'But then I do not like leaving her here on her own, either.' He furrowed his brow, and then said, 'We take a very careful look and then come back and get to a phone.'

'I thought you were all for riding in on a white charger?'

Dietfried said, 'That was before I saw the car tyres.'

387

'Toby, d'you think we're up against Karabas at last?'

'Well, we're up against something that isn't too worried about using strong measures to protect itself,' said Toby. 'Whoever slashed those tyres clearly didn't want Piers and the other two to make a quick getaway. Dietfreid, which way are the ruins?'

'They are on this path here,' said Dietfreid, setting off into the trees.

'Lead on, Macduff. Only do it quietly,' said Toby. 'Because I don't like this place much, and I've got the nastiest feeling that we're being watched—' He stopped dead.

From out of the trees, their slanting eyes shining, bounded eight of the wolf clan.

Felicity had used the narrow oblong of light outlining the panel as a kind of sand-glass; while it showed, it meant there was still daylight outside, and while there was daylight, Bryony would be safe.

The pain was grinding through her womb at regular intervals now and at one point nausea rose strongly in her chest, and with it, panic. Oh God, don't let me be sick! She swallowed hard and took deep breaths, forcing it down, because no matter how much fortitude you intended to show, it was impossible to vomit in silence. I *won't* be sick, I *won't*, said Felicity, over and over again. And then: I *will* endure this, and I *will* get out and find Bryony.

The sliver of light was starting to dim when she was aware of something happening in the room on the other side of the panel. She pressed her head against the scarred wood and heard Karabas's voice, and then a second voice, faintly accented like Karabas's, but lighter and younger. The change-over was taking place, and he must be about to go to wherever he had got Bryony and prepare for the ritual. Another wave of sickness hit her and this time she jabbed the fingernails of her right hand hard into the palm of her left, hard enough to draw blood. The sickness receded again. I've got to survive this to save Bryony, thought Felicity. I've *got* to. Anything else is unthinkable.

She heard Karabas say something that sounded like, 'Stay in this room – I think she's nearby.'

'Supposing she isn't?'

'Then at some point she'll have to return,' said Karabas.

'But she's here somewhere – hiding from us. I can *scent* that she is,' he said, and Felicity heard him cross the room. There was the sound of the kitchen door opening and closing, and then of the new guard sitting down in the same chair. Felicity heard the springs creak slightly.

The oblong of light was unmistakably fading. Soon it would be absolutely pitch-dark. Felicity, trying desperately to think of a way of outwitting her unseen gaoler, watched it, cold despair closing about her.

If I lose Bryony I shall have lost everything that matters. I'm losing this baby – yes, of course I am, I've known it for some time now – and I'll cope with that. But if Bryony dies at the hands of those madmen I shan't want to live, because there'll be nothing in the world anywhere, ever . . . She leaned her head against the wall, tears stinging her eyes. There was nothing she could do to reach Bryony, but there must be something, there must . . . And then, in the space of half a heartbeat, she caught a sound from the inglenook room, and her heart bumped with sudden hope.

The springs of the wing chair had creaked again, and footsteps had walked across the room. The guard, left by Karabas, had gone out of the inglenook room.

Felicity had no idea if he was just stretching his legs or if he had decided to search the rest of the house, or whether he was just being inquisitive. But wherever he had gone, it was now or never. She heard the gush of the tap being turned on in the kitchen – so you know enough to use the humans' plumbing do you, she thought – and then the chink of crockery. She would have to move and she would have to move *now*, even if all the torments of the damned were clawing at her womb. She slid the panel back and looked out into the shadowy room. There was a bad moment when she thought her cramped limbs would refuse to function quickly enough, and another when the pain jabbed viciously again, but she was operating on pure adrenalin now, and she managed to step out and cross the room to stand in the window recess, where she would be hidden by the long chintz curtains. She peered round the edge, looking round the room for a possible weapon. The lamp on Mad's sewing table was sufficiently heavy but it would be awkward to grab quickly and the flex might be too short. How about the large plant pot next to it?

Her heart was pounding so fast she thought she might be going to faint, but the pain was mercifully staying at a low ebb. The sickness had receded, but Felicity did not much care if she threw up all over the disgusting creature who was drinking her water and using her tumbler to do it.

His shadow fell across the floor as he came back into the room, and Felicity held her breath, pressing back into the deep recess. If he saw her then her plan would not work, but if he went straight to the yawning panel as she wanted him to— He stood in the doorway, still drinking from the glass of water he had poured. Felicity saw with angry irrelevance that he had used one of her best cut-glass tumblers, one of a set of six that had been a wedding present along with a matching carafe. She would take huge pleasure in smashing the glass to fragments when this was over.

For several seconds he stood in the doorway, scanning the darkened room. Felicity remained absolutely motionless. Would he sense that she was here?

And then he saw the open panel. He set down the glass and bounded across the room – Felicity registered with a sick shudder that he moved exactly like an animal attacking its prey – and he bent over, looking inside.

Felicity moved at once, her body ahead of her brain, snatching up the plant pot with both hands and lifting it as high as she could. It was a heavy clay pot, filled with soil, with white hyacinths growing up from it. Mad had brought the bulbs and Bryony had planted them, and the scent had filled the room each evening. Bryony . . . Don't flinch from this. Remember you're doing it for Bryony. Don't flinch.

She did not. As he heard her and started to straighten up out of the alcove, Felicity brought the pot smashing down on his head. He gave a grunt of surprise and pain, half slumping forward, flailing at the air with his hands. Felicity, sobbing and shuddering, dealt a second blow and then a third. He crashed to the ground, taking the little table with him, and Felicity stood poised, ready to deliver a fourth blow if she had to.

But he was either dead or beyond movement, and after a moment, she managed to put the pot down, her eyes still on him. The back of his head was a bloodied mess, splinters of bone protruding, and the scent of the broken hyacinths mingled grossly with the scent of blood. It was appalling. It was sickening and frightening and Felicity knew she would do it all over again if she had to.

Every muscle in her body was trembling as if she had been beaten with an iron bar, and there was an ominous dragging sensation at the pit of her stomach. She felt as if she might be bleeding as well, but there was no time to worry about that. Somehow she had to get to the road outside the cottage, and flag down the first car that came along.

Somehow she had to raise the alarm and send the police scouring the forest for Bryony all over again.

Chapter Forty-One

The sight of Dietfreid, with Priscilla and Toby, being brought into the underground room was like a cold blow across Piers's eyes. He stared at them, and for the first time faced the fact that they might not escape.

Priscilla and the two men were taken to the far corner of the cellar. 'I s'pose that's in case we get together and work out a plan to escape,' muttered Tybalt, crossly.

'We might be able to signal to them.'

'To do what?'

'I don't know,' said Nina, miserably. 'I wish they weren't here.'

'They look as if they wish it as well.'

Priscilla looked coldly furious, and Dietfreid was gesticulating excitedly. Toby appeared to be attempting to bargain with their captors. 'Fat chance of that,' said Tybalt, when Nina pointed this out.

But there was no opportunity to signal, or barely even to acknowledge the presence of the other three. Karabas's people tied the three new prisoners up, and turned their attention to replenishing the wall torches. There were sounds of movement from beyond the door at the head of the steps.

'It's starting,' said Piers, suddenly, and Tybalt felt his heart somersault into his mouth with fear.

'How do you know?'

'Can't you feel that it is?'

They could all feel it. The twisting flames burned up, and anticipation, raw and edged with sexual hunger, began to fill up the cellar. There was a sound from outside, as if people were assembling at the head of the stairs, and Piers sat up a little straighter, his eyes on the steps.

'Can't we do something?' said Nina, in desperation.

'Against this lot? With bound hands and feet?' muttered

Tybalt. 'We'd be minced up in about three seconds.' He said it softly so that Bryony would not hear, but Nina moved closer to Bryony; she tried to put her arms round the child, but her bound wrists stopped her. Bryony's little heart-shaped face was sheet white and, like Piers, she was staring at the stair. There's absolutely nothing we can do to help her, thought Piers, glancing at her. And if we get her out, unless she's got a very exceptional mother, she'll bear the mental scars of this for life. He suddenly found himself hoping that Bryony did have a very exceptional mother.

Into the underground room, moving with ceremonious solemnity down the stone steps, came a procession of six or eight of the older men, Karabas at their head. The fire-streaked darkness rippled over them, and both Nina and Tybalt thought that if they had not been aware of the fierce excitement of Karabas's people before, they were aware of it now. Tybalt stared at them, and thought: but it's all right really. They're only men and women. They're primitive and wild, and they radiate a peculiar power, but at bottom they're only people. And then the procession parted to make way for what walked at the rear, and Tybalt forgot about them being ordinary people and felt icy terror engulf him. For a moment the strange scene blurred. At his side, Nina said, in a tone of extreme horror, 'It's a wolf. Piers, it's a *wolf*. But – it's walking upright—'

'It's the shaman. He's wearing a wolf's head over his face,' said Piers at once.

'Are you sure?'

'God yes, of course I'm sure! It's the same thing I saw in the catacombs on Cruithin Island.'

'Yes, of course you did,' said Nina. 'Bryony, darling, it's all right, it's only a man dressed up – truly, that's all it is—'

'No, it's the wolf,' said Bryony, her eyes huge in her white little face. 'He's the one who ate up Edmund – in this room. And now he's going to make us eat up Mad. He *said* so.' Her lower lip trembled but she made a determined effort not to cry.

'Bryony, no one will make you do anything,' said Piers, and again she looked at him with such hope and such blind trust that the sheer futility of what he was saying slammed against his throat. But he said again, 'Bryony, listen to me, I've seen these people do this before – they dress up like wolves – it's a bit frightening to see it, but that's absolutely all it is.'

'Absolutely and truly?'

'Yes, absolutely and truly. That man is what they call a shaman. He wants his people to think he's a magical person – a sorcerer – and so he's put on that wolf-head so that he'll look a bit frightening. When this is all over, I'll tell you some really good stories about shamans.'

'Piers knows the very best stories,' said Nina.

'I like stories,' said Bryony, on a half-sob.

'So do I. And, listen, I promise we won't let anything bad happen to you either. We're all here with you, Bryony, we'll look after you—'

But he looked back at the macabre procession, and thought: but are we going to get out at all?

The shaman had taken up the position at the centre of the cellar, with Karabas at his side. With infinite slowness he removed the wolf-head and looked very directly at Piers. Nina, who was seated next to Piers, was aware of relief, because she had found it unbelievably grisly to have to look at the grinning wolf-muzzle. She stared at the shaman and felt the power that streamed from him, and then she looked fully at Karabas for the first time and saw him look at her. I hate you! thought Nina fervently. I hate you and I'm afraid of you! But below the fear, buried several layers down, was a dark sensual awareness.

The shaman turned to Karabas, rather in the manner of an elder statesman allowing a protégé to make his debut. Karabas inclined his head, and beckoned imperiously, and four of the men came out of the shadows. They each carried something which they set down at the centre of the room. Then they stepped back. By now there were easily twenty or twenty-five of them in the room, and in the relatively cramped space it was impossible not to be aware of the warm feral scent emanating from them.

'You see the blood jars of my people,' said Karabas, looking directly at Piers. 'They are ready.' A lick of hunger came into his voice. 'They are *filled and warm*,' he said, and Nina shuddered and felt sick, remembering Madeleine Foulsham.

From the other side of the room they heard Dietfreid's voice saying, disgustedly, 'Ach, so primitive.'

At the sight of the jars a low moan came from the watchers and several of them seemed about to leap forward. Piers's heart

394

missed a beat, in case this might create sufficient of a diversion for an escape attempt. But then he remembered that all of them were bound hand and foot, and that to get free they would have to cut the ropes around their ankles. The wolf creatures turned their heads towards the stair – they hear before we do, thought Piers, half-repelled, half-fascinated – and a sudden silence fell.

Down the stair, moving slowly and carefully, came six of the young men, carrying a carved chair. As they set it against the partly-demolished wall that Piers and Tybalt had broken down twenty-four hours earlier, flaring wall torches were lit on each side, bathing the chair in a pool of flickering light.

Seated on the chair was what, at first sight, looked to be a jumble of bones – a human skeleton carefully propped up as if it was about to hold court. Shreds of skin still clung to the bones in places.

But although the body was human, the head was not.

Piers stared at it in appalled recognition. 'So,' he said at last, 'you worship the rotting dead, do you, Karabas?'

Karabas had walked to the chair but when Piers spoke, he turned round, and in his beautiful, evil voice, said, 'That, Dr Adair, is your ancestor and mine. The one whose body you so helpfully disinterred for us last night. Marcus Fitzglen.'

Felicity had not waited to drag on a coat; she had not waited for anything. She was concentrating on getting as far as the main road without encountering any more of Karabas's people, and she was concentrating on coping with the clamping pain in her womb.

Because if I can just get to the road there'll be cars and people, she thought. I'll flag one down and ask the driver to take me to the nearest phone box to ring the police.

She repeated this over and over like a litany; it did not keep the pain much at bay, but it made it possible to keep going between the waves of the pain. I'll do it, thought Felicity determinedly. Somehow I'll do it and Bryony will be safe, because anything else is simply unthinkable.

The dark forest felt alien and the main road seemed to be a thousand miles away. The night seethed with faceless evil, and a tiny gust of wind brushed the leaves overhead, seeming to jeer at her.

Karabas has Bryony . . . Karabas has Bryony . . .

After a while the jeering whispers changed to, *You'll never find her . . . You'll never make it . . .*

But I must, thought Felicity, dizzily swimming in and out of the pain. I must.

Within the underground room, the shaman began to intone, and Piers heard that his voice had the same soft sibilance as Karabas's.

'In me is the spirit of the god, Fenrir, son of the great Loki, and to that spirit you must bow down.'

'I'll do no such thing,' came Priscilla's voice from the other side of the room, and then Toby's, saying, 'Bow down to a pack of wolves? Bloody cheek!'

Piers was overwhelmingly grateful to his companions for refusing to be daunted, but his attention was caught and held by the shaman's words.

Fenrir, he thought. Fenrir, sometimes referred to as Fenriswolf. The wolf who was bound by Tyr, but who will break loose when all the worlds end . . . Yes, *of course* they'd worship Fenrir! And even with the danger swirling all about him, and his mind working furiously to find a way of escape, he still experienced a thrill at hearing this immensely ancient form of ceremony.

'I am the immanent wolf of ancient times, the One who walked the wildwoods that once covered the earth and who could not be vanquished even by the Foljambes. You shall have no other gods but me. I shall send my curses and my vengeance upon the seed of those that do not serve me.'

Piers heard the eerie fusing of Christianity and paganism and prayed to every power he had ever heard of that he would escape to record the words. Keeping his eyes on the shaman he said, very softly, 'Tybalt, at any second they're going to haul me out to the centre of the room.'

'I know it.'

'I think they'll have to untie my feet,' said Piers. 'Which means they'll be concentrating on guarding me, not looking at you. Could you and Nina get to your feet then and inch your way to those wall torches? Brace your backs against the wall and push yourselves up if you can. Move smoothly so that they don't catch any movement, and then when I give the word, reach up to smother the flames.'

'How?' demanded Tybalt, looking at the wall torches thrust into crevices partway up one wall.

'Nina's wearing a scarf; if she can unwind it, it ought to do for one. D'you think you could get a shoe off for the other one?'

Tybalt was wearing slip-on moccasin-type shoes. He said he guessed he could get one off without attracting too much notice.

'Good. You'll have to reach both hands up,' said Piers. 'It'll be awkward, but I think it'll be possible – they haven't tied our wrists behind our backs which is one mercy. Wait till they take me to the centre of the room and then explain to Nina. Hush, they're coming over now. Watch for the signal.'

They untied Piers's feet but not his hands. Halfway free anyway. But once at the room's centre Piers had to fight down real panic.

Excitement was thrumming on the air, and when the shaman lifted his hands in the age-old gesture of supplication, Karabas's people fell to their knees.

'Fenrir, accept this sacrifice, and bestow on this human the mark of your bounty,' cried the shaman. On the edge of his vision Piers caught a movement and saw that Tybalt and Nina were both standing up. So far so good.

Piers said, 'Shaman! Before you get any further, shouldn't you consider something?' The shaman stopped at once, lowering his hands. Look at me! thought Piers, furiously. Look at me, damn you, and keep looking!

He said, 'Supposing I haven't inherited the blood of Marcus? Have you thought of that?'

The shaman smiled. 'Of course,' he said. 'But if you do not have the inheritance, you will die anyway.' He held out his hand, and Piers saw, with a cold chill, the dull gleam of the damson-shaped stone he had seen in the catacombs. The Stone of Destiny. The *Saxum Fatale*, the *Lia Fail*.

At the shaman's side Karabas held up his left hand. There was the bright glint of a knife-blade, and Piers stared at it in horror. 'The resurrection ritual,' he said, at last. 'Oh God, you're going to submit me to the resurrection ritual, aren't you? If the *Lia Fail* protects me from death you'll count that proof that

I'm of the same line and you'll kill me for the blood.'

'And if it does not, then it saves us killing you to protect our secrets,' finished Karabas.

'So I'm damned either way.'

'Yes. The Stone of Destiny will tell us what we need to know.'

Piers had to make a conscious effort not to look across to Tybalt. 'What about my friends?' he said. 'What will happen to them?'

'When this is over they will also be killed and their bodies buried in the forest or flung into the river,' said the shaman. 'We cannot allow them to betray what they have seen.'

'You'll be caught.'

'We shall be back on our island before the bodies are recovered. We are very used,' said Karabas, 'to covering our tracks, Dr Adair.'

'We want our people to continue living as their forebears,' said the shaman, and from his corner, Dietfreid said, 'Such pretentious rubbish. I have no patience.'

'And now,' said Karabas, softly, 'take in your mouth the Stone of Destiny.' He nodded to the shaman, who held out the Stone.

'No,' said Piers in a low voice.

'Do it,' said Karabas, and gestured to his brethren. At once they closed in, and Piers looked around the circle: at the narrow gleaming eyes, at the lips curled back showing the pronounced canine teeth. But beyond the circling wolf-creatures, he caught a glimpse of Tybalt and Nina, both almost at the burning torches.

Several of the wolf creatures were softly chanting, and words and rhythm beat insistently against Piers's mind.

'The Stone . . . The Stone . . .'

The shaman made a swift gesture, and two of the men stepped forward and stood on each side of Piers. Piers glanced at them, but before he could do anything they were holding his head in place and the shaman was forcing the gently glowing stone between his lips. He gasped and felt it slide into his mouth. At first it felt cool and then it began to radiate a thrumming heat.

At once the chant altered. *'Kill, kill, kill . . .'* it cried, spinning and echoing around the hot wolf-scented room. For a moment Piers saw everything in sharp clarity: the crimson-streaked shadows, the watching faces, the grisly pile of bones on the chair. The wolf-skull was grinning at him, and for a moment his vision seemed to distort, so that it was no longer a set of bones: it was a slender young man who sat there, watching everything with narrow dark eyes, smiling with the pointed muzzle of the dangerous creatures who had once prowled the wildwood . . .

Kill him . . . KILL HIM . . . See if he survives . . .

Piers blinked and the images vanished. There was only the hot firelit room and the avid faces of Karabas's people, and Karabas himself starting to raise the knife.

And Tybalt and Nina were reaching up to the wall torches.

Piers's head cleared. He brought his hands up and snatched the Stone from out of his mouth. A gasp went through the watchers, but before anyone could move, Piers lifted the Stone above his head, and using both his bound hands, he brought the Stone smashing down on the side of Karabas's head. There was a gasp of pain and astonishment and Karabas slid to the floor.

A howl of anguish rent the air – have I killed him? thought Piers, wildly. Is Karabas dead?

There was no time to find out. The shaman was whirling around, his eyes blazing with fury, crimson fire-shadows twisting eerily over his face, lending it the appearance of a thin slavering wolf-muzzle. Most of his brethren were crouching over the prone body of Karabas, but several were glaring snarlingly at Piers. Piers ducked away from the shaman's outstretched hands and darted towards Marcus Fitzglen's chair. He grabbed the wolf-skull, and dashed it onto the ground. It splintered into a thousand pieces, and a moan of anguish echoed round the room. The shaman bounded forward but Piers dodged aside and kicked out hard at the stone jars, tipping one of them up. Blood, dark and evil-smelling and horridly slippery, gushed over the stone floor.

'Tybalt!' cried Piers. '*Now!*' and Tybalt and Nina smothered the torch flames.

Darkness swooped down on the underground room.

Utter confusion reigned for several minutes. Karabas's people were plunging everywhere, several of them trying to re-light the torches, but slipping on the wet mess of blood and shattered bone. It was not pitch dark, but it was near enough.

Piers stood very still. The Stone was still in his hand: he could still feel its glowing power and with it a golden strength that was not his own pouring into him.

Karabas lay where he had fallen, and Piers bent to search for the knife. Had it been dropped and kicked aside? There was a moment of panic, and then his hand closed over it.

He began to move across the dark cellar, the knife held awkwardly but firmly in one hand, the Stone with it. He was prepared to knife any of the creatures who tried to stop him, but the Stone was shedding its own light and Karabas's people flinched and threw up their hands as if to shield their eyes. It's an optical illusion, thought Piers, wildly. Of course that's all it is. Hell, I don't care what it is if it holds those creatures at bay!

He reached Tybalt's corner unchallenged and thrust the knife into the boy's hands. 'Cut my hands free and then I'll cut yours. And then we'll free the others and let's get the hell out!' As Tybalt sawed frantically at the ropes around Piers's wrists, he sent a frantic glance about him. 'Quickly, Tybalt! I don't think these creatures will respect this Stone much longer.'

'It's done!' gasped Tybalt. 'Now for the rest!'

Carrying Bryony between them, Dietfried helping Nina, they ran up the stone stair.

'Don't stop!' cried Piers as they came out into the forest. 'They'll be after us at any second! We've got to outdistance them! Run and keep running until we reach the road!'

'And keep together!' shouted Toby. 'Hold hands! We daren't get separated!'

It was a wild nightmarish race through the old forest, but there was the sharp clean tang of the night all about them, and after the stifling, evil-drenched cellar it was invigorating beyond belief. Several times they thought they heard Karabas's people coming after them, but each time they paused to look there was no sign of them. Once Priscilla yelped as a low tree branch whipped across her face, and once Nina stumbled on a root but Dietfried pulled her up before she could fall, and they went on.

Tybalt was carrying Bryony. Piers glanced across at her and managed to say, 'Bryony, it's OK now. We're all safe.' He sent a swift glance into the dark trees. Were there creatures moving within the shadows? Slanting eyes watching them?

Toby said suddenly, 'Look; lights!'

'Where? What lights?'

'Flashlights,' said Tybalt after a moment. 'And cops by the look of it.' He gave a whoop of delight. 'Bryony, honey, we're about to be saved by the seventh cavalry!'

They slowed to a walk, dirty and dishevelled and out of breath. And then Bryony said in an uncertain voice, 'That's my mother,' and when Tybalt set her down, she ran as fast as her legs would carry her towards Felicity's waiting arms.

Piers, walking between Toby and Tybalt, saw that although she was pale and tear-streaked, and although she seemed to be walking with the assistance of a policewoman, Bryony's mother looked exactly as he had been hoping she would.

Chapter Forty-Two

Felicity set the table in the kitchen of Charect Cottage and counted plates and cutlery and wine glasses again. Nine adults were quite a lot, but at least in this weather they could spread into the garden. It was one of Bryony's green and gold days today, and although the May blossom had died, the lilac was already starting to scent the air.

Felicity's spirits rose, and for the first time since the nightmare in the forest and the hellish forty-eight hours in the gynaecology ward, she felt that life might one day be good again. Charect Cottage would certainly be good. She had asked the helpful builders to close up, once and for all, the priest's hole in the inglenook room, but on the outside wall, exactly in line with it, she had planted a small rosemary bush. Because rosemary's for remembrance, and because it's the only memorial I'll have of that little lost one . . . I'm sorry, said Felicity silently to the child. I'm sorry I didn't meet you, but each time I see this I'll think about you, because this is where you really died . . .

She would think about the wistful little ghost when she saw the rosemary bush, as well. She thought the ghost had not quite gone from the cottage; it might never go completely. But I quite like you being here. I think something fairly tragic happened to you, and I don't suppose I'll ever know what it was. But stick around, little ghost, in case there might be a bit of happiness due that you can share.

She and Bryony were going to plant something for Madeleine as well. Felicity thought it might take them a long time to get over Madeleine's death. She was still trying to get over the contents of Mad's will, bequeathed to her by a codicil dated one week after their first meeting.

'It's all yours,' had said the solicitor, smiling across the desk in the unfamiliar office in Ashbourne. 'The gatehouse and some shares and the island.'

'My grandmother owned an *island*?'

'Yes. It was purchased in – see now – 1540. By Sir Francis Foljambe,' said the solicitor, and Felicity had stared at him.

'It was just passed on down the family,' he said. 'Generation to generation. Nobody bothered about it much – I don't think it's known why Sir Francis bought it in the first place. Perhaps he wanted extreme privacy at times.'

'Perhaps,' said Felicity, but into her mind came the fleeting images she had glimpsed on that sun-drenched afternoon in the forest with Bryony and Mad. Francis Foljambe, who had been fond of the ladies, slight and clear-eyed, walking through the dappled greenwood shade . . . Had Francis encountered Karabas's people, and had he, with a superb blend of sixteenth-century extravagance and disdain, bought a faraway island in order to banish them?

'The agents say it's never brought in much revenue,' said Mad's solicitor. 'It's been a dormant file for decades – except when Dr Adair and his team got permission to go out there. Oh, and there's a record of some monastic order spending a day or two there fifteen or twenty years back. It's a very remote place, apparently.'

'It's a very remote place,' Felicity had said to Brother Andrew, seated in the familiar study with the comfortable book-lined walls and the inevitable tea-tray on the desk between them. 'But then you know that already, don't you?'

'Cruithin Island,' said Brother Andrew, softly.

'As far as I can make out Karabas's people have lived there since the dark ages,' said Felicity.

'As far as I remember it, Cruithin is still in the dark ages,' said Andrew, and Felicity smiled. 'My visit there gave Karabas's people the clue, didn't it?' he said, frowning. 'It told them about another of those – how did he describe it? – those pockets in the outside world where they could blend with the landscape? It's terrible to know we were responsible for Karabas coming to Bracken, Felicity.'

'But he would have left the island anyway. He was looking for me – for my husband, and for Bryony,' said Felicity, at once. 'It wouldn't have made any difference where he went. And actually, Bracken and the monks were exactly what I needed just then.' She leaned forward. 'Brother Andrew, some

403

years ago you considered Cruithin Island as a suitable place for a retreat centre.'

'Yes, but we decided it was impractical,' said Andrew. 'Hugely costly and massively complex to set it up.'

'Supposing you owned Cruithin?' said Felicity, carefully. 'I mean, supposing it was ceded to you outright? Could you create the retreat centre then?'

They looked at one another. 'Go on,' said Andrew.

'I've talked with Dr Adair,' said Felicity. 'He knows the island of course, and he thinks that nowadays the problems could be overcome without too much difficulty.'

Brother Andrew said, 'And Karabas's people?'

Felicity said, 'Karabas's people were rounded up by the police in the forest that night. The police asked me if I wanted to press charges; they asked Dr Adair and his team.'

'And?'

For an instant, Felicity's mind flew back to that night at Bracken.

Would you let them put me behind bars, Felicity? Karabas had said. *Would you really do that to me?*

'We all said we wouldn't press charges,' said Felicity. 'We said it quite independently of one another. They're a murderous bunch of savages, but—'

'But so were their ancestors,' said Andrew. 'So were our ancestors not too far back.'

'Exactly.' Felicity was grateful for this swift comprehension. 'My idea is that we lease their part of the island over to some kind of Trust dealing with wildlife or rare species or something of that kind. There must be a great many of those – Dr Adair's looking into that for me. I think the tribe should be allowed to live out the rest of its life on the island – guarded and prevented from leaving Cruithin, but in the surroundings they know. I don't think they should really be punished for what they couldn't help.'

Brother Andrew tapped the end of a pencil thoughtfully on the desk. 'And their descendants?'

'The Trust people would probably ensure there weren't any,' said Felicity, carefully.

'Ah,' said Andrew. 'Yes, of course.' There was a pause. 'We'd be mad to turn it down,' he said, and looked at her. 'What of Charect Cottage?' he said. 'Shall you want to go on living there? Because if we're to have Cruithin Island more or less outright—'

'Straight swap?'

'You'd be getting the bad half of the bargain. But could you go on living there? After all that's happened?'

'I don't know,' said Felicity.

She had no idea whether she and Bryony would be able to cope with living in Charect Cottage. There would be a lot of ghosts. But whether they stayed in Charect or went to live in the gatehouse, or whether they went to live somewhere else altogether, they would remember Mad. I didn't get to know you very well, said Felicity to Mad's memory. But I do know I won't forget you and I won't let Bryony forget you, either.

The supper tomorrow evening would dispel some of the ghosts, and perhaps set happier ones in their place. There would be Piers and his five assistants; and Morag Mackenzie and Brother Andrew were coming as well. Felicity had booked them rooms at the Prior's Arms, and she thought they would fit in quite well; there would be enough points of common interest between them and Piers's team to make a comfortable group. She had prepared a buffet supper and there was some really nice wine.

Bryony was looking forward to it. It would be lavishly good to have Piers and the others there to supper. She said this and then with one of her abrupt changes of mood, bent over a dish in which Felicity was mixing ingredients for a chocolate gateau and said in an unconcerned voice, 'Um . . . What actually happened to the wolf people after we all got out? Because it'd be pretty bad if they had to be put in prison, wouldn't it?'

Would you let them put me behind bars, Felicity . . . ?

Felicity glanced at Bryony. They had talked quite a lot about what had happened, but Felicity had let Bryony take her own pace. She thought that a good deal of the horror had passed over the child's head – she certainly thought the appalling intention of the blood jars had passed over her – and she was endlessly grateful to Piers Adair and to Nina and Tybalt for that. She was being careful to always have time to listen if Bryony wanted to talk, but she was also trying to let normality – school and lessons and the new puppy – start to weave back into Bryony's world.

Now, in answer to the question, she said, in an off-hand voice, 'They're going back to their island. The one I told you about.'

'The one Francis bought all those years ago for the wolf people?'

'What makes you think he bought it for the wolf people?'

'Well, I 'spect that's what happened. I don't suppose they'd come back here, do you?'

Felicity said at once, 'No, they can't ever come back. They're going to be guarded so that they can't leave the island ever again.'

'Karabas won't come back?'

'Not ever. He's dead.'

'Promise? Doubly promise?'

'Doubly promise,' said Felicity. She took the stirring spoon back from Bryony, and pounded at the mixture again. 'Darling, are you sure you didn't want to have the O'Callaghan twins here this weekend? You could have your own small party away from the grown-ups.'

'No, I told you. They can come later on, but tomorrow I'd like to have Piers to myself. And Nina and Tybalt and the others, of course. Tybalt's actually pretty nice-looking, isn't he?'

'Very.'

'He's not as nice-looking as Piers, but he's pretty nice.'

Felicity said, 'They're both terrific, darling.'

'Um yes. I thought,' said Bryony, 'that it'd be lavishly good to get to know him better.'

'Tybalt?'

'Piers.'

They looked at one another. Then Felicity said, 'Yes. Yes, I think it would be lavishly good as well.'

Bryony said, 'D'you know who Piers reminds me of?'

'Who?'

'Well, I didn't think it at first – not when we were all in that bad old cellar, but afterwards, after that ritual – it was *septic* that old ritual! – well, all of a sudden he looked quite a lot like dad.'

She looked up at Felicity as she said this.

Felicity was not looking at Bryony. She said, slowly, 'How remarkable. That's exactly what I thought the first time I saw him.'

Fear Nothing

Dean Koontz

Christopher Snow is athletic, handsome enough, intelligent, romantic, funny. But his whole life has been affected by xeroderma pigmentosum, a rare genetic disorder that means his skin and eyes cannot be exposed to sunlight. Like all Xpers, Chris lives at night – and has never ventured beyond his hometown of Moonlight Bay, a place of picturesque beauty and haunting strangeness.

Despite the limitations imposed by nature, he has always been determined to lead the fullest life and, with the help of family and friends, he has on the whole succeeded. But for Chris – and all the inhabitants of Moonlight Bay – a terrible change is about to happen; a change of potentially catastrophic proportions.

'Not just a master of our dreams, but also a literary juggler' *The Times*

'Plausibly chilling . . . Koontz at his best' *Express on Sunday*

0 7472 5832 5

Cat and Mouse

James Patterson

Psychopath Gary Soneji is back – filled with hatred and obsessed with gaining revenge on detective Alex Cross. Soneji seems determined to go down in a blaze of glory and he wants Alex Cross to be there. Will this be the final showdown?

Two powerful and exciting thrillers packed into one, with the electrifying page-turning quality that is the hallmark of James Patterson's writing, CAT AND MOUSE is the most original and audacious of the internationally bestselling Alex Cross novels.

'Patterson's action-packed story keeps the pages flicking by' *The Sunday Times*

'Patterson, among the best novelists of crime stories ever, has reached his pinnacle' *USA Today*

'Packed with white-knuckle twists' *Daily Mail*

'Patterson has a way with plot twists that freshens the material and keeps the adrenalin level high' *Publishing News*

0 7472 5788 4